serp[ent's kiss]

"Delightfully charming, Calliope Reaper-Jones is hysterical. One can't help but root for her to get the man, save the world, and get her heart's desire in the process. This character-driven addition to the Reaper-Jones series is truly fantastic."
— *RT Book Reviews*

"Amber Benson shines through her novel and entices readers. Calliope's personality is genuine, and readers will definitely love her." — *Nocturne Romance Reads*

"A thoroughly enjoyable, imaginative book, well-realized in both concept and execution." — *Assignment X*

"Fast-paced but filled with humor and pathos. A powerful, action-packed thriller." — *Genre Go Round Reviews*

"Benson has brought the series to a new, impressive height—dark, startling, and [with] plenty of shocking surprises. Urban fantasy fans should not miss this fantastic series."
— *SciFiChick.com*

cat's claw

"Callie bounces from twist to twist as she explores Benson's richly imagined world, where multiple mythologies blend and the afterlife is run as a corporation." — *Publishers Weekly*

"An entertaining, frenzied fantasy frolic that will have the audience laughing at the chick-lit voice of the heroine, who is willing to go to heaven on a hellish cause."
— *Genre Go Round Reviews*

"Benson is back with a second helping of her refreshing take on death and purgatory . . . Callie's offbeat humor and viewpoint guarantee a madcap romp." — *RT Book Reviews*

continued . . .

"A fun, snappy read to the tune of a chick-lit writing style, set in a colorful supernatural world. It's a charming mesh of several myths with an unconventional modern-day twist that hosts a cast of quirky, likable, and diverse characters."

—*Fantasy Dreamer's Ramblings*

"Sustains the style and pace of *Death's Daughter* but adds deepening characterization." —*The Monthly Aspectarian*

death's daughter

"Amber Benson does an excellent job of creating strong characters, as well as educating the reader on some great mythology history . . . a fast-paced and very entertaining story."

—*Sacramento Book Review*

"An urban fantasy series featuring a heroine whose macabre humor fits perfectly with her circumstances. Sure to appeal to fans of Tanya Huff's Vicki Nelson series and Charles de Lint's urban fantasies." —*Library Journal*

"A beguiling blend of fantasy and horror . . . Calliope emerges as an authentically original creation . . . The humorous tone never gets in the way of the imaginative weirdness of the supernatural events." —*Locus*

"In *Death's Daughter*, Benson provides a fun romp that defines the rules of an exciting new universe you'll be champing at the bit to dive back into time and again. There's action; there's intrigue, redemption, an adorable hell puppy, and even a hot guy or two. What more could you ask for?" —*Buffyfest*

"Amber Benson writes an amusing, action-packed, chick-lit urban fantasy loaded with more twists and curves than a twist-a-whirl . . . Filled with humor and wit, this is a refreshing, original thriller as double, triple, and nth crossings are the norm."

—*Genre Go Round Reviews*

Ace Books by Amber Benson

DEATH'S DAUGHTER
CAT'S CLAW
SERPENT'S STORM
HOW TO BE DEATH

how to be death

AMBER BENSON

ACE BOOKS, NEW YORK

THE BERKLEY PUBLISHING GROUP
Published by the Penguin Group
Penguin Group (USA) Inc.
375 Hudson Street, New York, New York 10014, USA
Penguin Group (Canada), 90 Eglinton Avenue East, Suite 700, Toronto, Ontario M4P 2Y3, Canada
(a division of Pearson Penguin Canada Inc.)
Penguin Books Ltd., 80 Strand, London WC2R 0RL, England
Penguin Group Ireland, 25 St. Stephen's Green, Dublin 2, Ireland (a division of Penguin Books Ltd.)
Penguin Group (Australia), 250 Camberwell Road, Camberwell, Victoria 3124, Australia
(a division of Pearson Australia Group Pty. Ltd.)
Penguin Books India Pvt. Ltd., 11 Community Centre, Panchsheel Park, New Delhi—110 017, India
Penguin Group (NZ), 67 Apollo Drive, Rosedale, Auckland 0632, New Zealand
(a division of Pearson New Zealand Ltd.)
Penguin Books (South Africa) (Pty.) Ltd., 24 Sturdee Avenue, Rosebank, Johannesburg 2196,
South Africa

Penguin Books Ltd., Registered Offices: 80 Strand, London WC2R 0RL, England

This is a work of fiction. Names, characters, places, and incidents either are the product of the author's imagination or are used fictitiously, and any resemblance to actual persons, living or dead, business establishments, events, or locales is entirely coincidental. The publisher does not have any control over and does not assume any responsibility for author or third-party websites or their content.

HOW TO BE DEATH

An Ace Book / published by arrangement with Benson Entertainment, Inc.

PUBLISHING HISTORY
Ace mass-market edition / March 2012

Copyright © 2012 by Benson Entertainment, Inc.
Cover art by Spiral Studio.
Cover design by Judith Lagerman.
Interior text design by Tiffany Estreicher.

ISBN: 978-1-937007-28-7

ACE
Ace Books are published by The Berkley Publishing Group,
a division of Penguin Group (USA) Inc.,
375 Hudson Street, New York, New York 10014.
ACE and the "A" design are trademarks of Penguin Group (USA) Inc.

PRINTED IN THE UNITED STATES OF AMERICA

10 9 8 7 6 5 4 3 2 1

how to be death

one

Call it a knack, a talent, a penchant . . . *a proclivity*. Call it what you will—my ability to inject myself into whatever nut-ball scenario crossed my path was, without a doubt, one of the most defining characteristics of my personality. If I were a wittier dame, I'd say that Trouble was my middle name, but since I'm more *Clueless* than femme fatale, I think I'll leave the film noir–isms to someone with a better grasp of the material. Needless to say, for those who've crossed my path . . . to know me is to wish you'd never met me.

The reasoning for this particular turn of phrase is two-pronged. While part of me is still a twentysomething girl who possesses a hard-core fashion obsession and a propensity for getting into ridiculous scrapes that invariably involve my friends—and even casual acquaintances—(Prong Number One), there is another, more all-encompassing aspect of my personality that's a real stinger of a Prong Number Two: I am, for lack of a better euphemism, *Death . . . the Grim Reaper . . .* or, just as aptly, *the Girl Who Can Wish You Dead.*

They all pretty much apply.

And now you see why most people wish they could go an eternity without stumbling across my path. There is no human being in existence—barring suicidal depressives and dooms-day cultists—who wants to get all up in Death's business, yet to humanity's consternation, I'm like a bad penny: I just keep turning up.

Death and taxes—you can count on us.

Now I haven't always been the head gal in charge of the passage of human souls from one plane of existence to the next. No, I was once a quasinormal human being wannabe who worked in a nice little white cubicle, honey-combed inside the right-angle confines of a tall Manhattan skyscraper, doing all the grunt work for the Vice-President of Sales at a company called House and Yard—they make the majority of the house and yard crap you see the overtanned, overplasticized hucksters who populate the Home Shopping Network shilling.

Being the assistant to a tyrannical boss who likes making your life a living Hell just for the fun of it, well, that sucks in its own right. But when your erstwhile boss turns out to be a Supernatural baddie who's been making your life miserable in order to keep you under her Wagnerian thumb just in case she ever wants to use your family connections to try and take over Death . . . somehow that's even suckier.

Hyacinth Stewart—said Wagnerian Blonde *and* plus-sized ex-model extraordinaire—had done exactly that. It was only sheer luck she and her cohort, a Japanese Sea Serpent God named Watatsumi, hadn't succeeded in doing away with me and assuming the Presidency of Death, Inc., in my stead after my father—the last Death—had been murdered by his arch-nemesis, the Ender of Death or "Marcel," as the bloodthirsty pain in the ass liked to be called. It was also a testament to the love and help of my friends Jarvis, Runt, and Kali and my younger sister, Clio, that I was still alive and kicking to take over my dad's job once all the fallout was over.

Without them—and one other person, who I won't mention because just their name dredges up an achy, hollow place in my heart—I would've been mincemeat. Which meant that because so many people had endured so much suffering and given so much of themselves (like their lives) to get me installed as the President of Death, Inc., I had no business disparaging the job, regardless of how badly I hadn't wanted to take it.

I just had to ignore the little voice in the back of my mind that liked to remind me of how unprepared I was for the job, that kept whispering: *You're just a girl—and not even an eru- dite one at that.* True, I loved the very pedestrian triumvirate of fashion, shopping, and food, but that didn't mean I was a total airhead, incapable of running the show—I had a college degree and I knew PowerPoint, for God's sake.

Still, no matter how much ammunition I gathered against its insidious undermining, the voice persisted, letting me know I had no business being in charge of Death, Inc., especially when it was run exactly like a corporation (hence the heavy-handed "President and CEO" title I now bore like a cross) and needed a boss with business acumen, smarts, and finesse. Three things I wasn't really sure I 100 percent possessed. Sure, I'd been a damn fine assistant in my day—for as much as I hated the job—but that didn't mean I was capable of assuming the helm of a multinational conglomerate and not running it into a sandbar.

Yet here I was, the titular head of a giant, multinational, multidimensional conglomerate, whether I wanted the job or not.

All these thoughts ran through my brain while I stared into the gaping interior of my Louis Vuitton overnight bag, trying to decide if the skimpy, white, rhinestone-encrusted string bi-kini I wanted to bring along on the trip made me look slutty or not.

The question of bikini sluttiness aside, my real problem wasn't *what* I was packing, but what I was packing it *in*. My obsession with high-end retail was legendary; I was a conspic-uous consumer right out of the pages of Thorstein Veblen's perennial classic, *The Theory of the Leisure Class*. Recently, I'd been working hard to curtail my excessive love of luxury brands in favor of a more economical shopping approach, but truth be told, I was finding it to be a very daunting task, indeed: the Louis Vuitton weekend bag was just another symptom of my luxury addiction gone out of control.

I'd seen it sitting all by its lonesome in the window of Barneys—seriously, I wasn't even in the store, I was standing on the sidewalk minding my own business, thankyouverymuch—and it'd just looked so darn cute and adorable I couldn't resist saving it. Besides, I was going to the Death Dinner, arguably the most important event on the Death, Inc., calendar, and I needed to look presentable now that I was the Head Honcho in charge of everything.

At least that was my rationale.

Being the President of Death, Inc., had its advantages—and a very generous living stipend was one of them—but before I'd accepted the job, I'd made a resolution to myself that I would get my shopping problem under control. To that end, my Executive Assistant, Jarvis, had put me on a budget.

A very *small* budget.

In my heart, I knew keeping my mitts off the money and doing exactly as Jarvis instructed were the only ways to make my resolution a reality, but it was just too damn hard—and I was too damn weak. When I'd put my corporate card down on the counter at Barneys and rescued the Louis Vuitton weekend bag, I'd blown Jarvis's budget for the month in one fell swoop.

As soon as I stepped foot out of the store, the guilt set in. *Hard-core.*

Using an old tactic from my shopping-whore days, I immediately ripped the tags off the bag so it would be harder to force myself to return it, but that made me feel even *guiltier*—and instead of being excited about my overpriced, monogrammed cowhide purchase, all I felt was ambivalence. I couldn't really enjoy the thing because it was a verboten purchase, but I couldn't bring myself to give it back because deep in my heart of hearts I *loved* owning something so deliciously extravagant.

Feeling the kind of shame a puppy does when it pees on the carpet, I'd hidden the bag under my bed (behind a bunch of dust bunnies and an old snowboard that I'd only used once, to deleterious effect—a broken collarbone that, because of my immortality, had healed in three hours instead of three months), but since Jarvis was so familiar with my predilections to excess, the subterfuge only lasted, like, two seconds.

Like a shark scenting blood in the water, he'd gone right to the source of my guilt, snagging the offending bag from under my bed and brandishing it above his head like Martin Luther with his ninety-five theses.

"And what is this, pray tell?" Jarvis said in his clipped British accent—an accent that still sounded strange coming out of the mouth of the lanky, hipster body Jarvis had appropriated after I'd accidentally wished him dead.

"It's, uhm . . . a *bag*?" I said innocently.

One bushy, brown eyebrow kinked in derision—and for, like, the thousandth time since Jarvis had acquired his new body, I marveled at how bizarre it was to see the old Jarvis expressions on this new, angular face.

"Oh, *really*?" he rejoined, trilling the *r* in "really" like no one's business, his voice dripping with sarcasm. "A *bag*, you say? I would never have guessed."

Jarvis had been an extended member of my family for as long as I could remember—growing up, he'd been my dad's long-suffering Executive Assistant and then, when my dad was kidnapped and I was named interim head of Death, Inc., in his stead, he'd become my own Man Friday. Over the past year we'd had our ups and downs, mostly because I'd had zero interest in running Death, Inc., and my bad attitude had peeved him to no end, but I knew when push came to shove and I needed someone in my corner, Jarvis would always be there. A fact he'd proven again and again as he'd helped me extricate myself from one ridiculous scrape after another, never once complaining about my ineptitude. Okay, he might've complained once or twice, but that was it and he was probably more than justified.

Anyway, it was still strange to think that the Jarvis I'd known as a child—the tiny four-foot-eleven frame, goat haunches (you read that right—Jarvis was a faun in his previous incarnation), and thick *Magnum, P.I.*–era Tom Selleck mustache—was gone, replaced now by the long-limbed, emaciated body standing in front of me, shaking the Louis Vuitton travel bag in my face like it was anathema.

"And wherever did you find *said* bag?" he'd continued, glaring at me.

"Uhm, wow, I have no idea how that got there . . ." I hedged, but this only garnered a "tut-tut" from Jarvis, whose hand-on-hip stance brooked no argument.

Jeez, I couldn't get anything past the guy. He knew my every trick, tell, and twitch . . . and he wasn't buying even a word of my dissembling. I might as well have just finished off every sentence with "And, yes, I'm a big fat liar!" and been done with it.

"Okay." I sighed, feeling bad for trying and failing to pull a fast one—mostly I felt bad about the failing part, but I wasn't going to tell him that. "I know exactly how that bag got there and it's not pretty."

Jarvis nodded, gesturing for me to continue.

"I fell off the wagon."

Jarvis raised the other eyebrow, making it seem as if two hairy caterpillars had overtaken his forehead.

I sighed.

"I didn't even go in the store—it was in the window and I couldn't just leave it there—so I used the corporate card—"

Jarvis winced, a pained expression pinching his face at the mention of the "corporate card," but I soldiered on.

"And now I feel like a jerk, so I put it under the bed and I can't even enjoy it. It's terrible," I said as I flopped onto my mattress, the fluffy purple comforter I'd bought online poofing out around me.

The pained expression slowly melted into a wide-lipped grin as I continued:

"I mean, I feel exactly like the dude in *A Clockwork Orange*—reconditioned to feel only disgust for my old, bad habits," I added, staring ahead glumly.

Having said my piece, I waited for the traditional Jarvis tongue-lashing to begin, but to my surprise, he circumnavigated my expectations and, with a weary sigh, sat down on the bed beside me, making the comforter poof even more.

As I batted at the comforter, trying to unpoof it, I decided the room I'd grown up in seemed much smaller whenever the new and improved Jarvis was in it. It was as if his long, skeletal frame took up space in the fifth dimension, displacing more matter in our third-dimensional world than it was supposed to.

"Keep it," Jarvis said, patting my shoulder.

Those two words were like a shot of adrenaline straight to my heart. I immediately sat up straighter, my brain wary and wanting confirmation on the validity of the words I'd just heard Jarvis utter.

"Really?" I said, not believing him, but really, really wanting to.

He shrugged, his shoulders encroaching on earlobe territory.

"We're attending the annual Death Dinner and Masquerade Ball and you'll need a carryall. So, I suppose it wasn't the worst of purchases."

It was weird to think the fake excuse I'd conjured up for myself as I stood outside the plate glass window of Barneys' happy-shopping-funland was now the exact rationale Jarvis was using to allow me to keep the bag.

It was like Jarvis had pawed his way into the confines of my mind and implanted a brainwashing device that scrubbed out the old Callie in favor of the more mature Callie 2.0. Or was the answer even simpler than that: Was I just embracing my new job with enough verve that I was starting to think like Jarvis?

Creepy!

this idea was kind of unsettling, but not as unsettling as I'd expected it to be. Over the course of the last few months, I'd found I had a bit of a knack for the whole Death thing. I mean, this was no "duck to water" scenario, or anything so instinctual, but with each new task or problem I overcame, there was the growing awareness I wasn't a total dunce at the job. My dad had set the reins of Death, Inc., in my hands for a reason and I was determined, now that he was gone, not to let him down.

Which meant in the future I was going to have to think a lot more like Jarvis than I wanted to—and I was also going to have to tamp down the persnickety voice in the back of my head that said I wasn't good enough for the job. If I could do those two things, then I might actually—Heaven forbid—have a chance at making a go of the family business.

"FYI: That thing totally makes you look slutty."

Startled out of my thoughts, I looked up to find my little sister, Clio, standing in the doorway to my bedroom, hands on hips, face squirming with disgust as she focused on the tiny, white rhinestone-encrusted bikini top I held in my hand. I quickly dropped the now noxious piece of fabric back onto the bed, watching as the long white ties dangled off the edge of the comforter like spandex mealworms.

"You really think so?" I said, knowing she was right, yet still wanting to take the damn thing with me anyway. It might've been a slutster piece of clothing . . . but it was *my* slutster piece of clothing, and besides, it made my butt look amazing.

"I know so," she shot back, rolling her eyes. "But don't let me stop you from embarrassing yourself."

I decided to let the potshot pass without comment. Instead, I stared down into the empty weekend bag, willing myself to get a move on. I had a wormhole-calling lesson in fifteen minutes and then Jarvis, Runt, and I were heading to the Haunted Hearts Castle, where the annual Death Dinner and Masquerade Ball were being held.

"I wish you were going with us," I said to Clio—and I meant it. I'd started to rely on her counsel, as far as the day-to-day running of Death was concerned, and not having her keen mind with me at the Death Dinner made me nervous.

She may have just turned eighteen that summer, but she was the smartest person, other than Jarvis, I knew. With her techno savvy (she could hack her way into any computer) and intuitive knowledge of how people operated, I'd been more than pleased when she'd decided to eschew college for a year to work at Death, Inc., helping me put the company back in order after it was almost demolished by the Devil and our not-so-dearly departed older sister, Thalia.

The two of them had staged a coup on Purgatory, murdered my dad—who'd been the President and CEO before me—and nearly destroyed the Hall of Death, where the Death Records for all of humanity were housed. They and their cohorts had worked hard to decimate the employee pool at Death, Inc., so that now we were dangerously understaffed, a problem we were still trying to remedy. I'd met with five possible replacements for Suri, the Day Manager of the Hall of Death, but none of them had had the chutzpah and class of the young woman who'd lost her life defending the records from my older sister's evil clutches.

And she'd been just one of the many casualties we'd had that day.

I'd inherited a job that was in flux, that needed my complete and utter attention—and since my old boss Hyacinth was officially MIA (she was actually spending her time jailed in Purgatory for the part she played in the Death, Inc., coup, but no one in the human world knew that), I'd gotten laid off from my assisting job at House and Yard just in time to devote myself full stop to rebuilding the company.

Because I'd been so busy, at first I hadn't missed my old life: the Battery Park City apartment I'd had to give up, my friends (who I never really saw anyway), and the City of New York itself. But now things had started to settle down and I was beginning to feel a burning yen for my past existence. I liked Newport, Rhode Island, where Sea Verge, the family mansion, was located, but the provincial city was *not* New York. There were no all-night diners, the shopping was boutique-centric, and everyone I'd ever known there had either fled or was married with a bunch of rug rats. So needless to say, the Mommy and Me crew weren't really interested in hanging out with a cosmopolitan, single gal newly arrived from the wilds of Manhattan.

Having Clio in my direct orbit made everything a lot easier. I could talk to her about anything, and no matter how dorky I sounded, she never judged. After my dad's death, she'd spent a few months living with her boyfriend, Indra, a Hindu God who'd carved out a human existence for himself making Bollywood musicals—hiding in plain sight, if you will—and though I'd pretty much written him off as a narcissistic jerkoid when I'd first met him, I'd had to eat my words when he'd shown himself to be a stand-up guy, sticking to Clio like glue during the crazy emotional roller-coaster ride she'd endured in the aftermath of our dad's death. I was a little shaky about the age difference—I'm talking millennia here—but other than that, I was all for the relationship.

But I would've been a liar if I hadn't said I wasn't a little disappointed when Clio chose to spend the weekend helping Indra shoot his new film rather than coming with me to the Death Dinner. I knew I was in good hands—Runt, my hellhound pup, was a master at sniffing out bad guys, and Jarvis was just aces, in general—but, still, I was gonna miss having my little sister to lean on.

"You know I'd go with you in a heartbeat, but Indra really wants me to be there for the shoot," Clio said, ripping me out of my thoughts again and back into reality.

"I know," I said.

"It's his first nonmusical and he's really nervous about it," she added, the tendrils of her short pink hair framing her face like starfish arms.

Clio and I were both part Siren, which accounted for Clio's stunning good looks and feminine demeanor (sadly, the stunning good looks had missed me by a mile), but even I could see that the gift of beauty was a double-edged sword. Clio had spent a good chunk of her high school career hiding her features behind thick, black plastic-framed glasses and a shaved head, in hopes she could stave off the bevy of lovesick men who followed her everywhere.

Not a chance.

Poor Clio, all she wanted was to be taken seriously—an impossibility when your high school teachers develop inappropriate crushes on you, giving you A-pluses even when you're purposely turning in D-minus work.

"Well, you know you'll be missed," I said, trying to hide my disappointment. "But I totally get it. Mr. Sex on a Stick needs you."

Mr. Sex on a Stick was what I called Indra whenever I wanted to rile Clio up. I hadn't coined the term, a magazine had that dubious honor, but it was still my favorite way to harass my sister. I don't think she particularly enjoyed the fact that her man was an object of sexual fascination to millions of horny housewives across the world.

"Gross!" she said, coming into the room just long enough to grab a pillow off my bed and lob it at my head.

"I'm just saying—" I bleated as the pillow connected with the side of my face.

"Get packed, butthead," Clio mock-growled at me. "Jarvis wants you down in the library stat for your wormhole-calling lesson."

And with that piece of info imparted, she flounced back down the hallway, leaving me to finish my packing in peace. I sighed and started pulling clothes from my closet, nicely folding a trio of light summer dresses and a white linen pantsuit into my weekend bag so they wouldn't get too wrinkled. Some PJs, socks, and underwear rounded out my wardrobe, but it wasn't until I'd pretty much filled the bag to the brim that I had a change of heart about my slutster status. Picking up the string bikini from its resting place on my bed, I covertly slid the wanton thing between the folds of the white linen suit, where it disappeared nicely inside the similar-colored fabric.

Slutster or not, I was gonna look *fine* in that bikini . . . and if the man-whose-very-name-made-me-nauseous-with-unrequited-love-whenever-I-thought-about-him was there and he just happened to see me looking all hot and sexy? Well, that was just an added bonus.

Eat your heart out, Daniel, I thought as I zipped up my bag and hoisted it off the bed, ready for whatever Trouble came my way.

I just hoped it was the kind punctuated by a capital *T*.
Hee-haw!

two

"You do understand the concept of folding space? Correct?"

Jarvis's voice had that smarmy "know it all" quality to it that really rubbed me the wrong way. He acted like I was supposed to just intuitively know/understand all these advanced physics concepts like "folding space" and "string theory." I got that all of these things were the framework upon which magic, time travel, etc., were based, but it didn't mean my brain was up for grasping the actual science part.

"I get that time and space are, like, ideas . . ."

I trailed off as Jarvis closed his eyes, trying to calm himself.

"Why do I have to know this stuff?" I asked again for, like, the three-thousandth time. We'd been working on the whole wormhole-calling thing for the past few months and the best I could do was set Jarvis's hair on fire.

I hadn't meant to do it, I'd just gotten frustrated—I'm good at the magicky stuff only when I'm feeling emotional or am in a high-stress situation—and then before I knew what was happening, Jarvis's hair was doing an impression of Michael Jackson at his infamous Pepsi commercial shoot. Luckily, Jarvis is way more adept at magic than me and was able to put out the fire before it did any permanent damage, but he'd watched me like a hawk ever since.

"You have to understand why spells and wormholes work

in order to fully control them," Jarvis intoned, in an exact repeat of what he'd said the first—and last—time I'd asked him the question.

Jarvis, his patience worn thin, sat down heavily on one of the library's wingback chairs, his long legs splayed out in front of him like he was a gangling schoolboy. Resting his elbows on the arms of the chair, he started massaging his temples as if that would make the lesson run smoother.

As much as I hated to admit it, I was a terrible Death student. I didn't like magic, I didn't like monsters, I was not a fan of the recently departed . . . and liking all those things kinda went hand in hand with running Death, Inc. I think my noninterest was the biggest reason why I sucked at wormhole calling—I once heard someone say emotion can't get through a tense muscle, and I was pretty sure you could supplant "emotion" with "magic" and it would wholly apply to my problem.

"Shall we try again?" Jarvis said finally, opening his eyes to look at me again.

I shrugged.

"I'm game if you are."

My answer did nothing to ease Jarvis's worry.

The key to calling up a wormhole so you could travel space and time without having to get in a car, train, or plane was to envision exactly where you wanted to go and then imagine yourself there. It didn't matter if you'd never been there before and had no clue how it looked. All that was important was holding the idea of the place in your mind. It was this link that enabled you to access the wormhole system and get where you wanted to go.

I was inept at this task. I could think of the place, get the idea in my head, and then two seconds later my mind was spinning off into other directions, my thoughts like buckshot. I didn't do this on purpose. I was just unfocused—a problem I'd had since I was a little kid. I guess you could say I had a touch of the old "attention deficit disorder." Unless I was just completely obsessed with something, I tended to get distracted super easily.

"Now, close your eyes—" Jarvis began in his clipped British accent, which contrasted so nicely with the lanky, young American body he now possessed.

I did as he asked, not wanting to get snapped at for day-dreaming, and closed my eyes, letting his words wash over me in waves.

"—and imagine you are in your bedroom at Sea Verge."

Just like that, my newly decorated bedroom magically materialized within the imaginary world of my mind's eyes. I smiled at the crème caramel carpet I'd just had installed, the polished redwood platform bed, fluffy purple down comforter, and matching redwood dresser and vanity Clio had helped me pick out. I had to admit the old bedroom was starting to look pretty tricked out, if I did say so myself.

When it had become apparent I was going to have to give up my Manhattan apartment for a full-time residency at Sea Verge, I'd decided the only way I could justify the move was to totally redo my old bedroom. I worried that returning to the wicker bedroom set of my childhood might trigger a full-scale regression, and I so did not need a new issue to add to the ones I was already dealing with. What I wanted was a clean slate—a new beginning—and trashing all my old stuff seemed like the perfect way to get the ball rolling in the right direction.

As usual, without meaning to, my brain had unintentionally left the confines of my bedroom and was on the move: An image of my old bedroom furniture sitting in the Goodwill waiting for someone to take pity on it overwhelmed my thoughts. Guilt welled up inside me. Had I made a bad decision? Was I supposed to keep all my old stuff forever and never move forward?

I'd had that stupid wicker furniture for eons. It'd been there waiting for me every summer when I came back from the New Newbridge Academy full of teenage angst and hatred at having to leave the boarding school that felt more like home than my actual home did. I'd spent hours moping around my room, writing in my journal and mooning over whatever male flavor of the week I had a crush on. That furniture and I had a lot of shared history, and what had I done? I'd just chucked it out like garbage.

I opened my eyes. Jarvis was standing above me, his foot tapping in staccato triplets that did nothing to hide his annoyance.

"You obviously were *not* thinking about your bedroom or you would be there now," Jarvis said.

"Well, I was thinking about it for a minute," I said.

Jarvis shook his head.

"I wish there were a way to make you focus," he mumbled under his breath. "Perhaps a pill that worked in the same fashion as a lobotomy."

Now, that wasn't nice, I thought to myself.

"A lobotomy?"

Surprised, Jarvis looked up sheepishly.

"Oh, you're still here," he murmured.

Was that a dig at my inability to call up a wormhole? I wondered.

"And where would I have gone in two seconds?" I said.

"To your bedroom, if you could call a bloody wormhole," Jarvis said, shaking his head.

Yes, it was a dig.

Annoyed with myself and with the dumb wormhole-calling lesson, I flopped down on the couch, releasing some of the tension my body had collected during the course of my myriad attempts to wormhole my way out of Dodge. Jarvis wasn't a bad teacher, but he was very demanding—which only added to my sense of failure when I was unable to do as he asked.

While I waited for Jarvis to give me another task to do or, more likely, cut our losses for the day and dismiss me, I appraised the space surrounding me. Sadly, I felt my dad's loss most keenly when I was here or in his study.

As little kids, my sisters and I had played hide-and-seek in the dark-paneled library, losing ourselves behind the intricately carved rolling mahogany wet bar—where my dad kept his excellent stock of buttery cognac and exotic ports—and falling asleep inside the hollow body of the large grandfather clock a Pope had given my dad as a thank-you gift. It was Pope John-Paul II, if you're curious, and he actually visited our house once when I was little, my dad making me sing my embarrassingly off-key rendition of "Fifty-Nifty United States" to entertain him.

Though the Pope's visit hadn't been one of them, I actually had a number of pleasant memories that revolved around me lying stretched out on the crème and oxblood Oriental carpet, reading some pulpy kid book, while my dad did his paperwork—apparently there was a lot of paperwork involved in running Death, something I'd discovered for myself my first week on the job. As my brain dawdled over fuzzy, childhood memories, I felt a cloud of melancholia settle over me, making me want to jump out of my own skin and play dress-up with someone else's life.

"I don't think I have any more in me, Jarvi," I said, resting my head on the back of the leather couch. "I'm beaten."

Jarvis came and sat down beside me, making the leather upholstery squeak. I couldn't help but grin—a move Jarvis did *not* appreciate.

"I think you enjoy being contrary," Jarvis said, his eyes trained on the large plate glass window overlooking the ocean. "You're so very eloquent at it."

Coming from Jarvis, I took that as a compliment.

I sat up and stretched, my neck and shoulders sore from overtensing. I opened my mouth to yawn, only to have my jaw crack in two places, startling me.

"It's not that I like being contrary," I said, trying not to sound trite. "It's just easier to say 'no' to something at first. But once I've let it sink in for a bit, I can usually be persuaded."

I didn't add that I'd said no to running Death, Inc., at first, too. Yet here I was, the acting President and CEO of that very company, happily doing a job I'd never in a million years have imagined myself doing, no matter what alternate universe I was living in.

"I suppose that makes sense on some level," Jarvis agreed. "You *are* reminiscent of an elderly human."

"Huh?"

Jarvis cocked his head and gave me a sly grin.

"Elderly humans are notorious for being stick-in-the-muds."

"I resent the implication," I parried. "For elderly people everywhere."

Above us, the grandfather clock chimed four times in slow succession, each strike like a fading heartbeat echoing in the darkened library. I'd forgotten to turn on the lights, and as dusk settled around us, there was an eerie feeling in the air. I shivered, gooseflesh pimpling as if someone were walking across my grave. A sense of foreboding made me reach over and turn on the green glass Tiffany lamp sitting on the nearby mahogany side table.

"Did you feel that?" I asked Jarvis, compelled by the strange knot of dread drawing tight inside my stomach.

Jarvis caught my eye, his face full of concern.

"Very odd," he murmured. "Very odd, indeed."

"I feel all cold and empty," I whispered. "Like someone just sucked all the good vibes out of the room."

Jarvis nodded, his eyes as wide as saucers of milk, each iris a pinprick orb.

"I believe out there, somewhere in the world, someone is plotting your Death."

"Not funny!" I said, glaring at Jarvis, who grinned sheepishly at me, the spell instantly broken.

"Well, it sounded spooky at any rate." He shrugged. "Besides, it's All Hallows' Eve 'Eve,' so someone should be enjoying themselves."

"Not at my expense." I glowered. "You're just peeved with me for flunking your wormhole course—as they say, Jarvis, those who can't *do*, teach, but I'm not sure what they say if you can't teach either . . ."

If the leather couch had had pillows, I'd have gotten one to the face for my comment. Instead, I was saved from a pummeling by the entrance of my favorite hellhound, Runt, who happily trotted into the room, carrying the handle of her pink leather overnight bag daintily in her mouth.

Dropping the bag at my feet, she sat back on her haunches, her black fur shiny and mint-scented from the bath I'd given her earlier in the day.

"Are you guys ready to go?" she trilled, her rich, feminine voice a dead ringer for Cate Blanchett's Queen in *Elizabeth*.

As cool as it was to have a talking hellhound for a friend, I did have to admit I still found it odd to hear a human voice coming out of an otherwise normal-looking dog. With her heart-shaped pink nose, shiny black coat, and doe brown eyes, Runt was more reminiscent of a black Lab crossed with a mastiff than a hellhound, but her keen intelligence, pleasant demeanor, and penchant for verbiage never let me forget she was also the daughter of Cerberus, the three-headed "former" Guardian of the North Gate of Hell, and not just one of man's faithful companions, the *Canis familiaris*.

Hellhounds usually started talking around their first birthday, so I'd known it was only a matter of time before Runt found her voice and started verbalizing—but, boy, did I get the shock of my life when she spoke for the first time . . . and out popped a reasonable facsimile of Cate Blanchett's voice. Apparently when Runt first moved to Sea Verge, Clio had been on a historical costume drama kick and all the "Mr. Darcy/Queen of England" action she'd exposed the pup to had affected Runt's learning curve way more than anyone had realized.

In my imagination, Runt's human incarnation was more in line with Cindy Brady than Queen Elizabeth, but who was I to judge? Just because I imagined the hellhound pup sounding like a ten-year-old girl—replete with blond pigtails, dimples, missing baby teeth, and an entirely pink wardrobe—didn't mean I couldn't accept the more regal version.

"I'm packed," I said, anticipating Jarvis's surprise and relishing it. Jarvis never expected me to be ready for anything, so it was nice every now and then to shock him with a little Boy Scout preparedness.

"And your dress?" Jarvis said, his tone sharp. "I should hope you had enough good sense not to *stuff* such an expensive garment in the carryall with all the rest of your toiletries."

"I'm not a lamebrain," I said, once again enjoying the idea that Jarvis had nothing to harass me about.

The dress—if you could even call it that; it was more like a fairytale princess gown than a frock—was still wrapped in the transparent plastic sheeting the dressmaker's assistant had delivered it in and safely packed in the black garment bag Jarvis had placed in my closet earlier that day.

I'd never had a gown made for me before. Heck, I'd never had *anything* made for me before, so it was with an ebullient skip in my step that I went to my first appointment with Mademoiselle La Rue, the seamstress to the Gods.

The day had gotten off to a shaky start when Jarvis had opened a wormhole leading directly to the Shakespeare & Company Bookstore in Paris—one of his favorite places in the whole world—and we'd emerged behind a row of books placed so haphazardly in their rows, I thought given the least provocation they might fall on top of us. To our surprise, we found two giggling American girls, each with dirty, straw-colored hair and the strong odor of patchouli in lieu of not having bathed, camped out behind the same shelf of disordered books.

The two girls were so involved with their own conversation that, at first, they didn't seem to notice the hulking, hipster man-child and the tinier, dark-haired Not-So-Grim-Reaper when we magically appeared beside them, but then, to my surprise, one of the girls gave us a wave.

"Want some 'shrooms, man?" she said, holding up a plastic baggie of brown, lichen-looking stuff for us to see. I'd never done mushrooms before, alcohol was more my poison of choice, but there was something very tempting about taking a break from my regularly scheduled programming to eat a few fungi and trip with these hippie chicks in the back of a famous Parisian bookstore.

"No, thank you," Jarvis bristled. "And you shouldn't be eating them either. They do terrible things to the human brain."

"Jarvis!" I said, smacking him on the arm. "Why do you always have to be such a Debbie Downer?"

"I am in no way a 'Debbie Downer,' as you say," he sniffed.

I rolled my eyes at the girl and she shrugged, turning back to her friend and ignoring us now that we'd identified ourselves as part of the establishment, not the counterculture.

"You didn't have to be so rude," I said to Jarvis as he hustled me away from the girls and toward the exit.

"I am not rude and I am not a Debbie Downer," Jarvis growled back at me as we hit the cool morning air, the shop door closing behind us with a soft *thunk*.

"Besides, you have an appointment to keep," Jarvis said brightly. "And you mustn't be late. It is a true honor for Mademoiselle La Rue to offer her services so freely."

"All right," I said, not wanting to argue with someone taller and snootier than me. "I'll be good and go see the French lady."

Jarvis smiled, pleased I was letting him win—because, more than anything, the ex-faun liked to win an argument. I think spending the majority of his existence as a faun, and a short one at that, had given him a Napoleon complex, making him testy and argumentative when he wasn't taken seriously. It was an annoying part of his personality, one you could *almost* overlook when he was small, but now that he was a supertall human with long, gangling limbs, it was less easy to ignore . . . and even more frustrating.

The hustle and bustle of Paris enveloped us as I followed Jarvis down winding cobblestone streets and open-air markets, past outdoor cafés crammed full of Parisians calmly sipping their espressos while, next to them, expatriates from North America and the rest of Europe hurriedly scribbled the pathos of their existential crises into dog-eared journals. It was like a mini-Shangri-la for the disaffected and disenfranchised of the world.

I'd only been to Paris twice with my family when I was a teenager, but each time we'd done the tourist thing: museums, Notre Dame, the Eiffel Tower, Versailles . . . in that order. I'd never been given free rein to go where I wanted in Paris before, had never walked down rambling old streets that seemed to lead nowhere then magically opened up to reveal seventeenth-century squares filled with tiny shops and cafés—and let me tell you, it was amazing.

"Do you like the city?" Jarvis asked as we walked underneath a crumbling stone archway and stepped into a tiny alleyway, the surrounding buildings so high they blocked out most of the natural light.

"Very much," I said as we picked our way across the ragged cobblestones, Jarvis in the lead.

As we walked, he grinned back at me, his eyes dancing with pleasure—and that was when I realized Jarvis could just as easily have opened a wormhole right into Mademoiselle La Rue's shop; instead he was giving me a treat, showing me the Paris he loved.

"Paris is awe—" I started to say, but wasn't able to complete the sentence because I had to prevent myself from running into Jarvis, who'd stopped short in front of a tiny wooden door.

"We're here," he said, pointing to a hand-carved sign hanging neatly above the doorway that read: SALON DE COUTURIER— PROPRIÉTAIRE: MADEMOISELLE LA RUE.

We stood there way longer than necessary because I was

waiting for Jarvis to open the door and go inside ahead of me, but he didn't budge.

"What?" I said, gesturing for him to go in first, but he shook his head.

"I'm not allowed inside. It's by appointment only."

"But you're with me and it's my appointment, so . . ." I trailed off.

Jarvis shook his head.

"You must go alone, Calliope."

I sighed, hating when Jarvis said stuff like that. Whenever ceremony dictated I do something alone, it usually meant the event was going to require a lot of sacrifice on my part and it was not going to be fun.

"It seems silly for you to wait outside . . ." But Jarvis was immovable. So with a feeling of growing disquiet, I reluctantly pushed open the heavy door and stepped inside, expecting the worst.

It was a tiny space, boasting wide, wooden plank floors and gorgeous, white plastered walls that looked as if they'd been installed before the French Revolution was even a blip on Marie Antoinette's radar. Just below the point where ceiling met wall someone had hand-painted a frieze of baby angels frolicking on fluffy cream clouds, masterful brushwork lighting their cherubic faces from within as they contemplated their surroundings with innocently manufactured expressions, their adorable derrieres and apple-round cheeks yummy enough to pinch.

While the rest of the shop was classic in its design, the space's good bones were overwhelmed by an ostentatious Louis XIVth desk and chair set, the golden gilt and scrolling so over the top, so gaudy, I had a hard time ripping my eyes away. A matching full-length mirror, dressed in the same eye-catching gilt as its desk and chair brethren, stood in the corner of the room, reflecting back the whole of the shop in the silvered expanse of its face.

My first impression was I'd have been happier shopping at Walmart than in this snooty shop—but we all know that the only princess gownage at Walmart is in the Barbie aisle.

As soon as I'd stepped into the room, the tinkling of the tiny silver bell above the front door had given away my presence, causing Mademoiselle La Rue to trot out from the back of the shop, her softly rounded body firm and supple as a racehorse. She wore her mane of light blond hair long and loose around her shoulders so that it seemed to float around her face in waves of softness, her pale pink lips, egalitarian brow, and aquiline nose instantly giving away her Gallic origins. Her large bosom and swollen hips were encased in a pale pink, watered silk wrap dress, cinched in the middle to show off a tiny, twenty-four-inch waist. Her legs were pale and smooth, her pink manicured toes peeking out shyly from within camel-colored peep-toe slingback pumps.

She smiled warmly at me, her pale lips curving slightly as she took in my Marc Jacobs blue jean dress and bright red ballet flats. My hair had finally started to grow again, the thick brown locks falling just above my shoulder blades and naturally curling inward a little bit at the ends, creating the illusion that it actually had some body. I'd worn my hair short for years, realizing it was easier to maintain a short cut than to spend hours in front of my bathroom mirror brushing rats' nests out of my long hair. But since I'd moved back to Sea Verge, I'd begun to let my hair grow again, and now I didn't even mind the morning detangling ritual; I found it cathartic even.

"You have modern tastes, yes?" Mademoiselle La Rue said, her English lightly accented, but impeccable.

I had trouble deciding how old the Frenchwoman was; her face was unlined, her body in the full blush of youth. In the timeless fashion of the French, she could have been twenty-five or forty-five, it was impossible to tell—but there was something about her voice, something *knowing* in the lilt of her words, that made me think she was much, much older than I even suspected.

She possessed a Marilyn Monroe nineteen-fifties vibe that was blatantly apparent in the contours of her shape (large bosom and hips, tiny waist) and the way she wore her makeup: heavy black liner and thick, painted brown brows. She could have been one of Alfred Hitchcock's cool, blond beauties ripped from her celluloid home and thrust into the modern era.

"If by modern tastes, you mean I'm more 'Alexander McQueen' Givenchy than traditional Givenchy, then, yes, I have *very* modern tastes," I said and Mademoiselle La Rue laughed, the gentle sound like the burbling of a mountain spring.

"Well, I can appreciate any couturier who can drape his own fabric," Mademoiselle said, "and Monsieur McQueen was a master."

With those words, I realized my mistake—the old adage "Don't judge a book by its cover" totally applied here. Mademoiselle La Rue may have owned a few pieces of gaudy French furniture and dressed like the heroine from *Vertigo* (and who says there was anything wrong with that?), but behind all the voluptuous beauty beat the heart of a true fashionista.

"Please call me Noisette," Mademoiselle La Rue said, smiling shyly at me.

I told her to call me Callie—and then we spent the rest of the afternoon drinking espresso and talking favorite designers while Noisette quietly sketched the outline of the gown I would one day wear to my first ever Death Dinner and Masquerade Ball.

So needless to say, I had not stuffed the gown in my weekend bag. I knew quality when I saw it and Noisette had made me the most beautiful gown I'd ever seen. As far as I was concerned, it was both a pleasure and a privilege to wear it.

"Shall we go then?" Jarvis asked, as visions of secret fashion assignations in Paris danced in my head.

I nodded, then shivered as the odd spooky feeling I'd had earlier returned to settle uncomfortably around my shoulders like an unwanted mink stole. I followed Jarvis and Runt out of the library, trying to dispel the morbid thoughts, but nothing I imagined was potent enough to displace the unease I felt. No matter what I did, I could not seem to unseat the gnawing dread that was starting to replace my excitement at attending my first ever Death Dinner as President and CEO of Death, Inc. Of course, I had no idea this was only a harbinger of what was to come, that I was about to spend the next twenty-four hours trapped in a blood-drenched whodunit.

three

The amount of luggage we had was ridiculous. Six bags for a three-person party—all because Jarvis traveled with way more luggage than any normal dude had a right to. Runt and I each had, like, *a* bag, but Jarvis had packed his entire wardrobe *and* the kitchen sink into four large, brown steamer trunks that looked like they'd have been more at home on the *Titanic* than in the twenty-first century.

"Are you sure you really need all that?" I'd asked as we stood in the foyer at Sea Verge, preparing to wormhole our way to the Haunted Hearts Castle, the location of this year's annual Death Dinner and All Hallows' Eve "Eve" Masquerade Ball.

Set in the heart of the California Central Coast, the Haunted Hearts Castle had been the chosen locale of the event for the last twenty years. The Castle's owner, Donald Ali, was one of those rare human beings intuitively aware of the Supernatural world. He came from a long line of truly psychic men and women who had made alliances with the purveyors of the Afterlife, creating a niche for themselves as liaisons between the human world and its Supernatural brethren. They weren't immortal and most of them had no magic-handling skills to speak of, but they were Sensitives, eager to engage with the unseen Supernatural world and collect all the "perks" that went along with working for and being socially involved with the Afterlife.

Even though I'd lobbied hard against it, Jarvis had insisted we take a wormhole to California. I'd begged him to consider a more traditional form of transportation, but my Executive Assistant was dead set on making me wormhole it to the Haunted Hearts Castle, telling me that no Grim Reaper under his watch was ever going to travel commercial to a formal Death, Inc., event. I offered a compromise which I thought was great: Death, Inc., could buy a personal jet and then we could all hit the West Coast in style—no commercial airlines, no TSA shenanigans; just luxury, luxury, *luxury*—but sadly, that suggestion was ixnayed, too.

Which was how I ended up on my knees in the middle of one of the Moroccan-themed courtyards at the Haunted Hearts Castle, throwing my guts up all over the hand-painted mosaic tile work—and let me just tell you that linguine backward is not a pleasant experience.

With that said, it's pretty apparent I am *not* a fan of traveling by wormhole and will do anything within my power to avoid it because, invariably, stepping into a great whirling mass of energy so I can be shunted into another time and/or place leaves me nauseous and unhinged. I know it's a necessary part of being Death, but I hate it with a passion reserved for cilantro and people that hit their pets.

Anyway, after I'd heaved the last of my lunch onto the gorgeous, blue-and-white mosaic tiles leading to the guest bedroom Runt and I would share for the duration of our stay at the Castle, I picked up my weekend bag—sans vomit, thanks to Runt's quick nose shove—and stepped into what I can only call a true masterpiece of opulence. We're talking sumptuous scarlet and indigo brocade tapestries on the walls, thick octagonal terra-cotta tile floors overlain by antique carpets chosen for the metallic accents that neatly dovetailed with the neo-Byzantium-styled gold leaf of the fireplace mantel; the place was an Oriental pleasure palace for the senses.

"Wow," I said, setting my bag down on one of the two full-size beds and running my hand across the smooth sheen of its deep burgundy, watered silk coverlet. "This place is unreal."

Runt followed me inside, dropping her pink leather bag on the floor beside the other bed while I went back and closed the courtyard door, extinguishing some of the natural light that had flooded the room upon our entrance.

"It's lovely," she agreed, her toenails click-clacking on the terra-cotta tile as she wandered over to check out the attached bathroom. To her pleasure, someone from the Castle staff had thoughtfully placed a water bowl and food dish filled to the brim with dog kibble underneath the white pedestal sink for her to use during her stay. On closer inspection we discovered the bowls were actually expensive white bone china soup tureens, their delicate fluted tops rimmed with a light cornflower blue pattern that blended perfectly with the minute blue-and-white mosaic tiles of the bathroom floor.

"Is that a closet?" I asked, sidestepping Runt's water bowl so I could open the white wooden closet door and peek inside.

"Not much to it," Runt said—and I had to agree. It was the thinnest closet I'd ever seen, not even seven inches in width by my guess, making it impossible to hang anything substantial inside it.

"What do you put in there?" I asked, but it was a rhetorical question. Obviously the closet, like many of the other decorative features of the Castle, was only for show.

Closing the shallow closet, we left the bathroom and returned to the bedroom.

"I think I'm gonna take a nap, Cal," Runt said as she hopped up onto her bed and circled three times, curling up in a tight ball of fluffy black fur in the center of the coverlet.

I looked out the window—there were two in the room, each separated from the other by a sliver of wall—and gaped at the beautiful panoramic view of the Pacific Ocean, marveling at how the sun resembled a pat of butter melting over the horizon.

"I'm gonna go for a walk, clear my head," I said, entranced by the view through the windows. "Maybe get a better look at that sunset."

My words fell on deaf ears. Runt was already snoring softly into her armpit. I lifted the edge of the coverlet over her, tucking it in around her prone form, then I slipped my sandals on and went outside for a better view.

* * *

"shit."

When you run into someone you don't want to see, there's something known as a ten-second rule: You have ten seconds to either hide, pretend you don't see them, or suck it up and say "hi."

I'd wasted nine seconds of my precious ten standing stock-still in the middle of the garden, my heart racing the Kentucky Derby inside my chest. I wanted to run—you could definitely lump that into the hiding category—but shock had bolted me to the walkway, my feet stuck to the brickwork like they'd been superglued there. As the final second came and went, I cringed, realizing I was screwed. I hadn't managed to make an exit, so now I was going to have to endure the suck-it-up-and-say-"hi" option.

Ugh.

I was trapped in one of the myriad sculpture gardens that graced the Haunted Hearts Castle—they all had specific names, but since they looked pretty much the same to me, I had no idea which one I'd stumbled into—so it wasn't like I could pretend I didn't see him as he stood by the edge of the garden, looking out at the vista that lay a thousand feet below him, the brilliant sapphire jewel tone of the Pacific Ocean edged with silver where waves crested and broke across the sandy lip of the beach.

He had his back to me, but from the rigid set of his shoulders, I could tell he knew I was there. His hair was still as dark and thick as I remembered, but now he'd cut it so short the pale skin at the nape of his neck was exposed, making him *seem* vulnerable even though I knew he was anything but. He was wearing an untucked white button-down shirt and a pair of loose khakis rolled up at the ankle, but my imagination immediately took liberties where Daniel, the former Devil's protégé, was concerned, and instead, I saw him the way I remembered him best: sprawled naked as a jaybird across the bed of my old Battery Park City apartment, a wry, seductive grin inked across his face. We'd spent enough time together that I knew every curve of his body, every hard place where muscle met bone and sinew. I'd licked and kissed every inch of him, and in the privacy of my dreams, I still did.

Daniel was the man whose very name made me want to cry because I'd loved him then lost him without even really meaning to. He was my big love—I knew that in my heart—and I'd fucked it up by letting some jerkoid finger me on a New York City Subway platform. I know it sounds crass—and it was—but it was the truth. I'd been scared of the magnitude of our relationship, had even, out of fear, pushed him away, and then I'd done the one thing he could never forgive: I'd cheated.

Therein lay my dilemma.

I was in love with Daniel—and he wanted absolutely nothing to do with me. Especially now that he was the acting Steward of Hell, looking after the Devil's former dominion while God figured out how to punish Lucifer for committing the ultimate faux pas: trying to stage a coup on Heaven and Purgatory. My friends and I, including Daniel, had foiled the Devil's plot, but during the course of the endeavor I'd lost a number of people I loved—including my man—and even though Daniel was still alive, he was as dead, at least to me, as all the others were.

My one comfort was that his new job had him so busy undoing all the evil stuff the Devil had done down in Hell, that it left him no time for any kind of a personal life—this important piece of info I'd wheedled out of Runt, whose father, Cerberus, had been granted the position "Hand to the Steward of Hell" for his part in helping to unravel the Devil's nefarious plans—and if anyone knew what Daniel was up to these days, it was him.

"How you doing, Cal?"

While I'd been mentally undressing him, Daniel had turned around—and the effect he had on my heart was devastating. My breath caught in my throat so it was all I could do to gurgle a strangled, "Hi, Daniel" back at him.

Though the sun was still out, its last rays keeping the night at bay, I felt frozen in place by the intensity of his gaze. "Paul Newman eyes" my mother had called them when she'd first gotten a look at Daniel's ice blue peepers. To my surprise, she'd given me a sly wink of approval—something I'd rarely gotten from her in the past and would be even more hard pressed to come by in the future since she'd left her old life behind and returned to the sea.

As much as I disliked how she'd handled the situation, I couldn't really fault my mother for ditching out on Clio and me—my dad's murder had pulverized her already-fragile psyche, and then my older sister's defection, and subsequent murder, had been the death knell. The dual blow of losing both husband and daughter had turned our mother into a wraith, a Milquetoast ghost of her former self. Clio and I hadn't known what to do with her, so we'd brought her back to Sea Verge—the home my parents had shared for so many years—and installed her in her old rooms, hoping it would somehow draw her out. Instead, it'd done the opposite: She'd burrowed even deeper inside herself, sitting for hours on end in an old Chippendale chair that looked out over the mercurial blue sea. And then one day she was gone. Back to the water from whence she'd come.

My hope was that she'd returned to the Siren family she'd disowned when she'd married my dad, but I had no idea of her true fate. The woman had borne more suffering than any one creature should ever have to—and being an immortal, instead of just one lifetime to mourn the loss of the thing she'd held most dear, she would have an eternity in which to do it.

"Oh, you know," I said finally, though I didn't have a clue what that meant.

There was an awkward pause as I stared at Daniel and he held my gaze. It took every ounce of strength I possessed not to start blubbering in front of him because just being near the man was the most exquisite torture I'd ever known. I'd never been an overly emotional person before, but these days I'd become a pro at crying over absolutely nothing. I was getting so good at it, in fact, that I was actually considering adding it to my professional skill set.

In the days after my dad died and Daniel broke up with me, I'd been numb, my brain set on autopilot just so I could get through the day, but as time had worn on, all the pain and frustration had returned full force and the grief I thought I'd escaped had come back to stab me in the heart.

"How have *you* been?" I asked, keeping my voice as level as possible—which was really frickin' hard when all I wanted to do was howl like a banshee.

Daniel shrugged, his eyes shifting downward, unlocking from my gaze.

"I'm all right. Keeping busy."

I nodded. What else was I supposed to do with that innocuous piece of information?

"Well, I'm good," I said finally, opting for a lie rather than the messy, mushy truth. "Been taking meetings and Jarvis has been giving me all these lessons, trying to get me up to snuff on all this Death stuff—"

I cringed, embarrassed by the extreme case of diarrhea mouth I'd just developed. God, I just couldn't seem to shut myself up.

"That's great, Cal," Daniel said, taking pity on me and interrupting my verbal barrage.

"Yep, pretty great," I echoed.

I suddenly felt very uncomfortable; my brain itching with the claustrophobic sensation of being trapped inside my own body, a sensation I could only imagine was reminiscent of being encased inside a too-tight spacesuit. I'd never experienced such an odd feeling before, and it made me want to rip my skin off so I could crawl out of myself. My light gingham summer dress, which I usually loved wearing, was now as heavy as a shroud, making my flesh squirm underneath the crinkly cotton fabric.

"How are you, really?"

Daniel's question caught me unaware. It was so pointed, so real, that it distracted me from the weird sense of internal entrapment I was experiencing.

"Uhm . . ." I started to say then stopped, wanting to answer him honestly. "Actually, not so great, really. If you want to know the truth."

He nodded like he'd expected as much.

"Me, too," he confided, finally looking me in the eye. "Not so great."

My throat constricted, the soft flesh of my tongue pressing firmly against my upper palate as I tried not to cry. It was a useless dodge; I wasn't strong enough to fight back the wave of utter misery that overwhelmed me.

"I, uh . . ." The words wouldn't come without bringing tears.

Daniel nodded again as if he knew what I was thinking. As if, in fact, he had the exact same emotions coursing inside him, too—though he seemed to have a much better handle on the crying part. He let out a shaky breath and grinned, but there was no happiness in his eyes, only my misery mirrored back at me. We stood like that, two people experiencing a shared, bone-aching pain, and in that moment, we were the only two people left in all of the world. I could feel my heart thunking like sludge, its steady beat drowning out all other sound as I stared into Daniel's eyes. We were in a vacuum, a lonely place of our own making, where nothing else existed but each other.

Then the moment was lost as he sighed and looked away. I sensed him trying to recollect his emotions, to blot out this brave new world our misspent love had created. When he looked back up at me, the connection had been severed, the thrum between us, which had been so strong that it shook me from the inside out, was gone and I was back in my own body, the itch to climb out of myself, no more.

"OMG! Is that Calliope Reaper-Jones?!"

The voice was loud and unmistakably feminine. I turned around to find its saucy-looking owner barreling toward me, her large, braless breasts jiggling inside a tight, blue spandex minidress that barely grazed the tops of her very tanned upper thighs. She was tiny, barely five feet on a good day, I guessed. Yet the dangerously high wedge heels she'd strapped on to her dainty feet made her much closer to my height.

"You didn't tell me you knew her," the girl chided Daniel as she slid between us and possessively took his arm, letting me know, without words, he belonged to her.

It was like a punch in the gut to see the girl hanging all over Daniel like he was her own personal jungle gym. She was laying on the classless sexual mojo act with a trowel, letting me know exactly where I stood as far as Daniel was concerned. And at least he had the decency to look embarrassed by the show.

"Aren't you going to introduce us?" she cooed, oblivious to the fact neither Daniel nor I had said a word since she'd sashayed her perky butt over and interrupted our little . . . *whatever* it was.

"Calliope, this is Coy."

She stuck her hand out and the charm bracelets she wore looped around her wrist jangled in concert.

"Hiya!" she chirped, her pouty red lips bunched together in what I realized, belatedly, was a smile.

With a feeling of resignation, I took her delicate brown fingers in mine and let her pump my arm up and down.

"Nice to meet you."

She did that pout/smile thing again, the corners of her eyes bunching up adorably around creamy, chocolate milk–colored irises and dark fringed lashes.

"Oh, it's just amazing to finally meet you," she giggled. "I've been following your career and you're, like, amazing."

My career? I thought to myself. *Amazing?*

"And what's so amazing about it?" I found myself saying, the snarky words snaking past my lips against my better judgment.

Coy missed the sarcasm.

"You're just a real inspiration, ya know? You were, like, nothing and then you were, like, *something*—it was amazing! Even in Mexico City we know all about the new Death girl!"

I tried to catch Daniel's eye, but the coward was too busy staring at his feet to acknowledge me.

"And how did you meet Daniel, Coy?" I asked, ignoring her overuse of the word "amazing" and steering us to what I hoped was a more banal topic of conversation.

Coy laughed, covering her mouth with her hand, in a move straight out of Anime Land. I'd seen a bajillion Japanese girls sport the same gesture to great effect, but it just seemed twee when Coy did it.

"Oh, Daniel and I just happened to run into each other one day. He was just so adorable I couldn't help myself."

"Uh-huh."

"Isn't he just precious?" she purred, reaching up and wrapping her fingers around Daniel's chin so she could turn his face in her direction and plant her cherry red lips right onto his.

Daniel looked startled and tried to pull away, but she held him firm. I wanted to barf. No, I wanted to punch her in the face. But the whole thing made me feel so horribly conflicted, I, therefore, could do absolutely nothing at all. Instead, I just stood there and grinned stupidly at Daniel and his new lover.

"Precious," I heard myself agreeing as I stared at the red lipstick imprint she'd left on Daniel's lips.

All I could think was: *Damn it, those are my lips!*

"I'm so excited to be here for the Death Dinner and Masquerade Ball," I tuned back in to hear Coy saying. "I couldn't believe it when Daniel asked me to be his date. Have you seen our room? OMG, it's just amazing."

They're sharing a room?! my brain screamed at me.

"And I brought the cutest little minibikini to wear," Coy was babbling. "It's white with tiny silver rhinestones . . . so adorable. I got it at Saks Fifth Avenue."

My gut clenched. Not only had the Mexican strumpet stolen my man, she'd totally usurped my slutster bikini, too. It was like I'd stepped into some alternate-universe version of *Single White Female*, only to find myself in the Jennifer Jason Leigh role—one more push from Coy and I'd be going all crazy attack bitch on her ass.

"Well, I gotta go," I said abruptly, turning on my heel and heading blindly in the opposite direction.

"Callie!" I heard Daniel call out behind me, but I ignored him. I had absolutely zero intention of letting him see how much he'd hurt me.

As soon as I was out of their line of vision, I started to run, stumbling into another one of the Castle's many sculpture gardens as the wet, hot tears began to course down my cheeks. My lungs burned from holding my breath as I fought back the racking sobs that threatened to spill out of me if I relaxed my vigilance for even a second.

I was so crushed by emotion I didn't see the old woman until I was on top of her. We collided with a bone-crunching *thwunk* and then I was sprawled on the ground at her feet, the back of my head throbbing in time to my heartbeat. How the old woman had managed to stay upright after our run-in, I had no idea, but there she was, looking down at me like I was intentionally blocking her path with my prostrate body.

"Sorry," I mumbled, cradling the back of my head with my hand as I tried to pick myself up.

The old woman reached out an emaciated mocha arm, her thin gray hair falling forward and across her weather-beaten face as she offered to help me up. I didn't want to offend her, so I grabbed the proffered hand, surprised when she easily pulled me to my feet. I'd misjudged her strength completely; this was *not* some fragile old lady with tissue paper skin and a delicate constitution.

She smiled at me, revealing two rows of solid white teeth that were all her own, though her dark skin was layered with the wrinkled folds of age and sun damage.

"Best be careful where you're going, Mistress Death," the old woman said, her words slow as honey dripping from a spoon. "There are evil spirits loose tonight."

I swallowed hard then nodded as the creepy feeling I'd been fighting all day returned with the old woman's words.

"You know what I mean," she continued, her Aboriginal accent giving her speech an undulating lilt. "Careful now."

She released my hand—I hadn't even realized she was still holding it—and made a funny clicking sound in the back of her throat. In my peripheral vision I saw a flurry of brown wings as a small owlet arced across the sky and gracefully landed on the old woman's shoulder. I took a step back and the creature's large amber eyes blinked thoughtfully at me, as if to let me know I had nothing to fear from it.

The old woman petted the top of the owlet's head and the bird turned its neck to get into a better position for scratching. It reminded me of some of the odd pretzel poses Runt wriggled herself into in order to have just the right spot scratched.

"Who are you?" I asked as the old woman cooed at the owlet, her dark eyes almost glowing in the twilight. She ignored my question, just continued ministering to her bird's needs as if I wasn't there. Maybe to her, I wasn't.

I tried another tack.

"I'm Calliope Reaper-Jones."

At this, the old Aboriginal woman finally looked up at me, her sturdy mud brown eyes locking onto my own with a fierce intensity.

"I know what you are."

The flat tone of her voice made my skin crawl. It was more than a statement. It was a pronouncement of something wicked yet to come.

"Okay," I said quietly, starting to back away. "I gotta go now."

My fear seemed to amuse the old woman and she started to

cackle, the rich honey of her voice turning to tar in her throat. I took off, not bothering to find out what other words of wisdom the old woman might be looking to impart to me.

But as I made my way down the mottled path, my feet speeding me away from the unsettling old woman as fast as they could carry me, I swear I heard these words drifting behind me like a malevolent curse:

"Best mind your head, Calliope Reaper-Jones."

four

I got back to my room without further incident, though it did take me twenty minutes to find Casa de la Luna, the building that housed the guest suite I wǎs sharing with Runt. I had to wander through two more sculpture gardens full of ancient Roman statuary—misshapen marble ladies and gentlemen without their arms, and in some cases heads, perched precariously among an assortment of flowering greenery—before I finally stumbled onto the main path.

It was once true that all roads led to Rome—and to borrow the adage: At the Haunted Hearts Castle all paths led to Casa del Amo, or the Master's House.

Aptly named, it loomed large over the rest of the compound, a quiet sentry composed of a bland limestone gray façade, but offset by a backdrop of startling azure sky. Inside, it housed a library, a massive room lined from floor to ceiling with dark wood bookcases, each crammed full of rare tomes from every continent, including an original vellum copy of the Guttenberg Bible sitting on a glass-enclosed pedestal near the door; the kitchen—the only modern space in the whole Castle—which was a bastion of efficiency with its stainless steel fixtures and industrial ovens, and the capacity to serve over seventy-five guests at one time; and, lastly, a formal dining room with heavy

African blackwood paneling and a long, rectangular oak table that could comfortably seat up to fifty.

There were over ten guest rooms in the Castle, as well as Donald Ali's master suite, which took over the whole of the top floor of the building and was only reached via a twisting, hand-carved circular oak staircase near the front entrance. I hadn't been up there, but from what Jarvis said, it was like a Moroccan palace—lots of Moorish details and hand-painted mosaic tile work mixed with medieval tapestries and curling Oriental rugs.

Built by a World War I war profiteer named Ezra Aaron Hearts in 1921, the Hearts Castle had been conceived as a Frankenstein's monster, if you will, of old-world architecture; a cannibalization of the most famous buildings and antiquities Ezra Hearts had collected during his many travels, so that he might admire them all in one glorious setting.

As a poor orphan eking out a hardscrabble existence as a breaker boy in Western Pennsylvania, he'd sworn that one day he would be rich beyond his wildest dreams, thus affording himself the opportunity to become the master of his own dominion. This was a seemingly unattainable dream for a dirt-poor boy from Pennsylvania, a boy whose life should never have included the realization of such a lofty goal, yet with the inception of the Hearts Castle, the confluence of all those fantabulous childhood imaginings was made real.

Ezra had chosen the site, a large outcropping of land over-looking the Pacific Ocean on one side and the small harbor town of Saint Simon, California, on the other, for its majestic views and plentiful grazing land—he had high hopes of bringing the American buffalo back from the brink of extinction by mass breeding them for commercial meat consumption, but sadly that vision, among many others, was never realized.

A construction worker discovered Ezra's body on the grounds of Casa del Amo early one morning in 1929. The mysterious nature of his death—had he jumped from the building's second-story turret window or had he been pushed—was never unraveled, but work was immediately halted on the munificent Castle. And when it was revealed that Ezra Hearts was bankrupt—even a war profiteer wasn't immune to the fluctuations of the stock market—the property sat like an empty shell, unfinished and unloved, until 1955, when a young entrepreneur named Donald Ali saw it while on vacation in Saint Simon and fell in love with the dilapidated structure. He bought the compound and all the adjoining land, using the original architectural plans to finally finish what Ezra Hearts had begun.

"Haunted" Hearts Castle had never been anyone's idea of a name for the property, but during the 1950s reconstruction so many workers reported seeing odd, unexplainable things during their time there that the name just stuck. Donald Ali had taken it all in stride, even commissioning a large ranch sign with the words HAUNTED HEARTS CASTLE in swirling wrought iron above the entrance to the private road leading to the grounds.

I was keen on picking up one of the battery-powered golf carts they kept for guests and going on a trip down the long private road so I could see the sign for myself. Gossip had it that the HEARTS—and only the HEARTS—part of the sign stayed a toxic rust red, no matter what anyone did to prevent it.

Spooky!

I followed the footpath until I reached Casa de la Luna, my emotions still running high as I threw open the door and found Jarvis sitting at the antique oak desk talking to Runt.

"There's a crazy lady attending this Death Dinner, isn't there?" I asked as I stood in the doorway, hoping I didn't look as unhinged as I felt.

Jarvis crooked an eyebrow in my direction.

"Describe her, please?" he said, crossing his legs and leaning forward thoughtfully.

"Uhm, she's crazy—"

"You already said that," Jarvis reminded me.

"Okay, sorry. Uhm, she's Australian and she has an owlet thing—"

Runt sat up on her bed and barked.

"Oh, oh! I know this one," she said, her tail wagging a mile a minute. "It's Anjea. She's the Vice-President in Charge of the Australian continent. And the owlet is really a mud baby."

"A mud-what?" I said, wrinkling my brow in confusion—though all I really wanted to know was if I was going to have to sit next to the woman at the dinner table and make awkward conversation.

"Her purveyance is mud, the creation of life from the primordial ooze if you will," Jarvis said, looking at me like I was slow.

I rolled my eyes.

"That means I am totally gonna have to shoot the shit with her at dinner, doesn't it?" I said, flopping down on the other bed and kicking my shoes off.

"Actually," Jarvis continued, "you will be sitting at the head of the table next to Kali—"

I sat up, feeling excited about something for the first time since we'd arrived.

"I didn't know she was coming tonight," I said, giddy that Kali was on board for the Death Dinner. If the Hindu Goddess of Death and Destruction was gonna be there, then the night was bound to get interesting.

"She wasn't supposed to attend, but Wodin found himself indisposed and Kali was selected to represent the Board of Death," Jarvis said, pulling a pair of pince-nez from his suit coat pocket and sliding them up his proboscis of a nose.

"Oh, please, not the pince-nez." I squirmed, disliking the tiny, templeless glasses a little more each time I saw them. I hadn't minded them so much when Jarvis was in his faun's body—the Tom Selleck visage and small stature actually made the pince-nez seem kind of roguish—but on his new Brooklyn-hipster-cool face, they just looked ridiculous.

"Am I going to have to use 'the hand,' Calliope?" Jarvis intoned, looking down his nose—and pince-nez—at me.

Jarvis was referring to his favorite quote of all time: a Fran Drescher, *Nanny*-era bon mot he liked to whip out whenever possible, regardless of the fact it was about as très passé as Vanilla Ice. Now, as much as I loved to tease my Executive Assistant, I'd actually been dying for him to trot out the Drescher quote because I'd had a little "surprise" made for him and it was best shared while "in context."

"Runt?" I said, turning to the hellhound. "Can you get that, uhm, *thing* for Jarvis, please?"

Runt, who was in on the surprise, hopped down from her

spot on the bed and began to nose around inside her pink leather bag until she found the prize I'd asked her to stow away for me.

"Clio, Runt, and I love you very much," I said as Runt carried the metallic gift bag over to Jarvis, who took it with only a smidge of healthy trepidation.

I didn't blame him. If the tables were turned and *I* was the one getting a nicely wrapped package from him, I'd be nervous, too.

"What is it?" Jarvis asked, holding the paper handle between two fingers like the thing was full of dynamite set to explode on a hair trigger.

"It's a present. For you," Runt said excitedly, sitting back on her haunches and patiently thumping her tail against the carpet as she waited for Jarvis to dig in.

The pup didn't have a mean-spirited bone in her body so she was oblivious to Jarvis's apprehension. In her world, friends never played mean pranks on each other. Thankfully, this was a world neither Jarvis nor I inhabited because as much as it sucked to be on the receiving end of an embarrassing incident, it was equally as joyous to be the one doing the embarrassing.

Jarvis cleared his throat—biding his time, I surmised—then he removed his trusty pince-nez from his nose and lovingly placed them in his pocket, where they would be safe from any indignities he might be about to suffer. With a sigh, he closed his eyes and stuck his hand into the bag, expecting the worst. When nothing terrible happened—no explosion, no animal attack, or steel trap shutting on his wrist—he opened one eye and looked down to see what his fingers had plucked from inside the bag.

With a sigh, he lifted the sea foam green T-shirt up into the air so it unfolded lengthwise, allowing him to see the quote I'd had screen-printed onto it especially for him.

"TALK TO THE HAND—IT'S NOT RETRO 'TIL IT'S ON A T-SHIRT," Jarvis read out loud, taking his time with the words as a funny look stole across his angular face.

Eyebrows scrunching together to form a solid line of bushy hair just below his forehead, Jarvis's lips pursed into that weird pretzel shape you make when you eat something supertart like a Sour Patch Kid. Though he continued to hold the T-shirt up in the air, his focus was definitely elsewhere.

Runt started to whine, pacing, as dogs are wont to do when they're nervous or confused. She and I had both thought Jarvis would love the T-shirt, so this kink in the plot was throwing her little world into retrograde. Darkness had begun to settle like a cloak around the room and the windows, which had shown me such a brilliant view of the sunset earlier in the afternoon, were now empty. I reached over and turned on the bedside lamp to add some warmth to the paltry yellow glow coming from the overhead lighting.

"Jarvis, are you okay?" I asked, my voice finishing half an octave higher than it'd started.

"I'm . . . It's just . . ." The words had left Jarvis's mouth of their own volition, and when they stopped, they were replaced not by silence, but by the trembling of his lower lip.

To my astonishment, one giant tear surfaced in the caruncle of his right eye, then slowly slid down the side of his face. The tension in his body seeming to dissipate with the release of the tear, he let out a long, shuddering breath before dropping his hands into his lap.

Runt got the message more quickly than I did. Instantly she was beside him, her textured pink tongue licking his hand as he began to cry in earnest.

"I thought it was going to be something terrible," Jarvis hiccupped as more tears snaked down his cheeks, the sobs making his skinny body shake uncontrollably.

I got up from my perch on the bed, picking my way over the luggage on the floor until I was beside my Executive Assistant, my arms wrapping around his shoulders.

"Well, that's the last time we get *you* a present," I cooed, trying hard to lighten the mood—my intention had been to make Jarvis happy, not send him on a crying jag.

Jarvis and I had been through a lot of pretty heavy shit together, but damn, I'd never have pegged him for a guy to get emotional over a T-shirt.

"I'm fine," Jarvis said, pulling away from me so he could wipe the tears from his cheeks. To his credit, he was able to compose himself pretty quickly.

With the T-shirt sitting like a talisman on his lap, he took a shuddering breath and smiled up at me.

"Thank you," he said, looking down at the T-shirt again. "Thank you both."

"And Clio, too!" Runt added—the kindest, sweetest hellhound in all history.

"And Clio, of course," Jarvis said, giving the back of Runt's head a pat.

"We imagined you having a totally different reaction," I said as I sat back, my butt against the desk. "More along the lines of 'happy, happy, joy, joy,' you know?"

"It is the nicest, most thoughtful gift *anyone* has ever given me," Jarvis said softly. "It truly is."

Now I was the one starting to feel all teary-eyed.

"It's just a T-shirt," I mumbled.

"But it took thought and planning and genuine affection," Jarvis said as he lifted the T-shirt up to his chest.

"And it's sea foam green, which is kinda, you know, an inside joke," I added quickly. "'Cause we have inside jokes."

After my dad was kidnapped, I'd been forced into completing three impossible tasks by the Board of Death to prove I was capable of handling the Death job until my dad was found. The first task had been to borrow Runt from Cerberus (obviously, I'd never really given her back) and the second was to collect this magical sea foam stuff from the God Indra (the same Indra who was now Clio's boyfriend). Jarvis had been instrumental in the tasks getting completed—more than instrumental, it wouldn't have happened without him—and I thought it would be cute to get the T-shirt in *sea foam* green 'cause I'm just a big, old, sentimental dork.

"That's not really an inside joke," Jarvis said. "It's more of a shared history."

"Same difference," I replied as Jarvis took off his suit coat and slipped the T-shirt over his blue button-down. I'd opted for a crew neck T-shirt in large and it seemed to fit my Executive Assistant perfectly.

"Does it look good?" Jarvis asked Runt.

She barked her approval.

"Should I wear it to the Masquerade Ball?"

I laughed.

"Then everyone will know it's you."

Jarvis considered this for a moment, then shook his head.

"That doesn't really matter in my case—and it might actually be nice to wear my catchphrase . . ."

I didn't want to encourage him—but I didn't want him to start crying again either—so I just gave a noncommittal nod and hoped better sense would prevail.

"Speaking of Masquerade Balls," Jarvis said, digging in his suit coat pocket and pulling out the dreaded pince-nez again.

"Uhm—"

"I need them to see, so bugger off," he said in response to my look of disdain.

Resting the glasses on the bridge of his nose, he cleared his throat, the light from the lamp refracting in his lenses.

"Now," he continued, pulling out a piece of neatly folded parchment paper from his pocket and reading from it. "Your schedule for the night is as follows: At nine o'clock you will attend the All Hallows' Eve 'Eve' Masquerade Ball. There you will greet the guests and make pleasantries—"

"Sounds like a blast," I said to Runt, who thumped her tail in agreement.

"Then you will come back to the room, and at eleven forty-five on the dot, I will accompany you to Casa del Amo," Jarvis continued, ignoring me. "I suggest that you ladies begin your toilet now. It's almost seven and I expect both of you to be ready and waiting when I come back to fetch you at eight thirty because we have a quick stop to make before dinner."

"Okay, I think we got it—" I started to say, but Jarvis bulldozed over me as he continued his directions.

"Your gown is hanging in the armoire, right here," he said, pointing to the art deco oak armoire in the corner before turning to Runt, "and your collar is in there as well."

"I think we can manage this," I said as Jarvis stood, pocketing both the parchment and pince-nez. "Right, Runt?"

"It's going to be a lovely evening," Runt said, her ears standing at attention. "I'm excited to see all the different dresses and masks!"

"I'm curious to see who's wearing which designer," I said to Runt as Jarvis gave us one more warning to be ready on time then left us to get dressed himself.

"I just wish we were wearing masks," Runt said sadly as I removed her plain, pink collar and slid the rhinestone one around her neck, adjusting it so it wasn't too tight.

"Me, too."

I really was a bit bummed about the whole mask thing. Everyone else got to be all mysterious and sexy . . . while I was forced to pull a Queen/hostess move and just stand at the door, unmasked, greeting everybody. Being the Grim Reaper had its perks, but this wasn't one of them. I may have gotten the awesome couture gown, but I'd be maskless for the entire All Hallows' Eve "Eve" Ball.

When Jarvis had first explained the evening to me, my first question had been:

"But why not have the ball on Halloween?"

That's when it was painstakingly explained to me that at midnight on October 31, magic ceased to work. People still died, but Death couldn't collect their souls until midnight on the following night when it officially became All Saints' Day. This was why people considered Halloween to be the time when the veil between life and death was at its thinnest—what they didn't realize was that the spooky stuff they encountered was due entirely to the presence of the recently departed souls who were left wandering around the Earth while they waited for magic to return. Once the second hand hit twelve on November 1, signaling the beginning of All Saints' Day, everything went back to normal and the transporters and harvesters I employed at Death, Inc., could then come and collect the orphaned souls.

It was a logical explanation for the existence of Halloween, but one I was perfectly fine ignoring in favor of the spooky, costume-wearing consumerism the Western world had accorded to the holiday. I wanted to see kids dressed like vampires and zombies, pretty princesses and Ronald Reagan, their jack-o'-lantern buckets, paper bags, and pillowcases exploding with candy and other treats. There was something deliciously unsettling about someone with half their baby teeth still in their head screeching "Trick or Treat" at you as they shoved their candy collecting receptacles in your face.

If you think I'm just being a sentimental human wannabe,

well, let me tell you, I acquired my love of the fiendish holiday directly from my dad, the former Grim Reaper himself.

Whenever I thought of Halloween, I had a very distinct memory of my dad dressed, for some odd reason, as a Wall Street banker, his mane of wavy blond hair curling around his handsome face, as he held my hand and carried Clio—who couldn't have been more than two—while we trudged through the darkness toward whichever unsuspecting house was next on our "hit list." Until I'd taken over his job, I'd never understood that for my dad, Halloween was his one and only night off the clock. When there were no Death duties to attend to, no bureaucratic problems that needed solving . . . magic was on hold, and for that one precious evening, he wasn't the Grim Reaper, but a normal man who cheerily spent his night of freedom hiking up and down Bellevue Avenue—and farther inland when the candy dried up there—making sure his daughters, the Cowardly Lion and Snow White, respectively, went home with an equal amount of candy in their buckets, so there'd be no squabbling over the spoils.

Now, here I was twenty years later, following in my dad's footsteps. I'd fought my fate for as long as I could, never realizing that maybe it wasn't such a terrible fate after all. Death was the great leveler between Heaven and Hell, Good and Evil . . . and it was up to me to make sure that things stayed in balance.

Of course, the nagging little voice chose just that moment to rear its nasty head.

If you're up for the job, that is, it whispered. *The balance will be kept only if* you *can manage it.*

Then with doubt simmering in my brain, I took Noisette's gown from the armoire and began to get ready for my first ever Death Dinner and Masquerade Ball.

five

The gown was delicate black gauze, spreading out around my feet in waves of fabric that simulated the nacre layers of a bed of oyster shells. The boning in the bodice held tight to my rib cage, dipping down to expose the rounded curves of my cleavage before nipping in at my waist and flowing sinuously over the arc of my hips in ragged swaths of material. In keeping with my position as Death, two large rhinestone skulls decorated the bodice. Except that, considering Noisette's bill, there was a good chance they were not rhinestones . . .

The gown swayed as I walked, the tattered gauze flowing around me like kelp caught in the undulating currents of the sea. I'd borrowed a pair of strappy black high-heeled sandals and some simple diamonds from my mother—heck, it wasn't like she was there to care if I raided her amazing, designer-strewn walk-in closet—but I'd eschewed any other adornment, thinking it would weigh down the ephemeral qualities of the gown.

"You look amazing," Runt said as she watched me snap on the back of my left earring then adjust the bodice of the gown so my cleavage was a little less exposed.

"It's the dress. Whoever said that clothes make the man, well, they were on the money," I shot back at her, but inside I was just as blown away as Runt was by how good I looked. Noisette was the couturier to the Gods for a reason, I decided. The woman had to weave magic into her creations because I'd never looked half as beautiful as I did in this gown.

Of course, I'd helped the gown out a little bit by doing a pretty bang-up job on my makeup and hair. After taking a quick shower, I'd set my lanky locks in hot rollers and applied a healthy dose of smoky silver eyeliner and shadow. Then I'd released my hair from the torture devices (the hot rollers) and used a spray borrowed from my sometimes-Goth kid sister, which darkened my usually fairly nondescript brownish hair to a mysterious glossy black. Then I blew it out, poufing it up far more than usual, then pulling down a few strands in what I had to admit were some pretty darn sexy wispy bangs. No denying it—I looked hot.

There was a rectangular mirror attached to the back of the delicate oak vanity and I stood in front of it, admiring my handiwork. In its surface, I could see the whole room reflected back at me: the two hand-carved teakwood beds with their glorious gold-and-scarlet coverlets, the gold gilt mantel, curving art deco armoire, and matching deco dresser that took over the far corner of the room, the delicate tracery desk and chair next to me—the whole space was a potpourri of dark wood paneling and spicy red-and-gold accents.

As I stood in my glittering black gown beside Runt, who was wearing her best dress collar (red, which looked especially nice with her fur), my dark eyes seemed lit from within. I surveyed the beauty that surrounded us and realized that I looked as if I was born for the part I was about to play.

There was a polite rap at the door—a patented Jarvis move—and Runt and I called out "Come in!" at the exact same time, which totally made us giggle.

The brass knob turned, hinges creaking as Jarvis, clad in a tailored black tuxedo, gold cufflinks, and shiny black dress shoes with gold buckles, swung the door open and stepped inside, instantly slipping his pince-nez onto the end of his nose so he could give us a quick once-over. Pleased by what he saw, he smiled and brought his hands together happily, rubbing them in anticipation.

"Noisette has outdone herself with that gown," he purred. "Do a spin, Calliope. I want to see the ruching in the back."

I rolled my eyes, embarrassed, but obliged him by doing a quick turn in place, the dress gracefully flowing around me as I baby-stepped in a circle.

"Perfect!" Jarvis said, giving me a wide smile. "Ladies, I have to say, you both look exquisite."

"You look great, too, Jarvis," Runt said. "And we were both ready on time just for you."

"Yes, and that impresses me most of all," Jarvis agreed. "Shall we go then?"

He offered me his arm, which I accepted, and the three of us left the comfort of the suite, stepping out into the tepid October night.

"who's that?" i asked as we passed a tall man I'd never seen before standing in the courtyard. He was wearing a dark suit and tie, an earpiece plugged into his right ear. He nodded to Jarvis as we passed by, his eyes giving my scantily clad upper body a discreet once-over that was both embarrassing and exciting.

Well, at least I knew the gown was a success.

"That," Jarvis said, once the man was out of earshot, "is a bodyguard. A human one."

"For who?" I said, trying not to trip over the bottom of my dress as I walked. I hadn't really thought much about mobility when I'd sat with Noisette in her shop, oohing and aahing over her concept for the gown, but reality was a bitch. It took everything I had to walk, talk, and not trip over myself at the same time.

"For whom," Jarvis corrected, as if he were a member of the grammar police.

"Yes, for whom, whatever."

"As you know, at midnight all magic ceases and for the next twenty-four hours you and all the rest of the immortals—"

"Including us," Runt chimed in.

Jarvis nodded. "Yes, that includes hellhounds and Executive Assistants, who happen to be immortal, too—"

As we left the courtyard, I tripped over a loose stone and Jarvis had to grab my arm so I wouldn't fall flat on my face.

"Stupid dress," I said under my breath, annoyed by how vulnerable being all gussied up made me feel.

"As I was saying before you almost wiped out back there," Jarvis continued, ignoring my glare. "For the next twenty-four hours we are all mortal—"

I stopped in my tracks, digging my heels in where I stood, wondering why Jarvis had left this crucial piece of information out of the, like, *five* previous briefings we'd had about the Death Dinner.

"Excuse me, but rewind please, Jarvis."

"Let's just keep moving," Jarvis said, but I'd staked my place on the walkway, and like a stubborn mule, I wasn't moving until I got some answers.

"Uh-uh, 'you got some 'splainin' to do, Lucy,'" I growled at him, doing my best Desi Arnaz impression.

Jarvis sighed, knowing it would be easier to do his explaining now rather than spend ten minutes arguing with me.

"I didn't want to frighten you—"

"Frighten me?" I interrupted. "You're not frightening me, you're just, like, leaving me majorly out of the loop. To the point where I'm gonna look like an idiot in front of the people you want me to impress."

"Oh, yes, I do see how that could—"

I cut him off.

"Jarvis, I'm here. I'm invested. I want to do this. I just need you to treat me like an adult and give me all the pertinent information so I can do my job correctly."

It took Jarvis a full minute of openmouthed silence to process what I'd said. He'd spent so long trying to convince me I could be good at the job, while, at the same time, kind of carrying me because I didn't *want* to be good at it, that now that the time had come to take the training wheels off, he was having a hard time letting go.

"Jarvis," I said, taking hold of both his upper arms and squeezing them gently. "Look at me."

He did. I gave him a reassuring grin. Screw the nasty little voice inside my head—I could *do* this.

"I can do this," I said.

Jarvis nodded, then repeated my words, but without as much conviction as I'd have liked.

"You can do this."

My grin got even wider.

"You say it like it's a bad thing. Be straight with me and I promise I won't let you down."

Jarvis swallowed.

"Your friend, Marcel, aka the Ender of Death, is back. I don't want to worry you, but you'll be very vulnerable tonight."

I looked down at Runt, who whined.

"You knew about this, too, huh?"

She nodded.

"Jarvis told me to be on the alert."

"And the bodyguards will be here to look after you, too," Jarvis added.

"All right," I said, shivering despite the not so chilly temperature outside. "Good to know."

Suddenly I was much more aware of my surroundings, my eyes scanning the darkness for bodyguards and/or enemies—though frankly, I wasn't sure which made me more nervous. A thousand feet below us, I could hear the crash of the surf against the cliffs, but the isolation, the idea of being so far removed from the rest of society, made me feel less secure, not more.

"I can't put him off forever, Jarvis," I said, my nerves not happy about this complication.

Jarvis ran his fingers through his dark hair and sighed.

"I know."

I'd made a promise to the Ender of Death—one I knew might not end well for me, but I'd had no choice. I'd been in the middle of trying to prevent my sister and the Devil from co-opting Purgatory and Death, Inc., for their own nefarious purposes, and in the spirit of good sportsmanship, I'd given the Ender of Death my word that I'd fight him mano a mano once I'd dealt with the situation. He'd been gracious enough to give me a respite and, until now, had been waiting patiently, biding his time and giving me the room I needed to sort out all the ancillary stuff I'd had to handle since I'd taken over the day-to-day running of Death, Inc.

But it seemed like my time-out was over. Marcel had reared his ugly head again and I was going to have to deal with him definitively, whether I was prepared to or not.

"I think we'd be smart to set a time and place rather than leaving that to Marcel," Jarvis said finally, and I could see he'd given the matter a lot of thought, but hadn't come up with a way of dealing with the problem that was satisfactory to him.

"Okay. Why don't you issue him a formal challenge then?" I offered. "As soon as we're done with the Death Dinner, I can start preparing."

Jarvis nodded, worry lines etching themselves deeply into his forehead and around his eyes. He knew this was the best—and only—option we had, but he didn't have to like it.

"Now that that's settled, shall we continue on with the evening?" Jarvis said, taking my arm again. "We have one stop to make before the ball."

the library at Casa del Amo made my dad's library at Sea Verge look like a closet. This was one large room and about ten thousand books.

"I can't believe this place," I said as I stood in the middle of the room, goggling at the humungous fireplace that took up the whole of the back wall. It was so big you could've roasted a whole pig in it and still had room to spit a couple of turkeys on either side.

"Agreed," Jarvis said as he ran his finger across the unprotected book spines, his eyes devouring each title he passed. "I believe it's the most comprehensive collection of Religious and Magical Arcana outside the Hall of Death."

Runt, who was never intimidated by anything, sat quietly by the door, her ears pinned back against her head.

"I don't like this place at all," she said quietly. "It smells funny."

But when asked to elaborate on what she meant by "funny," all she offered was: "It smells *dark*."

I had to agree with the pup. There was something odd about the place. It didn't smell "dark" to me, but it definitely raised the "weird" alarm.

I flopped down on one of the two red-and-gold-striped silk

couches that flanked the fireplace, bypassing the three brown leather armchairs, each placed conveniently by a bookshelf with an elongated, antique gooseneck lamp standing beside it to give illumination to the chair's occupant. I observed that two of the four walls were lined from floor to ceiling with bookcases, each bearing a multitude of multicolored tomes, their spines packed together like sardines in a can—but the other wall was a paean to the outdoors: stuffed animal heads and an assortment of antique hunting rifles. I liked the books, but I could do without the stuffed animal heads—especially the giant moose head (its antlers were more than four feet long!) that was the centerpiece of the hunting wall.

The octagonal tile we had in our guest room was continued here, but there were no Oriental carpets to up the warmth factor. The room was cold and sterile, like we'd stepped into the confines of a museum, leaving behind any idea that this was just a private house.

"Scholars from all over the world flock to the Haunted Hearts Castle," I heard someone say behind me, the voice sharp but feminine.

I whirled around in my seat to find a large girl in a shimmering purple gown standing behind me, her auburn hair in a tight chignon at the base of her neck. Her milky skin and translucent green eyes were heavily accented with shimmering bronze makeup, her full lips brushed with a touch of metallic peach.

I knew the girl, but I didn't know the name.

"Calliope," Jarvis began, instantly rushing to my side, "you remember God's assistant, Miss Munificent—"

"Ha!" I barked, then clamped my hand over my mouth when I realized I'd done it out loud. I wasn't trying to offend, I just knew "munificent" meant "generous," and that was the last thing I'd ever call *this* girl.

"Sorry about that," I said, removing my hand. "I'm Callie. Nice to meet you. Again. With names."

I stuck out my hand and the girl looked at it like it was a dead fish, but then she shrugged and took it anyway.

"Munificent, but you can call me Minnie—and if you say like the mouse, I'll cut you."

She delivered this line while giving my right hand, the one I'd proffered in friendship, a serious crushing.

"Ow! I get it," I yelped. "No mouse jokes."

She gave me a tight smile, then released my hand. She turned to Jarvis and winked at him.

"I told you, a little physical intimidation and you'd have her eating out of your hand."

It took me a moment to realize she was talking about me.

"Hey—" I started to interject, but she shot me a look that would've sent a zombie horde screaming back to their graves.

"Now, where was I," she said, returning her attention to Jarvis.

"The book . . ." Jarvis asked.

"Yes, the book," she said absentmindedly as she pulled her sparkly purple clutch out from under her arm and set it down on the back edge of the couch.

Runt took the opportunity to come and sit beside me, settling her butt down as close to my legs as she could before dropping her chin onto my lap. This was the universal signal for "pet my head." I did as I was asked and scratched behind her ears with my noncrushed hand. Runt, her chocolate eyes moving curiously as she watched Minnie undo the clasp of her purple beaded bag, whined into the gauzy fabric of my dress.

"Here you are," Minnie said, triumphant as she pulled a miniature, calfskin-bound book from within the bag's guts and handed it to me.

"What is it?" I asked, taking the book from Minnie, but directing my question at Jarvis.

There was a high-pitched, feminine giggle from outside and we all turned to see three women in long evening gowns, their faces masked, trundle across the courtyard, their bodies shaking with laughter. Beyond them, more partygoers emerged from the gardens, scattered buckshots of light marking the comings and goings of a hundred different wormholes.

"The Masquerade Ball is about to begin," Minnie said. "We better hurry this up."

"So, what's the book?" I asked again after realizing the lettering on the cover was in a language I'd never seen before.

"This is the original, fully annotated copy of *How to Be*

Death, written in the tongue of the Angels and untouchable by humanity," Minnie said tartly.

"It's all the basics that you've read in the translated copy your father keeps in the library, but with an added instruction manual on how to kick-start the End of Days," Jarvis added. "And it applies to any and all religions, not just Christians."

"Okay," I offered, but I was pretty uncertain as to why anyone was putting this kind of powder keg into my notoriously buttery fingers.

"You know that scene in *Raiders of the Lost Ark* when the guy's face melts off?" Minnie said suddenly.

"Uh-huh." I nodded, very intimidated by the aggressive lady in purple.

"That's what happens to human beings who touch this book," she said. "So don't let any human beings touch the book, okay?"

I nodded at what was obviously only a rhetorical question.

"She knows this, Minnie. There are many references to it in the translated copy—" Jarvis said then stopped, looking at me through narrowed eyes. "Oh, Lord, you haven't even read it, have you?"

I swallowed hard, wanting to lie even though I knew honesty was the best policy . . . maybe not the least confrontational policy but, in the end, always the best.

"No," I squeaked, cringing.

"I cannot believe you've gone this long without reading the book!" Jarvis pouted. "It's amazing to me how one person can be so incredibly mature one moment and such a child the next."

I cowered in my gorgeous black gown on the big red sofa, feeling like a total fake. Jarvis was right. I had to suck it up and read the damned book or I was just a poseur.

"I'll read it! I promise," I said. "Just stop making me feel like such a shit heel."

I'd forgotten Runt was there. I looked down at the pup's wide eyes and apologized.

"Sorry, I meant schmuck, not shit heel."

Damn, schmuck was, like, Yiddish for penis! That was as bad as shit heel, I thought miserably.

"Ignore me, Runt. I have a foul mouth and I should be duly punished."

"It's okay, Cal," Runt offered sheepishly. "They say way worse things on cable."

From the mouths of babes.

"So, now that I have the, uh, book what am I supposed to do with it?" I asked.

Jarvis began to pace in front of the fireplace, looking serious, though I caught him sneaking a few quick glances in Minnie's direction when he thought no one was watching.

"The book becomes the property of the new Death upon the transfer of the presidency of Death, Inc.," Minnie intoned. "Your father brought it back to God only hours before he died and now—"

A sharp pain lanced my heart. So my dad had known exactly what he was doing when he'd let Marcel, the Ender of Death, destroy him. He'd even given back the original copy of the Death guide so it wouldn't fall into the wrong hands after his death. I sat motionless on the couch, my brain awash with questions I knew I'd never, ever have the answers to.

"So you must protect it with your immortal life."

"What?" I said, looking up. I'd missed Minnie's explanation entirely.

"You look after the book and keep it safe," Runt chimed in.

"Thanks, buddy," I replied, patting her head.

Outside, the courtyard was filling with more revelers wandering around in pairs and small groups. There was an air of restlessness about them and I wondered if they were somehow waiting for me.

"No one knows I've transferred the book to you tonight," Minnie said. "Don't tell anyone you have it. It's not common knowledge that Death is its keeper."

"The Board of Death and a few others know, but otherwise the world believes the original was destroyed when the Romans burned down the library in Alexandria," Jarvis added. "So this book is more of a legend—"

"Or not such a legend," I said, looking down at it. "So why here, why now?"

"The book can only be transferred to the new Death on All Hallows' Eve 'Eve.' That's why it's been in Heaven until now."

The Afterlife was riddled with all kinds of stupid stuff like that—rituals that had no real reason to exist, but existed and were adhered to nonetheless.

"All righty then," I said, using the arm of the couch to hoist myself back onto my feet. "I guess that's that. I'll just put the book away—"

I wedged the tiny book in between my cleavage, where it was perfectly concealed beneath a wad of gauzy fabric.

"And then we'll get this show on the road."

Jarvis and Minnie looked at each other. I fully expected one of them to protest the cleavage-book scenario, but they remained silent on the subject.

"I promise I'll put it in a safe place when we get back to the room," I added, and this seemed to ease the tension somewhat.

Jarvis nodded, gesturing with a wave of his arm.

"Well then, after you, my dear."

They waited for me to take the initiative—probably so they could give each other more "knowing looks" behind my back—but I didn't need to be told twice. With Runt at my side, and doing my best to ignore Jarvis's and Minnie's palpable disapproval, I quashed all the nervous thoughts whirling around my brain. Then, with my head held high, I sashayed out the door and into the madness of the All Hallows' Eve "Eve" Masquerade Ball.

six

They'd arrived in droves, milling about the Castle's gardens and courtyards in their black-tie best, giddy at first, but now starting to get restless. I could hear the complaints and rowdy catcalls as I tried my darndest to follow Jarvis's retreating back. Somehow in the confusion of bodies outside the library, he and Minnie had gotten ahead of us, so that Runt and I were now forced to play catch-up.

Well-dressed men and women—mostly humanoid, but there were other creatures, too—swarmed around us like ants. I felt goose bumps rise on my arms as the night began to cool, making me wish I'd brought a wrap even though once we got where we were going, I knew I wouldn't be cold anymore. The sounds of the waves below us and the chatter of five hundred impatient revelers waiting to be led to their destination were brighter than anything I could see with my eyes, save the moon, which was a pat of butter high above us, cold and full as it floated in a pitch-black sky.

We were headed for the far end of the property, where there was a large flat piece of land overlooking the sea. It was here that Jarvis and I would meet up with the six Continental Vice-Presidents—one each for Africa, Asia, Australia, Europe, North America, and one for South America and Antarctica—and together with Kali, the representative from the Board of Death, we would open a semipermanent wormhole into another historical period in time.

Everyone was forced to meet in one spot, the Haunted Hearts Castle, which was the only access point to the event. Here, all comers with the proper invitation would be marked with a magical sigil that expired at 11:30 p.m. sharp—that's when the wormhole closed and everyone was magically returned to their own homes. It was done this way so no one got stranded at midnight when all magic ceased for the following twenty-four hours.

The Death Dinner and access point were always at the Haunted Hearts Castle, but every year a new spot was chosen to host the Masquerade Ball itself. Last year, it had been in a tent at the New Orleans, Louisiana, 1884 World's Fair—I hadn't gone, but Jarvis said it was eerily beautiful. I couldn't see anything too weird about New Orleans as a locale, but this year, the Executive Board of Death, Inc., had decided to hold the Masquerade Ball in a place I thought was a very strange choice, indeed. We were going back some 30,000 years in time to Southern France, where in the Chauvet-Pont-d'Arc Cave, which was playing host to our Masquerade Ball, some of the earliest known cave paintings ever discovered on Earth had just been freshly painted.

It was a neat idea, but I had my reservations about five hundred plus partygoers being stuffed into one cave like a bunch of sausages. Still, the Masquerade Ball was one of the highlights of the supernatural calendar. A time for all the creatures/beings who'd worked with/for Death, Inc., to come together for an evening of good-hearted debauchery. I'd never been invited before, but my older sister, Thalia, had been a fixture, notorious for her racy costumes and diva behavior. I'd learned this tidbit of gossip from Kali, who'd never cared much for Thalia—though she had admired my sister's apparent single-mindedness when it came to seducing the opposite sex.

Thalia and I had been as opposite as two human beings could possibly be. She was a vain, type A personality with enough ambition to take over the Afterlife—something she'd almost succeeded in doing until I'd gotten in her way. While I, on the other hand, was an average-looking, average-achieving, and pretty much average everything else, too, gal with zero ambition to take over the Afterlife. She was blond and beautiful; I was mousy brown. I loved food and she only drank protein shakes. The only thing we actually had a similar interest in was clothing, but we diverged there, as well: I loved window-shopping for designer duds, while she actually had the cash to buy them.

After she'd finished her MBA at Rutgers, Thalia had joined the family business, slowly working her way up to Vice-President in Charge of Passage—a subset of the Harvesting and Transporting Department—and though the job had been cushy and respected, it hadn't been enough for my sister. She'd been too ambitious, had seen herself rising to the very top of the corporate ladder, becoming the President and CEO of Death, Inc., and running the company when our dad stepped down.

It wasn't until she was promoted to the Vice-Presidency of Asia and met the nefarious demon Vritra—who would shortly thereafter become her husband—that she discovered the truth: Her younger sister (me) was actually the one with the birthright to become the next Grim Reaper. Until then she'd had no idea her dreams were unattainable—that no matter how much flesh she pressed or how hard she worked, she would never attain the job she so desperately wanted . . . at least, not through any traditional means. So in her desperation to succeed, she'd done the unthinkable. She and Vritra had kidnapped our dad . . . and that's how I'd gotten dragged into the whole mess.

In every generation there are two (sometimes three) beings born with the propensity to become Death. Most of them never know their true nature because the reigning Grim Reaper is granted immortality, and someone who gets that kind of perk usually tends to stick with the job for a long, long time. But sometimes there's a cock-up (or a kidnapping), and the two (or three) "potential Deaths" are called up to vie for the newly available position.

Trying to become Death is a real pain in the ass, with tasks to complete, magic to learn, and monsters to slay—not something I'd ever have seen myself pursuing as a career choice, but somehow Jarvis and Clio had talked me into it. While I was out trying to save my family's immortality, Thalia was busily working to set me up as the fall guy for our dad's kidnapping.

And she'd almost succeeded.

If it weren't for Daniel (who was another potential Death), Jarvis, Clio, and Runt, my older sister would've thrown me under the bus, stolen Death, Inc., and destroyed the Afterlife. Instead, the shoe got put on the other foot: We killed Vritra, found Dad, and dive-bombed Thalia's nasty little plan before it even got started. I like to think if fate had been different, if Thalia had been the true heir and not me, she would've been satisfied with waiting for our dad to step down of his own accord—and none of the horrible things that happened later would've ever been set into motion.

I said, I *like* to think that . . . but I know it's not reality. Fate is fate and people are people—and there's no changing either one of them. Thalia would've found a way to get rid of my dad one way or another.

So here I was, stepping into my dad's job and running the business my older sister had so fiendishly plotted to steal away from me—

"Hey, watch where you're going!"

The rude voice knocked me out of my thoughts one second before the rude voice's owner knocked me off my feet. I went down hard, throwing my hands out to keep my chin from slamming into the blue mosaic tiles I'd been walking on only a moment before. I heard Runt barking in my left ear, her furry black form rushing in to separate me from the person I'd run into. I laid a hand on her flank to calm her, but she continued to bark, the sound dry and throaty and full of menace.

"It's okay, Runt," I said, "I'm all right."

I looked up to see who or what I'd run into, but the man was already on his feet, his back to me as he quickly began to walk off into the crowd. I felt a pair of strong hands grab me under the armpits, easily lifting me back up on to my feet.

"Thank you—" I started to say, but stopped when I saw my savior was wearing a golden lion mask, the mane and whiskers made from real, curling lion hair. To complement his choice of mask, he'd chosen an elegant black tuxedo with a black cummerbund.

My heart started to beat faster as I tried to get a look at the flesh beneath the mask. I wondered who he was—he was obviously a flash dresser and he'd stopped to help a damsel in distress, so he was chivalrous, too.

Hmmm.

"Uhm, thank you," I said again, trying to look into his eyes, but my new friend was shy and kept looking away.

I leaned forward to give him a chaste kiss on the exposed flesh of his cheek, but he moved and I got the crook of his neck instead. Then, before I could say anything else, he bowed and melted back into the crowd. I opened my mouth to protest and that's when I realized Runt was gone. I whirled around looking for the hellhound pup, but she'd taken off, probably trying to catch the guy who'd knocked me over.

"Runt!" I called. "Come back!"

But it was no good. Runt was gone.

"Mistress Calliope, are you okay?"

Jarvis and Minnie were suddenly at my side, having doubled back once they'd realized we were missing. Jarvis kept glancing around us, his eyes scanning the crowd for suspicious characters.

"Some jerk knocked me over and Runt took off after him," I said in a rush, starting to get really worried about the hellhound.

There were just so many people running around the gardens and I didn't know who or what 99 percent of them were. Anyone could just snatch up a little pup—well, she wasn't *that* little anymore, actually—and haul her off to God knew where. There were so many wormholes popping in and out of existence around us, the bad guy had a thousand choices for his escape.

"We have to find Runt," I said, feeling frantic.

"She's a big girl," Minnie said, putting a hand on my bare shoulder, but I shrugged her off.

"I don't care. She's a puppy and anyone could take—"

Off in the distance we heard loud, persistent barking and then Runt, her tongue hanging out of her mouth as she panted, slalomed her way through the crowd.

"Runt!" I yelled, squatting down to hug the pup as she stopped not two inches from my face. I pulled her to my chest, nuzzling the back of her neck.

"I tried to . . . get him," Runt panted, "but he was . . . too fast for me."

Jarvis knelt down to dog eye level.

"Did you see what he looked like?" he asked. "Was it—"

He didn't finish the sentence because Runt was shaking her head.

"It wasn't the Ender of Death. I *know* what he smells like and this guy wasn't him."

Jarvis relaxed visibly after that, but this time, as we continued on, he kept a firm hand on my elbow. Minnie stayed on my other side, physically blocking me from view with her voluptuous body. Her green eyes scanned the crowd with a feline insouciance, but I could feel the tension thrumming through her body.

"Maybe we need to issue this challenge sooner rather than later." I sighed, raising an eyebrow in Jarvis's direction as we headed toward the meeting point. "You're a nervous wreck, Jarvi."

Jarvis shook his head, his dark eyes serious.

"I'd rather work for you than for the Devil's protégé . . . or God forbid, your friend, Frank, so you can see my dilemma."

I knew exactly what Jarvis's "dilemma" was: He had no interest in kowtowing to someone he didn't respect. He'd given me the benefit of the doubt and had been open to helping me develop my talent only out of respect for my father. In the end, I'd like to think I'd earned Jarvis's loyalty through my own actions, but it'd been touch and go a few times. I knew if I hadn't been willing to work on my bad attitude and selfishness, Jarvis wouldn't have stayed with me. He was too smart and too surly for that.

I'd learned so much from my dad's former Executive Assistant, was really in Jarvis's debt for all he'd taught me, that it was hard to be objective where he was concerned. Part of me didn't want to stop being a perpetual student; was all for sitting back and letting Jarvis do the heavy lifting while I rested on my laurels and "learned." With his take-charge personality, Jarvis would relish "helping" me run the show. He wouldn't even realize he was being manipulated if I played my cards right . . . but I would know and that just wasn't gonna happen.

At some point, Jarvis was going to have to let me go and *I* would have to help *him* with the transition, not the other way around. I needed to show him I could stand on my own two feet and make smart decisions about the fate of Death, Inc., become the kind of leader I knew my dad had been. Not that I discounted any of the help and support I'd gotten from Jarvis. He'd been integral in helping me discover my true destiny and I knew I was a better, stronger person because of him, but I couldn't let him become my crutch. Whether I liked it or not, Death, Inc., was only as strong and capable as I was.

It was time to get my butt in gear.

The crowd had bunched together near the access point—a large, white rented tent staked into the dirt by a series of heavy wooden spikes—and they were making it almost impossible to get where we needed to go. Weaving our way through the throng of overeager partygoers, the trip took two minutes when it only should've taken twenty seconds.

As we reached the tent, Minnie gave my hand a reassuring squeeze.

"You'll be great," she whispered—then she gave Jarvis a wink before melting into the restless masked crowd.

Minnie's thoughtful gesture took me by surprise. My last experience with the woman would not have led me to believe she possessed an ounce of empathy within her overlarge bosom, but as usual, I was learning (the hard way, of course) not to judge a book by its cover; until push came to shove, you just never knew *who* was gonna have your back.

To my surprise, Runt gave my hand a lick then followed Minnie out into the masses, leaving me in Jarvis's more than capable hands. I swallowed hard and followed my Executive Assistant as he made his way over to the small band of men and women who were obviously waiting for us to arrive as they huddled under the safety of the rented tent.

Upon our arrival, Jarvis immediately started introducing me to the four Continental Vice-Presidents I didn't know. I'd had my superweird run-in with Anjea, the Vice-President in Charge of Australia, earlier in the night, but Jarvis had either forgotten or didn't care because he went right ahead and introduced me to the Aboriginal woman as if we'd never laid eyes on one another before.

With her long, unkempt hair and wizened face, Anjea was still as creepy as I remembered from our last encounter, but at least she'd changed into a nice silk robe that matched the silvery strands in her hair. She nodded her head as Jarvis introduced us, her unearthly eyes boring into mine with so much intensity I thought she might attack me. To my relief, she stayed aloof, only her eyes telegraphing her interest in me.

"Calliope, you look so glamorous," a tall Native American man in a navy tuxedo said as he stepped up to greet me, holding a crow's beak mask at his side, the string pinched between the fingers of his right hand.

His deep-set brown eyes—eyes that had seen more than their share of suffering—crinkled at the edges as he smiled down at me, his tiny chin coming to a beardless point below a wide-lipped mouth.

"Naapi," I replied, letting the tall man embrace me, careful not to smush his mask against the folds of my dress.

The Vice-President in Charge of North America had been a friend of my father's for as long as I could remember, and when I was a little girl, he'd been a frequent visitor to Sea Verge, staying for days at a time to confer with my dad and Jarvis about Death, Inc., business. His trips might originally have been intended as just "business," but this changed once Clio and I discovered he was a master storyteller, one who could keep us entertained for hours on end with all the thrilling tales he knew about the American Old West. Clio and I'd harassed him unmercifully, begging him to tell us story after story—not realizing until much later that they all came from firsthand experience.

He had a myriad of tall tales, but our favorites included ghostly Buffalo Men who roamed the desert plains, scalping any white man who dared cross their path; young braves who went on vision quests but got lost in the land of the spirits, unable to return to their grieving families; a young woman who married an Indian brave from another tribe only to discover her new husband was actually an evil spirit. Naapi bewitched our impressionable young minds, weaving his tales with deft hands until we looked upon those stories as if they were a part of the tangled skein of our own memories.

Not long after my dad's death, Naapi had come to Sea Verge offering his condolences and his services should the need ever arise. I knew Jarvis and my dad had considered him an ally, and I bore only positive memories from the time I'd spent with him as a child, so I'd accepted his offer graciously. In truth, he was one of the few people I was actually looking forward to seeing here at the Death Dinner.

After Naapi and I'd dispensed with the pleasantries, Jarvis had introduced me to the rest of the Vice-Presidents.

There was Yum Cimil, the Vice-President in Charge of South America and Antarctica, a small, tight-lipped old man with dark orange skin and the kind of gravity-defying back comb-over you could only marvel at for its sheer aerodynamic ingenuity. When Jarvis introduced us, he wouldn't speak to me, just glared at me like I'd said something rude.

"He doesn't speak to women," a tall, good-looking man standing beside him said, taking my hand and pressing the smooth skin of my knuckles to his mouth, the dark bristles of his mustache tickling my sensitive flesh. "I'm Fabian Lazarev, Mr. Cimil's second in command, and I, on the other hand, have a healthy appreciation for the beauty of a young, vulnerable woman."

Young and vulnerable? I wanted to laugh, but one look from Jarvis shut me up. Over the years, I'd developed a nasty habit of saying exactly what I was thinking without any filter and the habit was proving a hard one to break.

The next man Jarvis introduced me to reminded me of a prizefighter. He had a barrel chest and thick, muscular legs, which seemed just about ready to burst the seams of the tailored tuxedo pants they were encased in. Handsome in a rugged, outdoorsy way, he had high cheekbones and chiseled features, but the most striking thing about him was his penetrating almond-shaped hazel eyes.

"I'm Erlik, and Asia is my bag," he said as he bowed deeply from the waist, his eyes never leaving my face.

His unadulterated gaze was a bit disconcerting, but I curtsied in return, knowing the ladylike display would win points with Jarvis.

Next, I was introduced to a handsome African man in a pale blue dashiki. He had wide cinnamon eyes and blindingly white teeth that overwhelmed his generous smile. He held out his hand to me, his smile only widening as he gripped my fingers. "I'm Ogbunabali, but please call me Oggie. All my friends do."

"Nice to meet you," I replied, giving his hand a good shake. Surprised by my strength, he raised an eyebrow.

"On my continent, the women work the hardest of all—and their grip is as firm as yours," he said. "Someday it would be my honor to host this reign of Death as I hosted your father before you. You must come visit."

I nodded.

"That would be awesome."

Oggie grinned, shaking his head in amusement.

"Yes, I agree. It would be 'awesome.'"

Oggie was a very charming man, but that didn't make me like him. What drew my interest was the way he didn't seem to be judging every word that came out of my mouth, unlike Yum Cimil, who'd stared me down like I was the second coming of the Antichrist. Oggie had taken me with a grain of salt and hadn't been at all put off by my unorthodox verbiage. Or maybe the truth was even simpler than that. There was something about the handsome man that reminded me a bit of Daniel: charming, kind, and interested in the people whose dominion he oversaw.

Oh, Daniel, I thought miserably, my heart breaking all over again.

All throughout our relationship, Daniel had begged me to approach God about intervening on behalf of the creatures down in Hell. The ones subjugated to the Devil's nasty and selfish whims. They'd been subjected to all kinds of dictatorial behavior, and Daniel had implored me to ask God to place limits on how the Devil was allowed to treat his people. I'd hemmed and hawed until the Devil and my sister had staged their siege on Purgatory and Death, Inc.—but by then my chance to do the right thing had slipped away. In the end, Daniel had gotten his wish, but not through any help of mine. In the wake of the Devil's unsuccessful bid to take over the Afterlife, God had made Daniel the Steward of Hell, so that now all of Daniel's energies—*except for the energy he was apparently expending on his new lady friend,* I thought sarcastically—were taken up righting all the wrongs that had occurred in Hell during the Devil's dominion.

"I thought there were six Continental Vice-Presidents?" I whispered to Jarvis after I'd finished my chat with Oggie.

"There are," he replied. "Morrigan is in charge of Europe, but she seems to be late."

"I'm right here, little Jarvis de Poupsy . . . Death's 'Executive Assistant.'"

At the sound of the purring feminine voice, we turned to find an elegantly dressed Irish woman with flaming red hair and an icy smile, standing behind us. Her milky skin glowed in the moonlight, nicely setting off the emerald green of her low-cut gown, but though she was made of living flesh and blood, there was something infinitely cold about the woman. She appeared to be only a few years older than me, but I got the distinct impression this was merely a glamour, that her real countenance was a gnarly thing, indeed, and better never inquired about.

"I'm Callie," I said, offering her my hand—which she blatantly ignored.

"Shall we get this circus moving, Death?" she said evenly, her lips never varying from that cold curl of a smile.

I shrugged, trying not to show how intimidated I was by the older woman. She was all ice and cold beauty, the veneer of disdain she wore, unwavering.

"We're just waiting for Kali—" I started to say, but was interrupted by the weight of a heavy hand settling on my shoulder.

"Don't put that crap on me, white girl," Kali said, her black hair piled on top of her head to show off the sensuous curve of her exquisite neck, her pale cream sari a diamond-encrusted sparkler. "I've been here waiting for your white girl ass all bloody night."

She gave my shoulder a friendly squeeze, but unmindful of her strength, the squeeze was more painful than playful. Luckily, her appearance seemed to subdue Morrigan, who stepped back in line with the other Vice-Presidents, though her eyes stayed glued to me with a quiet contempt.

"It's time," Jarvis said, nudging me with his elbow.

I swallowed hard, nerves making my mouth as dry as the deserts down in Hell. I stepped forward, holding the billowing skirt of my dress so I didn't step on it, and cleared my throat.

"Here," Jarvis whispered, palming me a megaphone, which I took happily.

The noisy crowd, all of them masked now, began to settle

down as they saw I was about to speak. Pressing the megaphone's mouthpiece to my lips, I cleared my throat again, the
sound carrying like wildfire in the newly born silence.

"Uhm, hello, you guys."

The sound of insects chirping was my only response as my
voice echoed around the temporary encampment, harsh and
loud even to my own ears.

"So . . . my name is Calliope Reaper-Jones . . ."

I trailed off, the crowd seemingly nonplussed by my war-
bling introduction, the beginning of a light drizzle only adding
to the awkwardness.

Shit, I thought nervously. *Now what?*

And then I had a flash of unscripted brilliance: I decided
what the crowd *really* needed was a little encouragement! I
took a deep breath and just went for it.

"Are you guys ready to party?!" I screamed, the megaphone
multiplying the sound of my voice a thousandfold—and to my
happy surprise, a cheer went up from the crowd, proving that
my pandering was well worth the effort. Until that moment,
they'd been a cold, bored (and now wet) mess, but with that one
phrase I'd gotten their engines revving on high all over again.

I caught Jarvis's eye and was pleased to see that even he was
mildly amused by my antics. With a nod, he signaled for me to
step back and I did as he asked, handing him the megaphone as
I hopped back in line with the others: Kali on one side and
Naapi on the other. They were already holding hands with the
rest of the Vice-Presidents, so that when I took their fingers in
my own, it completed a magical circuit of unparalleled power.
I felt a burst of electricity rip through the ether as, behind us, a
loud *boom* shook the ground and a violent swirl of gray-green
energy began to form inside the tent. Buoyed by another cheer
from the rowdy assemblage, I screamed at the top of my lungs:

*"As your new Grim Reaper, I would like to invite you all to
the All Hallows' Eve 'Eve' Masquerade Ball!!"*

•

Out of darkness a new world was born; one that was unlike any other I'd ever seen, full of lingering shadows and the brilliance of a thousand flickering lights. Leaving behind the chilly drizzle of Central California, I stepped into a Wonderland that was more "prehistoric" than "Disney-centric."

Thirty thousand years ago the Chauvet Cave was not cut off from the outside world—that would come later, with the advent of a giant landslide that sealed the cave away until it was rediscovered in the late twentieth century. We were experiencing the cave in the time before its forced retirement, when it was a series of carved niches in the rock wall, the ceiling only a protective stone overhang that kept out the worst of the elements. Hidden in its nooks and crannies, their brightly colored bodies the reason why the cave had become a protected archeological site in our time, were the gorgeous painted renderings of wild horses, cave lions, bears, bison; all creatures that haunted and sustained the early men and women who peopled the Earth. Though the cave was empty now, the paintings remained, their presence like a ghostly afterimage pressed into the backs of the eyelids, giving voice to the human beings who once inhabited this place.

In the semidarkness, the paintings seemed alive as they shifted and shuddered in the glow of a hundred wrought iron candelabras brought in to illuminate the cave for the party. They'd been placed strategically throughout the space, their gray metallic frames blending in with the cavern's walls. All around them dancers whirled like dervishes, their bodies lithe as cats, the animal masks they wore—modern replicas of the creatures that graced the walls around them—hiding their true identities.

I was exempt from the fun, forced to stand by the entrance to the wormhole—there was no chair in sight—and greet each new person who entered the cave. After the introductions, I then got to watch as my new masked "friend" moved off toward the writhing mass of bodies. After a while, I got bored with fake smiling at all the masked and anonymous, so I switched to a look that was full-on gravitas, hoping it would speed things up, but it only caused people to malinger, taking my hand and offering me their condolences on my dad's passing. The contrived sympathy was way worse than the ache I'd gotten in my jaw from the fake smiling, so I immediately switched back.

At least the music was good. I was enjoying the classic rock cover band Death, Inc., had hired for the event. They were playing Great White's version of "Once Bitten, Twice Shy," which was definitely a toe-tapper.

"Except for the band, this sucks," I said to Jarvis in between meet and greets, happily taking the proffered glass of wine he was holding and downing it in one sip.

"That was my wine."

I guess he hadn't been proffering it to me after all.

"Sorry," I said, stifling a burp as I set the empty wineglass down on a passing tray. The young woman who was carrying the tray did a double take when she saw me then flashed a quick grin. I returned the smile, but I didn't know if her grin meant she knew who I was or if she was just flirting with me—ah, the trials and tribulations of being Death: You didn't even know where you stood with the caterers.

"Are you sure this 'no masks' thing is really necessary?" I asked. "It would be so much more fun if we could wear them, too, Jarvi."

Jarvis was consigned to the boring side of the party with me. As my Executive Assistant, he had to stand nearby and whisper people's names in my ear as I greeted them, so no one felt shortchanged. Since they were all masked, I had no idea how he was able to tell them apart, but somehow he was able to point out all the important Gods and Goddesses and members of Death, Inc., so they wouldn't realize I didn't have a clue as to who they were.

Runt was keeping close, too, splayed out on the ground beside my feet, panting lightly. At first, I tried to get her to go out and dance instead of hanging out in boring land with Jarvis and me, but she just looked hurt by my suggestion.

"I want to be where you guys are," she'd said, plopping down on the floor next to me—and I'd left it at that.

It was warm in the cave; too many bodies crammed into a too small space, making me glad I hadn't brought a wrap because I was already starting to sweat like a pig. I wiped my upper lip with the back of my hand, my eyes peeled for another waiter bearing drinks. There was no food at this shindig, but the alcohol was free-flowing. I'd seen a couple of drunk staggers intermixed with the dancing and knew the way the crowd was drinking, it wouldn't be long before I saw more.

"Why *is* everyone wearing masks?" I asked suddenly. It was the first time I'd wondered why, exactly, the whole mask thing was so important—and once the bee was in my bonnet, I wanted an answer.

Jarvis was quiet, his dark eyebrows knitting together in consternation. I could tell by the look on his face he was having a hard time deciding how much information to divulge. This response was the opposite of how Jarvis usually handled info—he loved to lecture, it was his raison d'être—so I knew there was something naughty he was gonna try and hide from me.

This is going to be interesting, I thought curiously.

"Well, uh, you see, Calliope, the reasoning behind the masks is, well . . ." He struggled with his words, not an everyday occurrence, and I relished it.

"Yes, Jarvis?" I said, baiting him.

He gritted his teeth, his jaw tightening.

"One word, Death," a feminine voice purred. *"Ritual."*

Jarvis stopped stammering, foisting a nasty glare on Morrigan, who'd sidled in between us, her emerald green dress almost black in the candlelight setting off the pale smoothness of her skin. Unlike the rest of the crowd, she wasn't wearing her mask.

"Ritual?" I asked.

Jarvis closed his eyes, waiting for the inevitable.

"In the old days, All Hallows' Eve 'Eve' was a Bacchanal, where the Gods and their human supplicants came together in honor of creation, an appeasement to the Mother Goddess," she said matter-of-factly, "so they could be assured their magic would be returned to them on All Saints' Day."

"You used the words 'supplicant' and 'appeasement,'" I said. "Are you talking, like. human sacrifice stuff?"

Morrigan's laugh was throaty and mellifluous.

"Nothing so trite, Calliope," she replied. "Fucking. Lots and lots of fucking."

I was taken aback, not prepared for her answer. Next to me, Jarvis sank down into his shoes, embarrassed . . . or maybe there was something more to it than that.

"Jarvis, you should share your history with Calliope," Morrigan purred, enjoying Jarvis's discomfort immensely. My Executive Assistant blanched, his normally tan face white and pinched.

Morrigan was harassing Jarvis on purpose, putting him on the spot because she knew something personal about him that he didn't want to have to divulge to me. Now, normally I would've been annoyed with Jarvis for withholding pertinent information, but I didn't like how Morrigan was railroading him, and my annoyance at being left in the dark again was forgotten in the wake of all the defensive feelings she'd roused in me on my Executive Assistant's behalf.

In this world, only *I* was allowed to tease and/or torment Jarvis—not this haughty red-haired bitch. She wasn't more than an inch or two taller than me, so I figured I could take her in a fight.

"Well, thanks for the info, Mortimer," I said, taking a step closer to the Celtic Goddess, so I was pretty much invading her personal space. "But I think you best move the show along before *I* say something *you* regret."

Morrigan stared at me, openmouthed, and I couldn't tell if her shock came from my bluntness or from the fact I'd just called her Mortimer. For a minute, it seemed as if she was going to attack me, but then her entire countenance changed and she visibly shrank away from me.

Score for the Reaper-Jones team! I thought happily, but my self-congratulatory pat on the back was cut short by the realization that I wasn't the one responsible for the redhead's change in demeanor. As I followed her gaze, I saw that Morrigan's eyes were locked on a tall, statuesque woman moving quickly toward us through the crowd, her patrician face, high cheekbones, and short dark hair making her look like approaching Byzantine royalty. She was holding a golden horse mask in her right hand, obviously having just taken it off.

"Morrigan, darling, you haven't introduced me to your friend," the woman said as she joined the huddle, taking Morrigan's arm and giving it a loving but firm "warning" squeeze.

The tension in the air was palpable, but the new woman ignored it, not waiting for Morrigan to introduce us, but holding out her hand for me to take.

"I'm Caoimhe O' Donoghue," she said, a crackling *snap* of electricity flowing between us as I grasped her hand. Her grip was solid, her fingers warm to the touch as we engaged in a very traditional handshake, but I got the sense that, for her, this was something more.

"Calliope Reaper-Jones," I said when she finally released my hand—an action I had to initiate. She seemed so loath to let my hand go that, frankly, I wouldn't have been surprised if she'd decided to take it with her as a prize.

"It's a pleasure to finally meet you," Caoimhe said as she begrudgingly returned to Morrigan's side. To my surprise, her eyes were moist with emotion, her smile wavering.

"Nice to finally meet you, too," I replied, not sure who the hell the woman was, but not wanting to hurt her feelings.

"Time to go, Caoimhe," Morrigan said as she tried to maneuver the other woman out of my orbit.

"You're just . . . *you're lovely*," Caoimhe said, the words pouring from her mouth as if she couldn't contain them.

It wasn't very often I got a compliment, but I'd learned from Jarvis that the polite thing was to just say thank you. So I did.

"Thank you," I replied, embarrassed.

"Let's go," Morrigan said as she physically had to drag the other woman away.

"Bye, Mortimer!" I called out after them, unable to stop myself from throwing one more potshot at Morrigan's retreating back.

"What the hell was that all about?" I asked as the two women finally disappeared into the crowd.

"I haven't the faintest," Jarvis said, his shoulders loosening. Out from under Morrigan's thumb again, he had started to relax.

"Bullshit," I said, but Jarvis didn't take the bait.

"Okay, whatever," I said, annoyed that Jarvis was stonewalling me.

I knew the redhead had hit a nerve because he'd been so strangely silent during the exchange, his lips pursed unhappily. But even after I'd defended him against a marauding party, he was still choosing not to elaborate—so whatever the Goddess had on him must've been big.

"If you don't want to share, don't worry about it," I continued, coy now. "I'll just ask Naapi to explain."

I started to scan the crowd for the Vice-President of North America, knowing it was gonna be hard to pick him out of the crowd, the sea of masks dissolving all individuality.

"No, don't!" Jarvis said, grabbing my arm. "Morrigan may have been blunt, but she wasn't wrong. The Bacchanal was real . . . is *still* real."

That got my attention.

"Still real?" I asked, warming to the subject. Jarvis didn't want to elaborate, that was more than apparent, but he'd already moved past the failsafe point in the conversation, so there was no going back.

"The Bacchanal is how many of the half-breeds are created . . ." Jarvis said, trailing off. "It is how I was conceived."

Jarvis looked down at his feet, shame dark in his eyes.

"Jarvis, I didn't mean—"

He waved me away, his voice low.

"It's nothing."

But he was lying. This was obviously a big deal to the ex-faun, something he didn't want to share with the world, but was now being forced to do by the bitterness of Morrigan's wrath.

I decided to change the subject, or at least, change the thrust of the conversation.

"So, it still happens, the Bacchanal?"

Jarvis, relieved I wasn't going to pin him to the wall and watch him wriggle, nodded his head.

"The masks keep one's identity a secret, so all are equal on this night. Couplings between Gods, humans, and supernatural creatures are encouraged."

I looked around, noticing for the first time that couples seemed to be pairing off and leaving the dance floor, their masks keeping the hookup totally anonymous.

"Are they going off to have *sex*?" I sputtered, starting to understand for the first time why Jarvis and I were maskless, why Runt hadn't wanted to go off and "have fun," but instead was sticking to my side like glue.

Jarvis perked up, smelling blood in the water.

"Shall I get you a mask then, Miss Calliope?" he sang, enjoying my unease, milking it for all it was worth.

"Shut up," I seethed.

"But don't you want to have anonymous sex with a stranger?" Jarvis said, his eyes brimming over with glee.

"No, I do not—" I shot back.

"But you really seemed to want one of those lovely golden masks—"

I took the opportunity to punch Jarvis in the shoulder, hard.

"You win," I growled. "So shut up now."

The night had soured on me, the beauty of the cave and its glorious artwork tainted by all the crazy sex I imagined people having in the shadowy corners and hidden nooks. The candles weren't just for ambience; their flickering incandescence was being used as a tool to keep the sex stuff secret, and the music I'd been enjoying was only a cover-up for all the grunting and grinding.

Ugh . . . so not *my cup of tea.*

"How long do we have to stay here?" I asked, feeling kind of dirty just being in the cave. I wasn't a prude—far from it— but orgies were *not* in my repertoire.

"Eleven fifteen is the earliest we can get away with departing," Jarvis replied, the look on his face telling me he was feeling just as skeevy about the evening as I was.

My mind was reeling, unable to focus on anything but the sex I knew was happening nearby. I wondered how my dad had dealt with this kind of thing—had he been repulsed by it or had he just accepted it as part of the job?

"This must've been weird for my dad," I said. "Standing here all night, knowing what was going on around you."

Jarvis got noticeably uncomfortable.

"It was a part of your father's job."

Well, that's no kind of an answer, I thought to myself.

"Sure," I said, not wanting to argue with Jarvis, but sensing once again there was more to the story than my Executive Assistant was willing to share with me. "What about you? You ever partake in the mass orgy?"

Jarvis shuddered, his distaste palpable.

"Never," he said, a bite to his words. "I would never contribute to something this destructive."

"How is it destructive?" I asked. "It just seems kind of gross and it's definitely a repository for a ton of sexually transmitted diseases."

"Like the Gods care about that," Jarvis mumbled.

"Sure, they're immortal, so it doesn't really affect them," I agreed. "But the humans and other creatures, they're susceptible."

"As I said before," Jarvis repeated. "Like the Gods care."

"So, explain to me the destructive part?"

Jarvis sighed, looking down at Runt. He must've decided the pup had already heard too much naughty stuff, so what was the point in stopping now.

"The offspring born of this night, they never know who their true fathers are."

This problem hadn't occurred to me before, but when Jarvis voiced it, it made sense. Especially when I remembered that Jarvis himself was a member of this fatherless club. I may not have loved everything about my parents, but at least I knew they were my parents.

"You never met your father?" I asked, not wanting to press, but also curious to learn more about my Executive Assistant's upbringing. Jarvis knew everything about me while I knew absolutely nothing about him—and this was something I wanted to remedy.

"Never. I have no idea who he might be," Jarvis said, a pained expression on his face.

"Maybe we could find out—" I started to say, but Jarvis cut me off.

"No. No meddling, Calliope Reaper-Jones. My life is perfectly fine as it is."

I didn't believe him, but he'd sounded so adamant, I wasn't going to push it.

"All right, no meddling," I said, trying to placate his ruffled feathers.

"Thank you."

"What time is it anyway?" I asked, letting Jarvis off the hook. I was itching for eleven fifteen to arrive as quickly as possible.

"It's not even ten yet." Jarvis sighed, looking at his wristwatch.

Why is it when you want time to speed by, it's as slow as molasses, but when you're really enjoying something, it goes into overdrive, moving so fast the fun stuff is over before you even know it? Well, this party was going to be a molasses night and there was nothing I could do about it.

Daniel.

His name popped into my head, unbidden. Was he here now, having hot sex with someone—his date, Coy, possibly, or maybe a masked sex bomb he didn't even know—right under my nose? Oh God, the idea made me sick to my stomach. To my horror, I couldn't stop myself from looking around the cave, trying to catch sight of him in some secluded corner, pounding away.

Stop it! I thought to myself, but the image of Daniel, boffing some nameless girl whose very existence I would detest for all eternity, was burned into my consciousness. No matter what other, happier, thoughts I tried to blot it out with, it just wouldn't go away.

"What time is it?" I asked Jarvis, barely containing my antsiness.

"Nine fifty-five."

One hour and twenty minutes of sheer suffering.

"What time is it?"

Jarvis glared at me.

"Nine fifty-six."

It was going to be a long one hour and nineteen minutes.

eight

At eleven fifteen on the dot, Jarvis, Runt and I took our leave. In the intervening hour and nineteen minutes, the party had really started to heat up, with more couples sexing it down in the darkness than chilling on the dance floor. The band had kicked it up a notch, eschewing the slow songs for the heart rate–accelerating dance hits—probably vibing off the sexually heated atmosphere. Of the caterers, there was no trace, and any alcoholic beverage you might've wanted had gone with them.

The masks I'd so envied earlier in the evening had now become only a harsh reminder of the strange new world I'd become embroiled in when I'd taken over my dad's job—a world where supernatural ritual trumped sexual mores, where children were conceived without the benefit of knowing their parentage. These weren't the ethics my parents had instilled in me as a child, or the moral lessons I'd learned at boarding school. I mean, *I* was the kind of gal who was horribly tortured by my one "cheating" mishap—and I'm not even talking full-on intercourse—so being thrust into the middle of masked orgy land was way out of my comfort zone.

Judge not, lest you be judged, right? And I didn't want to be known as a sanctimonious prude. Maybe this wasn't the lifestyle choice I wanted for myself, but it seemed to work for some people and who was I to condemn them? I mean, I'd been a party to a cheating episode, so I was guilty of being naughty, too.

"Do we have to do anything? Or can we just go?" I asked Jarvis as he checked his watch for the final time, nodding happily at what he saw.

"Best to go now while they're otherwise engaged," he said, ushering Runt and me toward the exit. "They'll be finished soon enough as it is."

The loud music pounding in my ears, I gave the crowd a faux military salute.

"Thanks for a great time," I said, sarcasm dripping from my tongue.

Sick of the dress I was wearing and disappointed in my first All Hallows' Eve "Eve" Ball experience, I decided this wasn't an event I looked forward to hosting again in the future. Maybe I could talk Kali into running it for me next year. She was good at getting her hands dirty and a master at carnage, so I knew hosting an orgy would be right up her alley.

Speaking of the Hindu Goddess of Death and Destruction, I realized I hadn't seen her or any of the other Death, Inc., executives since the ball had begun. They'd been around for the first few minutes of the initial meet and greet, but once that'd petered out, they'd disappeared and I wondered if they, too, had gone off to partake in the "fun."

As for Daniel, I didn't even want to think about him anymore. I'd been obsessing about my ex nonstop since I'd realized what was going on around me. I finally decided if he really was out there in the groping throng getting his hands—and other body parts—dirty, then I didn't want to know about it. The only thing that had saved me from an out-and-out breakdown was the fact that a few of the masked revelers hadn't joined in when the sex-jinks had started, but instead had remained on the dance floor, drinking and enjoying themselves without disrobing. My hope was that Daniel had been among this levelheaded minority. Of course, with sexpot Coy as his date, I had to admit to myself that this wasn't a very likely scenario.

"Let's go, Cal," Runt said, nuzzling her snout against my hand, silently encouraging me to stop scanning the crowd for Daniel and Coy—not like I'd be able to tell it was them with their masks on, but I just couldn't help myself.

"Okay," I said absently, my eyes still locked on the crowd. I knew she was right, that I was torturing myself by remaining in the cave any longer than I needed to, but it was so hard to drag my eyes away.

I scanned the dance floor one more time, just in case, but if I thought I was going to have my jealous feelings resolved one way or the other, well, I was sadly mistaken. Runt pressed her wet, heart-shaped nose against my palm and I patted her head, her soft fur a balm against all the nauseous emotions roiling around my gut.

"Calliope?" Jarvis said, his words breaking through my obsessive thoughts.

I gave him a pleasant smile, one I hoped would mask all the turmoil I was feeling, but Jarvis was a sharp little bastard and knew exactly what was going on.

"Calliope, I think it's best if we go now. You have a long night ahead of you, and you need to prepare."

Jarvis and Runt were right. I needed to get my head on straight and stop trying to control something I had no power over. My dad would never have gotten mired down in something as petty as whether or not Daniel was doing the nasty. He would've put the job ahead of any romantic notions of love or destiny—and if I was going to be as good a Death as he was, then I was going to have to stop being such a putzhead.

"All right," I said, shoving any thoughts of Daniel out of my mind as I followed Jarvis and Runt toward the shimmering wormhole.

"Let's get the hell outta Dodge."

the trip back to our room was uneventful. We passed through the wormhole without incident, though I noticed both Jarvis and Runt scoping the scene as they led me out of the cave and into the overcast gloom of the Central California night. There was no one manning the white tent, helping to make sure the partygoers found their way inside. Instead, a tall man in a gray suit and sunglasses, headset plugged into one ear, was waiting for us just beyond the shadow of the tent, his face as hard as granite. He nodded to Jarvis as we passed then fell into step behind us.

It was disconcerting to be dogged by the cold mercenaries Jarvis had hired to guard us and I wondered out loud where he had found them.

"They come highly recommended," Jarvis whispered as he glanced back anxiously at the man trailing us. "They were in Iraq and Afghanistan. Extremely skilled at the art of warfare—and bloodthirsty."

"Are you sure these are the kinda guys you want guarding us?" I asked, uncertainty giving buoyancy to my words.

"That's exactly *why* I wanted them guarding you," Jarvis replied, his tone brooking no argument.

I sighed. As disturbing as it was to be shepherded along in the darkness by a man wearing sunglasses (this wasn't a goddamned Corey Hart video, people), I guess it was better than the alternative. I really didn't want to have to deal with a surprise Ender of Death attack, especially now, when I was in such an emotionally vulnerable state.

Runt stuck to my side the whole way back to the room. I could tell she didn't like the bodyguard situation, either. She believed she could do a much better job of protecting me than any human could—and she was probably right.

"We're almost there, Cal," she said, trotting along beside me, her dark coat causing her to blend in with the night, leaving only the tapetum lucidum of her eyes visible in the darkness.

"Once we get inside, I suggest you put the, uhm, book somewhere safe," Jarvis whispered as we crossed paths with the bodyguard standing watch over the entrance to our suite. He nodded at Jarvis as we passed, but otherwise he didn't move a muscle as his compatriot joined him at the door.

I waved at the men just to annoy Jarvis, but I quickly dropped my hand when my Executive Assistant glared at me.

"Sorry," I mumbled, holding the door open so Jarvis and Runt could follow me inside.

"I'm freezing," I said through chattering teeth as I grabbed the coverlet off my bed and threw it over my shoulders, beginning to warm up immediately. My flimsy dress had left a lot of my skin exposed to the elements, so in just the few minutes it'd taken us to walk back from the tent, I'd started to shiver.

I rubbed my hands together until they'd lost their chill, then

I dropped the coverlet back onto the bed, rooting around inside the bodice of my dress until I found the book where it had settled in beside my right boob. Snagging the small, square object, I brought it out and held it up to the light so I could study it.

"It's so small," I said, flipping through the pages. "Why make something so important, so small?"

Jarvis was used to my ignorance—actually, I think he counted on it so he could lecture me without guilt—and was more than prepared to explain the provenance of *How to Be Death: A Fully Annotated Guide*.

"After the fall of Lucifer, God asked the angel Metatron to create a treatise giving implicit instructions on how one might end the reign of humanity on Earth, now and forever," Jarvis began as I unhooked the bustle of my long skirt and shrugged out of it, letting the heavy material fall to the floor around my feet. With the skirt gone, the bodice was instantly transformed into a cute little minidress version of the gown. *Très chic!*

"Metatron created an instruction manual on how to kill humanity?" I asked, confused because I'd always thought God was, like, humanity's biggest fan.

"There must always be balance in the universe, Calliope," Jarvis replied, loosening his bow tie as he sat down on the edge of Runt's bed. "And God has to prepare for every eventuality. At least if this knowledge is contained in one book and that book lies in the possession of a nonbiased party—Death—then there is some modicum of safety."

"So Death is the only thing keeping humanity from destroying itself?"

Jarvis nodded his head.

"As Minnie said earlier, humanity is incapable of reading or touching the book—"

"The big face melt-off, I remember," I interjected—and I could tell Jarvis was pleased I'd been paying attention. To show my continued interest, I picked the tiny book up from where I'd set it down on the dresser and flipped it open, the strange Angelic language as indecipherable now as it'd been when I'd first looked at the book.

"But Metatron took pity on humanity," Jarvis went on. "Wanting to give them some knowledge of the fate awaiting them, he imparted a generalized version of the book to the human, Enoch, who transcribed Metatron's words into what would then become the *Book of Enoch*."

"But the *Book of Enoch* doesn't have the instruction stuff in it," I said, starting to catch on. "So it's kind of a warning without any teeth—but *this* copy of the book, the one Minnie gave me, it's the real deal. It has all the missing information in it."

Jarvis nodded.

"Exactly. And the safest place for it is in the Hall of Death."

Jarvis's words caused my mind to start whirring, realization dawning inside me.

"Wait a minute," I said, waving the book in front of me. "This thing is supposed to live in the Hall of Death?"

"Yes—" Jarvis began, but I cut him off.

"*This* is what my sister was looking for, isn't it?" I said, my throat tight with emotion. "This book was the reason why Suri and all the others in the Hall of Death had to die—so Thalia could find this book and keep control of humanity's fate for herself."

Runt had hopped onto my bed when we'd first come inside, curling up in a ball next to my pillow and shutting her eyes, a nod to the fact that it was way past her bedtime—but when she heard the urgency in my words, she instantly opened them again. Assessing the situation and deeming it urgent, she eased herself off the bed and trotted over to me, dragging her side against my leg before settling her butt down on top of my left foot, in a gesture of consolation.

"Yes, I think the book was the reason your sister stormed the Hall of Death while the Devil was countering our attack down in Hell." Jarvis sighed, his eyes morose.

I saw that Jarvis had come to this conclusion much earlier in the game than I had. Probably because he'd been in possession of all the pertinent information, while I had remained in the dark until now.

It had been a bloody, horrible day—and one that would be forever etched in memory. Jarvis, Cerberus, and I had released all the souls from Hell as an offensive tactic to get the Devil to leave Purgatory and return to his own dominion. It had worked, but it had left his coconspirator (my sister, Thalia) and a small retinue of Bugbear guards free to lay siege to the Hall of Death, killing everyone inside except for Tanuki, the giant man who ran the Death Record filing system.

"Why didn't you tell me before?" I said, sadness welling inside me. "Don't you think I should've known this?"

Jarvis dropped his eyes, his hands tightening into two curled fists on his lap.

"You should have been told," he murmured. "It was wrong of me to keep this information from you."

I didn't know what to do with his apology. It did nothing to ease the sense of anger-fueled guilt I was experiencing.

"Whatever," I said, turning away from him and dislodging Runt from my foot in the process.

"Calliope," Jarvis said, "I only withheld this because I didn't want to burden you. You've had so much to deal with these past few months. It seemed irrelevant now—"

"Nothing is irrelevant, Jarvis," I said. "Not anymore."

I could see Jarvis's face reflected back at me in the tiny art deco makeup mirror that sat on top of the dresser. He looked miserable, shoulders slumped, eyes downcast. Sensing my scrutiny in the mirror, he lifted his head and grimaced, but I didn't drop my gaze.

"I haven't made this easy for you, Jarvi. I know that," I said. "But I'm ready to do this thing the right way."

Jarvis nodded, looking a bit less morose.

"You were put into an untenable situation, Calliope, and I have been trying very hard to make things easy for you, to not overwhelm you," Jarvis said. "I think of you as if you were my own daughter, and I only wanted to make the transition as painless as possible."

I sat down on the bed beside my Executive Assistant and sighed.

"I guess you did the right thing, Jarvi," I said, putting my arm around his shoulder. "At least, I think my dad would have approved."

Jarvis swallowed, a single tear streaking down his cheek.

"I miss him very much, you know," Jarvis said.

"Me, too," I replied, my throat constricting even as I fought to stay strong.

We sat in the deepening silence, each lost within the maze of our own thoughts, Runt a lump of snoring fur between our feet. There was no assuaging the guilt I felt, so I let my mind wander instead, surprised that it kept returning to the two armed human bodyguards waiting outside the door, their sole focus to keep me out of harm's way for the next twenty-four hours—a notion that was at once comforting and extremely unsettling.

"So what do we do with the damn thing while we're stuck at the Death Dinner?" I said finally, tired of the extended silence.

"Any magic we worked would dissolve once the clock struck midnight," Jarvis said thoughtfully. "That means there would be no point in concocting an obscuring spell."

"It has to be a clever hiding place in its own right," I agreed, my eyes searching the room. "Someplace no one would ever think to look."

Runt's ears perked up at my words.

"I know where to hide it," she said, thumping her tail happily. "It's perfect!"

She stood up and stretched, waving her rump in the air like a flag, then took off, her paws padding on the soft fibers of the Oriental carpet. Jarvis and I followed her as she made a beeline for the white, mosaic-tiled bathroom. Once inside, she promptly clicked her way over to the closet and plopped her dark bulk down in front of it.

"There's a false bottom. Open it and see," she said, waiting for one of us to slide the closet door open for her. I took the bait, sidestepping her tail so I could inch the wooden slider down its track.

"How do you know it's a false bottom?" I asked her, shaking my head because I just couldn't see a way to pop the bottom up or slide it out.

"I noticed it when we were checking out the bathroom earlier," she said, cocking her head as a fiery gleam came into her bright eyes. "Try opening one of the little drawers, Cal."

I did as she said, slowly pulling out one of the built-in drawers set into the wood just below the sliding door, but nothing happened.

"Do the other one, too," she said.

I pulled the other drawer out of its wooden frame, so that now both drawers hung out in the air—and suddenly there was a sharp *click*. A cylindrical piece of wood that I'd originally taken for a knot in the closet's molding slid upward into the air.

"Whoa," I said, impressed.

"It's a dowel," Runt said matter-of-factly, and I wasn't about to argue with her.

"Now watch this."

Runt lifted her paw, setting its weight down on top of the dowel, then giving a happy yip, she pushed it back into the molding, the false bottom sliding open to reveal a hidden compartment built into the wall behind the closet.

"You're amazing!" I said as I knelt down to give the pup's neck a squeeze. I'd forgotten that Runt was such a master at hide-and-seek, so it was only natural she would be the one to discover the best hiding spot in the Castle.

"Looks as if someone else has been using it for safekeeping, too," Jarvis said as he rooted around inside the secret compartment, up to his elbow in dismembered cobwebs. A moment later his fingers grasped their prize, a tarnished silver locket, and pulled it up into the light. He cleared the dust off with one powerful puff, his large fingers fumbling with the clasp until it popped open.

Inside the locket was the small black-and-white portrait of a woman with long, dark hair and a mysterious Mona Lisa smile, the turned-up corners of her lips giving only a hint at her personality.

She's beautiful," I said, staring at the picture.

Jarvis flipped the locket over, looking for any kind of inscription, but there was nothing; not even a name had been etched into the silver.

"She's nameless, too," Runt said.

"And no one seems to have breached the compartment until now," Jarvis said, indicating the cobweb detritus he'd scraped off his sleeve. "So it appears as if we've found our hiding place."

We waited as Jarvis returned to the bedroom, fetching the book so I could set it inside the false bottom with the mystery locket—we'd decided to let sleeping dogs lie, so the locket went back in, too. I closed the two drawers, one after the other, and we watched as the dowel reset itself, sealing away the hidden compartment from even the most prying of eyes.

"Let some bad guy find it now," I proclaimed to the world

at large as I grinned at my coconspirators, proud of the bang-up job we'd done. I didn't think we could've found a better hiding place if we'd tried.

It was only later, upon closer inspection of the strange events that transpired during the course of the evening, that I wondered if I hadn't jinxed us.

nine

"Time to go," Jarvis said as the small desk clock reached a quarter to the hour and Runt yawned sleepily, the heat in the room making everyone tired.

We'd been sitting around for the last ten minutes—Runt and I curled up on my bed, Jarvis sitting ramrod straight in the desk chair—waiting until it was absolutely time to leave the safety of the room for the quick jog over to the main house. Neither the pup nor I wanted to leave the toasty room, but since neither of us could come up with a good enough argument to get me out of the Death Dinner, it was a moot point. So one after the other, we got up and trooped after Jarvis as he stepped out into the chill of the October night.

Taking a key from his suit coat pocket, he locked the door—which was the only entrance to the suite—then deposited the key back into the same inside coat pocket, patting his breast to make sure the key was safely entombed. I thought the whole thing was overkill. We had two bodyguards, and one of them was going to be stationed by the door at all times, so what was the point of locking it?

"And what if something happened to the guards?" Jarvis said, looking piqued. "You want anyone to be able to just waltz into your room and lie in wait for you?"

I shook my head, but I thought the scenario was a little far-fetched. Still, I'd learned it was always easier to let Jarvis have his way than to fight him over superfluous details.

"It's freezing," I said, wrapping my arms around myself and trying my best to keep up with the nimble-footed ex-faun, the first bodyguard trailing behind us like a silent wraith.

Keeping my eye on the man who was supposed to keep his eye on me, I decided that the word "mercenary" was the perfect descriptor for the two fellows whose charge was to keep me safe from the Ender of Death for the next twenty-four hours.

Even though I knew the bodyguards were a (probably) necessary fashion accessory for the evening, I still hated feeling like I'd stepped into the middle of a John Le Carré novel. All the cloak-and-dagger stuff had never been my cup of tea, and as the bodyguard's shadowy presence dogged us across the courtyard and onto the stone path leading up to Casa del Amo—his compatriot had remained behind to guard the door like I'd anticipated—I couldn't help feeling like there was something "wrong" about the men, a subtle, malignant energy I didn't like, swirling around them like a swarm of aggressive wasps.

"Stop," Jarvis said abruptly, holding out his arm to block my path, but only succeeding in jarring me with his arrested movement, so that I misstepped and tripped over a raised stone in the path, accidentally slamming my elbow into the small of his back as I fought to remain upright.

With a strangled grunt, Jarvis fell to his knees, his hands grasping blindly at his back as he searched for the tender spot I'd gouged. Runt, who'd been following along at my heel, was more graceful than either of us, entirely circumventing the mini–traffic accident with a little hop.

"I'm sorry, Jarvis!" I squeaked, trying to help him up—but he waved me off.

"Stay away—"

I took a step back, giving him room to collect himself. I didn't want to get blamed for any further mishaps.

"Is it bad?" I asked as he gritted his teeth and palpated the spot with his fingers. Guilt swelled in my chest and I felt terrible—like I'd accidentally hit a baby or something.

"It's . . . all . . . right," Jarvis said through clenched teeth, his usually pale complexion red with pain. After a few moments, when it appeared that nothing was busted, I held out my arm, hoping he'd see it as a peace offering. With a sigh, he reached out and took the proffered hand, letting me help him climb back onto his feet.

"Why'd you stop like that?" I asked as he brushed the dirt from the knees of his tuxedo pants. Unlike me, he was still in the same clothes, not having had a chance to change since the ball.

He didn't answer me. He didn't have to—because ahead of us, I could hear the tinkling of Coy's giggle as it floated down to us from where she and Daniel stood, blocking the entrance to Casa del Amo.

"Oh, God." I winced, wanting to turn tail and run, but Jarvis grabbed my arm before I could get away. "I don't want to see them, Jarvis. *Please.*"

Jarvis's grip tightened on the flesh of my upper arm, not unpleasantly, but hard enough to keep me from fleeing the scene.

"Calliope Reaper-Jones, Daniel will be a part of your business affairs for as long as he remains in charge of Hell," he hissed through his teeth. "So you'd best get used to dealing with him—*and* whatever trollop he might have on his arm."

"He's right, Cal," Runt said, her tone neutral, but she was definitely telling me to suck it up and act like an adult.

I don't wanna go, I thought miserably, but with both Jarvis and Runt ganging up on me, I didn't stand a chance of squeaking out of it.

"Ready?" Jarvis asked as he stapled a warm smile of greeting onto his face, then giving my arm a gentle tug, he forced me forward. I inhaled deeply, hoping the influx of fresh air would unstick my brain, but it backfired, a whiff of Coy's heady floral perfume making me sneeze.

"Bless you," Runt whispered, but Jarvis didn't deign to reply.

"Let's go," he said as he led me toward utter emotional ruination.

"I think I'm gonna be sick," I moaned, half walking, half cowering behind my Executive Assistant.

Ahead of us, Daniel had finally noticed our arrival—I guess

they'd been too wrapped up in each other to see our Laurel and Hardy routine down at the bottom of the path—and he instinctively took a step away from Coy, almost as if he didn't want to offend me by standing too close to her.

It was only as we approached the two of them that I realized something important—something I should've realized when I'd first met the woman but had been too oblivious to notice during our previous encounter. Coy wasn't just some run-of-the-mill girl Daniel had met in a bar, chatting her up over peanuts and a light beer.

No, Coy was a Goddess.

How I knew this, I don't know—but there was just something reminiscent of Kali about her and that's what clued me in.

"Shit," I mumbled under my breath as we overtook them, my brain screaming at me to run as far away as possible from this potential heartbreak disaster. Panicking, I tried to imitate Jarvis's pleasant smile of greeting, but I was so miserable all I could manage was a half-formed grimace.

I must've slowed down—heartache turning my legs to jelly—because Jarvis dug his nails into the sensitive skin of my naked arm, the tiny talons enough of a threat of potential violence to keep me on my feet.

"Good evening," Jarvis said, nodding to Daniel as we passed.

"Good evening," I echoed morosely.

Daniel started to say something, but was interrupted by his date's chirpy voice:

"Hi, Calliope!"

Coy batted her long eyelashes at me then took Daniel's arm and cuddled against it, closing her eyes with pleasure. I swallowed hard, my eyes searching out Daniel's, looking for reassurance that this was some kind of a joke, that Coy was just a very cruel figment of my own imagination, but I got nada. Daniel refused to even look at me.

"We shall see you inside," Jarvis shot back then trundled me past them as quickly as he dared.

Jarvis could've let go of me then, but he didn't. He continued to hold on as we made our way up to the front entrance of the building and passed through the wooden door leading into the foyer. He didn't hold on to me because he was worried I would run away or cause a scene and embarrass myself, but because he knew his strength was the only thing keeping me on my feet.

There was no time for talking once we stepped inside. I may not have been involved in the details of the Death Dinner, but Jarvis was, and we were immediately swept up in the preparations. Upon our entry, a tall woman with a head of bushy blond hair and a long, pointy nose sashayed into the room, a white apron tied around her waist, her mouth set in an unbroken line. She was holding a typewritten menu in one hand and a bunch of springy golden marigolds in the other.

"Taste this," she said, stuffing a marigold bloom into Jarvis's unsuspecting mouth.

"Hmmm," he said as he chewed, then nodding his head in approval, he swallowed the bloom, the marigold's spicy flavor having withstood his expert appraisal.

"You like them." It wasn't a question.

"For the salad?" Jarvis asked the woman, who pursed her lips and gave a barely perceptible shake of her head.

"Garnish for the cold carrot soup."

Jarvis thought about this for a moment then acquiesced.

"I approve."

The woman hadn't seemed worried, and I expected she thought Jarvis's approval was already a foregone conclusion. Without another word, she turned on her heel and departed, the folds of her black Mao jacket flapping behind her as she marched down the hall.

"Was that Zinia Monroe?" Runt asked, her question laced with excitement.

"That's exactly right, Runt," Jarvis said, patting her head. "It's amazing luck on our part because Mr. Ali has been wooing her for years to be his personal chef. Then, only four months ago, out of the blue, she sold her latest restaurant to a Japanese conglomerate and finally accepted his offer."

"How do you know who she is?" I asked Runt, but I thought I already knew the answer.

Clio and Runt were Food Network junkies. Neither one of

them could cook worth a damn, but on a number of occasions I'd found them sitting in front of the television in Clio's room, watching celebrity cooking shows until their eyes crossed.

"She makes the most amazing Mexican hot chocolate cake," Runt said, her eyes glazing over as she described the dessert. "Layers of rich, runny chocolate flavored with cinnamon, sitting atop a flourless cake base—"

"I gotcha," I said, my stomach starting to growl. "Although you can't have actually tasted this cake if you only watched her make it on TV."

The sound of Zinia's low-pitched voice, coming from farther down the hall, cut into our conversation.

"Jarvis de Poupsy, are we going to my kitchen or not?"

"I really don't like leaving the two of you like this," Jarvis confided, looking worried. "I should go to the kitchen and make sure everything is in order before Zinia has my head, but I *could* always—"

"We're okay," I said, interrupting him before he could offer to bottle-feed Runt and change my diaper. "Go do what you need to do. We can look after each other."

I was starting to calm down from my Daniel-Coy run-in and I didn't need Jarvis hovering over me like a recalcitrant mother.

"Are you sure?"

I could sense him waffling, so I pushed a little harder.

"I'm fine," I said, hoping to reassure myself while I reassured him. "Besides, I can always scream if there's a problem."

Jarvis didn't like that idea at all.

"No screaming," he said, running a hand through his thick hair. "Just send Runt to find me if things get out of hand."

I saluted him.

"Will do, Captain Kangaroo."

He cleared his throat, not enjoying being called "Captain" anything, let alone Captain "Kangaroo," but he sensed I was starting to revive—the beauty of the Castle was working its charms on me—and decided now was as good a time as any if he was gonna take his leave.

"Just follow the hallway and it will lead you directly to the drawing room," Jarvis called over his shoulder, pointing down the hall. "Have a cocktail and relax!"

Runt and I watched Jarvis's retreating back, both of us wondering when he'd been replaced with this Stepford Wife version of himself. I was not known for my ability to hold my liquor, so the guy had to be either really worried or really distracted (or both) if he was encouraging me to partake of an alcoholic beverage.

"This Castle is spooky," Runt said as we left the safety of the foyer and followed the curve of the hallway toward the drawing room.

"Spooky, but beautiful," I agreed as we crossed the intricately constructed Moroccan mosaic tiled floor, the tiny blue-and-green squares glinting like polished fish scales beneath our feet.

Whitewashed plaster walls stretched elegantly above the heavy, brown wood wainscoting, while gilt-framed Dutch baroque realism portraits lined the hallway, each set of luminescent eyes silently observing our progress as their rounded faces glowed from within.

The claustrophobic hallway gave way at the end of the corridor, and we found ourselves inside an octagonal room with ornately carved hardwood from floor to ceiling. Cabinets, their thick wooden doors blending seamlessly into the wood veneer walls, lined the circumference of the room, while beveled shelves were fitted above every cabinet, each one home to a flight of neatly shelved books. Some interior designer had probably fished the tomes out of an estate sale, carefully selecting them for the intact brilliance of their spines and nothing else. Even the ceiling had gotten in on the action; octagonal shapes resembling inverted, overgrown mushrooms were cut into the wood above our heads, making it feel as if we'd stepped into an upside-down wooden forest.

A petite woman with a pixie face and fine, closely cropped silver hair that perfectly outlined her scalp—giving her head the appearance of a denuded skull—greeted us at the door, a massive tray of miniature antique cut-crystal sherry glasses filled with a jewel-hued, reddish-brown liquor balanced precariously on the fans of her upturned palms.

"Sherry?" she said in a squeaky voice, her too big white blouse and black skirt making her resemble a country mouse. Eyes downcast, she proffered the tray at me, sloshing some of the liquid out of the glasses and onto the floor.

"What is it?" I asked uncertainly as I took one, surprised at its heaviness.

"It's a Palo Cortado. A very rare sherry, but quite delicious," said the only other occupant of the room, a rotund man with snowy white skin and a nasty smile.

He was perched on one of the two red-and-gold upholstered love seats that sat in the middle of the room, happily warming his great bulk against the crackling fire someone had thoughtfully laid in the wrought iron grate of the fireplace—probably the woman carrying the tray of sherry. He had on an expensive tailored tuxedo, but it'd been incongruously paired with a red bolo tie, making it look trashy, not classy. In fact, the shiny charcoal fabric was so slick and unforgiving that his hairless body resembled an albino sausage wrapped in a gray bun with a dollop of ketchup (the bolo tie) on top.

To add to his odd taste in clothing, there was something cold and reptilian about the man. I almost expected him to flick out a forked tongue and test the air for my scent, but instead he gave me a frosty, gap-toothed smile, his bald pate glistening with sweat.

"Sounds drinkable," I replied, putting the glass to my nose and giving it a good sniff. I'd been burned once by a Midori Sour and it'd made me pretty finicky about what I put in my system, alcohol-wise.

"It's divine," the reptilian man said, closing his eyes as he rolled his head from one side to the other, each movement eliciting a firm *crack*.

I ignored the gross sounds by fixating on my drink. It smelled all right, Reptile Man was drinking it, and I'd selected a glass at random from the tray, so I figured it was okay to taste. With one casual flick of my wrist, I put the glass to my lips and let the liquor slide down my throat. Though the alcohol made it burn a little, the sherry had a warm, nutty flavor that titillated my taste buds.

"Mmm, that's good," I said, starting to reach for another glass of the sweet liquor, but Runt's tail slapped painfully against my calf, scolding me into setting my empty glass back down on the tray instead.

"It should be savored, not downed like a shot," Reptile Man said with a frown.

I shrugged.

"I'm not much of a drinker."

Reptile Man didn't like my answer, giving me a disdainful sniff as he snottily sipped his sherry. Suddenly, from somewhere deep within the belly of the building, a clock began to chime the hour in long, elegiac peals, making my teeth vibrate. As I waited for the clock to suspend its doleful dirge, I counted the twelve booming strikes that meant it was now midnight:

There would be no more magic for the next twenty-four hours.

I searched inside myself, wanting to see if I felt any different now that magic had ceased to be relevant to my life, at least temporarily. But no, I felt no different than I did twenty seconds earlier when magic was still viable.

"Well, that was loud," I said as I walked over to one of the red-and-gold upholstered armchairs and sat down, the soft cushion cradling my butt. Runt followed me over to the chair and plopped down on the floor at my feet, her tongue protruding adorably as she panted.

"That's the end of magic for now," the serving woman said abruptly, her words cutting into my thoughts. Curious, I looked over at her, but she took the opportunity to busy herself with the drink tray.

"And the beginning of a whole new era of Death," Reptile Man purred, looking meaningfully in my direction.

I'd purposely chosen a spot out of touching range but just close enough that I could still comfortably carry on a conversation with my new "friend"—and boy, was I pleased with my choice. His lecherous gaze told me if I'd been any closer, he would've been trying to pat my arm or my leg—or any exposed body part he could reach with his sweaty white fingers.

"I'm Calliope," I said, changing the subject *and* trying to wipe the lechy look off Reptile Man's face, but it was a no go.

"I know who *you* are," Reptile Man said softly, his voice a low hum. "But the real question is: Do you know who *I* am?"

I had no idea who he was. Jarvis had given me a bound booklet with the names and pictures of all the dinner guests before we'd left, but I'd just kind of scanned it, something I was cursing myself for now. I'd figured Jarvis would be there to whisper names, etc., at me, but here I was totally on my own and clueless.

I decided hedging was the best I could do given the situation, so I gestured for the serving woman to come closer.

While we'd been talking, said serving woman had inched her way into eavesdropping range, the tray balanced precariously in one hand, the glasses tinkling uncomfortably. I was surprised they'd hired her for this job, not because she didn't look adorable in her too large clothing, but because she didn't seem to have much serving experience. Even *I* saw she was cruising for a bruising when those expensive, cut-crystal glasses ended up in sticky shards on the floor.

"Can I have another sherry, please?" I asked, plucking one off the tray while Reptile Man only rolled his eyes.

"Do I know who you are?" I repeated, nervously swirling the sherry in my glass just like I'd seen wine connoisseurs do it in the movies. "Do *I* know who you are?"

Reptile Man leaned forward on the love seat, waiting to see where I was gonna go with this.

"Please, elucidate, Miss Reaper-Jones."

I cleared my throat, feeling the effects of the first glass of sherry starting to stifle my good sense.

"Well, I obviously know a lot of things, being the new Grim Reaper and all," I offered. "So, it only stands to reason I would know who you are."

"Yes," Reptile Man hissed. "Go on."

"I'm the President and CEO of Death, Inc., and since you're here, right now, drinking that sherry you're so fond of," I babbled, "then you must work for me. And that is my final answer."

Reptile Man opened his mouth to reply—I could see the confusion on his face, his brain clicking away as he tried to make sense of what I'd just said—but I was saved from the executioner by the entrance of my dad's old friend, Naapi.

"Calliope," he said, grinning widely at me. "I'm so glad you're early. I would like to introduce you to my consort, Alameda Jones."

The lanky young woman on his arm stepped forward and I could see her underwear—or lack thereof—through the long silky dress she was wearing.

"It's nice to finally meet you," the girl breathed, her frizzy golden hair bunched into a knot on the top of her head.

She was of mixed race, with warm honey skin that glowed in the firelight and wide, full lips stretched taut over pearly white teeth. Her liquid caramel eyes took in my minidress and makeup, and I saw approval etched across them.

"Lovely dress," she said, coming over and grasping my hand as I stood to meet her. "Noisette? Am I right?"

We grinned at each other, connecting on the shallowest of pretensions: fashion.

"She's amazing. Am I right?" Alameda continued, reaching out and touching the ruching at my back lovingly.

"She's unreal," I agreed, starting to enjoy myself for the first time since we'd arrived at the Castle.

"Who is this?!" Alameda said suddenly, her eyes snapping open with excitement. "Aren't you just the most adorable thing ever!?"

She dropped down to her knees, her fingers effortlessly finding the sweet spot behind Runt's ears.

"Is she a hellhound?" Alameda asked. "I'd heard you had one, but to see one outside of Hell . . . amazing."

"Her name's Runt," I said, crouching down beside Alameda, so I could give Runt a pet, too.

"Can she talk?" Alameda inquired, then without waiting for my answer, she turned to Runt. "I'm Alameda. It's lovely to meet you."

"Hi," Runt said shyly, unsure about all the attention Alameda was lavishing on her.

"I met your father once," Alameda said, her voice all honey and dulcet tones. "Cerberus. A great man."

Runt gave a short yip and nuzzled her head into the back of my knee, hiding her eyes.

"Wow, I've never seen her get embarrassed before," I said, amused.

"I knew you ladies would get on," Naapi interjected as he stepped behind Alameda, helping her to her feet. I stood up, not wanting to be the only one on my knees, but I had a hard time keeping my balance because Runt kept burrowing her face into my leg, pushing me forward.

Behind us, Reptile Man cleared his throat, displeased at being ignored for so long.

"Hello, Uriah," Naapi said absently. "I didn't see you there."

Because he was such a large and creepy presence, it was hard to miss him, and I got the impression Naapi had been purposely ignoring him.

"Yes, Mr. Drood and I were having a splendid conversation about sherry before you guys came in," I said, pleased Naapi had supplied me with Reptile Man's first name. It was easy to identify him after getting that piece of information. He was Uriah Drood, the all-powerful Head of the Harvesters and Transporters Union—and a slimy creepoid who I knew Jarvis detested with every ounce of his being.

"I wouldn't go that far, Mistress Death—" Uriah began, but any disparaging remark he was about to make was silenced by the arrival of my favorite goddess, Kali, her milky cream sari a blood-soaked mess.

"Shut your mouth, white girl." She glared at me as I stared at her, openmouthed, my skin crawling at the thought of where all that blood had come from. "Because it's not like *this* isn't all your fault anyway."

ten

"My fault?" I croaked.

I may have been responsible for a lot of screwups in my own life, but I couldn't quite fathom how Kali being drenched in blood was my doing.

"Well, it is," she said, running her hands through her plasma-soaked hair, which now hung freely down her back in long, curling waves. "I'm here at this Death Dinner because of you and now I smell like skunk and tomato!"

Well, that took me a moment to process. *Skunk and tomato?* What about all the blood . . . but then my nostrils were assailed by the familiar stench of skunk spray and everything clicked into place.

Oh, shit, I thought. *Some poor, unsuspecting skunk just sprayed the bejeezus out of the Hindu Goddess of Death and Destruction.*

"Kali," I sputtered, but she held up a warning hand.

"Skunk," she spat at me, her eyes full of fury. "And tomato juice that your stupid serving girl poured all over my head!"

I looked around, realizing for the first time the serving lady with the sherry was MIA—I guess she'd slipped out while I was talking to Alameda—obviously finding herself something way more exciting to get caught up in.

"I'm so sorry, Kali," I said, but inside I was thinking it

might've been better if she'd actually been covered in blood like I'd first suspected.

"I don't want your sorry, dipwad," she growled at me, her lips pressed into a flat line. "I want you to make me smell like a goddamned daisy!"

"Well, why don't we just get Jarvis to magic the smell away . . ." I trailed off, realizing what an idiot I sounded like when we all knew there would be no magic making to speak of for the next twenty-four hours.

"I don't think that's an option, white girl," Kali said, adjusting her lids into two malevolent slits as she went all cat-eyed with wrath.

I looked around the drawing room, hoping for some help from the assemblage, but none was forthcoming. Without realizing it, the rest of the class had just voted me "most likely to de-skunk a pissed-off goddess."

Thanks, guys.

"Okay," I said, slowly moving toward the stinky goddess. "Why don't we get you into a shower and then I'll get my phone out and do a little checking around, see if we can't find a better option than tomato juice."

Kali looked skeptical.

"Look," I continued, "if there's one thing I'm good at, it's digging up info online. I mean, I wasn't the Assistant to the Vice-President of Sales at House and Yard for nothing!"

If I thought my fierce rallying cry—go, House and Yard!— was gonna stir things up a bit and get the peeps on my side, well, I was sadly mistaken. Nonplussed was the expression of choice from the peanut gallery. Even Kali looked uncertain, but she tried to cover it by giving me a watery smile.

"I stink, white girl," she wailed, her lips curling downward as she fought back tears. "What will become of me?"

I was shocked. I'd seen the woman bathed in blood, ripping the heads off her enemies and gorging on their entrails; I was not prepared to see her felled by the likes of a little skunk spray. To calm her down, I pulled my BlackBerry wannabe out from between my cleavage and began to type "skunk," "spray," and "removal" into the web browser. Instantly, a bunch of possible websites popped onto the screen and I started to scroll through them.

"All right, I think I got it," I said—and since no one else was gonna help us out, I took Kali by the arm (damn the stench!) and led her toward the door. Runt, not wanting to be left in the drawing room alone with a bunch of strangers, took off after us. As we passed through the doorway, I inclined my head in the direction of the kitchen.

"Tell Jarvis what's going on and see if he can get me these supplies," I said, reeling off the list of household materials I'd need to permanently delete the stench of skunk from Kali's flesh.

"Will do!" Runt said, happy to be of use. She trotted off in the other direction—apparently, even a muddled Kali was protection enough against the Ender of Death—while I guided my charge farther into Casa del Amo, hopefully in the direction of a bathtub.

"You wanna tell me how this happened?" I asked, for lack of anything better to talk about. Kali's face turned beet red and she shook her head vehemently.

"Oh, come on," I whined, "I'd tell you all the good stuff if it were me."

Kali shook her head again, shivering as we passed through the library and into another corridor.

"There is no 'good stuff,'" Kali said, her voice flat. "And it's embarrassing, dipwad."

"More embarrassing than getting finger-banged in the middle of the New York City Subway?" I said.

Kali considered this for a moment before conceding:

"Yes, you may well have the more embarrassing story, white girl."

"So, dish then," I said as we wove our way through the labyrinthine corridors, stopping every now and then to try a closed door—but all were locked.

"I was spying," Kali said, eyes downcast.

I tried the next door we came to, intricately carved wood set far back into the plaster wall, and when I cranked the doorknob, it pushed right open, revealing the interior of an unoccupied guest bedroom. I didn't wait for an invitation, since none was going to be forthcoming, but just banged the door all the way open and dragged Kali inside.

"Go on," I said, my eyes searching for the telltale signs of an adjoining bathroom and finding two closed doors for possibilities. "You were spying?"

I left Kali standing in the middle of the room, dripping tomato juice and skunk stink on the Oriental carpet, as I tried the first door, which only yielded a closet stuffed to the brim with men's clothing

"Not it," I said, slamming the door then stalking over to the other possibility.

Kali watched the proceedings with growing doubt, but before she completely lost her faith in me, I hit pay dirt.

"It," I called as I threw open the second door to reveal a beautifully appointed, mosaic-tiled bathroom with a sunken tub and matching pedestal sink and toilet.

"Jackpot!" I said, going back to my charge and pulling her into the pristine whiteness of the bathroom.

Together, we unwrapped her sari, pulling out the pleated front from her skirt waistband—which was drenched in skunk spray—and letting it fall to the floor, where the polluted fabric pooled into a bunch at my feet. Using the toe of my shoe, I kicked it away from us, sending it between the toilet and the pedestal sink. Next, I helped her shrug out of her shirt and skirt, both of us wrinkling our noses at the horrible mixture of tomato and skunk.

"Oh my God," I gagged. "I have to open a window."

As Kali climbed into the bath, I ran over to the bathroom window and unlatched it, throwing both sides open to get the maximum amount of ventilation into the room.

"So, tell me who you were spying on," I badgered as I stood at the window, inhaling the untainted air.

"Forget it, white girl, I don't want—" she said, turning on the faucets full blast, the sound of running water drowning out her words.

I didn't get a chance to ask her to elucidate further because Jarvis and Runt chose that moment to burst into the bathroom, carrying a brown cardboard box filled with all the household chemicals I'd asked for.

"My God, the stench," Jarvis said, reeling at the intensity of the skunk-tomato smell.

He set the box down on the bathroom floor, then quickly

backed away, his sensitive nose keeping him sequestered in the bedroom. Runt, whose olfactory senses had to be way more acute than Jarvis's, came right into the bathroom, unfazed.

"Wow, that smell is pungent," she said, settling down next to the bathtub. "But it sure made it easy to find you guys."

"Thanks, Runt," I said, petting the pup's head as I squatted down next to the cardboard box and started digging out the stuff I'd need to make the de-skunking concoction I'd found on the Internet. "You are officially my go-to person 'in case of emergency.'"

"Don't forget Jarvis," she said, watching me mix hydrogen peroxide and baking soda in an empty plastic two-liter soda bottle. "He got all the stuff you wanted and he didn't even blink when Zinia yelled at him for leaving."

"Thanks, Jarvi," I called out, not sure if he could hear me over the flowing water. "You're aces!"

"Hurry up!" Kali yelled at me, her dark hair plastered to her head like a skullcap as she sat hunched in a ball next to the flowing faucet. "And close the window. I'm naked and it's bloody freezing in here!"

"Jeez Louise," I mumbled under my breath as I added the last ingredient to my de-skunking solution and watched it fizz.

"I'm waiting, white girl!" Kali said, her teeth chattering. The Hindu Goddess had done a lot for me over the past year, but I was pretty sure this was going to make us even-steven.

"Okay, where did you get hit?" I asked, holding up the plastic two-liter bottle.

Kali glared at me.

"How am I supposed to know that, Calliope Reaper-Jones? Does it look like I was taking notes for posterity?"

Fine, be a bitch, I thought, my nose burning from the foulness of the smell wafting from the bathtub. *See if I de-skunk you next time!*

"Do a sniff test, give me ballpark," I said.

"It's time for the Death Dinner to begin," Jarvis yelled from the bedroom. "Are you nearly done in there?"

"No!" Kali, Runt, and I all screamed back at once—which Jarvis took as a sign to keep his thoughts to himself. The synchronicity of our "no" definitely made Kali relax a little, and instead of the megabitch attitude I'd been getting, she started to mellow, even allowing herself a small grin at the absurdity of the situation.

"All right, white girl." She sighed, shaking her head. "I guess my hands and arms got it for sure."

She sniffed her fingers and grimaced.

"More than for sure, actually," I murmured as I poured the stuff in the bottle over the afflicted area and watched it fizz.

"Are your hair and face okay?" I asked.

She nodded.

"They're fine. That's just the tomato juice the dumb bitch poured all over my head."

Once again I found myself wondering how the woman got the job. Wasn't she supposed to stay in the drawing room with her sherry tray? Not go skulking around the halls, looking for trouble. I made a mental note to ask Jarvis about the woman after we were done with the whole Kali-skunk debacle.

Luckily for the Goddess, most of the spray was on her clothes and not her skin. I could see oily secretions on the hem of her skirt and on the sari, itself, where they lay crumpled in a ball on the floor, so I suggested dousing her feet and calves in the solution—then we sat quietly, waiting for my jerry-rigged de-skunker to do its job.

"I think it's working," Runt said, her more highly developed sniffer awarding us success.

"Why don't you wash the tomato out of your hair and we'll go find you something else to wear," I said to Kali. "Maybe there's a way to get the smell out of the sari—"

"Burn it," she said matter-of-factly, picking up a bottle of rose-scented shampoo from the side of the tub and squirting a dollop into her hand, massaging it into her hair.

"Are you sure?" I asked. "I bet we could get—"

She waved me away with her hand.

"I have a thousand more like it."

I shrugged and grabbed the clothes off the floor, wadding them into a ball and shoving them into the bottom of the card-board box alongside the empty bottles of hydrogen peroxide, dish soap, and baking soda. I picked up the box, thinking I'd carry it out to a garbage can, but the stench was so overwhelming I changed direction, walking over to the casement window and dumping the whole thing out into the shrubbery.

"Did you just litter?" Runt asked me, eyes wide.

I shook my head.

"It's not littering if I plan to pick it up later."

Runt looked at me curiously, trying to assess the veracity of my statement.

"If you say so, Cal."

"We'll be right back," I called to Kali, leaving her to finish her shower in privacy as Runt and I returned to the bedroom to harass Jarvis into getting her some replacement clothing.

Jarvis sat up when he heard the door shut, looking sheepish that we'd caught him admiring the octagonal-tiled terra-cotta floor while he perched on the edge of the bed, waiting for us to finish in the bathroom.

"Clothes? Any extras hanging around for Kali to wear?" I asked, flopping down on the bed beside my Executive Assistant. "Or maybe the bodyguard dude could run back to our room and get something of mine?"

"No," Jarvis said, shaking his head. "I want him no more than thirty seconds away from you at any given time."

"Okay, sorry," I mumbled, annoyed—I guess that meant the bodyguard was lurking out in the hallway somewhere.

"I don't understand why this couldn't have happened earlier," Jarvis harrumphed. "When I could still use magic."

I shrugged, hoping I looked sufficiently contrite, but inside I was dancing. I didn't want to be all sour grapes, but I actually liked the fact we'd landed in a magic-free zone. I wasn't the most adept at wormhole calling or spell making or monster defeating—okay, I wasn't adept at all—but I *was* a great gal to have around when it came to traditional (i.e., nonmagical) problem solving. It's what I did when I worked at House and Yard, and it was something I could do now when everyone else was at such a disadvantage, their magical abilities on hiatus.

"I know it's tough, Jarvi," I said, patting him on the back, "but we'll get through it. I promise."

Jarvis shot me a dubious look, but I just smiled back at him innocently.

"You appear to be taking this turn of events in stride,

Calliope," Jarvis said, his eyes narrowed. "It wouldn't have anything to do with your disregard for magic, would it?"

"I don't disregard magic," I scoffed. "I just don't love it, that's all. And it's not my fault I'm not good at it—"

"Ha!" Jarvis shot back at me. "There it is! Excuses, excuses, excuses!"

"It's not an excuse, Jarvis, when I'm just not good at something—"

"You're not good at magic, Calliope," he interrupted me, "because you have an emotional block against it. It's a purely Freudian concept."

"Oh, brother," I moaned, flopping back on the bed, the soft down comforter cradling my head and making me want to forget the stupid Death Dinner so I could just lie there all night. "No psychoanalysis, Jarvi. I can't bear it right now."

"Fine," he said, giving up entirely too easily, which made me uneasy. "Shall we find our stinking rose a new outfit for the evening then?"

He stood up, my head bouncing twice on the comforter.

"Yup, let's do this thing," I replied, using every ounce of energy I possessed to make myself get up off the way too comfortable bed.

"Hey, Runt, stay here and make sure Kali doesn't decide to pull a naked lady at the dinner party act," I said, giving the pup a wink. In the bathroom, we could hear Kali singing Cee Lo Green's "Fuck You" in time with the loudly cascading faucet.

"Dinner has been delayed, but not indefinitely, so let's make it snappy," Jarvis said, walking to the bedroom door and opening it.

I pointed at the bed, which still held the imprint of my shape, and said:

"Hey, Jarvi, I think I gotta get me one of these beds. Très comfortable."

Jarvis rolled his eyes.

"Leave it to you to fixate on the furniture."

"But it's so comfortable, Jarvis," I snickered, glad he wasn't harping on my lack of magical ability anymore.

When Jarvis was in his old faun body, I'd been quite a bit taller than him and able to outwalk him without working up a sweat, but now that he was in his new, taller body, I was the one left in the dust. I had to take two giant steps to match his one, and frankly, when he was peeved with me, he walked superfast, making it very exhausting to keep up with him—especially as we maneuvered our way back through the labyrinthine corridors of Casa del Amo.

"Can you slow down?" I moaned, my high heels click-clacking like buckshot on the tile floor as I tried to keep pace. "I'm doing this backwards and in heels."

Jarvis shook his head, bewildered.

"I don't know where you come up with these things. Ginger Rogers, you are not."

"I know," I said, out of breath as I tried to catch up to him, "but it's such a good quote I had to use it. Besides, the 'heels' part was true."

Jarvis clucked his tongue, still shaking his head.

"Here we are," he said, stopping abruptly in front of a doorway half-concealed behind a cornflower blue woven tapestry. If Jarvis hadn't pointed it out, I would never have noticed it.

"What's in there?" I asked curiously.

Jarvis grasped the hammered tin knob and turned, pulling the door open to reveal a closet stuffed with maids' uniforms. I snorted, covering my mouth with my hand, the giggles rolling out of me as I imagined Kali wearing one of these cotton monstrosities to the Death Dinner.

"Uhm, Jarvis," I said, clearing my throat to stifle my laughter. "You do know who this is for, don't you? Kali? The Goddess of Death and Destruction who bites men's heads off with her teeth?"

Jarvis ignored me and began to pick through the clothing, disregarding all the peach pastel and royal blue dresses with their preattached white aprons and lacy collars. I didn't know what he thought he was going to find by digging around in that closet, but I stood back, letting him do his thing.

"Wait!" I said when he flipped past a mustard yellow one with a black Peter Pan collar and a cute little black tie encircling the waist. "Pull that one."

I pointed to the yellow dress and Jarvis lifted it off the closet rail, holding it up so I could get a better look at it. I inspected the fabric (polished cotton, not my favorite, but not too terrible), making sure there were no stains or other flaws.

"This is it," I said, nodding. "It'll work fine for the dinner and then she can borrow something of mine after."

Having found a reasonably presentable dress for Kali to wear, we followed the same circuitous path back to the bedroom. When we got there, the door was still open and Runt was pacing back and forth in front of the bathroom door, waiting for Kali to come out.

"She takes forever," Runt said, padding over to me so I could rub her ears.

"She's high maintenance," I commiserated, knocking on the bathroom door to get Kali's attention. "But she's worth it."

The door opened and Kali, her head wrapped in a fluffy white towel and another draped over her body, stepped out of the bathroom. She scowled at me then held out her hand.

"How do I smell?" she asked.

I took one for the team and sniffed at her wrist. To my surprise, it smelled faintly of roses, the skunk stench almost completely gone.

"You smell great," I said, thrusting the mustard yellow dress at her. "And here's your dress."

Kali stared at the dress in my hand, pursing her lips, but wouldn't take it.

"No way."

"It's just temporary," Jarvis chimed in, but I glared at him, willing him telepathically to shut the hell up and let me handle the situation.

"It's a new designer, very hot right now in New York City, totally hip—"

Kali wasn't buying it one bit. She continued to gape at the dress, her nose upturned.

"If it's so hip, white girl, why don't you wear it?" she said tartly, raising an eyebrow at me.

"Well—" I started to say, but she just stood there, shaking her head.

"No, no, no, NO!" she shrieked, ripping the dress out of my hands and throwing it on the floor. "I will go nude or will not go at all."

She dropped her towel, revealing a very toned, very sexy example of the feminine form, her large breasts swinging like pendulums as she huffed and puffed, a close approximation of an angry bull about to go into the ring.

"Okay, stop," I said, seeing disaster on the horizon and trying to avoid it. "I have an idea."

Somewhere down the hall the tinkling of the dinner bell filtered back to us and Jarvis tensed, his body going taut with the weight of Executive Assistant–centric responsibility. I could sense him just dying to usher us out of the bedroom and toward the dining room, but the problem of how to clothe Kali so dinner didn't devolve into a nudist retreat trumped his need for order.

"So," I began, three sets of eyes staring back at me as the dinner bell tinkled again, a little more urgently this time.

"Here's what we're gonna do . . ."

eleven

And that is how yours truly ended up attending the Death Dinner in a very fetching, mustard yellow maid's uniform.

I do have to say Kali looked extremely pretty in my Noisette-designed minidress with its tight bodice and tattered fabric, her loose dark hair and tanned skin nicely offset by the delicate black of the material. Her boobs, which were larger than mine, spilled over the edge of the bodice, causing her to resemble, oddly enough, a high-class Ren Fair serving wench, so every time I looked over at her, the phrase *"Huzzah to the big tipper!"* ran through my head.

It hadn't taken much persuasion to get Kali into my dress, and after a quick switcheroo, we were ready to go to the dining room. Once more, we trailed through the interlocking corridors of the building, past the winding circular staircase that led to the upstairs master suite, and bisected the library before finding our way into the dining room.

Like the rest of the rooms, the dining room was gaudy and elaborately appointed: African blackwood wainscoting, red-and-gold Oriental carpets lying across the tiled floor, tapestries from medieval France—depicting the progression of a very gory wild boar hunt—hanging from the walls, and a long rectangular table the length and width of two school buses taking up the bulk of the room.

Though it could seat far more, tonight the table was only set for sixteen, but what the dinner party lacked in populousness, it more than made up for in peculiarity. It was a truly unique assemblage of individuals, and I included myself, Runt, Kali, and Jarvis in this observation.

"Where do I sit?" I whispered to Jarvis as the four of us—the last ones to arrive, of course—entered the room, interrupting the dinner conversation already in progress.

"That is your chair, Calliope," Jarvis said, pointing to the place setting at the head of the table. To my horror, Uriah Drood was on one side and Daniel on the other.

That's *my seat?!* I thought miserably. *Shit, shit, shit!*

"I don't want to sit there," I said under my breath, but Jarvis was already shoving me toward the empty chair.

"I'll be right there with you, Cal," Runt whispered, sliding underneath the table just as Jarvis set the heel of his hand into the small of my back and pushed me into my seat. As I adjusted myself into my chair, I felt her wet nose press against my calf—her doggy way of reassuring me that everything was going to be okay.

I watched as Kali took a seat between Anjea (the spooky Aboriginal woman) and an old man with full white mutton-chops, bushy white eyebrows, and jaundiced-looking skin, while Jarvis was relegated to the end of the table, next to Yum Cimil, the old man who wouldn't talk to me because I was a female.

"So good of you to finally join us," Uriah Drood said, his voice rich with sarcasm, his pale hand inching entirely too close to my own for comfort. I instinctively snatched my fingers away, grabbing my napkin and disengaging it from its heavy silver napkin ring so my actions wouldn't look too suspicious, but I was pretty sure Reptile Man knew exactly what I was doing.

"Anytime," I replied, flashing him an insincere smile—*jeez, the man grossed me out!*

As I looked around the room, I realized the only person I didn't know was the older man in muttonchops next to Jarvis. I assumed he was Donald Ali, the man who owned the Haunted Hearts Castle, but that was only because I'd met everyone else. Though he appeared to be in his middle seventies, his pale gray eyes emanated a lively intelligence that belied his age. Radiating power, he reminded me of someone who was used to getting whatever he wanted and damn the consequences. I'd experienced this quality before in other grotesquely wealthy men and women, and as enticing as all that power could be, I actually found it to be a very frightening quality.

At the end of the table, half-hidden behind the ostentatious ostrich feather and purple orchid table centerpiece, I saw Jarvis trying to get my attention. I stared, my curiosity piqued, as he mimed looking at his watch then scanning the crowd before nodding his head, twice.

"What?" I mouthed, confused. I had no idea what he was trying to tell me—and the Marcel Marceau act was not helping.

Jarvis took a deep breath, gritting his teeth as he sat there, contemplating other ways of communicating his thoughts to me when suddenly I felt Runt licking my leg. I gently pushed her head away from my calf, but she persisted until I finally had to lean down and put my head under the table, so I could glare at her.

"Knock it off," I whispered, annoyed at her.

"Speech, Cal," she said and I covered my mouth with my hand—I'd totally forgotten that since I was the host of the Death Dinner, I was supposed to make some kind of a speech to get the ball rolling. That's why everyone was sitting around in silence, waiting. I was screwing the whole thing up and Jarvis and Runt were both trying to save my neck.

"Sorry, everyone," I said as I sat up and pushed back my chair so I could stand.

"I would like to thank you all for joining us here at the Haunted Hearts Castle for the, uhm . . ."

I paused, my brain spinning as I tried to remember how many years they'd been having the damn thing. I knew Jarvis had told me the answer at some point, but I couldn't pull it out of my head for anything in the world.

"How many years have you guys been doing this thing?" I asked then waved away my own question. "Uhm, it doesn't matter. It's the annual Death Dinner and we're all here together, so, yay!"

Jarvis sank down in his seat, mortified. Across the table, Kali snickered.

"I'm honored to be your host this evening—even though it's late and we're all pretty tired—"

Jarvis cringed. If he could've hidden inside the centerpiece, he would have.

"Anyway, I'm glad to be here, though it is a sucky way to get a job. You know, having your dad die—"

Next to me, Daniel bit his lip to stop from laughing.

"Don't you laugh at me." I scowled at him, forgetting where I was for a moment, but when I looked up again, all eyes were riveted on me.

"Uhm, I just want to say thank you all for coming tonight," I said, reverting back to my opening again. "I'm honored to be here, hosting the, you know, Death Dinner tonight 'cause if we don't stick together, well, then where does that leave Death?"

I was crashing and burning right there in front of all the people I was supposed to impress. Jarvis was going to kill me!

"I'm Calliope Reaper-Jones," I blurted out. "And though you don't really know me, I hope to use this opportunity to remedy that."

"So we can all stick together?" Uriah Drood said just loudly enough for everyone to hear.

If there's one thing that gets my blood boiling, it's being mocked in front of other people—especially people I don't know very well.

"Excuse me?" I said, turning on Uriah, my eyes glowing with unfiltered anger. "Were you just mocking me? 'Cause I think that's what you were just doing. Was that what you were doing?"

Uriah Drood stared at me, his eyes wide. I guess he'd thought I'd be some kind of shrinking violet.

"I'm not—" he started to say, but I cut him off.

"I didn't think so, Drood." Then turning my attention back to the others, I said: "Now, what was I saying?"

"Opportunity to remedy . . ." Daniel replied without a trace of irony.

"Thank you," I said, nodding. "Now, as I was saying, let's take this evening to get to know one another, to find out how we can best fulfill our obligation to the universe and maintain the balance of Good and Evil within the human world."

I paused, my brain quickly searching every neural pathway for a means of ending my disastrous speech on a high note . . . but this was all I could come up with:

"So, let's eat!"

The room was silent as the whole table stared at me, not sure if this was some kind of joke or if I'd actually just done exactly what they thought I'd done. To my surprise, it was Anjea who put her hands together first. I just assumed she was the doing the whole "ironic" clapping thing, but when Caoimhe and Naapi joined in, I realized she wasn't—and I decided I was more than happy to have a mildly mediocre finish than a complete and utter failure.

Instead of letting the applause fester into awkward silence, Jarvis picked up a miniature crystal bell and rang it twice, ending the speechifying section of the dinner and bringing on the beginning of what promised to be an amazing meal.

"Nice speech," Daniel said under his breath as the tiny serving woman from the drawing room reappeared, balancing a large tray of Dungeness crab salads on one hand. She seemed unsteady on her feet, the tray almost as big as she was, but she managed to make it to the table without falling over, which was impressive.

"You're a schmuck," I said, sitting back so she could put a plate down in front of me.

"So are you," he replied, picking up his fork and moving the greens around on his plate so he could inspect them.

"What are you? Two?"

"I don't like hearts of palm," he said stubbornly. "You know that."

"Then don't eat them."

I watched him pick the small discs out of his salad, setting them to the side then forking some of the remaining Dungeness crab and greens into his mouth. Annoyed, I picked up my own fork and took a bite, enjoying the silence brought on by the arrival of the food.

"How will you handle the upcoming strike Mr. Drood is proposing?"

The masculine voice sliced through the clinking of cutlery and I looked up, not understanding, at first, that the question was directed at me. Erlik, the barrel-chested Vice-President in

Charge of Asia, was gazing at me intently, his lips parted in anticipation.

Once again, all eyes were on me, curious to see if I was going to mess up this part of the dinner, too.

"Miss Death?" he said, his hazel eyes dark and unreadable.

I realized he was testing me, that this was some kind of power play and it was up to me whether I passed or failed. I set my salad fork down on my plate and cleared my throat, trying to come up with a succinct, but intelligent answer. I didn't want to say too much and show my hand, but I also didn't want to start babbling.

At least I wasn't in the dark on this subject. Jarvis and Kali had briefed me in a casual, yet intense breakfast meeting, which, when translated, meant they'd basically talked *at* me while I tried unsuccessfully to eat my eggs Benedict: the thrust of the matter being that the Harvesters and Transporters were talking about striking in protest to the unorthodox actions I'd undertaken during the Devil's failed attempt to hijack Purgatory and Death, Inc.

Okay, let me explain.

In the middle of all kinds of craziness, when it seemed like the balance between Good and Evil was going to be undermined by personal greed and bitter revenge, I threw what I can only term as a "Hail Mary Pass." I asked Cerberus and the Harvesters and Transporters to unleash all the damned souls from Hell, thinking this would cause complete and utter chaos down in Hell and force the Devil to abandon his hold on Purgatory and return to his original dominion.

To my utter surprise, my ruse had worked, but unbeknownst to me, asking the Harvesters and Transporters to get involved in the battle had gone firmly against the provisions in their contract. I'd argued with Jarvis, not understanding why the Union had a problem. In my mind, I'd seen a crisis and had tried to avert it, but in the Union's eyes—i.e., Uriah Drood's eyes—I'd violated the terms of a legally binding agreement.

I've never been good at politics, I don't really comprehend the art of corporate management, and I'm not great at chess. All three of these things are strikes against me being able to run a giant company like Death, Inc.—but maybe none of that really mattered. Maybe because I looked at the world through rose-colored spectacles and believed the universe was comprised of an inherent sense of fairness and a clearly defined idea of what was right and wrong—well, just maybe I was the perfect person to turn the engine around and start the train on a whole new course.

You see, over the years, I'd learned the hard way that lying only caused more problems than it solved and I was determined not to play that game anymore. Instead, I was gonna be a transparent leader, probably the first one in the history of Death, which meant I wasn't just going to sit back and let the shits like Uriah Drood try and manipulate the system; I was gonna force them to work within it.

"If Mr. Drood goes ahead with his strike, then we will just have to appeal to the Harvesters and Transporters themselves," I said, sitting up as straight as I could in my chair. "They were there. They saw what the Devil intended to do to Purgatory and to Death, Inc. If they feel what I asked of them wasn't a necessity, that the unwitting violation of their contract outweighed the eventual outcome, then I will cross that particular bridge when I get to it."

Jarvis caught my eye and winked at me. Erlik nodded, seeming to appreciate the brevity of my answer.

"Isn't this salad delicious?" I said, smiling at Yum Cimil and his charming second in command, Fabian Lazarev.

Yum Cimil gave a slight shake of his head, but I wasn't sure if that meant he liked the salad or if it was just a tic I'd misinterpreted.

"Interesting choice of words . . . rather diplomatic of you, surprisingly," Uriah Drood said as he placed a forkful of crabmeat into his mouth and chewed slowly, savoring the bite.

I'd expected him to be a voracious eater, but the head of the Harvesters and Transporters Union was actually a delicate nibbler, a food and wine sniffing relisher of all things epicurean—something I should've realized when he'd been so pedantic about how I drank my sherry.

"I just think we can resolve things amicably," I said, trying to appear thoughtful when what I really wanted to do was dump my salad over his head.

Jarvis believed Drood was the engineer behind the strike,

that without him pushing, the issue would be dead in the water. The only thing Jarvis and Kali couldn't figure out was what his motivation was: Why was Uriah Drood so hell-bent on causing problems for the new reign of Death?

"Maybe so," Drood mused, pushing his empty plate away. "Maybe so."

The serving woman came around to collect the dishes, her small hands having a hard time getting a grip on the oily plates, and again, I wondered how she'd gotten the job.

"Well, I have some news," Naapi said from his spot at the other end of the table.

Turning in his chair so he could get a better look at me, I had a strange premonition that the Vice-President in Charge of North America was about to say something I did not want to hear. I watched as Alameda placed a manicured hand on her consort's sleeve, as if she were physically willing him not to speak (or maybe I was just reading into it), but Naapi only patted her hand and forged onward.

"I have decided to resign from my post."

A gasp went up from the assembled crowd. This was big news, news that should have been shared with me in the privacy of a closed-door meeting, not here in front of all these people. I'd just assumed Naapi was loyal to my dad—and through him, me—but I'd forgotten that most people (even Gods, no *especially* Gods) are loyal to themselves first and the greater good second.

"I've wanted to retire from the post for a long time," he continued—and of course, now that he had the floor, he couldn't help doing a little grandstanding. "In fact, I'd spoken at length about my reservations with your father, Calliope. Both of us were of the mind I should remain until the end of the year and after that we would find my replacement."

Everyone turned back to me, itching to see what my response would be. I choked, my brain going blank . . . and then my mouth started moving of its own accord.

"Well, my dad actually filled me in on all this, so Jarvis and I have already put together a list of possible replacements."

Crack! Like a Ping-Pong match, all eyes shifted back to Naapi now that the ball was on his side of the court.

"Oh, really?" he said uncertainly.

Obviously, he'd been under the impression this piece of information was going to be a total surprise.

"Of course," I said gamely—and my total transparency/no lying resolution went right out the window. "My father and I talked over many, *many* things before he was murdered."

The temperature in the room dropped ten degrees and I could taste the fear as it seeped out of terrified pores, wafting in the air like a heady perfume. If I was ever curious about what these people expected of me—and my abilities—this was the answer. They'd all assumed, rightly, that I'd been dragged into the family business against my will; therefore, I was going to be a nonstarter as far as running Death, Inc., was concerned. They weren't expecting me to actually be on top of my business.

Well, screw them, I thought angrily. *I'm my father's daughter and they are gonna learn the hard way that it's best not to tangle with me!*

Jarvis quickly rushed to my defense, a welcome life raft in the middle of a turbulent sea.

"We have a list of possibilities ready and waiting," Jarvis said primly. "But as this is a dinner party, we'll save any announcements until we've conferred with the Board of Death further."

At my feet, I felt Runt's tail thump against my ankle. Well, at least I had two people firmly in my corner.

"Yes," Kali interjected. "We at the Board of Death are looking over the names on the list and a choice will soon be forthcoming."

She grinned at me, eyes glinting with mischief as she embellished upon the lie already in progress. And now I had *three* friends firmly in my corner. If I hadn't been sitting at a formal dinner party, working overtime to keep myself one step ahead of the madding crowd, I would've cried.

Jarvis rang the crystal bell to call for the next course, bringing this uncomfortable line of dinner conversation to an end. As the server—a young Hispanic guy now instead of the odd woman—arrived with a tray loaded down by heavy soup bowls, Anjea stood up. Though she wasn't a large woman, she moved with the deliberateness of a dictator, commanding your undivided attention.

There was a moment of uncertainty as everyone looked around, trying to gauge what was going to happen next: Was the old woman going to make a toast, or was she gonna open fire with a tommy gun? To no one's surprise, she went for the tommy gun—well, not literally, but her verbal tirade had the same emotional impact.

"Don't be blind, Death. Use your eyes or be forever damned!" she said, raising a bony finger and pointing it in the direction of my heart, her gaze dark with intention. Our eyes locked, and I found I couldn't look away. I was nailed to my chair by the intensity of her stare.

As suddenly as Anjea's outburst had begun, it ended, an awkward silence ensuing as she lowered her arm and sat back down, pulling her chair forward so she could reach her water glass, which she downed in one long swallow.

Up until that moment, Daniel's new friend, Coy, had been a silent party to the Death Dinner, sitting obsequiously in her chair while the rest of us sparred. But now her delicate hand clamped onto Daniel's upper arm like a vise, her bright pink lips molding into a perfectly formed *O*. She blinked hard, the color abruptly draining from her tan face.

"I think I'm going to be sick," she said, using her hands to push herself away from the table, her whole body shaking uncontrollably.

Without waiting for an answer, Coy stood up and wobbled toward the exit.

twelve

I have to say, for me, Anjea's bizarre invective was the highlight of the Death Dinner. It was like she'd dropped an atomic bomb on the room, and no matter how hard Jarvis tried to jump-start the conversation again, there was no coming back from it.

We ate the chilled carrot soup (and its spicy marigold garnish) in silence, the cacophonic slurping of fifteen people the only soundtrack. The next course was rack of lamb accompanied by fennel mashed potatoes and a mint glace—all of which went down without anything more than a few polite queries about how everyone was enjoying their food, etc., etc. At one point, Anjea resettled in her chair and everyone stopped eating, waiting to see if she was going to go all *Carrie* on us again, but she merely picked up her fork and dove back into her lamb.

You can tell a lot about someone by the way they eat—and when someone is concentrating on their food, not talking or listening to conversation, it's as if their eating style gets distilled down to its very essence:

Uriah Drood was a fastidious eater, cutting his meat into perfect squares that he then speared with his fork and ate with unvarying deliberateness. Daniel, on the other hand, ate very normally, nothing precise or regimented, just someone enjoying their food because it tasted good and gave them energy.

Daniel had almost missed the soup course because of Coy's

freak-out. He'd followed his date (and her five-inch heels) out into the corridor to make sure she was all right and their conversation had been loud enough for everyone at the table to overhear. Thankfully, it'd been of the standard "Are you okay?" and "My stomach aches a little, so I'm going to go lie down" vibe (no cooing and drippy pet name calling, thank God), making exposure to it a nonmortifying experience.

I wondered how many of the people sitting around me knew about our shared history, that Daniel had been my lover once upon a time—Jarvis, Kali, and Runt for sure, but the others? I had no clue. It made me feel squeamish just thinking other people might be cataloging and judging my sex life behind my back.

Gross.

When Daniel returned to the table, he'd seemed frustrated by his conversation with Coy—and I'd actually kind of felt sorry for him—but then I'd noticed the smudge of pink lipstick hiding just below the curve of his jaw like a glossy petroleum-based bruise and I'd seen red. It was all I could do not to go chasing after his little Latin Lolita and show her exactly what a real stomachache felt like—because I had a hard time believing her "illness" was anything other than a bid for Daniel's attention.

The sudden clatter of cutlery to my right caught my attention and I looked up to see Fabian Lazarev, his handsome face flushed a bright tomato red, gripping the handle of his steak knife, the business end pointed across the table at Erlik's heart. The two men appeared to be engaged in a very heated conversation, the threat of physical violence notching up the tension in the room tenfold. They were both angry, but the Vice-President in Charge of Asia seemed to have gotten the upper hand, having driven Fabian Lazarev into such a rage he'd felt it necessary to pick up a weapon in order to make his point.

"You know nothing of which you speak," Fabian spat across the table, brandishing the knife so the sharpened surface of its blade caught the light, a sheen of silvery dots reflecting back across the dark wood of the tabletop.

"I think I know exactly what I'm 'speaking of,'" Erlik replied, his face relaxed as he sat back in his chair, unconcerned. "So back off, Lazarev . . . before I make you."

Fabian stood up, holding the knife out like a sword, and leaned across the table. He was too far away to do any damage, but his intent was clear: He wasn't going to be bullied by anyone.

"You cannot make me do anything, you sorry excuse for a man!"

Erlik didn't move a muscle. He just sat there, lounging in his chair like some giant African cat, totally cool right up until the very moment of attack. Without any warning, he was suddenly out of his chair, his lithe body snaking forward, glasses and plates flying as he grasped Fabian's wrist and snapped it backward, sending the steak knife clattering to the table. Fabian cried out, his hand bent awkwardly in Erlik's grip.

"Stop, please, I beg you . . ." Fabian whined, but Erlik ignored him, using the other man's wrist to reel him in closer, their noses almost touching.

"I can make you do anything I want," Erlik breathed, his voice even. "And don't you forget it."

He shoved Fabian back across the table, the Russian crying out in pain as he was slammed bodily into his chair. Erlik continued to stand there, watching the other man whimper and cradle his hurt wrist.

"The show is over," Erlik said, eyes still locked on his wounded opponent before turning abruptly and stalking out of the room.

No one said a word—I think we were all in shock.

"Someone do something, please . . . my hand," Fabian said weakly. The color had drained out of his face and he seemed to be in a lot of pain.

"There's nothing we can do for you, idiot," Kali said, rolling her eyes. "No magic."

I got up and circled around the table, gesturing for Jarvis to ring his crystal bell, so the servers could start collecting the broken china. I knelt down beside the wounded man. At first, he shied away from me, not wanting me to touch his hand.

"Come on. Let me see it," I said, coaxing him into letting me examine his wrist.

I could tell immediately it wasn't broken, and once All Hallows' Eve was over, his immortal body would heal itself within a matter of hours. In the interim, I could make him a splint—like

I'd learned in the first aid class I'd taken at the Y two summers earlier—and load him up on Tylenol or some other over-the-counter analgesic.

"Can someone hand me their butter knife," I said, picking up Fabian's own from its spot on the table.

Jarvis was immediately at my side with another butter knife and a couple of cloth napkins. He'd realized what I was doing and was already two steps ahead of me.

"Tear them up into strips for me, will you?" I said to Jarvis as I gently turned Fabian's arm over and started to place the two butter knives lengthwise under his palm, wrist, and forearm.

I'd taken the first aid course with my ex-neighbor, Patience, a very well-intentioned, but slightly vacuous lawyer who was always on the prowl for a man and was most proud of the fact that she naturally possessed 2 percent body fat. Though I make her sound a little self-involved, she wasn't a selfish person by a long shot. She volunteered for all kinds of charitable organizations, giving as freely of her time as she could, and was an especially big proponent of helping underprivileged children get a leg up in school. So when she was offered the chance to tutor urban elementary school students on the weekends, she jumped at it—which was how I got roped into the first aid course. One of the stipulations of the tutoring program was that you had to have a first aid certificate, something Patience did not possess, so she signed herself and her unwitting accomplice (me) up for a first aid class at the local Y.

I'd been terrified at first, afraid I was going to accidentally puncture someone's lung or wrap a wound too tightly and permanently cut off the circulation to someone's appendage, but by the end of the first class, all my fears were allayed—it seemed that I was pretty good in a pinch and didn't get all freaked-out over blood and saliva like a few of the other people in the class.

"What're you doing to my linens?" Donald Ali said, breaking my concentration with his rumbling voice.

"Making a splint," I said, giving him a steely glare that dared him to contradict me.

"We have a first aid kit in the kitchen," he replied, amused at my fierceness.

"Oh."

Probably should've asked about that before *I got Jarvis ripping,* I thought to myself. *Note to self: Ask first, rip later.*

"It's fine," our host said, smiling back at me. "Besides, they're only reproductions of the originals after all."

I looked down at the scraps of napkin Jarvis had given me, wondering why anyone would ever make a reproduction of a napkin.

"The originals belong to the set of linens Archduke Ferdinand of Austria breakfasted on the morning of his assassination," Donald Ali continued as if he were reading my mind. "Historically significant as this led directly to the beginning of World War One."

"That's just morbid," I said, but before I could finish binding the splint, Lazarev pulled his arm away, the butter knife clattering to the floor.

"No," he said softly, shaking his head. "I appreciate what it is you're doing, but enough."

"Suit yourself." I sighed, thinking about the poor ruined napkins as I got up and went back to my chair.

". . . it's just history," I heard our host saying as he smiled oddly. "Though I suppose that's something you immortals wouldn't understand."

"We understand more than you think, Donald," Naapi said, moving his glass out of the way so the server could set dessert down in front of him. "It's why I'm looking to retire. Longevity isn't without its flaws."

Donald Ali snorted, dismissing Naapi's comment.

"You would last ten minutes as a mortal."

"Well, we shall have to see about that," Naapi replied, looking down at his hands. "When I step down, I plan to renounce my immortality as well, so . . ."

This comment sent the room into a tizzy. Everyone started talking at once—the overriding sentiment disbelief as they chided Naapi for his foolishness. Only Alameda Jones and Donald Ali seemed immune to the agitation, both quietly watching the scene play out, but never giving a clue as to how this startling news really affected them.

"Settle down," I said. "Leave Naapi alone and enjoy your dessert!"

It was like dealing with a bunch of unruly kids; no one listened unless you shouted at them. Finally, Jarvis shook the crystal bell, and this seemed to get their attention, bringing a little order to the chaos.

"Thanks, Jarvis," I said quietly, my annoyance lowering to a simmer now that everyone had stopped screeching at each other.

Taking a deep breath to calm my agitation, I checked out the bowl sitting in front of me.

"What are you?" I asked the dessert, but it was Uriah Drood who answered.

"It's affogato with homemade vanilla gelato," he said, spooning the goopy-looking stuff into his mouth with relish.

I raised an uncertain eyebrow, but decided since there was vanilla in the dessert, it couldn't be too bad. I lifted my spoon and took a bite, wrinkling my nose at the bitter espresso taste. Apparently, I wasn't a huge affogato fan, the combination of espresso and vanilla not really doing it for me—but the home-made vanilla bean meringue cookies that came with my affogato? Now those were amazing. My mouth watered as I nibbled on the delicious, flaky cookies, and I couldn't help marveling at how insanely delicious they were. After I'd eaten the two tiny ones off my own plate, I was seriously tempted to steal Jarvis's bell and ring myself a to-go container of the confections.

"I'd really like to talk to you after dinner. Is that possible?" Daniel asked as he leaned toward me.

I swallowed, biding my time as I tried to figure out his angle. Why did he want to talk to me alone and (hope against hope) did this have anything to do with us getting back together again?

"Give me your cookie and I'll think about it," I said finally, not knowing what else to say. A simple "yes" would probably have been fine, but there was something about Daniel that brought out the argumentative side of my personality.

He gave the lone cookie on his plate a long, lingering glance then slid it in my direction. Popping it into my mouth, I sighed as I let the taste of vanilla bean melt on my tongue.

"These things are scrumptious," I said, my mouth full of cookie. "Thank you."

Daniel raised an eyebrow, but didn't comment on my lack of table manners. I dabbed at the corners of my mouth with my napkin, letting him sweat a bit. I very much wanted to spend time with him, but I wasn't about to let him get what he wanted so easily. Besides, I was peeved at him for bringing Coy to the Death Dinner. It wasn't like he didn't know I was going to be there (I was the host, for God's sake) and that having her on his arm *and* sharing his room with her was going to make me feel like crap.

"So, we can talk? In private?" he said, glancing over at Jarvis, who was in the middle of a conversation with Caohime. I thought I heard her say the words "Sea Verge," "mother," and "Calliope," but they were too far away, and their tones too hushed, for me to be certain.

"Sure, whatever," I said, still focused on the other conversation.

He looked pleased, his hand covering mine so he could give my fingers a gentle squeeze. Well, that shifted the focus back to our conversation and pronto. At the feel of his touch, my heart lurched in my chest, a lump forming in the back of my throat. I clenched my teeth together to fight off any tears that might be lurking, wondering if Daniel had any idea how painful all of this was for me. He seemed fine with our situation, as if getting over me had been the easiest thing in the world for him. For me, it'd been one of the most painful experiences I'd ever had, up there with my dad getting killed and my older sister betraying me.

"Okay, I'll walk you to your room," he said, and then, as an afterthought, he added: "And I know Runt isn't going to want to leave your side this evening, so she should come, too."

"Fine. Whatever."

He looked a little hurt by my curtness then he shook his head, releasing my hand and returning to his coffee.

While we'd been talking, everyone else had finished their affogato, making me the only one who was still nursing the dessert. Since I wasn't going to finish it, I pushed the plate away, the small crystal bowl holding the espresso and gelato concoction shuddering against the plate with the force of the movement. Tired and heartsick, I realized it was time to bring this disastrous dinner to a close. I cleared my throat, forcing all ancillary conversations to an abrupt end, and stood up, making Runt snuffle and shift position under the table.

"Once again, thank you all for coming," I said, looking around the room, but trying not to catch anyone's eye. "I hope the evening and the meal were enjoyable. Jarvis, what's next on the agenda?"

My Executive Assistant graciously accepted the gauntlet.

"Please feel free to retire to the drawing room for after-dinner liqueurs," he said, beaming at the assemblage. "Our servers will meet you there."

Jarvis rang the crystal bell, signaling the end of dinner and everyone stood up, shuffling out of the room. I hadn't realized how stressed out the evening had made me, but as soon as the room had cleared and only Jarvis, Runt, and I remained, I let out a huge sigh of relief.

"Jesus, that was awful," I said, resting my elbows on the table and dropping my chin into my hands. "Do I have to go to the drawing room, too? I don't think I can bear it."

Jarvis shook his head.

"I'll go on your behalf."

"You're the best," I said, blowing him a kiss. "Remind me to give you a raise."

Jarvis laughed, coming around and patting my shoulder.

"The bodyguard will be waiting out front for you. Do not try to ditch him, please."

I rolled my eyes.

"I would never do that." Not true. I was notorious for flouting Jarvis's direct commands.

"Just be very careful," Jarvis said, his two caterpillar eyebrows scrunching together with worry. "Now is an extremely vulnerable time for you."

"I get it," I said. "I promise I'll be good."

Jarvis wasn't totally convinced—I could tell by the nervous glint in his eye—but he nodded and let it go. Using the back of the chair like a ballet barre, I stood up and stretched, yawning with exhaustion.

"By the way, what happened to your friend Minnie? She didn't stay for the ball or dinner?"

Jarvis turned a shade of hot pink I'd never seen on a human face before.

"I, well, er . . ."

I narrowed my eyes, smelling weakness.

"Jarvis, are you and Minnie . . . Are you, *you know*?" I nee-dled him, making Jarvis turn an even brighter shade of pink.

"Oh, you *so* are doing naughty things with Miss Minnie," I continued, very much enjoying Jarvis squirm.

"You have no idea what you're talking about," he splut-tered. "Our relationship is purely platonic!"

I snorted.

"Platonic, my ass—"

"She is almost finished with her novel and I'm helping her with the copyediting—"

"But that's not all you want to help her with," I shot back.

"Silence!" Jarvis yelped. "Don't be so crude."

"I bet she didn't go to the ball because you were stuck with me and couldn't play with her—"

Jarvis covered his ears with his hands, making a beeline for the exit.

"Filthy . . . you have a filthy mind, Calliope Reaper-Jones!"

"Of course I do!" I yelled after him as he crossed the threshold and disappeared down the corridor. "That's why you like me so much!"

I grinned to myself, pleased with my ability to still get a rise out of Jarvis.

"It's why I like you, too, you know."

I turned around to find Daniel standing in the doorway that led to the kitchen.

"It's why you *liked* me," I corrected. "Past tense."

Daniel opened his mouth to reply, but I cut him off.

"C'mon, Runt," I called, waking the sleeping dog up. "Time to go back to the room."

She made a cute little yipping-yawn noise and stood up, stretching as she padded out from her spot underneath the table.

"You have ten minutes," I called over my shoulder as I strode toward the exit. "Starting now."

And for the record, I didn't care if he followed me or not.

thirteen

I'm a notoriously fast walker, and that evening, trying to out-pace Daniel, I was at my fast walking best. At first, he kept up with me, but when he realized I wasn't going to slow down and that talking was going to be at a minimum, he gave up, drop-ping his own gait to a saunter so that after a few seconds I'd far outstripped him. Runt, who was much faster than me on a bad day, had no problem keeping up.

As the path stretched out ahead of us like a grayscale ver-sion of the yellow brick road, I started to feel guilty about leav-ing Daniel in my dust. I didn't know what he wanted to talk to me about, maybe it was important business stuff, and here I was, acting like a spoiled baby and totally blowing him off.

In my heart I knew I was just rationalizing my need for at-tention from Daniel: bad, good, or business—I would take any of it. I was in denial about my true feelings, so I was going to allow my unconscious need for contact to override any feelings of anger I might have. Slowing my pace, I looked behind me to see if Daniel was still following. He was, but he was so far down the path it was gonna take him all night to catch up. I took a deep breath, exhaling through my nose, and then I headed back the way I'd come.

As I approached him, Daniel was ambling along the path,

checking out the statuary illuminated in the rich amber glow of the outdoor lights that dotted the landscape.

"Okay," I said when I was five feet away. "What do you want?"

Daniel grinned at me. He knew he'd won that hand, and I knew that he knew that I knew.

"Nice of you to join me."

I crossed the last few feet remaining between us and stood directly in front of him, arms crossed over my chest.

"I hope you know that it's cold and I'm tired and Runt's tired—"

"No, I'm not," the pup said, looking up at me.

"Yes, you are," I shot back, giving her a warning look. She gave a short yip that let me know she thought I was being a pain in the ass then she trotted a ways down the path to give me and Daniel a little privacy—something I didn't want.

"Look, I'm not trying to keep you out in the cold any longer than I have to, but there are a few things we need to talk about," Daniel said, pulling his own coat off and holding it out to me.

"I don't want it," I said, gesturing at the coat with my chin, my arms still folded across my chest. "But I do want you to say whatever you have to say and be done with it. By the way, if you try anything weird, there's a human bodyguard shadowing my every move. So consider yourself warned."

"Okay, I will consider myself warned," he said, trying not to laugh. I guess he thought the idea of him doing anything untoward to me was some kind of joke.

"It's not funny," I said, annoyed because this was supposed to be quick and painless and now Daniel was purposely dragging it out to make me feel bad.

"That you would think I'd do anything bad to you," Daniel said, shaking his head. "That's absurd."

"Just forget it," I growled, turning away, but Daniel grabbed my arm, pulling me back.

"Cal," Daniel said, his breath hot on my cheek. "Just relax."

We stood there, both of us breathing hard, then he let me go. I took a step back, putting some much-needed distance between us, and smoothed the short skirt of my yellow maid's uniform down so it wasn't riding up my thighs.

"I liked your other dress better," he said, his voice low and gravelly as he stared at me, those ice blue eyes piercing my very soul. "The way it pushed your breasts up was very . . . sexy."

I swallowed hard, my body turning on against the better judgment of my brain. I took another step away from him, hoping the cold air would cool me off before I got too heated up down below.

"Thanks," I said, working hard to keep my voice even. "I liked it, too. But it was either loan it to Kali, or stare at her nipples during dinner."

Daniel snorted, not expecting the word "nipple" to pop out of my mouth.

"What are you talking about?"

I shrugged my shoulders, goose bumps taking over my skin.

"She got sprayed by a skunk and it ruined her sari. There wasn't time or reinforcements to get her an outfit from my room, so I picked this from one of the closets—" I indicated the maid's uniform. "But she said she'd go nude before she'd wear it. So, trading with her was the only option."

"How do you always end up in these ridiculous situations?" Daniel asked, amusement dancing in his eyes—and I had to physically restrain myself from reaching out and touching his cheek.

It was the kind of thing I'd done a thousand times before when we were together, touching his face or stroking his hair. I never even thought about it, I just did it. Now, touching him was an off-limits experience, something I didn't have permission to do anymore.

"I guess it's just a habit," I said, falling into the easy banter we'd enjoyed as a couple. "Something I was born to do."

"You're freezing," Daniel said, holding out his coat again.

This time I took it, ashamed that I'd been so rude before. He'd been trying to do something nice and I'd thrown it in his face. I slid the jacket over my shoulders, engulfing myself in Daniel's scent—a spicy, masculine smell I knew better than my own perfume. I inhaled deeply, letting the warmth from the jacket, and the familiarity of his musk, envelope me.

There was just something about Daniel that made me giddy with happiness one moment and ready to deck him the next. I didn't know if that connoted love, but I had a feeling no one else in the whole universe could make me as happy as Daniel could—and me, the idiot, had to go and screw the whole bloody thing up. I wanted to scream at myself for being such a numb-skull, for letting someone as wonderful as Daniel slip away—but instead I shoved all the feelings welling up inside me back down and out of sight.

"Your girlfriend is really pretty," I said, tucking an errant strand of hair behind my ear. "Took me a little while to realize she was a Goddess."

Daniel started to say something then shook his head and closed his mouth again.

"What?" I asked.

"Let's just . . ." he said. "Let's talk about something else."

I nodded, trying to act like those words didn't break my heart into tiny pieces, but it was useless. A big, fat tear slipped out and rolled down my cheek.

"No," Daniel said, his face stricken. "Please don't cry. Please, Cal."

He reached out and brushed the tear away. My mouth crum-pled and I looked down at my feet, fighting back the cascade of tears trying to escape, my resolve quickly deteriorating.

"I hate it when you cry," he continued, looking kind of teary-eyed himself.

"I can't help it," I hiccuped, my throat constricting so I could hardly get the words out. *"I miss you."*

I wasn't imagining things; Daniel's eyes were as misty as my own. He sniffed and shook his head, trying to shake off the emotion he was feeling, too.

"I can't talk about this right now, Cal," he said, brushing away the wetness on his cheek with the back of his hand. "I want to talk about it, but not tonight. Please."

I nodded, not really understanding what he meant, but just so goddamned happy to be connecting with him again.

"Okay," I said, nodding. "We can talk later."

"Thanks, Cal," he said, smiling at me. "I do need to talk about something else, though. Is that all right?"

"Yeah," I said, nodding again. "You can talk to me about anything."

Daniel bit his lip, his face twisting into a grimace of pain.

"Why does everything you say just hit me right here?" he said, indicating the place where his heart was hidden beneath sinew and rib bone.

I shrugged, but I was secretly pleased I was affecting him so much.

"I don't know. I guess we just have simpatico. Whatever the hell that means."

"Ha!" Daniel said. "*That* we don't have—because sometimes I just want to put a muzzle on you, you drive me so damn crazy."

I knew the feeling. Daniel was a master at making me so mad I wanted to punch him.

"Whatcha want to talk about?" I asked finally, after we'd stood there kind of grinning at each other for a while. Whatever feelings my question called up inside Daniel, it made him instantly tense up, his jaw tightening like a screw.

"The Ender of Death, I mean, Marcel—"

"What about him?" I interrupted.

Daniel ran a hand through his hair, making the cowlick at the crown of his head stick up.

"Well, let's just say I was really pleased to hear that Jarvis had taken some precautions."

"What? You mean the bodyguards?"

Daniel nodded.

"And Runt, of course. She's a better watchdog than any human bodyguard."

"What are you talking about?" I asked, looking across the yard where Runt was sprawled underneath the moonlit shadow of an Egyptian obelisk.

"What do you think hellhounds do, Cal?" Daniel said, scrunching his eyes together with curiosity.

"I don't know," I stammered. "They hang out in Hell . . . I don't know. Tell me."

Daniel laughed—and his entire face lit up.

"They're the greatest guard dogs in the universe. Why else do you think the Devil had Cerberus guarding one of the Gates of Hell?"

I'd actually never stopped to think about it before, but what Daniel said made sense. Runt had been guarding me in some capacity or other from the very first day we met. Without her,

I'd have been mincemeat many times over. She must've realized we were talking about her because she sat up and started thumping her tail.

"She's a really great and powerful supernatural creature, Cal," Daniel continued. "And she's chosen to stay on Earth and look after you."

There was something underneath what Daniel was saying, something I was in the dark about.

"What else could she be doing . . . if she weren't, you know, looking after me like you just said?"

"She would be in Hell with her family, helping us clean the place up again after—" Daniel said, but I cut him off.

"You said she'd be with her family," I blurted out. "Don't you just mean her dad?"

Daniel looked at my quizzically.

"Runt has a whole family down in Hell—brothers and sisters, aunts and uncles, cousins. She's part of a very large hell-hound tribe."

I was shocked. No one had ever told me that Runt came from a whole tribe of hellhounds, all of whom probably missed the crap out of her. I felt terrible. I'd unwittingly forced her into staying on Earth when, of course, she'd no doubt want to be back in Hell with her family if she'd been given her druthers.

"I had no idea," I said, the positive vibe I'd been grooving on quickly dissipating. "No one ever said anything to me before."

Daniel reached over and squeezed my arm—but it felt like an empty gesture, something you did when the other person was too wrapped up in themselves to see reality.

"She wants to be here with you," he said.

I shrugged his hand away then took off his jacket and handed it back to him. He seemed confused by my abrupt mood change.

"Cal, what did I say?"

"Nothing." I shrugged, my tone flat. "Go on with what you were saying about the Ender of Death."

It took Daniel a moment to catch up.

"Uhm, well, I wanted you to understand the danger you were in," he began.

"Already on it," I replied. "Anything else?"

My moodiness made him uncomfortable. He started to shift back and forth on the balls of his feet nervously.

"As your diametric opposite, Marcel is at the zenith of his power for the next twenty-four hours," he said, lowering his voice so only I could hear him. "That means he's gonna come gunning for you while you're at your weakest."

"Everyone is at their weakest right now," I mumbled.

"That's true," Daniel nodded. "Magic isn't accessible and so the power that protects our immortality wanes, but I don't think anyone here is as vulnerable as you are."

"What's that supposed to mean?" I shot back. My teeth were starting to chatter, but I clamped them together so he wouldn't see how cold I was.

"You have a lot of enemies, Cal," Daniel said, his tone hardening. "Whether you want to hear this or not, it's true. There are a lot of people who would wish you dead."

"Okay, this conversation is officially over," I said, waving his words away.

"Cal—"

"Nope, I don't want to hear any more," I said, starting to walk away. "Runt, let's go!"

Runt didn't need to be told twice. She was beside me so fast I hardly had time to miss her.

"I'm not letting you walk by yourself," Daniel said, catching up to us as we traipsed down the path, the darkness like a living, breathing creature all around us.

"Fine, do what you want," I said then proceeded to ignore him.

We walked in silence for a few minutes, Runt's panting and the crunch of gravel under my heels our only accompaniment. Suddenly, Daniel was grabbing my arm and yanking me back from the path and into the shadow of a neighboring hedge.

"What—" I tried to say, but Daniel put a finger to his lips, miming for me to be silent. When I'd calmed down enough that he trusted me to actually be quiet, he lifted his hand and pointed to a spot just beyond the hedge where two people stood, their identities hidden in the shadowy folds of the semidarkened statuary garden.

"Who are they?" I mouthed, but Daniel only shook his head and shrugged.

"Not sure," he whispered.

We watched as the figures moved in closer to one another,

their shadows starting to blend together until they weren't two people anymore, but one.

"Are they . . ." I asked.

"Kissing, yes," he whispered back at me, nodding.

Runt whined at our feet. She didn't like us hiding in a hedge and spying on people, and I had to agree with her, it wasn't the classiest way to spend an evening. I did feel a tad bit like a voyeur, staring out at the kissing couple from the privacy of a hedge, but the lure of being so close to Daniel held me in place.

Like everything that concerned Daniel, I was completely ambivalent. One minute I was so mad at him I could spit, the next I was trying to stand as close to him as humanly possible. God, it really wasn't fair.

The hoot of an owl jerked the necking couple out of their embrace and they pulled away from each other with the abruptness of two people caught doing something illicit. It gave me the feeling that whoever they were, they weren't supposed to be here under cover of darkness, making out with each other.

The owl hooted as it landed on a tree branch high above us, shaking the leaves so they allowed a ray of moonlight to pierce the inky night, revealing the identity of one of the shadowy figures. For a fleeting moment, I saw the bewildered visage of Alameda Jones as plain as day, her honeyed skin and flashing eyes unmistakable in the opalescent glow of the moonlight. She blinked as the tree shuddered once more and then the owl took off, the branch it had settled on snapping back into place and blocking the moonlit ray's progress once more.

"Alameda Jones," I mouthed to Daniel, who nodded his agreement. He'd seen her face, too.

But when I looked back again after the brief exchange, I saw that the couple had disappeared. If I hadn't had Daniel and Runt there with me to verify what I'd just seen, I'd have thought it was a hallucination. No matter where I looked, there was no sign anyone had been standing there at all, let alone had had a secret assignation right in front of my eyes.

"Where'd they go?" I whispered to Daniel.

"Don't know," he said. "It's like they vanished into thin air."

We spent a few minutes trudging through the underbrush, looking for an escape route, but we found nothing—and it was strange to think no magic had been used to cover up their flight.

"I think we should get you back to your room," Daniel said finally, after we'd exhausted all avenues. To my surprise, even Runt's powerful sniffer hadn't been able to trace their path.

"I wonder who her special friend is," I said out loud as we picked our way back to the path, trying not to knock over any of the precariously perched marble busts that littered the statuary garden.

"Well, he was taller than her, so that leaves out Yum Cimil, Uriah Drood, and Fabian Lazarev," Runt chimed in.

"Good use of deductive reasoning," I said, giving her a quick pat on the head.

"It can't be Daniel because he's here with us," she continued. "Oh, and it might've been a tall woman."

The only tall women I could think of were Caoimhe—and Morrigan.

"Morrigan, maybe?" Daniel pitched in, thinking along the same lines. I smiled back at him just as the Moroccan elegance of Casa de la Luna rose ahead of us like a beacon.

"Well, this is our stop," I offered as we stepped off the path and into the courtyard leading to our room.

"Thanks for talking to me, Cal," Daniel said, all seriousness now. "I was really worried about you."

"I'm fine," I said as we crossed the courtyard, the darkness pushed far into the corners of the building by the bright outdoor lighting.

The other bodyguard was standing a few feet away from the door as we approached. He gave us a brief nod then went back to his original position: bodyguard statue.

"I'll see ya later, alligator," I said as I took my own key from the front pocket of my maid's uniform and unlocked the door. Turning the knob, I eased the door open so Runt could pad inside ahead of me.

As the light from the open door hit Daniel, illuminating his wistful countenance, I felt my heart melt into mush inside my chest and the need to be close to him overwhelmed me. Sensing my mood, he stepped away from the doorway.

"I have to go."

Giving me a slight wave, he swiveled on his heel and walked back out into the night. I looked over at the bodyguard, wondering what he'd made of our little good-bye, but I couldn't read anything on the man's face.

"Nice night," I said, but the bodyguard merely nodded. I guess engaging in idle conversation with the gal you were supposed to be guarding wasn't in the job description.

I sighed, looking out into the darkness, hoping to catch one last glimpse of Daniel, but he was gone—and I was alone again, left to wallow in my screwed-up relationship misery all by my lonesome.

I went back inside and shut the door, luxuriating in the warmth of the heated room. Runt was curled up on her bed, trying not to look curious about my talk with Daniel, but failing miserably.

"I'm so tired," I yawned. "Let's talk about Daniel in the morning."

Runt's tail started thumping against the comforter as I rummaged around in my carryall, pulling out some soft red cotton Paul Frank pajamas to wear to bed.

"He still likes you, you know," Runt said, hopping off the bed and following me into the bathroom—and I knew I wasn't going to get out of this interrogation so easily.

"Hey, I'm gonna take a bath—"

"You can talk while you bathe," Runt said, as if that solved everything.

"Grr," I growled, shutting the bathroom door behind us. "You're a pain in the butt."

Runt curled up in a ball on the bath mat and waited for me to dish.

"Well," I said, taking off the maid's uniform and folding it into a neat square that I placed on the back of the toilet. "He was worried about me . . ."

Runt snorted and banged her tail unhappily.

"I heard that part, Cal. What *else* did he say?"

I sighed, reaching into the tub and turning both taps on high. I waited for the water to get hot then I dropped the plug into the drain and stepped into the watery warmth. As I eased myself into the tub, pressing my back against the cool porcelain, I tried to get my bearings. What exactly had my conversation with Daniel meant?

"I think he might . . . miss me," I said, my voice almost drowned out by the sound of the running water from the faucet.

"I think so, too." Runt agreed. "He didn't want to go. He wanted to stay and talk to you all night."

I grinned, pleased Runt had gotten the same impression I had.

"But why didn't he want to talk about Coy?" I said.

"I don't know. Maybe he felt guilty about bringing her here for the Death Dinner."

"He was probably banging her at the Masquerade Ball." I sighed, lowering myself so only my eyes and nose were above the rising waterline.

"I don't think so," Runt said. "Daniel's not like that."

I wanted her to be right. I wanted him to be the kind of guy who eschewed group orgies in the middle of ancient French caves, but I wasn't so sure. I reached up and grabbed the bottle of peach shampoo I'd left on the side of the tub with my other toiletries earlier in the evening and squirted some of it into my hand, lathering it into my hair.

"I think you just have to have a little faith, Callie," Runt said as she laid her chin down on her outstretched paws. "Sometimes things have a way of working out—even when you least expect them to."

I took a washcloth from the ledge of the soap dish and poured some body wash into its cottony folds, rubbing it together until it was a white foamy mess. As I lathered my body, I couldn't help wishing Daniel were in the other room waiting for me.

Leave it to the hellhound pup to be the wisest person in the room, I thought wryly as I dunked my head under the water and disappeared into the soapy oblivion of my bath.

fourteen

Still wet from the bath, my body felt completely relaxed as I slid into the soft cotton pajamas I'd brought into the bathroom with me. I'd stayed in the tub far longer than I'd intended, not getting out until the water was tepid. Then I'd pulled the plug and watched the dirty liquid whirl down the drain as I wrapped my hair in the thick white bath towel I'd dried off with, and then padded over to the sink.

I'd been in the bathroom for such a long time that Runt had fallen asleep on the bath mat, the rise and fall of her breathing the only indication she was still among the living. I stepped over her and she whined in her sleep, but didn't wake up, her eyes flicking back and forth underneath her eyelids. I plugged my hair dryer into the electrical socket and turned it on, the superheated air blowing a hole in the fog that coated the mirror so I saw half of my face in fuzzy reflection. I pulled the towel off my head, draping it over the towel rack to dry, then proceeded to burn my scalp with the blow-dryer.

"Crap!" I yelped, turning the dryer to low.

My yelp and the noise from the hair dryer finally woke Runt up and she yawned, squeaking as she stretched out across the floor.

"What time is it?" she asked over the drone of the dryer,

raising herself onto her haunches and shaking her head, her ears flopping back and forth.

I had no idea what time it was. I assumed it was pretty late since the dinner hadn't officially started at midnight like it was supposed to and it had gone on for what seemed like forever—but since I never wore a watch, anything I said would only be a guesstimate.

"Not sure," I said, turning the hair dryer off and unplugging it even though my hair was still slightly damp. "I'll go check."

I opened the bathroom door, the steamy air eddying out in front of me, and took a step into the bedroom. I didn't take another one. Instead, I froze where I stood, my hand wrapped around the bathroom doorknob, my body unable to move. It took me ten seconds to process what I was seeing and then ten more to actually get my mouth to start working again.

"Runt?" I whispered, my voice trembling. "We need to go get Jarvis."

"What's wrong, Cal?" Runt said, padding out of the bathroom. "It smells like blood—"

Damn right it smelled like blood—because there was a growing pool of the stuff seeping out of the beheaded corpse lying facedown and spread-eagled across our bedroom floor.

"Who is it?" Runt whispered, staying as close to me as she could, her tail between her legs.

I knew exactly who it was. I'd recognized the dress as soon as I'd come out of the bathroom. It was made of dark green sequins, and when I'd last seen it, it had barely covered the well-proportioned body wearing it. Even now, amid all the carnage, it was hanging off one supple shoulder, revealing a tanned chunk of shoulder blade and side boob.

"It's Daniel's date," I said, swallowing hard. "Coy."

"Where's her, you know . . . *head*?" Runt asked, both of us refusing to move any farther into the bedroom. I shook my own head—glad it was still attached to my neck—and shuddered.

"You got me," I said, taking a tentative step forward. "I hope the bad guy didn't take it."

Normally, a harvester would've already come to collect Coy's soul, but since we were in the middle of All Hallows' Eve, this wasn't the case. Had this happened at any other time,

I would've at least been able to see and talk to her newly departed soul and reassure her everything was going to be okay, but the cessation of all magic had made that impossible. Wherever her soul was, it was just going to have to wait awhile for collection.

"I think she was a Goddess," I told Runt.

"She smells immortal," Runt said, sniffing the air, nostrils flared.

"She does?" I asked, curious what immortals smelled like to a hellhound.

"Yes, she smells like burnt sage and rose petals," she replied. "Very faint now, though. The iron scent of the blood kind of overwhelms."

Tired of standing in the bathroom doorway like a terrified teenager, I walked into the room, careful not to get my bare feet in any of the blood.

"I'm gonna look for her head," I said, skirting over a long finger of blood on the run from the original pool. I'd seen enough *Law & Order* to know touching anything would be considered compromising the crime scene—and I knew Jarvis would punch me if I did that.

I stayed close to the edge of the room, keeping my hand on the wall as a guide. I let my eyes drift over the headless body, the garish green sequined dress giving the corpse a surreal appearance. Beneath it, the cold dead flesh seemed almost rubbery, like it wasn't a real person, but one of those animatronic caricatures you saw populating *The Pirates of the Caribbean* ride at Disneyland. In fact, I kept expecting the body to get up and wave me on to the next part of the ride—*creepy!*

"Do you see it anywhere?"

"Nope," Runt said and whined unhappily.

"Me neither," I said, finally making it to the bedroom door, which of course was on the other side of the room. Here, I was afforded another vantage point, one that gave me a view of the space between my bed and the wall.

"Nothing over here, either."

I unlocked the bedroom door and opened it, letting in a blast of chilly air.

Outside, the courtyard was calm, the chirp of crickets pervasive as I left my bedroom—which in my mind had now become a charnel house—and tiptoed out into the night. Behind me, I heard Runt's toenails clicking on the tile, and then she was next to me, her flank quivering.

"It's creepy in there, Cal," she whispered, brushing up against my leg.

"I know," I agreed, patting her head.

I looked to my left and saw the bodyguard standing at the entrance to the courtyard, his eyes fixed on our door. I waved in his direction, gesturing for him to join us, and he nodded, moving toward us with military efficiency.

"What do you need, ma'am?" he said, his voice gruff. He had a thin, ratlike face, and up close, it looked like he Bryl-creemed his hair.

"Has anyone entered this room since we got back?" I asked, keeping my tone even.

The bodyguard shook his head.

"Not a soul."

Interesting choice of words, I thought to myself.

"Well, somehow someone got in," I said, gesturing to the open doorway.

"Jesus Christ," the bodyguard said, his blue eyes wide as he stared at the headless corpse lying on my bedroom floor.

"I went to take a bath and the room was empty," I continued. "When I came out, this was waiting for me."

The bodyguard shook his head again. This time more adamantly.

"No one went into this room, ma'am. Not on my watch."

I believed him. The bodyguard had no reason to lie, and besides, he looked as shocked by the whole thing as Runt and I did.

"We need to alert my Executive Assistant," I said, shivering in the cold night air, but not at all interested in going back into the warm bedroom. "Can you call up your buddy on that earpiece thing and get him to bring Jarvis over here?"

The bodyguard nodded, putting his hand to his earpiece.

"John, can you give me a location on Jarvis de Poupsy?"

Even under these horrible circumstances, Jarvis's last name made me want to giggle, but I stifled the urge, not wanting to seem callous. There was a dead girl lying a few feet away, her head missing in action, and as the embodiment of Death, I owed her some respect, even if I hadn't really liked her all that much in life.

"He's on his way, ma'am," the bodyguard said, reaching out and closing the bedroom door. "Until then, this is a crime scene and I need you to stay out."

i'd left the room in my pajamas with no shoes and socks, my hair still damp from the shower, so by the time Jarvis and the second bodyguard arrived, I was freezing.

"Calliope? Where is your coat?" These were the first words out of Jarvis's mouth when he saw us standing outside the bedroom door waiting for him.

"Inside," I said, pointing at the closed door. "But it's a crime scene so we can't go in."

"Open the door," Jarvis said, frowning at the bodyguard who'd locked us out. "I need to see what's happened and then we can decide how to proceed."

The rat-faced bodyguard opened the door and I got to see Jarvis's face blanch as he was introduced to what was left of Daniel's date. Seen from outside, the body looked even more jarring; the jagged edge of flesh where Coy's head had been severed from her neck was on grisly display, bone and sinew making a bloody tableau.

"My God," Jarvis gasped, covering his mouth with his hand. "What happened?"

"No one entered the premises since Ms. Reaper-Jones and her dog returned," Rat Face said, his gaze steady, his eyes betraying nothing. "I haven't been inside the room, but when we did reconnaissance earlier this afternoon, we ascertained there were no other exits from the location besides this door and the windows."

"We didn't want to touch anything," I said, "so I didn't check to see if the windows were unlocked or not."

"Actually, ma'am," Rat Face continued, "no one could enter or leave via the windows without a key—they've been fitted with special locks to prevent theft. Apparently, they had a break-in a few years ago and three Ming Dynasty vases were stolen."

"Let's check them anyway," Jarvis said, pushing the door

all the way open and stepping inside. The bodyguards followed Jarvis inside, Rat Face stopping to pick up the coverlet from the foot of Runt's bed and passing it back to me so I could wrap up in it.

Runt and I watched from the doorway as Jarvis and the other bodyguard checked the windows, discovering that they were, in fact, still locked from the inside, adding another layer of mystery to how Coy got into the room . . . and how her murderer had gotten out again.

"Calliope, you and Runt were in the bathroom, correct?" Jarvis asked and I nodded.

"I took a bath and Runt stayed in the bathroom with me—the body was there when I got out."

"I think we'd better call the police," Rat Face said, reaching in his coat pocket for his cell phone, but Jarvis stopped him.

"Not necessary. I already took the liberty of contacting the authorities."

Rat Face returned his cell phone to his pocket.

"A detective from the Bureau happens to be vacationing in nearby Cambria and they're sending him up now," Jarvis continued. He didn't explain that "the Bureau" he was talking about wasn't the FBI, but the Psychical Bureau of Investigations—the supernatural version. "So, we'll wait for him to arrive, but until then I think we should seal the room."

The bodyguards seemed happy to comply with Jarvis's suggestion, but before they could begin, Jarvis crooked a finger at me.

"Calliope, I would like you to go into the bathroom and get your shoes."

I stared at him. My shoes? What the hell was he talking about? I didn't have any shoes in the bathroom.

"Go now," Jarvis said firmly.

Not doing what I'd normally do—openly question him in front of strangers—I did as he asked, hopping over the drying bloodstain and going back into the bathroom to look for my nonexistent shoes.

I stood in the middle of the bathroom, looking at the toilet and tub, trying to figure out why Jarvis had sent me back in here. My toiletries were where I'd left them, the wet washcloth and towel hanging on the towel rack to dry, Runt's untouched bowls of water and food were on the floor next to the closet. Everything was exactly as we'd left it—and then it hit me. Jarvis had sent me in here to collect the book!

I jogged over to the closet and slid the door open, revealing an empty wooden bottom. Kneeling down, I jerked open both of the tiny bottom drawers, popping the dowel out of its hiding spot. I used my body weight to push the dowel back into the molding, the hidden compartment in the bottom of the closet opening wide. I stuck my hand inside its shadowy recess, my fingers feeling around for the book.

"Crap!" I muttered, leaning forward, so I could peer down into the compartment, my face inches away from all the dirt and cobwebs.

But I had no luck: Someone had cleaned us out. Both the book and the old locket were gone.

"Crap, crap, crap," I hissed, shutting the two bottom drawers as quietly as I could and sliding the closet door back into place.

This was bad. Really, really, *really* bad.

I stood up, my heart hammering in my chest as I tried to figure out the order of events. When had someone come into my room and stolen the book . . . and did this have any connection to Coy's murder? I figured since the book had been placed in the hidden compartment *after* the Masquerade Ball, the theft could only have occurred from the Death Dinner onward, so that limited the suspect pool to the high-level members of Death, Inc., and their dates, plus Zinia Monroe, the two servers, and Donald Ali.

I hadn't included Daniel in this list because . . . well, because I didn't think he was capable of stealing anything or hurting anyone. I knew that I was being naïve, but until someone gave me hard proof Daniel was involved in any way, I wasn't counting him.

I left the bathroom empty-handed on all fronts. Luckily, Jarvis had the two bodyguards rechecking the window locks, so I was able to tiptoe over and grab a pair of sneakers from beside the bed and slip them on before anyone noticed.

"As soon as they're done, we're all supposed to go up to Casa del Amo and wait for the detective to arrive," Runt said when I had my shoes on. She was waiting in the doorway, her pink eyes uncertain. I nodded and followed her outside, leaving Jarvis and his security team to secure the room without us.

As soon as we were clear of prying eyes, Runt looked at me expectantly. I shook my head.

"Gone. Someone must've gotten in while we were at dinner and taken it then," I said.

"Or maybe whoever killed Coy was still in the room, and when we left, they took the book."

I hadn't even thought of that possibility. Either way, someone had their hands on a very important, very dangerous piece of Death arcana, and Jarvis was not going to be happy to hear it.

A moment later, Jarvis joined us outside, his eyes ringed with exhaustion.

"Let's go," he said, motioning for us to follow him.

"What about the bodyguards?" I asked.

"One of them will stay here," Jarvis said, moving quickly, his body a tension rod that seemed about to snap. "That way no one can get into the room without permission. The other will start notifying the rest of the guests and ask them to meet us in the drawing room at Casa del Amo."

The landscape lighting was still on, making it easy to adhere to the path, but the bright lights left me feeling exposed, so I waited until we were absolutely alone before I told Jarvis about the missing book.

"It's a disaster," Jarvis whispered, his shoulders slumping forward in defeat.

"Runt thinks the murderer might've still been in the room and waited for us to leave before grabbing the book."

This piece of information didn't make Jarvis feel any better.

"If the two crimes are even connected." He sighed. "Neither of the bodyguards saw anyone enter or leave your room all night. Which makes me think magic has to be involved—"

"But there's no magic, Jarvis," Runt said. "Not since midnight."

Jarvis sighed, slowing his pace, his body riddled with worry.

"I know that, Runt," he said sadly. "I just have no other explanation."

Jarvis was always in possession of a good hypothesis, so the idea that my know-it-all Executive Assistant didn't have an answer for something was chilling.

"So, what happens now that someone else has it?" I asked, changing the subject. "What damage can they do?"

"It depends on who is in possession of the book," Jarvis replied. "If it *is* someone truly terrible, they could immediately begin the Apocalypse and thus end this world as we know it. That is the worst-case scenario."

"I don't like that one," Runt said.

I didn't like it, either, but I decided the other possibility was almost as bad.

"Now, if it fell into the hands of someone interested in controlling Death," Jarvis continued, "it's a different matter entirely. The book could ultimately be used to manipulate the Harvesters and Transporters into doing that person's bidding, which would leave you out in the cold. We must get the book back in your possession by midnight, Calliope, or else it could get bad. Very, very bad indeed."

"Shit," I said, starting to understand exactly why Jarvis was so worried.

At that moment we arrived at the entrance to Casa del Amo and Naapi came rushing out to meet us.

"We just heard the news," he said, grasping Jarvis's arm and giving it a squeeze. "I'm terribly sorry this has happened tonight of all nights."

Jarvis started to thank him for his concern, but Naapi wasn't finished.

"I hope my revelation at dinner didn't have anything to do with this atrocity."

"I doubt it," Jarvis said. "We don't really know what happened—"

"So, it definitely wasn't an accident—"

"No one gets beheaded by accident," I mumbled, but Jarvis shot me a nasty look and I shut up.

"Beheaded?" Naapi cried. "So it was murder."

Jarvis was still sending me angry looks, so I let him explain.

"We don't have enough information to say for certain," he said, moving toward the front door. "But the Psychical Bureau of Investigations is sending Edgar Freezay. Which makes me feel very comfortable that this will be resolved in a timely fashion."

"Edgar Freezay," Naapi repeated thoughtfully. "A truly great man, though I heard he'd retired from the Bureau."

Jarvis opened the door, the heat from the building snaking out to beckon us inside.

"He did, but he still consults for them from time to time," Jarvis replied. "Besides, he's a close, personal friend, so the call was an easy one to make."

Naapi nodded, looking relieved.

"I'd best go tell the others. They're in the drawing room."

He took off down the corridor just as the door closed ominously behind us. Jarvis waited until Naapi was gone, then he took my arm and led Runt and me into a hidden alcove just out of eavesdropping range.

"We'll be in good hands," he whispered, giving me a smile for the first time since we'd discovered the body. "Edgar was a great friend of your father's . . . and he adores your mother."

fifteen

The crackle of logs combusting in the fireplace filled my ears as I sat curled up in front of the roaring blaze, letting the heat defrost my freezing hands. I knew the coverlet had been no-where near Coy's body, but for me, it was tainted—and I didn't want it near me any longer than necessary, so I'd set it down on one of the ottomans, preferring to roast in front of the fire to stay warm.

We'd entered the drawing room to find Morrigan, Caoimhe, and Yum Cimil already inside, waiting for us. Jarvis had stayed on with this core group after dinner, drinking Chambord by the fire and discussing Naapi's impending resignation, when the bodyguard had swooped in to tell him about the death.

Only Caoimhe seemed upset by the news, her already pale face whitewashed in the firelight. The others were calm, openly discussing what they thought might've happened to the young woman they'd just shared dinner with.

One by one, the rest of the guests found their way back to the drawing room, each looking more curious than the next about what had happened, but Jarvis was refusing to divulge any more details until the detective arrived.

Alameda Jones had taken the time to change into a pair of soft brown leather pants and a thick, camel-colored chambray sweater, her wet hair slicked back against her scalp, while

Erlik and Oggie were still in their formal dinner clothes. Uriah Drood ambled in behind Donald Ali, both men in robes and pajamas, but only Donald Ali looked as if he'd been woken from a deep sleep, the whites of his eyes bloodshot and yellow; Uriah Drood's hooded ones were as fresh and lively as a newborn baby's.

Anjea never showed up—no one had any idea where she and her owlet had gone—and Kali only popped into the room for a minute to confer with Jarvis before disappearing as mysteriously as she'd come.

Fabian Lazarev was the last to appear. Hair unkempt and shirt half tucked into his pants, he sat down in one of the armchairs and undid his bow tie, letting it hang limply around his neck, his hurt wrist, red and swollen. Dazed, he stared blankly into the distance, elbows on his knees and chin thrust forward from slumped shoulders. He reminded me of a prizefighter who'd just lost his final bout.

With a full house, the chatter in the room was deafening, so I kept my gaze on the fire, tuning out the white noise of their staccato voices in favor of my own thoughts. Beside me, Runt lay stretched out on her back, her belly exposed as she enjoyed the absentminded tummy-scratching session I was treating her to. As I sat there, I found it harder and harder to block the voices out, my annoyance quickly turning into anger as I listened to them bitch about the inconvenience of having to wait for some detective to show up—not even taking two seconds out of their complaining to say a silent prayer in the name of the recently departed. Part of me wanted to stand up and start yelling at them to shut up, but instead of causing a scene and incurring Jarvis's wrath, I retreated inward, moving closer to the fire and keeping to myself. If being Death meant I was in charge of these assholes, I was going to have to rethink my interest in the job. These were the high-level members of Death, Inc.; they were supposed to give a shit about human life—or any life, for that matter—not act like a bunch of disgruntled barnyard hens, squawking all over the place when something bad happened.

It was a bit sad to think my fervor came from being a convert. Up until recently, I'd been as obnoxious as the rest of them, self-involved and totally unaware of other people's needs, but in the past few months I'd learned that the internal struggle for selflessness was the only thing that kept the universe in balance. I'd watched my older sister disappear into her own selfishness, almost taking our world with her in the process. As it was, my dad's death had been part of the collateral damage from her conniving for power—and it was something I didn't think I could ever forgive her for. Not that I was going to get the chance. She, too, had become the victim of her own greed—dying at the hands of one of her compatriots in what was truly a horrific finale to any human existence.

The memory of her death made me shudder, but it'd been the ultimate lesson in how *not* to live your life—and I decided the people in this room could learn a lot from her gross, incendiary end.

"Calliope?"

I looked up to find Daniel standing above me, eyes red-rimmed

"I'm really sorry," I said, my voice breaking as I reached out and patted his shoe, wanting to touch him and finding that his foot was the closest thing.

"Thanks, Cal," he said, squatting down beside Runt and petting her flank. Her tail started thumping lazily against the carpet.

"It wasn't pretty," I said.

He nodded. I guess someone had already filled him in on the details, maybe Kali.

"I'm the reason she was here," he said, looking into the heart of the fire, where the flames burned the bluest. "It's my fault."

I didn't know what kind of relationship they had. Whether he was in love with her or just "enjoying" her company, but it didn't really matter anymore. She'd died a horrible death and she deserved my respect.

"It's not your fault," I said, taking his hand in mine and marveling at how warm it was. "And we'll find out who did this. I promise."

To my surprise, Daniel let me hold his hand and we sat there quietly, two people lost in their own thoughts, waiting for something to happen that would drag them out of their lonely, interior worlds.

There was a knock at the door and the room went still, the myriad of voices silenced by expectation, but when Jarvis turned the knob, it was only the chef, Zinia Monroe, and her two servers, each bearing a tray of coffee and tea.

"Tea?" Erlik said, looking with marked disdain at the silver tea service the mousy woman was carrying. "Don't you think something stronger would be more appropriate?"

"I have just the thing," Donald Ali said, getting up from his spot on the couch and, at four in the morning, moving with a halting, exhausted step toward the sideboard that sat in the far corner of the room.

He opened the bottom cabinet door, taking out a squat cylindrical glass bottle of brown liquid stamped with a pale beige label. He opened the bottle and held it up for everyone to see.

"One of Shackleton's bottles of Mackinlay's single malt whiskey, left in the ice of Antarctica after the expedition failed," he said, grabbing a thickly rounded tumbler from the sideboard and pouring himself a shaky finger from the bottle. "It's over a hundred years old. Cost me a fortune, but I was able to bewitch them out of seven bottles. 'Cause seven is my lucky number."

He took out more tumblers, setting them up in a horizontal row.

"Anyone else care to try?" he asked, gesturing to the waiting tumblers.

"Please," Erlik said, joining Donald Ali at the sideboard.

"I'd like a taste as well," Uriah Drood agreed, but he remained where he was, perched on one of the couches, playing with the sash of his robe, which was belted tightly at the waist.

Yum Cimil motioned to Fabian Lazarev, crooking his finger then pointing in the direction of the whiskey. It took Lazarev a moment to focus, but when his master's wishes eventually bored through his malaise, he was up like a flash, asking Donald Ali for two glasses of the rare vintage—one each for both him and Yum Cimil.

"Some coffee, miss?"

I looked up to find the male server from earlier standing above me, the coffeepot perfectly balanced on his tray. I hadn't paid him much mind when he'd originally appeared at dinner, but as he stood above me now, waiting for an answer, I found myself giving him my full attention.

"Yes, I'd love some," I said, even though I didn't really want any—there was just something intriguing about the petite, birdlike man. Something mysterious about the way his brown, almond-shaped eyes tilted downward, making him seem perpetually sad.

"Milk and sugar?"

I nodded, watching as he poured coffee into a fragile bone china cup and saucer, my eyes lingering on his dark Mesoamerican features: a high, clear forehead; chiseled cheekbones; and wide, pale peach lips. I had a sense of the familiar, like I'd seen the man somewhere other than the Haunted Hearts Castle, but before I could ask him if we'd ever met, he'd handed me my drink and was on to the next person.

I looked at Daniel, hoping he might have an idea who the man reminded me of, but his gaze was elsewhere, his eyes still lingering on the fire.

Over by the sideboard, Erlik and Donald Ali were engaged in conversation and I frowned, not pleased by the tone of what I was able to catch.

"You would think the women, with their delicate natures," Erlik was saying, "would be the ones to need something to steady their nerves."

I guess I wasn't the only one paying attention to their conversation because as I watched, Morrigan sat up in her chair, disengaging her hand from where it rested high on Caoimhe's thigh. She glared angrily at the Siberian Vice-President in Charge of Asia.

"Delicate natures?" she said frostily. "There is nothing delicate about any of the women you see here tonight and I resent your sexist implications."

Erlik laughed, a throaty guffaw of condescension that made my blood boil. Morrigan took instant umbrage at the affront, and before anyone could stop her, she was out of her seat and across the room, her pale white fingers around Erlik's meaty throat. As she squeezed, she leaned in very close to his face and grinned at him, her face a malevolent mask.

"I could disembowel you so quickly, your guts would be steaming at your feet long before you even realized they were gone."

Erlik tried to respond, but Morrigan's fingers were like stone and he could only manage a strangled growl.

"Morrigan, please, let him go," I found myself saying as I realized I was on my feet and already marching toward her.

She turned her head, her auburn hair red as blood in the firelight. Even though I was still halfway across the room, I stopped moving forward, truly frightened by the vehemence in her gaze.

"Stay away from me, little Death," she snarled, her claws tightening around Erlik's throat.

As powerful as Erlik's appearance made him seem, he was no match for Morrigan. She was aggression unbridled, her murderous grip just an extension of the all-consuming rage I saw reflected in her eyes—rage that was now directed entirely at me. In a flash, she'd released Erlik from her cruel embrace and was heading toward me, her movements as fluid as a predatory cat.

I didn't know if I was supposed to run away or stand my ground, but it all happened so quickly I was forced into the latter. I felt, rather than saw, Morrigan's hands reaching for me—and my body reacted before my brain could screw me over and tell it to freeze. I crouched down, dropping my chin into my chest to protect my vulnerable neck from Morrigan's grasping fingers, then I shot forward, using all my strength and Morrigan's own forward motion, to ram the top of my head into the soft fleshiness of her gut.

My head butt was more than effective. Morrigan made a funny gurgling noise as she clutched her belly then dropped to her knees. Instantly Caoimhe was on her feet, but she looked torn: Should she go to Morrigan or to me? I shook my head, letting her know I wasn't the one who needed her attention. She frowned and turned away from me, but not before Morrigan had seen the exchange, her eyes rigid with pain and rage.

Afraid she was going to come after me again, I took a step back, but Caoimhe's calming touch seemed to ease her aggression and she dragged her murderous eyes away from my face, her attention now on her lover.

"Calliope," Jarvis cried, making his way over to where I knelt, my knees still aching from their impact with the floor after the head butt, the Oriental carpet having given them no padding at all. "Are you all right?"

I nodded, not trusting my voice. I was shaken by the attack, my body trembling from the shock of almost having my throat ripped open by a woman's bare hands. I felt a wet nose pressing against my shoulder and I looked over to find Runt beside me. She started to whine and I looped my arms around her neck, burying my face in the warmth of her midnight coat.

"I'm okay, Runt," I said, my face against her flank.

I felt a pair of strong arms encircle my waist, lifting me back onto my feet—and I leaned into the heat the other body was giving off, enjoying being in such an intimate embrace.

"You did good," Daniel whispered in my ear as he let me go, the heat from his body dissipating so fast it felt like it had never existed.

I staggered for a moment, miserable at being wrenched apart from Daniel, but then I found my footing and was able to clear my head. Now was not the time to be getting all mushy over a man—especially when his date was the reason I was trapped in the drawing room with this bunch of crazy people.

"Thanks," I said to Daniel, smiling up at him, his ice blue eyes anchoring me in place.

The peal of the doorbell echoed throughout the drawing room and my skirmish with Morrigan was forgotten in favor of finding out who was at the front door. Jarvis took the reins, telling everyone to stay where they were.

"I'm sure it's Detective Freezay, so everyone please remain here in the drawing room until I return," Jarvis said, looking pointedly in my direction.

Jeez, did the man really think, after all that, I was gonna go jump out a window or something?

"Why do we have to stay here?" Uriah Drood said huffily, once Jarvis was gone.

"Because this is a murder investigation now and the detective will want to talk to us all," Daniel replied. I could tell Drood wanted to argue the point, but he knew Daniel's logic was unassailable.

"It's four thirty in the morning," Alameda said, yawning. "And frankly, I'm exhausted."

"I second that," Oggie said, nodding in Alameda's direction. "Everyone is exhausted after the ball and dinner—it's been a very long night. Maybe we could adjourn now and take this up in the morning?"

Erlik remained silent on this topic, too busy trying to breathe through his bruised windpipe to stir up any more controversy. I looked at the others, waiting for them to weigh in, but all complaints ceased as the door opened and Jarvis returned with what appeared to be a bear of a Nordic man trailing behind him. The man possessed a shock of white-blond hair and muddy green eyes the color of ancient swamp water, the dark green polo shirt and baggy gray-and-black-striped woolen suit pants he wore making him look like a golf caddy. To complete the odd outfit, he had a solid black bowler hat, ringed with a fuzzy red band, perched jauntily on top of his head. As I studied the new addition, he was busy doing the same thing to the rest of the room, his eyes all over the place, taking in the fire, the hellhound, the whiskey, and the assembled guests in their various states of dress. I sensed no judgment, just a healthy curiosity about everything he encountered.

"Detective Inspector Edgar Freezay from the Psychical Bureau of Investigations," Jarvis said, presenting the detective to the group.

"Thank you, Jarvis, for the introduction, but you may all call me Freezay," Edgar Freezay said, his gaze lingering on each face in turn as he continued to study the contents of the room. "I try not to stand on ceremony, especially in cases like this. I want you all to feel like you can tell me anything that flits through your pretty little heads. Regardless of how absurd you might think it is."

I instantly liked Edgar Freezay. He was an odd bird, but I sensed there was more to the man than appeared at first glance. I would've bet a hundred bucks he didn't miss anything, his eyes constantly flicking here and there, curious about everything he saw. With his towhead and unlined face, it was hard to tell just how old the detective was, but I gathered he was somewhere in his mid- to late forties—though with supernatural creatures, there was no way to know if their physical appearance related to their biological age; because usually it didn't.

"Now, who of you don't I know?" Freezay continued,

pointing to Naapi, Morrigan, and Donald Ali in turn. "You, I know. You, I know. And you, I don't know."

"I'm Donald Ali and this is my Castle."

Donald Ali was getting testy, either from exhaustion or from the fact that someone didn't know who he was.

"Nice spot," Freezay said, then he pointed at the whiskey bottle still open on the sideboard. "Excellent taste in whiskey. Nice to know those stolen bottles made it to a good home."

Donald Ali's mouth dropped. I'd never seen a man of his caliber looking so flummoxed before. Usually they were the ones doing the flummoxing, not the other way around.

"I assure you, this bottle is not stolen—"

Freezay shook his head.

"Nope, still stolen. Even if you paid for it, the guy whom you bought it from did not."

"This is outrageous!" Donald Ali said, his face turning a surreal shade of green. "I want this man out of my house!"

Jarvis stepped in, trying to calm the old man down—though I thought Jarvis had a better chance of calming a raging bull than someone like Donald Ali.

"We are lucky to have Detective Freezay—"

"Just Freezay," Freezay said.

"Yes, well," Jarvis went on. "We are lucky to have Freezay here to help us. I and the Board of Death trust him implicitly."

Donald Ali walked up to Jarvis, shoving his finger into my Executive Assistant's chest.

"Now you listen here," he bellowed. "I will not be talked to this way in my own home. I am going upstairs to bed, where any sane person should be at this hour."

He removed his finger and stormed out of the room on slippered feet, glaring at the detective all the way to the door. The rest of the room was silent as he nearly slammed the door off its hinges on his way out.

"I suppose he's right . . . this *is* his house," Freezay said, looking thoughtful as he chewed on a thumbnail. Then he twisted his head in my direction and gave me a sly wink. "But from this moment forward, I'm in charge. And that means no one, and I mean *no one*, is leaving the Haunted Hearts Castle until I say so.

"Now that we've settled that," Freezay continued, smiling, "I'm going to want to speak with everyone individually, so stay in the main house or on the nearby grounds because I don't want to have to chase any of you down."

Donald Ali's departure had put a seed of disquiet in the group. No one wanted to stay at the Haunted Hearts Castle if there was a murderer on the loose—especially when everyone's immortality was null and void for the remainder of All Hallows' Eve.

Uriah Drood was the first to protest the enforced quarantine.

"I'm not staying here one minute longer than I have to," he said, pulling his robe tightly around his middle and heading for the door.

"And how do you plan on leaving?" Freezay asked curiously. "Do you have a car?"

"Well, I . . . I . . ." Drood spluttered. "You know I don't have a car. Who needs a car when they can just call up a wormhole?"

Freezay leaned against the mantel of the fireplace, arms folded across his chest.

"I have a car. I'm sure Donald Ali has a car, but you, my friend?" Freezay grinned. "You're shit out of luck. No wormholes until midnight, so unless you plan on walking down to town, I don't think you, or anyone else here for that matter, are going anywhere."

Uriah Drood glared at Freezay, unhappy with the way he'd been shot down so succinctly.

"Anyone else want to argue the point with me?" Freezay asked.

There were no takers.

"Good," he continued. "And let's make one thing clear. I will listen to anything you have to say, but if you waste my time with bullshit claptrap, well, let's just say, I don't suffer fools gladly."

"Freezay," Jarvis said, indicating the drawing room, "why don't we make this our interview room since everyone knows where it is?"

"Makes perfect sense, Jarvis," Freezay agreed. "Now, first things first: Who discovered the body?"

I raised my hand.

"I did."

"Me, too," Runt added.

"All right, let's clear the room, folks," he said, dismissing everyone with a wave of his hand. "Then we can get this investigation on its feet."

Everyone started to clear out, Runt and me included—but Freezay called us back.

"Not the two of you," he said, pointing at Runt and me. "And, Jarvis, you'll stay, of course."

I watched as the rest of the group shuffled out, most of them probably going back to their rooms to get a little shut-eye, something I found myself really envying.

"It's nice to see you again," I heard Freezay say to Caoimhe as she made her way to the door.

"You, as well," she said, smiling shyly at him.

"Things have been . . . good?" he asked, taking off his hat and running the brim through his fingers.

"Very good," she said, nodding.

He swallowed hard, looking down at his hat.

"Good," he said. "Well, I'm sure I'll be speaking to you again shortly."

"I'm sure you will," she said mysteriously—and I watched, curiously, as Freezay followed her to the door, shutting it softly behind her retreating back. It was an odd exchange—and since I'd been having my own odd conversations with Caoimhe, I decided to file it away for more thought at a later date.

"My God, *that's* a group," Freezay said, once everyone was gone. "I was afraid if I didn't get them out fast, they were going to get chummy and then I'd never be able to get them to do anything. Conquer and divide. That's my mantra."

With that said, he flopped down on one of the couches, looking very pleased with himself.

"So, you're Calliope," he said, taking in my unkempt hair and pajamas. "And you and Giselda, there, found the body."

"I prefer Runt," Runt said. Though her given name was Giselda, I'd coined the nickname "Runt" and somehow it'd just stuck.

"You and Runt found the body," Freezay said, correcting himself. "Give me your first impressions."

I looked down at Runt, not sure *what* my first impression had been, other than shock.

"She's a Goddess," Runt said quietly. "She smells like burnt sage and rose petals and that's how all the others smell, too."

"Do I smell like that?" I asked, but Runt shook her head.

"You just smell like you," she said.

Freezay held up his hat for us to return to the subject at hand.

"I didn't do it and neither did Runt," I said suddenly—the realization that he might think we'd killed Coy hitting me like a bullet. "I mean she was dating my ex, Daniel, but that wasn't a reason to cut her head off."

"Calliope!" Jarvis squeaked, but Freezay only laughed.

"I don't think either of you killed this woman," he said, clearing his throat. "I knew your father very well—and I know Jarvis. And if the ex-faun over there says you're aces, then I have no doubts. Besides, the whole supernatural world knows what you did for Purgatory and Hell—and it gives me a pretty good idea about the true nature of your character."

"But shouldn't you suspect everyone?" I asked.

"I've been doing this a long time, and I tend to trust my gut when it comes to people and their psychological motivations. Very infrequently am I wrong."

"Okay. If you say so," I replied, taking him at his word. "So, first impressions. It's a mystery how the murderer got in and out. Runt and I were in the bathroom the whole time and we didn't hear a thing."

"The water was running and it was pretty loud," Runt added.

"Good, good," Freezay said, nodding as he spun the bowler hat around on his pointer finger. "Now, how would the two of you feel about helping a very astute detective, like myself, actually, during the course of his investigation?"

"Hell yeah," I said, excited to actually be a part of the action rather than sitting around waiting for someone else to do the solving.

"Me, too!" Runt chimed in.

I looked at Jarvis, not really needing his approval, but kind of wanting it anyway.

"If you're careful, and you stick with Freezay, then I think it might be the safest thing given the situation," Jarvis said, resigned to us helping the detective with his investigation.

And with that settled, we moved on to the first order of business: seeing the last place Coy had called home.

Daniel's room.

sixteen

"Daniel, Daniel, Daniel . . . two beds for one night? Seems a little prudish to me."

Freezay, Jarvis, Runt, and I were standing just inside the doorway to Daniel and Coy's room, in what amounted to a near mirror image of the one Runt and I'd been given on the other side of Casa de la Luna. The only difference was that there were clothes everywhere, suitcases (five of them) in various states of disarray, underwear draped across the bedside lamp, curlers plugged into the electric socket next to the bed that were still on and set to "High"—it looked as if a fashion tornado had hit the room and left it for dead.

"I guess that makes me a prude, then, Freezay," Daniel said, embarrassed by the state of chaos Coy had created on her side of the communal space.

I stared at Daniel, a wellspring of hope filling my heart. If he hadn't wanted to sleep in the same bed with Coy, then maybe they hadn't been that serious after all. I mean, what normal person made their lover sleep in another bed while they were on a hot, romantic getaway?

Answer: no one in their right mind!

"Separate beds, that sadly, no one will get to use," Freezay said, walking through the disaster area and picking up random bits of detritus Coy had left behind.

When he got to the underwear, he retrieved a pen from the night table, using it to spear the lacy undergarment through the leg hole and lift it from the lampshade. He raised the bit of lace to his nose and sniffed, cocking his head.

"Very interesting," he said.

Very gross, I thought.

"What did you find?" Jarvis asked expectantly. I think he was hoping Freezay had solved the crime with one sniff of a pair of panties.

"Our victim ate asparagus sometime in the past twenty-four hours."

Daniel caught my eye and I knew exactly what he was thinking: Freezay was as crazy as a loon.

"And she was also an immortal. There are traces of burnt sage in her scent, which is all over this room," Freezay said, using the pen as a fulcrum to pinwheel Coy's underwear in a circle around his head. "A telltale sign of immortality, as Runt pointed out. So we know her death could only have been brought about by two means: Either someone knew her immortal weakness and planned this murder . . . or it was an accident, her killing an unintended consequence of something else."

"How can you know that?" I asked, raising my hand like a schoolkid.

"Why, it's very simple," the detective said, spinning the underwear so fast it flew off the tip of the pen and sailed across the room. "We assume her immortal weakness isn't something as pedestrian as decapitation—"

Distracted by something he'd seen poking out of one of Coy's suitcases, he paused mid-sentence to pick his way through the mess, throwing open the suitcase lid and extracting what intrigued him from its innards.

"This is fascinating," he said, holding up a blue foil package bearing the words "Bubu Lubu" in bubbly white script, the image of a white ghost in a red scarf skittering happily underneath the font. He ripped open the top, extracting a long brown log from inside the foil packet and popping half of it into his mouth.

"Just as I expected," he said, his mouth full. "Delicious."

He finished off the piece in his hand and pulled another one from the package, eating that one, too, before crumbling the empty packet into a ball and throwing it back into the suitcase.

"As I was saying," Freezay continued, wiping his mouth. "Assuming the murderer didn't use her immortal weakness to kill her and since her appearance at the dinner wasn't planned—"

"How did you know that?" Daniel said, genuinely shocked by Freezay's pronouncement.

"The tags and receipt in the suitcase," he said, pointing to the same suitcase he'd just opened. "They're from a store downtown—one I know well—and the date is yesterday's."

He pulled a crumpled receipt from his pocket, brandishing it for us to see.

"Did you grab that when you opened the suitcase to get the candy thing you just ate?" I asked.

Freezay shrugged.

"I saw the receipt first, the candy was a surprise."

The detective was quick, his mind moving a thousand miles a minute, processing the information his senses collected and coming up with logical presumptions based on what was inputted. I decided that he and my baby sister, Clio, would get along like gangbusters; they both worked on a level I could barely comprehend.

"It's true," Daniel said, pulling the chair out from under the desk and sitting down heavily on it. "I invited Coy to come yesterday morning, though she'd been pestering me for weeks for the invitation."

"And why did you invite her on such late notice?"

A deer caught in a truck's headlights couldn't have looked more uncertain than Daniel did about answering the detective's question.

"We don't have all night," Freezay added, frowning.

Daniel sighed, shoving his hands into the pockets of his pants.

"I met Coy when I was staying with Callie in Manhattan—"

I tried not to show my shock, but I couldn't believe Daniel had been spending time with another woman when he'd been *my* houseguest. That little shit!

"It was very benign . . . at first. She worked for a Mexican import-export company and was only in town occasionally.

She stayed in a place not far from Callie's when she was in the City and I would run into her at the little coffee place down the—"

"That was *my* little coffee place!" I cried, even though I knew I was going to have a hard time establishing ownership over a public business.

"Anyway," Daniel continued, embarrassed. "It was all very friendly, but I could tell she wanted more, and then when she found out I was coming to this, she kept pushing me to invite her."

"How'd she know who you were?" I asked, feeling very catty about Daniel's "benign" little friendship with Coy.

"I knew there was something supernatural about her—and the community is very small," Daniel hedged, but Freezay saved him from having to explain any further.

"And now we know why she bought the dress she was murdered in only today and not previously," Freezay agreed. "She brought lots of possibilities, but someone with her personality wouldn't have been satisfied with any old thing. She'd want something new and shiny to show off in."

"That's what I'd do," I said. "I mean, as a girl who likes clothes, which is a passion Coy and I obviously shared."

Freezay nodded, pocketing the receipt again.

"I would agree with that assessment wholeheartedly, Calliope. It does take one clotheshorse to know another."

Normally, I would've been up in arms over that kind of comment, but Freezay had a way of disarming me with one knowing smile.

"That's pretty astute," Daniel said to Freezay. "Deductive reasoning, right?"

"Deductive something," Freezay said, picking up a beaded bag from the floor where Coy had dropped it. "Tell me again how you found the body?"

He was looking at me then his eyes shifted to Runt, who'd plopped down on a pink faux fur coat Coy had left in a ball next to the bed.

"Both of you tell me again," he said again, snapping his fingers.

I stood up straighter, looking at Jarvis, who nodded.

"There's something we didn't tell you before," I began, "in the drawing room."

"Yes, I know that," Freezay said, unclasping Coy's beaded bag so he could look inside. "Go on."

Jarvis nodded for me to continue.

"Well, as Death, apparently I'm in charge of the original, fully annotated manuscript of *How to Be Death* . . . you know, the one that's written in Angelic script and that no human can touch and is supposed to be a legend, but isn't—"

"Go on," Freezay said again, sticking his face into the beaded bag, so he could look for who knew what inside it.

"My dad gave it to God for safekeeping when all the shit hit the fan a few months ago—"

Freezay dropped the bag on the bed, stepping over a mound of clothing so that he was standing directly in front of me. Then he took my hand in his and raised my fingers to his heart.

"Though your father was a true friend, I didn't feel the need to travel to your doorstep and share my grief with you," Freezay said, pressing my palm against his chest. "He knew I loved him and that was all that was important to me."

He dropped my hand, his speech finished, and stepped back over the mound of clothing so he could return to his beaded bag. Acting as if we hadn't just shared an emotional moment together, he picked up the bag and stuffed his hand into its beaded guts.

"You did send a card," I heard Jarvis say from the doorway where he was standing. He abhorred a mess and Daniel's room was disgusting.

Freezay nodded his agreement.

"I did, didn't I? Were there kittens on it, cavorting with a ball of string?"

"Yes, that's the one," Jarvis said.

"And when you opened it up, it read: 'When you lose a four-legged member of your family, it's as if a part of your heart dies with them . . .'?"

I stared at Jarvis. Was this guy serious? Sending me a pet sympathy greeting card in response to my dad's death . . . *weirdo*!

"I liked that card," Freezay said as he ripped the black silk lining out of the beaded bag, pulling out a jade arm cuff carved into the image of a double-headed serpent. "*This*, though, I don't like so much."

"It's so cold," I said as Freezay dropped the piece in my hand, the weight of the jade heavier than I'd imagined.

"It's a funerary cuff," Jarvis said. "Aztec, I believe."

The cuff gave me the creeps and I was more than happy to hand it back to Freezay, who set it on the night table, where the twin set of dragon eyes stared malevolently back at us.

"Interesting once again," Freezay mumbled before fixing his gaze on me again. "So finish your story about the book, though I think I already know the denouement."

"We hid it in the bathroom," I said, indicating Jarvis, Runt, and myself. "But when I went back to get it after Coy died, it was gone."

"And that gives us the answer to our first question," Freezay said, rubbing his hands together excitedly. "We know the murder was tangential to the real crime—and that was the theft of the book."

"Explain that again?" Daniel said, and I noticed he seemed tense, something that was unusual for him.

"This was no elaborate murder," Freezay said, not bothering to explain his theory further. "I think we should adjourn to the scene of the crime."

He didn't wait for us, just opened the door and stepped out into the night. I poked Runt lightly in the butt with my toe and she raised one eyelid sleepily.

"I'm so tired, Cal," she yawned, stretching. "This is the longest night ever."

"No kidding," I agreed. "But we gotta get a move on."

The pup got up and went with me to the door, Daniel right behind her, but as he moved to follow her over the threshold, Freezay called back to him, his tone firm.

"Not you!"

"What the—" Daniel said, stopping in the doorway. "What do you mean 'not you'?"

Freezay was back like a shot, weaving around Jarvis and me, until he was standing in the doorway, facing Daniel, his hat bunched tightly on his head.

"I don't care what you do," he said, "but you're not coming

with us. Don't argue or get combative, just take it with my apologies and know that I actually like you."

Freezay patted Daniel's arm affectionately, but this only confused Daniel more. I watched as his urge to argue was tempered by the realization that cool logic would serve him much better in this particular situation.

"Okay, fine. I'll stay here," he said quietly. Then he turned to me, his eyes imploring me to listen. "Be careful, Cal. Please. Just be really fucking careful."

Daniel rarely cursed. Not that he was uptight about it, but it just wasn't his bag. So the idea he'd just used the word "fuck" in a sentence meant he was really worried about me—and worry, the insidious snake that it is, doesn't like to announce its presence, but just springs, fully blown, into your brain and starts whispering its secrets.

And now I was infected with it—*crap!*

"I'll be careful," I said, trying to reassure him *and* myself at the same time—and not doing a very good job of either.

"I'm serious, Cal," he said, unexpectedly crossing the divide between us and pulling me into his arms.

The hug lasted only a moment, but I savored his nearness as if it were the finest of wines—and just as suddenly as it had begun, the hug was over, and dazed, I was following Freezay, Jarvis, and Runt out into the misty dawn.

the two bodyguards had dutifully maintained their watch during the night, neither one seeming the worse for wear, though this was probably because they were trained to handle every eventuality—even bizarre situations like this one. Upon our arrival, Jarvis had introduced them to Freezay, who looked even more bizarre in the burgeoning daylight, both men giving him a polite nod. For the most part, Freezay had ignored them, pushing his way into the murder room as soon as the door had been unlocked.

Jarvis asked the bodyguards to remain outside, closing the door behind him as he stepped into the room, allowing Freezay the freedom to work without curious or prying eyes distracting him.

"Oh, she's dead all right," Freezay said as he circumvented

the puddle of sticky arterial blood, heading straight for the bathroom instead of the corpse.

I looked at Jarvis, who shrugged, then together we followed Freezay into the bathroom.

"Now, show me how this works," the detective demanded as he stood in front of the closet door.

"It's very simple," I said as we all crowded around behind him. "You just slide the door"—I slid open the cabinet door—"and pull out these drawers."

I knelt down, my fingers curling around the metallic drawer pulls as I eased both drawers open, their rollers squeaking as the dowel began to protrude from its hiding place within the molding.

"You just press this and voilà!" I said, putting my palm over the dowel and pressing it back into place, the bottom sliding away to reveal the hidden compartment beneath it.

"It's very ingenious how they've done this," Freezay said, letting his muddy green eyes roam over the hidden compartment, then using his fingers to dig where his eyes could not. "I wonder if the whole compound isn't riddled with things like this, hidden compartments, et cetera."

"But the book?" Jarvis pressed, eyes skittering nervously between the three of us. "Do you think it can be found?"

Freezay stood up, rubbing the dirt from his hands onto his pants, the thick fibers of the wool trapping it and adding another, darker, layer of striping to the pattern of the fabric. He took off his bowler hat and the shock of white-blond hair stood up at attention.

"I need a haircut," he said, ignoring Jarvis's question and running his hands through his hair before ramming the bowler back down onto his head. In the light of day, I could see faint age lines in the crevices of his face. He had no pores to speak of, his skin as smooth as a baby's bottom, except for a hint of raggedy blond stubble on his chin.

"I don't mean to harp on this," Jarvis tried again, "but there's something more you should know."

I'd thought we were all up to speed, but it appeared Jarvis had held a few things back from the rest of us.

"We don't need to get the book back just for safekeeping,"

Jarvis continued, falling effortlessly into lecture mode. "It actually serves another purpose. When it's in Heaven, it's power is anodyne—but upon its return to Earth, the magic it contains becomes fecund, so that on All Saints' Day, the day after it is placed in the hands of the next Death, it binds itself to its new owner and will remain within that master's power for the next three hundred and sixty-five days."

Well, that put things in a whole new light.

"Jarvis, please, you have to stop withholding information," I said, exasperated by his unwillingness to be frank with me. "What else aren't you saying?"

"That's the last of it," he said, looking sheepish. "But now you understand the urgency."

At my feet, Runt let out a loud yawn that ended in a whine.

"Sorry," she said, embarrassed. "It's just so bright out now and it was so dark when we started."

Freezay didn't seem too troubled by Jarvis's admission.

"As frightening as the information you just disclosed is, we can't let it sway us from the other matter at hand," Freezay said, reaching down with a large, calloused palm to pat Runt on top of the head. "We find the murderer and, I guarantee you, we find the book. The two go hand in hand—of that, I'm convinced."

"He's right, Jarvi," I said. "We can't just sit around freaking out over what might be."

"But the book takes priority—"

I shook my head.

"They *both* take priority."

"Agreed," Freezay said. "You'll see, Jarvis. One will illuminate the other."

Jarvis didn't seem convinced, but he let Freezay lead us out of the claustrophobic atmosphere in the bathroom and into the open environs of the bloodstained bedroom.

The murder room was just as we'd left it the night before. Dried blood the color of rusted metal was everywhere, congealing on the Oriental carpet and around the meaty globules of viscera that comprised the rent bone and muscle of Coy's neck. I'd never seen a decapitation before, but if the aftermath was any indication, it was an experience I could do without.

I watched as Freezay fell onto his hands and knees and

sniffed the bloody remains, his bowler-hatted head only inches from the corpse. He made a face and sat back up, resting his hands on his knees.

"Her head is somewhere in this room," he declaimed, scratching his nose. "Probably in your suitcase."

"My suitcase?" I squealed. "I don't want her head in my suitcase!"

Leaving the corpse to its eternal repose, Freezay got up and, waving my hysteria away like an excitable gnat, stalked over to my overnight bag (my new, expensive Louis Vuitton overnight bag) and unzipped it. I closed my eyes, not wanting to see any of my clothes covered in gore.

"Yup, there she is," I heard Freezay say—and I cringed, knowing this did not bode well for the future of my new bag.

Opening my eyes again, I found Freezay hunched over my bed, his hands inside the innards of my Louis Vuitton travel bag. He'd set the bag on top of the sheets, opening it wide enough for everyone to see Coy's severed head, sitting upright in a nest of my bloodied clothing, looking like someone's sick idea of a booby prize.

Thankfully, the vertebrae and exposed gristle of the neck were hidden beneath the fabric of my white linen pantsuit—which made up the first layer of the severed head nest—so, if you wanted to, you could kind of pretend the rest of Coy's body was hidden underneath the mattress like some kind of grotesque magician's trick. That is, until you turned around and saw her actual body splayed out on the floor, a Death-centric installation art piece of the macabre.

Upon closer inspection—once I'd swallowed back the bile of horror the first glimpse of her head had produced—I noticed her face was relatively free of blood, but that her dark hair was another matter entirely, the ends sticky with congealed gore and gunk. In death, her irises had rolled up behind the orbital bones, leaving only the bloodshot sclera visible between dark, fringed lashes. Lips were drawn back in a frozen rictus of horror, exposing hot pink gums and a set of strong teeth—teeth, I noticed, that were white in front, but markedly yellow from the incisors back.

"Somebody whitened her teeth," I heard myself saying and instantly felt guilty for pointing it out.

"The nose isn't hers, either," Freezay said matter-of-factly.

"How do you know that?" Jarvis asked and Freezay pulled Coy's driver's license out of his pant's pocket. The picture was an older one, and in it, Coy was in possession of a real honker of a nose.

"Found this back at the other room. The California DMV is notorious for not updating your photo—even when you accidentally/on purpose lose your driver's license," he replied. "See the date? Poor thing's been stuck with this picture for a long time. Must've driven her batty."

"Why didn't she just use a glamour or a spell or something?" I asked, confused. If she was a Goddess, then she could easily change her appearance without surgery.

"A glamour doesn't change what you feel on the inside," Jarvis said, trying to answer my question. "And there are many supernatural creatures who can see through them, so they're worthless in certain situations."

This window into Coy's insecure world made her seem more human—more vulnerable even—and I found myself wondering who, exactly, the real Coy was. I hadn't given her a chance, hadn't tried to get to know her because I'd hated her on sight for being with Daniel. But maybe if I'd met her under different circumstances, where there was no romantic rivalry to divide us, I might've actually liked her. She and I had definitely shared a love of fashion and we obviously had the same taste in men.

"Why would someone do this?" I said, guilt squeezing my insides. "Why take off her head and then stuff it in my travel bag? Why not take it with them?"

To my disgust, Freezay reached into the travel bag and, grasping the head by the hair, hoisted it up into the air so he could get a better look at the point of disarticulation. He'd made the move so unexpectedly, I hadn't had time to cover my eyes, so now I found myself staring at the head, fixated by the bizarre image as it hung there in all its grotesque glory, like a particularly unsettling Halloween mask or a Miss Mofet reject from *The Silence of the Lambs*.

"You've seen a cat covering its feces in a litter box," Freezay said, the head swinging by the hair as he examined the neck. "Almost as if it's embarrassed by what it's done? I would apply the same principle here."

Freezay released his grip on the head and it dropped into my bag with a soft *thunk*, the sound making the skin on the back of my neck crawl.

"And then, of course, there are the ritualistic aspects of the murder," he continued. "The killer has set up the scene to lead us in a very particular direction—"

Freezay stopped speaking, his focus somewhere else entirely for a good ten seconds, and then suddenly he was grinning up at us, his pale features arranged into an expression that was more demon than detective.

"I need to turn the body over," he said, eyes gleaming with excitement. "I think there's more to this than just a simple decapitation!"

seventeen

"You say that like it's an awesome thing," I said and Freezay nodded his head eagerly, the bowler hat sliding down low over his forehead.

"Of course it's an awesome thing," he cried, shoving the hat brim out of his eyes. "The more clues the better. Now take her arm, Jarvis, and let's do this thing."

Jarvis blanched, a red splotch magically appearing on the apple of each cheek. My Executive Assistant was a peach, but when it came to getting his hands dirty with bloody stuff, well, it wasn't really his strong suit.

"I don't think I, really, I . . ." he murmured, clearing his throat twice and looking markedly uncomfortable.

Jarvis did so much for me and required so little in return, I decided saving him from further embarrassment was a good way to say thank you.

"I'll do it," I said, squatting down beside the body.

"If you would be so kind as to take the other one," Freezay said, his hands already wrapped around Coy's upper right arm. I grabbed the left one, the skin cold and clammy to the touch, and together, we hoisted the body up onto rigid legs.

"Oh, Lord," Jarvis cried, leaning against the wall for support.

"What?" I said, trying to look across the body.

"Her heart's gone, Cal," Runt said, padding over to Jarvis and licking his trembling hand.

"Let's lay her onto her back," Freezay said, but Coy's legs had locked into rigor mortis, making them stiff and unwieldy.

"Not . . . working . . ." I said, straining against the weight of the dead body and silently cursing Jarvis for being such a wuss.

Sometimes I couldn't believe the situations I found myself in: Here I was, at roughly sixish in the morning, wearing my pajamas and dragging a dead body all over the place when I should've been happily snoozing the morning away.

Amazing.

"One more time, but first—" Freezay drew his right foot back, kicking first the back of one knee and then the other, cracking the rigor so we could lower the headless body to the floor.

"That's so gross," I said—then I finally saw the gaping hole in Coy's chest—the place where a heart should be, but wasn't— and I realized *that* was way grosser than Freezay kicking the rigor out of her knees.

"A knife," Freezay said, able to examine the wounds now that the corpse was on its back. "The assailant wielded it in his left hand and once the body was on the ground, they stood over her and stabbed downwards."

Bile rose up in the back of my throat, but I couldn't look away. I watched, fascinated, as he ran his finger along the grizzled edges of the wound, the congealed blood and gore not fazing him one bit.

"Next, the assailant worked the knife through the neck, severing the flesh and muscle, but they had to flip her over to have a better go at the vertebrae."

I should have been grossed out watching Freezay inspect Coy's body, but instead I found myself mesmerized. There was a hyperreal quality about the scene, the lights brighter, the shadows deeper . . . the blood redder than it should've been. My eye was drawn to the glint of one single emerald green sequin that had somehow detached itself from the bodice of Coy's dress and found its way into the gory mess that used to be her heart.

Of that ventricular muscle, there was no trace—and we savaged every nook and cranny in the place, upending furniture, opening drawers, and lifting up bed frames—but still, we came up empty-handed.

As we wrapped up our search for the missing heart, Runt discovered something interesting: a clue that would make no sense until much later in the investigation when even more tragedy had struck.

What's this?" she said, standing over a tiny droplet of blood that had somehow found its way inside the grate of the fireplace. It was a minute island of red far removed from the original blood puddle.

Freezay squatted down beside the hellhound, sticking his finger in the middle of the droplet.

"How did it get all the way over here?" Jarvis asked, but Freezay was too busy sniffing the speck of blood, behaving as if he were some kind of forensic chef who'd just tasted a particularly divine treat.

"All right, I think we're done here," Freezay said suddenly, ignoring Jarvis's question as he wiped his bloodied finger across the leg of his pants. "Time to start collecting lies."

"Lies?" I asked.

"Oh, no one ever tells the truth when you question them," Freezay said rather absently, his mind seemingly elsewhere. "Who saw our victim last? We can establish a timeline and see where that leads us."

"Something startled her. Or she wasn't feeling well—I couldn't tell which—and she left before dessert," Jarvis said, something I'd totally forgotten in the wake of everything else that had happened; for me, the Death Dinner might as well have occurred another lifetime ago.

"And Daniel went outside to check on her," I added before I realized this might put Daniel in a bad light. "But he came back and finished dinner with us then walked Runt and me back here . . . so it couldn't have been him."

Freezay shook his head sadly.

"Just because you're in love with someone doesn't mean they can't commit murder."

"i didn't touch Coy," Daniel said. "I swear to God."

Jarvis had sent one of the bodyguards to fetch Daniel from

his room. His hair was wet from the shower and he'd changed into a white button-down shirt and gray corduroy pants, but there were dark smudges under his blue eyes. He looked worn out, but he winked at me when he came into the room.

Freezay had commandeered the drawing room for his "lie detections" as he liked to call witness interviews, saying that: "They lie to your face, they lie on their mother's graves, and they lie to themselves . . . but the truth is always there, just below the surface, waiting to be teased out of them whether they know it or not." Now I knew cynicism had its place in the universe, but I liked to think the majority of us were a relatively honest bunch and that the "lies" Freezay was referring to were mostly just differences in perspective. Maybe that was just me being naïve—it wasn't like I hadn't seen people in my life resort to conniving, evilness—but I didn't want to live in a world where bad behavior was the norm.

"You were the last one to see her alive, were you not?" Freezay asked Daniel, continuing the interrogation as he bit into a piece of hot buttered toast.

Upon our arrival, Freezay had badgered Jarvis into ordering coffee and toast from the kitchen. Amazingly, Zinia Monroe was already up and cooking, happily making us a beautiful continental breakfast of buttered toast, croissants, strawberry preserves, and coffee.

"Yes, I talked to her outside the dining room," Daniel agreed, holding a cup of coffee in his right hand. He'd refused the food, but he'd jumped at the offer of a caffeinated beverage. "But all she said was that her stomach ached and she was going to go to our room. That was it."

"What about the kiss?" I chided him and he looked at me blankly. "I saw lipstick on your jaw. Pink glossy stuff."

Daniel took another sip of his coffee and smiled mysteriously.

"Not Coy."

And that was all he would say on the matter. Freezay didn't seem to think my question was pertinent, so he didn't force the issue. Instead, he zeroed in on what Daniel remembered of Coy's departure.

"So, you said you'd see her in the room later and went back to the dinner?"

Daniel nodded.

"That's it. That's all that happened, and when I went back to the room, she was gone. I never saw her again."

Freezay dipped his toast in the coffee and sat back in his armchair, plunking his feet down on top of the coffee table.

"Anything else? Anything we should know before I send you on your merry way?" Freezay asked.

"Well," Daniel replied, "I don't think it was a stomachache."

"Me, neither," Freezay agreed, yanking his feet off the coffee table and sitting up, so he could lean in close. "Did anyone else see the two of you talking?"

Daniel was thoughtful for a moment, eyes pensive, then he sat up straighter in his chair.

"The two servers. They were clearing the dishes. They walked right by us."

sitting in front of us on the love seat, hands folded primly in her lap, Connie Silver looked even smaller now than she had the night before. She was still in her serving outfit, her face haggard from lack of sleep, but she seemed calm, a secret smile playing at the corners of her lips.

Next to her, the other server, Horace Perez, was still as death, his lips compressed into a minimalist smile, though for the life of me, I couldn't fathom what he had to be smiling about. Horace's silent green gaze remained fixed on Freezay as the detective asked him questions, his eyes hardly ever blinking. He was lean and compact, his lithe body packed into a tight white T-shirt and cuffed dark-washed jeans. He reminded me of a leopard perched high on a tree branch, preparing to leap upon its unsuspecting prey.

"What were they arguing about?" Freezay asked again and Connie blinked, her eyes skittering around the room, her brain finally processing the question.

"No, I told you before. They weren't fighting," she said haltingly, her mouth dry as tissue paper. She swallowed and licked her lips, but that didn't seem to help. "He was just trying to make sure she was okay."

She couldn't keep her fingers still as she talked, massaging her right wrist like it was an avocation.

"The man, he was, shall we say, *worried* about the woman," Horace interjected, and it was the first time he'd spoken since the interview had begun. "She insisted she was fine and he went back into the dining room. She left . . . by herself."

Connie stared at the man sitting next to her on the love seat, her eyes blinking furiously.

"You weren't there when they came in," she said, her tone accusatory. "I was the only one there."

Horace tsked quietly to himself, shaking his head as if he were expressing regret for a friend's unfortunate mistake.

"She has misspoken, but it is not on purpose," Horace said, smiling benignly at Connie, who glared at him. "My partner was very distracted last night. She would not have noticed my entrance as she was too busy eavesdropping on the couple."

"I was not—" Connie protested, but Freezay held up his hand for quiet.

"No petty squabbling, Ms. Silver. It's unbecoming. Now, did either of you see which direction the victim took when she left? Perhaps she exited by the front entrance?"

"I don't know where she went," Connie Silver said, annoyed at being reprimanded. "I went to the kitchen."

Horace shrugged his shoulders, cocking his head to the side in apology.

"I don't know where she went, either," he said. "I'm sorry."

Freezay fell back into his chair, jarring the cup of coffee he held in his hand and slopping the lukewarm brown liquid out onto his woolen pants.

"Get out of here," he barked. "Both of you."

Connie shuddered, twisting her hands together nervously as she stood up. Horace, cool as a cat, rose from his seat, unflustered by Freezay's outburst.

"I hope we were able to aid you in your investigation," he said as he followed Connie to the door.

"You helped me more than you can know," Freezay said, throwing the sentence away like it was nothing—but it seemed to have a profound effect on Horace, who paused midstep and turned back around to stare at Freezay.

"Excuse me?" Horace said, eyes narrowed.

"Might I see your tattoo before you go?" Freezay said, smiling innocently up at the other man.

Horace bit his lip, shaking his head as if to say he had no idea what Freezay was talking about. Connie Silver stood in the doorway, her curiosity piqued now that Freezay's steel trap of a mind was fixated on someone else.

"And what tattoo is that?" Horace asked finally.

Freezay fluttered his long blond eyelashes like a flirtatious slattern and said:

"Why, the one of the dragon on your upper bicep, of course, silly."

The odd smile returned to Horace's lips and he nodded. Then slowly, seductively, he rolled up the left sleeve of his white T-shirt to reveal that, yes, indeed, his bicep was ringed by the curving green body of a double-headed dragon.

"Happy now?" he asked, the vein in his left temple ticking in time with his heartbeat—and suddenly the room was pulsing with energy; power, unbound, coursed through the drawing room as Horace dropped his mask, all pretense at appearing human disappearing as a frisson of pure energy pulsed out of every pore. Then Horace pulled the plug, letting the raw power dissipate until all that remained was the unassuming young man with the weird smile.

"Yes, very happy," Freezay said, holding Horace's gaze a tad longer than necessary.

"Good. Then excuse me," he said and walked over to where Connie was waiting for him at the door.

No one said a word until the door had closed behind them—and then Jarvis, who'd been standing by the fireplace, came over and sat down on the edge of the love seat they'd just vacated.

"Amazing," Jarvis said, shaking his head in disbelief. "How could you have known about the tattoo when I had a clear view of his left side and I never noticed a thing?"

Freezay grabbed a croissant from the breakfast tray and took a bite, the pastry flaking onto his lap.

"Neither of those servers is a caterer by trade. That I can tell you for certain," Freezay began, wiping buttery croissant residue from his upper lip with the back of his hand. "Did you notice the way she rubbed her right wrist, as if it were a nervous tic?"

I nodded.

"She was obsessed."

Freezay shook his head.

"Not obsessed. In pain. I suspect carpal tunnel syndrome. She usually wears a brace on that hand—you can tell by the slight difference in skin color between the wrist and the fingers—yet she hasn't been wearing it. Why?"

Runt sat up. I thought she'd been dozing by the fire, but she'd apparently been awake the whole time.

"Don't you get carpal tunnel from typing?" she asked.

Freezay clapped his hands together happily.

"Precisely."

"She almost dropped the tray of sherry she was carrying twenty different times last night," I added, sitting back in my own armchair, pleased I was able to contribute. "I remember thinking she wasn't a very good server, that there was something off about her."

"She isn't a server," Freezay agreed. "That's what's off about her. I think she works with a computer. In a job that causes repetitive stress on her wrists, forcing her to wear the brace."

"Now what about Horace and the tattoo?" Jarvis asked. "How were you able to deduce that?"

"The tattoo was an educated guess, based on contextual clues."

"Like what?" I asked, sipping my coffee, which had started to get cold and chalky.

Freezay stood up, coffee cup in hand, and began to pace in front of the fireplace, careful not to step on Runt, who was splayed out beside the hearth.

"His accent," Freezay said, stepping over Runt's tail. "Very slight, but distinctly Mexican, specifically Mexico City—and he smells of sage and rose petals, am I correct, Runt?"

The pup yipped her agreement.

"I knew one of them was a God!" she said, thumping her tail.

"And a God would never sling coffee and Danishes," Freezay said, stroking the stubble on his chin.

"No argument there," Jarvis said—and I could tell he was very much enjoying this game of "whodunit." I wouldn't have pegged my Executive Assistant for a Sherlock Holmes fan, but he was clearly having a blast.

"Hey, just FYI, I got coffee *plenty* of times for my boss—" I said.

"You're not a God," Jarvis replied before I could get another word in edgewise.

"Add to that our victim, Coy, hailed from Mexico, where she ostensibly worked in the field of import-export, though that was probably just something she created to entice Daniel," Freezay said, hitting up the coffeepot for its last greasy dregs. "Do you know anything about Aztec ritual sacrifice?"

This wasn't where I was expecting the conversation to go, but Jarvis seemed to have gotten a hold of the same thread Feezay was trailing.

"The head and the heart . . . of course! You think she was ritually murdered," Jarvis exclaimed.

Freezay downed the last of the coffee then set his cup back on the breakfast tray.

"The funerary arm cuff leads me to suspect so, yes," Freezay said. "And the nature of the killing itself can't be ignored."

Someone cutting off your head and stuffing it into a bag was just a miserable way to die, ritual or not—although I suspected if Coy had known her final resting place would be a Louis Vuitton travel bag, it might've made her feel slightly better about her untimely end.

"I'd noticed earlier that Horace was left-handed, and assuming he actually had the tattoo I *thought* he might have," Freezay continued, "well, I made the educated guess it would be on his dominant arm."

"Amazing," Jarvis said, impressed.

"So, you think Horace killed Coy," I said, putting into words what I assumed everyone else was thinking, too—but Freezay wasn't ready to slap the cuffs on Horace just yet.

"It's still too early to tell," he said, drumming his fingers on the mantelpiece. "I suggest we speak to the other guests before we rush to judgment. These things always have a way of getting more complicated than we expect."

"But the book? Do you think Horace has it?" Jarvis asked.

"If that man wanted the book," Freezay said, raising an eyebrow, "I don't think you, or anyone else in this room, could keep it from him."

Freezay was right. If that mini show of power was any indication, Horace was not a man to be trifled with.

"Luckily," Freezay continued, his brows knitting together in thought, "I believe he came here for an entirely different purpose."

"And what's that?" I asked.

Freezay shook his head, a smile flitting across his lips before morphing into a frown.

"I have absolutely no idea."

eighteen

Leaving the warmth of the drawing room behind as Jarvis led us through the snaking corridors of Casa del Amo in search of our next interrogation victim, I couldn't help but feel slightly claustrophobic in the semidarkness of the narrow halls. To make matters worse, whenever Jarvis was nervous, he went into hyper–lecture mode, superfluous information leaking from his mouth like water through a sieve.

"And this lovely oil is another Titian. You can tell by the subtle shading of . . ."

I rolled my eyes, trying to filter out Jarvis's voice so I wouldn't have to listen to his single-subject monologue, detailing the provenance of every piece of artwork we encountered as we wound our way through the building.

"Jarvis, no more art talk. You're killing me," I said, my words coming out more harshly than I'd intended.

Jarvis got all pouty, his feathers ruffled by my comment, but before he could regress into full-on squawkiness, Runt had trotted ahead of us, giving a short yip to let us know we'd arrived at our destination. Startled out of his snit, Jarvis hurried over to join her in front of the closed door.

"Yes, good job," Jarvis said, patting Runt on the head. "Now, I need to telephone Wodin and the rest of the Board of Death to let them know what's transpired, so I'll leave you to it."

I'd never seen Jarvis use a telephone before—mostly because he was a stickler for handling things in person; he was always popping off via wormhole to see someone about something—so the idea of my Executive Assistant forced into using a telephone was almost enough of a novelty to make me want to tag along for the show.

"I think we can handle this one on our own, Jarvis," Freezay said, stepping over Runt and knocking on the door three times in quick succession. "Go do whatever you need to do."

Jarvis seemed a little hurt that no one begged him to stay and help with the interviews, but he didn't pout about it.

"Well, you know how the Board of Death likes to be kept in the loop," Jarvis said, though no one had asked. "And Kali's gone off, so that puts it all squarely on my shoulders."

"Well, have fun with the phone," I called after him as he took off down the hall—but he ignored me, still peeved about my "art talk" comment.

Ah, the silent treatment. Jarvis is going to make me pay for that one, I mused.

Freezay knocked again as we heard someone rustling around inside the room, and then, a moment later, the door opened to reveal Naapi standing in the doorway, eyelids drooping from an interrupted bout of sleep. He was dressed in a red silk robe and matching slippers, the robe's sash hanging out of one loop and dangling almost to the floor.

"Please come in," he said as he ushered us inside, rubbing the sleep from his eyes and pointing to the sole chair in the room: a desk chair he'd dragged into the middle of the floor for the occasion. Freezay inclined his head in my direction, indicating I should take the chair, and he went to stand against the wall, next to a large armoire.

The room that Naapi and Alameda had been given was in the main house just down the hallway from where I'd de-skunked Kali. Like the skunk bedroom, it was decorated in a Moroccan motif, incorporating a rich color palette of indigo blue, sea green, and gold in the mosaic tile work and textiles. It was larger than the room Runt and I shared, but it wasn't half as opulent. Of course, our bedroom also boasted a dead body, so the Vice-President in Charge of North America and his lady friend were the clear winners on that front.

"I can see that we've come at a bad time, sir, so I'll make this short," Feezay said, pulling off his bowler hat and running its brim through his fingers as he spoke.

"Thank you," Naapi said, instantly warming to the deference Freezay was paying him.

There was a rattling sound behind us, and the door opened to allow Alameda Jones to enter the room. If she seemed surprised to find us there, she didn't show it.

"Excuse me," she said, making a beeline for the bathroom and shutting the door firmly behind her.

Upon her exit, Freezay returned to his questioning.

"We just need to account for everyone's movements last night, so if you can be so kind as to tell me where you were after dinner . . ."

Naapi nodded, more than willing to cooperate.

"I was in the drawing room after dinner," Naapi said, sitting down on the edge of the bed, legs crossed, his scarlet robe open to show off the red silk pajamas he was wearing. "You can ask Yum Cimil, Jarvis, Morrigan. I never left the room."

The bathroom door opened and Alameda came out, her lithe body wrapped in a saffron-colored kimono. Long limbs moving with the easy fluidity of a swimmer or long-distance runner, she crossed to the bed and climbed inside, yawning sleepily.

Freezay nodded, as if he had no doubts about Naapi's alibi, then he turned on Alameda, all deference gone now.

"And where were you, Ms. Jones?" Freezay said as he leaned against the wall, arms folded across his chest, nothing casual about his tone.

Tucking her long legs up to her chest so that her chin balanced neatly on her knees, she shrugged.

"I was in the drawing room with Naapi and the others," she said, biting her lower lip. "But my sandal strap snapped and I came back to the room to change my shoes. No one saw me and I saw no one."

As she shifted her position on the bed, her kimono fell open, revealing a strappy bruise-purple silken negligee that showed off her mocha skin and taut, muscular body. It was such a blatant show of skin that I was embarrassed for her.

Sitting up in my chair, I opened my mouth to tell her that

actually someone had seen her kissing someone—who obviously wasn't Naapi—in the sculpture garden, so she was a big fat liar, but Freezay shot me a "shut it" look and I closed my mouth.

"Thank you, Ms. Jones," Freezay said, tipping his hat. "Your movements are duly noted. Now—"

Before Freezay could finish the sentence, there was a frantic knock at the door and then Jarvis burst into the room, eyes wild with uncertainty.

"Freezay, a word," he said breathlessly. "In the hallway, please."

"One moment."

Freezay didn't bat an eyelash, just followed my Executive Assistant out into the corridor, shutting the door behind them.

"What was that all about?" Alameda asked, curiosity ablaze in her warm caramel eyes.

I shrugged, reaching down to stroke the back of Runt's neck. The pup had staked out a spot next to me, curling up in a large ball beside my seat. But Jarvis's frenzied interruption had jarred her out of a light doze and now she was up on her haunches, just as curious about what was being discussed out in the hallway as the rest of us were.

"I don't know," I said, but I knew it wasn't good, whatever it was.

"So, did you see the body?" Alameda asked, sliding onto her knees to get closer to me. "Was it horrible? Someone said she was eviscerated, her intestines strung out over the Oriental rug."

I shook my head.

"Not eviscerated . . . decapitated."

"That's horrific!" Naapi said, getting up so he could pace in front of the door. "I don't understand why someone would do such a thing. It's so senseless."

I could've gone into lurid detail about why a person might murder someone in such a fantastical and gory fashion, but I chose to treat Naapi's question as if it were a rhetorical one.

"Does the detective have any idea why someone wanted Coy dead?" Alameda asked.

"He keeps his cards very close to his chest," I replied, not wanting to share anything with Alameda that might get me in trouble later.

"But he must've said something, had some idea why she was murdered?" Alameda went on, pushing me for more information.

I shook my head.

"I honestly don't know."

Alameda wasn't buying my lack of knowledge.

"I think we have a right to know what happened here tonight," she said snidely. "We're all immortals and that entitles us to a certain level of treatment—"

"Alameda," Naapi said, his tone warning her to back off, but she frowned at him, her beautiful face twisting into something less than pleasant to look at.

"Don't tell me what to do," she said to him, crawling across the bed to scowl at me like an angry child. "I know you think being Death means you're better than me, but I'm here to tell you that you're just a half-breed human, who only got her immortality by the luck of the draw. Nothing more, nothing less."

I wasn't going to argue with her. It was true. I'd had immortality foisted on me by my parents and it was mine only so long as I remained Death—but I didn't feel like that made me better than anyone else. To me, immortality was a cross to bear; one I would've happily given up in favor of a shorter, finite human existence. I hadn't wanted to be Death. I had fought tooth and nail against it, but I'd been railroaded into the job by fate and my father—and now I was just trying to do the best I could with an unwelcome situation.

"You speak the truth," I said earnestly, sitting back in my chair.

Go chew on that for a while, I thought, pleased by the look of consternation my words had conjured on her face. Most people, when put on the defensive, engaged their attacker with an equally aggressive response, but I hated fighting and I'd learned that doing the unexpected was a great way of shutting an argument down before it started.

Luckily, the door opened and I was saved from having to deal with her bad attitude any longer.

"Calliope," Jarvis said, crooking his finger for me to get up. "Let's leave Naapi and Alameda to finish their nap."

"Well, it was lovely chatting," I said. "But I'll have to catch you on the flip side."

I gave them a wave as I followed Runt out into the hallway, glad to escape the look of pure poison Alameda was giving me.

"What's going on?" I asked as soon as the door closed behind me, but Jarvis was already striding down the hallway, Freezay hot on his heels.

"No time to explain now," Freezay shouted back at me. "Just follow us!"

We caromed down the hallway like silver balls in a pinball machine, retracing our steps until we reached the library.

"Prepare yourself," Jarvis said as he threw open the door and we all followed him inside.

"Holy shit," I said, my mouth hanging open as I stared at the dead body draped over the couch.

The flesh was rent in a hundred different places, blood leaking in dark red tributaries from its torso and neck, not even its arms and legs spared from the deep gashes that filleted muscle and skin from bone.

"She was exactly like this when I found her," Jarvis said, the only color in his face two blotches of red high on his cheekbones.

"But we just talked to her," I whispered, my brain still trying to process what I was seeing.

"It wouldn't take long for her to bleed out," Freezay said, bowler hat in hand. "With the internal jugular severed, exsanguination can occur within two minutes. It's odd about the shallower cuts, though. They look different, weaker."

Connie Silver had not died an easy death. Eyes wide open, gagged mouth fixed in an "oh" of horror, she was the living-dead version of that Norwegian painting *The Scream*.

"It must've happened right after we spoke to her," Freezay said, squatting down beside the corpse and squeezing the bowler hat back onto his blond head. "The blood is already starting to congeal and no rigor mortis has set in. This is very, very recent."

"Why would someone murder the serving girl?" I asked, wondering what the connection was between Coy and this new, bloodless corpse.

"Hmm . . ." Freezay said, but it wasn't in response to my question. "This is odd."

He was standing over the corpse's head, his eyes fixed on its bloody nose. Suddenly, his hand shot out and plucked the nose right off the dead woman's face.

"Interesting," he said as he squeezed the protuberant rubber nose between his fingers. "A false nose for a false server. I wonder what else isn't real."

He went for the hair next, the short gray wig coming off easily in his hand, revealing a panty hose stocking cap pulled down over the skull. Freezay yanked the stocking cap off and a cloud of blond curls *poofed* around the dead woman's face. Jarvis gave a squeak and clamped his hand over his mouth, causing Freezay to look up at him curiously.

"You know this woman?"

Jarvis nodded.

"Who is she, Jarvis?" I asked.

He dropped his hand to his heart, the shock slowly dissipating from his face.

"Constance Partridge."

"How do you know her?" Freezay asked.

Jarvis walked over to an armchair and sat down heavily. The light that came in through the library windows illuminated the fear on his face.

"She worked for me at Death, Inc.," Jarvis said. "In your father's office, Calliope. She was a very sweet, but *very* ineffective young woman, so after a few months, I had her transferred to another department."

Freezay walked over to where Jarvis sat, putting a hand on his shoulder.

"What department? Where did she go after you transferred her?"

Jarvis swallowed hard. He knew what Freezay was getting at and it frightened him.

"She worked in the Hall of Death . . . in the rare items room . . . where we kept 'the book.'"

Freezay jumped up and down in place, gleeful at what he'd just learned.

"Hazzah! We have a connection!"

Jarvis took a deep breath and shook his head.

"Unbelievable," he murmured. "Is no one an honest employee anymore?"

I went over and put my hand on his shoulder, giving it a squeeze.

"You are."

He gave me a small smile and patted my hand.

"You're a role model," Runt said, trotting over and nuzzling his hand.

It was cheesy, but it was exactly what Jarvis needed to hear. Runt was the smartest dog in town, hands down.

"There's more," Jarvis said, the color returning to his face as he sat up in his chair. "She left Death, Inc., and you won't believe where she went next . . ."

Freezay grinned down at him.

"I can't even imagine, so I hope you're going to tell us."

Jarvis leaned back in his chair, hands folded tightly in his lap.

"Constance Partridge became Uriah Drood's Undersecretary at the Harvesters and Transporters Union."

we found uriah Drood sitting outside by the pool, enjoying a solo breakfast.

He'd chosen a garden table, one of the many scattered around the yard, sitting out in the open sunlight rather than hidden within the shadow of the tall Greek sculptures that loomed over the circumference of the Olympic-sized aquamarine swimming pool. He appeared unconcerned by our arrival, not at all put off as the four of us crowded around him like a posse cornering an outlaw.

"Oh my, you've found me," he said dryly, his great bulk resting in one of the tiniest white wrought iron chairs I'd ever seen.

It was incongruous, the large man and the miniature outdoor furniture, but Uriah Drood seemed oblivious to the picture he made as he sat underneath the watchful eye of the marble statuary, sipping from a dainty cup of tea and munching on croissants. Even though we had him surrounded, he continued to eat as if we weren't there, as though he had all the time in the world to sit and enjoy his repast.

"She's dead," Freezay said, throwing Constance's gray wig down on the wrought iron table like a gauntlet.

Uriah Drood stopped chewing, the cup of tea halfway to his lips. He stared down at the wig for a moment then set the cup back into its saucer, resting his hands on top of the table and giving the detective his full attention.

"I have no idea what you're talking about," he said, then he reached for his white cloth napkin and dabbed at his lips with it.

"Constance Partridge," Jarvis said. "She works for you."

"Oh, yes, Constance, of course. You say she's dead? However did it happen?"

There was no shock, no recrimination . . . just calm nonchalance. His reaction would've given anyone watching the impression that Constance Partridge was nothing to him but a far removed business associate.

"She was tortured, you schmuck," I snarled. "Someone filleted her with a knife and then left her to bleed to death from her wounds. And we have no idea why . . . not that you give a shit."

How could he sit there, basking in the sunlight like an obese version of Uncle Fester from *The Addams Family*, sipping his tea and munching on croissants when someone he knew had been tortured? I wanted to cross the three feet between us, rip the dainty little cup of tea out of his hands, and dump it on his head.

"What was she doing here?" Freezay asked. "She was working for you. You should have some idea as to why she was here, pretending to be someone else."

The large man shrugged, bending his lips into an apologetic frown.

"I have no idea why Constance Partridge would be here, pretending to be someone else. I don't usually get involved in my employees' personal lives."

I was sick of this charade. Uriah Drood was lying through his teeth and I wasn't gonna let him get away with it. Not giving myself any time to question my decision, I walked right up to the table and grabbed a croissant from the tray, holding it in my hand like a softball. Only I wasn't about to throw this pastry. No, I had a much better idea where to stick the flaky-crusted beauty I was holding in my hand—and that place was right down Uriah Drood's throat.

Smashing the croissant into his face, I pushed the pastry into his open mouth. He gagged, shoving me away with his hands, but I was relentless, forcing the croissant past the barrier of lips and tongue so that the soggy, crumbling pieces slid farther and farther down into his gullet.

No one moved to stop me, so I took that as a sign to continue what I was doing. I picked up another croissant from the plate and smashed it on his bald pate while still keeping up the full-frontal croissant-mouth assault with my other hand.

"Listen to me, you jerkoid," I spat, grinding the greasy croissant into Uriah Drood's scaly scalp as he squealed like a little piggy and tried to fend off my attack with flailing arms. "I want to know exactly what Constance Partridge was doing here and I want to know NOW!"

The croissant I'd stuffed into his mouth made it hard for him to speak, and I could see he was ready to talk, so I released him. Tears streaming down his pudgy face, he began to retch chunks of pastry onto the table, some of them finding their way into his teacup. I watched, gleeful, as the croissant I'd ground into his skull slid down his forehead and landed in his lap, where he quickly swatted it onto the ground.

"I . . . I . . . you're a terrible creature," he sobbed, pointing a thick finger in my direction. "How dare you?!"

Trying to look as menacing as possible, I made a grab for the last croissant on the tray and he shuddered, shrinking away from me.

"Don't make me use this," I said as I held the croissant aloft, letting the weight of my implied threat settle over him.

"Fine!" he shrieked. "You want to know what Connie was doing here at the Haunted Hearts Castle? Will that ease your mind, Ms. Death?"

"Yes, it will," I yelled back at him. "It would ease my mind greatly!"

Uriah Drood sat very still, eyes unblinking as his gaze bored into mine. There was something dark and frightening about the man, a hidden malevolence only hinted at by the calm superciliousness of his stare.

"She came here under my orders," he whispered, then paused for effect.

"She came here to steal your precious book."

nineteen

In a surge of anger, I lobbed the last croissant at his face. It barely made a sound as it hit his chin and fell to the ground, unblemished.

"Where is it? What'd you do with the book?" I said, but I'd just thrown my last weapon away without a thought as to how I was going to intimidate Uriah Drood empty-handed.

"I don't know," he replied, picking up his napkin. It was soiled by orangy-brown retch residue, but he didn't seem to notice this as he wiped his mouth with it. "Constance wouldn't give it to me."

Freezay rested a hand on my shoulder.

"Calliope, why don't you sit down."

It wasn't a question.

He led me over to a wrought iron patio chair—a twin of the one Uriah Drood was sitting in—and pushed me down into it, leaving the heels of his hands pressed into my shoulders as he stood behind me. I didn't know if he was punishing me for the croissant incident or if he was trying to calm me down, but I let him hold me in place even though I felt like a bug, pinned and wriggling, on the wall.

The sunlight reflected off the white of the tabletop and I closed my eyes, letting the meager warmth and my exhaustion overwhelm me.

"Why don't you start at the beginning?" I heard Freezay say, the pressure from his palms remaining steady against my shoulders. I took a deep breath and let it out slowly, my whole body relaxing under the powerful sway of those large, sensitive hands.

Things weren't supposed to go down this way. The Death Dinner was supposed to be a relatively enjoyable, easy introduction to some of the men and women who worked with and/or for me at Death, Inc. Instead, it had morphed into some Mephistophelian murder mystery extravaganza—all because of some stupid book.

Freezay released my shoulders and I opened my eyes, looking up to find him smiling down at me. I hadn't really noticed how handsome he was before. He had a rugged Nordic sensibility and the white-blond hair and unsettling green eyes to go with it. He was definitely what you would call eccentric, with his bowler hat and odd ensemble and totally not the type of man I usually thought of as attractive—and he was quite a bit older than me, for sure—but I had to admit there was something very intriguing about Edgar Freezay. And I got the sense from the way he was looking down at me that he found me just as fascinating.

Who knew my dexterity with croissants could be such a turn-on? I thought.

My juvenile, boy-crush musings were interrupted by Uriah Drood, who sniffled once before spilling the details of the plot he'd conjured up with Constance.

"We all know that Naapi has been circling retirement," he said from his tiny wrought iron perch, eyes lingering on the cool blue of the swimming pool as he spoke. "And Death—your father, that is—was well aware of my interest in the soon-to-be-vacated position."

Runt chose that moment to leave Jarvis's side and cross over to where I was sitting, putting her dark head in my lap. I reached down and began to stroke her neck, the warmth of doggie breath hot on my pajama leg.

"Constance was the one who told me about the book and she was the one who set this whole miserable affair into motion."

"I can't believe you're blaming the dead person for this," I said, and Runt snorted her agreement.

"I'm not blaming anyone for anything," Uriah Drood said. "I'm just explaining myself. From the beginning. As the detective asked me to."

"Calliope," Jarvis said, warning me to keep my mouth shut. "Go on, Mr. Drood."

I noticed the back of Jarvis's neck starting to turn pink from the sunlight, but I didn't call attention to it, not wanting to get sniped at for opening my mouth.

"Constance decided to get a job serving at the dinner. She would use her time to watch you, new Death," he said, glowering at me. "And then when she was sure you had the book, she would steal it from you. She'd placed tiny wireless cameras in your room, so we could monitor your every move. Needless to say, we thought we'd missed the whole thing when you made the swap in the library and not in your suite. But then we caught you hiding the book in the bathroom and we were back in business—"

"If by 'business' you mean blackmailing Calliope into giving you the Vice-Presidency of North America," Freezay finished for him.

Uriah Drood started to protest, but then he stopped and nodded.

"Yes," he said, resigned to the truth. "Only once Constance had the book, she decided to double-cross me, that bitch—"

"So you killed her," I blurted out.

Uriah Drood giggled, girlish snorts of laughter issuing through his fingers as he covered his pink lips with his hand.

"Why would I do that? I didn't have the book yet," he giggled.

I looked over at Jarvis, who shrugged. I didn't want to admit that Uriah Drood's logic made sense, but it did.

"So who killed her then?" I asked, but Uriah Drood had no answer for me.

"Sorry, I don't know who killed Constance . . . Oh, and if you're thinking we caught that other woman's murder on tape, think again. Once we got the book, we turned the recording devices off, so you're out of luck there," he said snidely as he stood up and brushed croissant crumbs off his gray suit coat. "And now that you've ruined my brunch, I'd like to go back to my room and freshen up."

Freezay let him go without another word. When we'd seen the last of his lumbering gait, Freezay sat down in Drood's chair and picked up the undamaged croissant from the ground, examining it for a moment before setting it back on the tray.

"Well, we know two things now that we didn't before: Connie Silver, aka Constance Partridge, was murdered for the book, and Calliope Reaper-Jones is a damn fine shot with a piece of pastry."

I couldn't help but smile at Freezay, pleased, at last, to have someone acknowledge my acumen with pastry products. Jarvis's reaction, on the other hand, I was not looking forward to. I took a deep breath, totally preparing myself to get blasted for my unladylike behavior.

"That was a very pleasurable experience," Jarvis said, surprising me. "I almost clapped when you greased his scalp. Just lovely stuff, Calliope."

That was very high praise, indeed, coming from Jarvis.

"I couldn't take the hedging," I said. "I knew he was lying about Constance and it made me so mad I just had to do something."

"It was amazing, Cal," Runt agreed.

As much as I was enjoying the adulation, I was also exhausted. I'd been going since early the day before, and the lack of sleep was finally catching up with me. Even poor Runt could barely keep her eyes open.

"What's my problem? I'm so tired, I could fall asleep right here at this table," I said, yawning. "This never happens to me."

Jarvis offered me his hand and I stood up, yawning again.

"All the supernatural qualities you possess are hindered now by the lack of magic in the world—and it will be like that until All Saints' Day," Jarvis said.

"Well, that's a bummer," I said, leaving the site of my first ever pastry attack behind me.

Jarvis sighed, scratching the back of his neck—which had turned from a reasonable shade of light pink to a bright burnt red.

"Yes, a bummer," he agreed. "Is my neck burnt?"

I nodded.

"To a crisp."

"Damn." He sighed.

"So this book is pretty popular," I said—wanting to know exactly what I was going to be dealing with if I didn't get it back. "Constance and Drood were after it, and maybe Coy, too."

"Whoever controls the book controls the Harvesters and Transporters," Jarvis said quietly. "It's why Uriah Drood was so intent on getting a hold of it. He could easily have blackmailed you into naming him Naapi's successor in exchange for its safe return, and the world would've been none the wiser."

"And if I hadn't given in to his blackmail plot? What then?" I asked as I felt time slipping away from me. Above us, the sun, having already reached its zenith for the day, began its slide toward the horizon.

"If someone else possesses the book at the stroke of midnight, then it will be another three hundred and sixty-five days before Death can collect it again. During that time, Death will have no dominion over the Harvesters and Transporters—"

"But what happens to all the souls if no one comes to collect them?"

"During the Middle Ages, the year 1347 to be precise," he said—and I could feel the beginnings of a lecture coming on. "The book was stolen by the angel Azazel, who used it to bring about the beginning of a plague called the Black Death—"

"I'm not an idiot," I said, stopping to turn up the cuffs of my pajama pants so I wouldn't keep stepping on them as I walked. "I *have* heard of the Black Death, thankyouverymuch. I mean I did see that Bergman film *The Seventh Seal* like twice."

What I didn't add was that I'd slept through the movie the first time I saw it and made out with a really cute guy all the way through my second viewing.

"Well, what you *don't* know," Jarvis said, continuing, "is that for the next ten years, Azazel was in charge. Basically blackmailing Death into doing whatever he wanted in exchange for making the Harvesters and Transporters do their jobs. This injustice continued until the next Grim Reaper took office and recovered the book from Azazel."

"Okay, so not interested in that scenario," I said, fuming at the injustice of it all. "We gotta find the book because I don't want to be bossed all over Heaven and Hell by the likes of Uriah Drood."

"My thoughts exactly," Jarvis agreed.

Our conversation was abruptly cut short by the sudden appearance of Erlik striding aggressively down the path toward us.

"What's happened in the library?!" he bellowed as soon as he was in shouting distance. "First Coy and now this? You're supposed to stop the murderer, not encourage him!"

But verbal antagonism wasn't enough for the likes of Erlik. He was a big hotheaded asshole who wanted to be taken seriously—and that meant physical intimidation.

"I want an answer from you!" he growled, his face turning scarlet as he jammed a finger into Freezay's chest.

It was a mild October day, not superhot, but warm enough to work up a sweat if you exerted yourself. The look Freezay gave the enraged man made me shiver.

"Your tone is unacceptable," Freezay said, his muddy green eyes flashing with barely concealed anger. "You either calm down and we can have a reasonable conversation, or you can incur my wrath. Something I would encourage you to avoid."

Erlik stared at him, weighing his options. The men were an even match when it came to physical size, both tall and solidly built, but where Erlik was all cultivated muscle, his biceps the size of Easter hams, Freezay was rangy and lighter on his feet. I'd watched Erlik get his ass handed to him by Morrigan the night before and I was pretty sure he didn't want to find himself in a similar situation with Freezay.

"Fine," Erlik said, stuffing his hands into the pockets of his blue jeans and turning his anger down a couple of notches.

"Now what can I do for you?" Freezay said.

Erlik nervously shifted back and forth on the balls of his feet, all the energy he'd just tamped back down inside himself having nowhere else to go.

"I want to know what you're doing to find Coy's murderer."

I wanted to know what we were doing to find Coy's murderer, too, so I listened intently to Freezay's answer.

"Can I ask you one question first?" Freezay asked, his tone light. "And then I promise to tell you what you want to know."

Erlik considered the question, trying to figure out if this was just a dodge or an actual legitimate request.

"Go ahead." He sighed, finally deciding he had nothing to lose by answering the detective's question. "Ask your question and we'll see."

"I'd like to know exactly how long you were involved with Coy."

Well, that came out of left field, I thought.

Erlik bowed his head, the muscles in his neck straining.

"How did you guess?" he asked, looking up again, his lips trembling.

"No man rages like a bull over the death of a woman he doesn't know."

Erlik nodded, realizing he'd given himself away by his own aggressive behavior.

"What can you tell me about her? Something I wouldn't be able to guess, but that a lover would know implicitly," Freezay asked, patting the large man's arm, a show of sympathy for the bereaved.

Erlik took a moment to collect his thoughts, probably sifting through all the things he knew about his ex and separating out what was fit to tell a detective from what was too intimate to divulge.

"She's a Goddess. From the Aztec Pantheon," he said. "Her given name is Coyolxauhqui and she's estranged from her family, so I never met any of them."

I noticed Erlik used the present tense when he spoke of Coy. Freezay seemed aware of this, too, and even though he was simmering with questions—I could see the anticipation in his eyes—he tempered his interrogation with kindness.

"You should know that she died quickly," he said simply— though I wasn't sure if he was telling the truth or just trying to spare Erlik's feelings. "And that any mutilation to the body was done postmortem."

Eyes welling with unshed tears, Erlik was unable to speak, merely nodding that he'd understood.

"Is there anything else we should know?" Freezay asked, more gently now.

It was strange to watch a muscle-y macho man cry. It felt like we were intruding on something we had no business seeing, but before I could suggest that Jarvis, Runt, and I give them some privacy, Erlik had gotten control of himself again, swiping at his eyes with the sleeve of his yellow Oxford shirt.

"There's someone here who could easily have done her in," Erlik said, his brow ridged with tension. "He leaves a trail of devastation wherever he goes, a real womanizer who got his hooks into Coy and never let her go again. And when he's done with them, his women have a strange way of *disappearing*."

"And who might that be?" Freezay asked, curiosity alive on his face.

As if Erlik had prearranged it with fate, a cloud passed over the glaring sun, cloaking his face in shadow.

"Fabian Lazarev, of course."

Freezay raised an eyebrow, but didn't comment. Instead, he asked Erlik where he had gone after dinner.

"Didn't you hear what I just said?" Erlik asked, less than thrilled with Freezay's reaction.

"I heard you," Freezay said. "And I will look into it."

Erlik shook his head, miffed by Freezay's apparent lack of interest in Lazarev, but he didn't push it.

"I left the dining room with everyone else," he said sullenly, "but I went outside, stood in one of those sculpture gardens, and had a cigarette. So if you're fishing for an alibi, I don't have one."

Ah, the beauty of immortality, I thought. *You could smoke all the cigarettes you liked and never get lung cancer.*

Freezay seemed satisfied with Erlik's answer.

"I think that's all I need from you right now. But I might have to speak with you later in case I need anything confirmed," Freezay said. "Be around."

"And what about that bastard, Lazarev?" Erlik asked, not wanting to go until Freezay had assured him on that front.

"I promise he will be the next person I speak to," Freezay said judiciously. "Now run along and stay out of trouble."

Erlik did not like being condescended to. Brandishing a fist in Freezay's face, he said: "Don't push it, Detective."

And then he pivoted on his heel and was gone, his thick, muscular legs moving him quickly out of our view.

"You think there's anything to what Erlik said about Lazarev?" Jarvis asked.

"Only one way to find out," Freezay said. "Ask."

"Hey, what about the bodies?" I asked.

"What about them?" Freezay said, eager to get back up to the main house and talk to Fabian Lazarev.

"We can't just leave them where they are. It's disrespectful."

"The Harvesters will pick their souls up at midnight, Calliope," Jarvis said, trying to reassure me. "We can magically deal with the bodies afterward. Until then there's no point in moving them just to move them."

I started to protest, but I could see my argument wasn't going to get support from anyone.

"I still feel bad—"

"Speaking of feeling bad," Jarvis said, pushing up the sleeves of his dinner jacket, "I have to find Kali and let her know what Wodin said when I telephoned him. I was actually on my way to brief her when I discovered Constance's body."

"So we're not gonna move the bodies and you're just gonna leave?" I said, trying not to be a baby about him going. "Like right now?"

"You'll be in Freezay's capable hands—"

"Okay," I said, feeling annoyed.

"Don't pout," Jarvis said. "We'll all be back together in the drawing room before you know it."

Jarvis didn't wait for me to protest, just took off before I even had a chance to state my case.

"Whatever," I said under my breath.

"You think he's just going so he can take a nap?" Runt asked, and I laughed, feeling my anger starting to dissipate.

"Why don't *you* go to the drawing room and take a nap," I suggested when I noticed the poor pup's eyes drooping.

"I'm okay," she said, yawning.

"Then how about fetching Fabian Lazarev from his room and meeting us in the drawing room," Freezay said. "That'll keep you on your feet."

Runt looked more than happy to oblige.

"On it!" she said, perking up. She liked being needed and was probably excited about doing something other than just following me around.

"Shall we?" Freezay asked as we watched the hellhound pad off down the corridor.

"Only if you promise that the night will get better from here on out," I said.

Freezay laughed, shaking his head.

"If you're with me, then your night is already off to a better start," he said—and then he gave me what I can only term a "saucy" wink, before taking my arm and leading me down the hall toward the drawing room.

twenty

Being with Edgar Freezay was nothing like being with Daniel; there was no crazy sexual electricity, and no feeling of being utterly connected to another human being—but that wasn't to say it was all cold fish, either. There was definitely *something* sexy about the detective that drew me to him. He was intuitive, smart, and I liked the eccentric way he presented himself.

He was a hot "weird" dude.

But as much as I wanted to forget about Daniel and not give a damn who he was shacking up with, I just couldn't seem to move on. Even when I had the perfect opportunity to scrub him from my mind—Edgar Freezay, for example—I just couldn't do it. I was stuck waiting around for the man who I knew was my soul mate to realize his life just wasn't as sweet without me in it.

"So I heard what you said to Jarvis and I want you to know that there's nothing to feel bad about. You can't do anything for them until All Saints' Day starts," Freezay said, scratching at the blond stubble on the bottom of his chin. "But at least you know their souls are going to continue on, that they're going to be recycled through the system. Imagine dealing with death and having no proof that there even *is* an Afterlife. Before I got conscripted into the Psychical Bureau of Investigations, I was a normal policeman, working cases without a clue that the supernatural world even existed—"

"Wait, you were a real policeman?" I said, pretty sure the Psychical Bureau of Investigations wasn't known for bringing normal human beings into its ranks.

"My father, Wodin, is notorious for taking up with human women, never enlightening them to the fact that he's a God—even after impregnating them," Freezay said dryly. "So I had no clue about my heritage until I was contacted by Manfredo Orwell, the head of the PBI's Crimes Against Humanity Division when I was twenty-six. I'm sure you, of all people, can imagine my surprise at finding out exactly who and what I was."

And I thought I'd had it bad. I'd always known who I was and what my family was capable of . . . I'd just chosen to ignore it. Freezay, on the other hand, had lived in isolation from others of his kind, probably having all kinds of odd experiences that he couldn't share with anyone because no one would believe them.

"You must have had an inkling about your true nature," I said, but Freezay shook his head.

"I thought I was crazy. As a child, I'd see things I couldn't explain, and then I'd share them with my mother, who was a no-nonsense second-grade teacher and had no idea the man she'd picked up in a Detroit bar one dark and stormy night was a God. It felt like I'd spent my childhood in a psychiatrist's office—until I turned ten and realized people would leave me alone if I just kept my mouth shut."

"Wow," I murmured.

"Believe me, magic makes the job much more interesting," he said. "And you don't have to follow the rigid procedural stuff you're forced to adhere to with traditional police work. You'd have never caught me touching a body without gloves when I worked a murder scene in the real world."

"Jarvis said you retired. You seem pretty young to be a man of leisure," I said.

Freezay laughed, but it wasn't a pleasant sound.

"A man of leisure I am, but not of my own volition. I didn't retire. Let's just say I was asked to leave the PBI and let it go at that."

We reached the door to the drawing room and Freezay held it open so I could go inside first. It was just as we'd left it: fire dying in the grate, dirty breakfast dishes spread across the coffee table.

"Well, here we are, Ms. Death," he said, closing the door behind him and smiling at me.

"Who do you think did it?" I asked, plopping down in an armchair and "resting" my eyes for a moment.

"I have no idea who did this," he said, sitting down on the love seat across from me. "But I believe the book is at the epicenter of it all. Follow the book and you'll find our killer. Find our killer and the book will present itself."

"So, if Constance, aka Connie the Server, stole it, then what did she do with it? Why not give it to Uriah Drood like she'd planned?"

"You got me," he said, throwing his hands up in mock surrender. "I haven't got a clue why people *really* do the things they do. I mean, I can logically take the crime apart and see its psychological aspects, but when it comes to motivation, the details vary so greatly, all you can do is quantify them into the big three basics: money, love, and power—but that never gives you a free pass into their psyches."

The rest of our conversation was put on hold by a knock at the door.

"Come in!" Freezay called.

Runt entered the room first, followed by Fabian Lazarev and his boss, Yum Cimil.

"He wouldn't let him come on his own," Runt whispered to Freezay, gesturing with her nose at Yum Cimil as she came in and sat down by my chair.

I could understand why Yum Cimil didn't want his employee left to his own devices: Lazarev looked like a different man. His face was drawn, exhaustion hollowing dark gouges into the flesh above his orbital bones, making it appear as if someone had punched him in both eyes. He slumped forward where he stood, his loose white V-neck shirt and black linen pants hanging like rags on his taut frame.

"Please have a seat," Freezay said as he got up and gestured toward the love seat. Yum Cimil stared at the recently vacated spot, but Lazarev, who moved like a man in a fog, did as he was told, sitting down and putting his head in his hands.

Dressed in a modified version of an undertaker's uniform—black suit and high-necked white button-down shirt—it was hard to tell what Yum Cimil was thinking as he looked around the room, but I guessed he was none too happy about being included in our little soiree.

"If you're not into the love seat," Freezay said, "please, be my guest and sit wherever you'd like."

Yum Cimil furrowed his brow, his eyes shifting back and forth between me, Freezay, and Lazarev. After a few moments of interior debate, he seemed to decide that this wasn't a trick question and shuffled over to the love seat, sitting down next to his second in command.

"As you know, Coyolxauhqui was murdered last night—"

Fabian Lazarev sat up at the mention of Coy's true name, his mustache twitching as his normally tan face went a pale, milky white.

"But that's not the end to the tragedy," Freezay continued. "Constance Partridge—Uriah Drood's Undersecretary at the Harvesters and Transporters Union *and* the serving woman here at the Haunted Hearts Castle—was killed this morning."

Lazarev looked confused, his dark eyes unfocused.

"I don't . . . understand," he mumbled. "Why was Drood's secretary here? And why did someone kill her and the serving woman?"

Freezay leaned against the fireplace mantel, twisting the brim of his bowler hat in his hands.

"The serving woman and Uriah Drood's Undersecretary are one and the same."

Lazarev glanced at Yum Cimil, who frowned, the lines around his mouth deepening into furrows.

"You guessed this?" Freezay asked, his ability to read Yum Cimil's facial expressions, impressive.

Yum Cimil stared at him for a second then leaned over and whispered something in Lazarev's ear.

"Yes, I understand," Lazarev nodded. "Okay."

He returned his gaze to Freezay, licking his dry, cracked lips.

"She was wearing a wig. We noticed at dinner she kept scratching her head. Not so good for hygiene and food cleanliness."

Yum Cimil was way more observant than me. I'd only noticed her nervousness and lack of grace with a tray full of sherry, but he'd seen through the artifice of her façade.

"Does her death have any connection to Coy's murder?" Lazarev asked, this question his own.

"We don't know. We have to assume that two separate murders in the same location within a twenty-four-hour period are not coincidental," Freezay replied. "You looked surprised when I called Coy by her given name? Why?"

Lazarev, if it were possible, got even paler, his lower lip trembling uncontrollably.

"I . . . well . . . I knew Coy. She is . . . was my girlfriend, until she was seduced by another, more recently than I'd like to admit."

"Erlik stole her away from you," Freezay said—and it wasn't a question.

Lazarev swallowed hard then looked down at his hands.

"Yes. He told you, I assume."

"Actually, he said you'd stolen her away from him," Freezay said.

"Ha!" Lazarev nearly shouted as emotion brought him to his feet.

Erlik had been upset by Coy's death, but there'd been something almost selfish about his reaction. Lazarev was a different beast altogether. He was devastated by Coy's death— you could see it in the hunch of his shoulders and the gaunt look in his eyes—and it made me feel sorry for him in a way that I hadn't for Erlik.

"He said women you've dated have a way of disappearing—"

"He said that?" Lazarev cried. "He truly said that?"

Freezay nodded. "He truly said that."

"An unbelievable monster," Lazarev spat, "to say *that* about *me* when he is the one . . ."

Lazarev trailed off, his energy waning, as he sat back down beside Yum Cimil.

"A projection of himself onto you?" Freezay offered—and Lazarev nodded his head weakly.

"I suppose."

"Where were you last night when Coy died?" Freezay asked, abruptly changing the subject.

Lazarev's eyes flicked around the room, his brain working overtime to cobble together a timeline of his evening that wouldn't get him in trouble.

"We know *you* were here in this drawing room with Jarvis, Caoimhe, Morrigan, and Naapi," Freezay continued, turning his gaze on Yum Cimil. "But of Mr. Lazarev's whereabouts—"

"I went into the kitchen. Zinia Monroe and the two servers were there. They can tell you," Lazarev cried.

"Well, one of your witnesses is dead," I said. "So hopefully the other two can back you up."

Lazarev glared at me.

"Don't judge me, Death," he snarled. "You know nothing about my life."

I didn't like being growled at, but I knew the man was suffering, so I tried not to take it too personally.

"We'll definitely be talking to—" Freezay started to say, but his words were interrupted by the sound of raised voices in the hallway.

A moment later, Morrigan threw open the door and stormed inside, her mouth puckered in anger.

"But I have to tell her," Caoimhe cried as she entered the room right behind her. "It's my right—"

Startled by our presence in the drawing room, both women came to an abrupt stop, silence stealing over them as they realized they had an audience for their argument.

"Hello, ladies," Freezay said, his gaze sliding over Morrigan and settling onto Caoimhe. "Nice of you to join us."

"We didn't know anyone was in here," Morrigan said, glaring at the detective. "We'll just go—"

"No, stay," he said, his gaze riveted to Caoimhe's face. "You're on my list, and since we've just finished with Mr. Cimil and Mr. Lazarev, your entrance is pure perfection."

Lazarev stood up stiffly, anger buzzing through him as he continued to glare at me. Yum Cimil got to his feet and put a restraining hand on Lazarev's arm, the younger man's rage diminishing at the touch.

"I'll probably need to speak with you again," Freezay said

as the two men departed, passing the women without a glance. "So don't disappear on me."

As they reached the doorway Yum Cimil turned around, shooting me a cool, appraising look. I held his gaze until Lazarev tapped him on the shoulder.

"Let's go, sir," he said, offering his arm to the older, smaller man.

Yum Cimil accepted the proffered arm, disengaging from our staring contest to follow Lazarev into the corridor. As I watched them go, I decided that Yum Cimil was a weird old man. Specifically weird because he dressed like a mortician and always had a sour look on his orange face. I didn't know what the schmuck had against womankind, in general, but I knew *I* was not a fan of his—and it had nothing to do with him having a penis.

"We were in the drawing room when all the shit went down," Morrigan was saying when I tuned back into the conversation. She was facing the fireplace, resting her hands on it as she spoke, her bloodless fingers pressing into the mantel.

Behind her, Caoimhe was on the edge of the love seat, her hands in her lap as she listened to her partner speak. Her patrician profile and dark coiffure made her look like a model half her age, and I could see exactly why Morrigan had chosen her as a consort; she was beautiful, polished, and full of life. Sensing my gaze, she caught my eye, giving me a shy smile. I smiled back at her, enjoying the shared moment, but as soon as Morrigan turned back around, Caoimhe's gaze flicked away from mine.

As a modern woman, I couldn't help but be bothered by the subservient way Caoimhe behaved around Morrigan. I found it degrading and odd that a woman who had so much going for her was cowed at the hands of her lover. It was just weird.

"Yes, I know where you were last night, but this morning?" Freezay asked, pushing Morrigan for an answer.

"Why don't you ask your little poppet how she murdered that girl in her bedroom?" Morrigan hedged, throwing me under the bus to get the attention off herself. "Who else would've killed her? She was shacking up with Ms. Death's old boy toy, so there's your motivation right there—"

"Morrigan!" Caoimhe shouted at her, the intensity of her reprimand rippling through the room.

"I didn't touch Coy," I said, though I wasn't able to muster much energy, my frustration already having given way to exhaustion. I was tired of always having to defend myself—and just plain tired, too—and this once I knew I was totally innocent; no one could throw any of the responsibility for the two murders in my direction.

"But I don't really care if you believe me or not," I continued. "I have nothing to prove to you or to anyone else."

Freezay winked at me.

"Now as I was saying—"

There was a knock at the door, interrupting Freezay's train of thought and freeing Morrigan from having to answer immediately.

"Now what is it?" Freezay moaned under his breath, striding over to the door and throwing it open.

Zinia Monroe was standing on the other side, her hand raised as if she meant to knock again. Her blond hair was in a messy bun on top of her head, her Mao jacket mussed from her having worn it through the night. She had a pair of black thick-framed glasses perched on her sharp nose, a silvery chain hooked on to the end of each temple and looped around her neck, keeping them in place.

"Yes?" Freezay said, frustrated by the interruption.

Zinia ignored his uncivil tone, looking past him at me.

"I need help in the kitchen. I'm sure everyone is hungry, and since one of my servers is dead and the other is MIA, I'm short staffed. Can you help me out?"

"I can help you, sure," I said, standing up—I couldn't have come up with a better excuse to get out of the hot seat if I'd tried.

"Well, come on then," she said, beckoning me forward. "The food isn't going to sit there all day waiting."

She spun on her heel, marching back the way she came. I shot Freezay a questioning look, but he merely nodded his head for me to go on.

"I'll see you ladies later," I said, heading for the door. I expected Runt to follow me as she usually did, but the pup was out cold, her back rising and falling gently as she slept. I didn't have the heart to get her up; she was still little and needed her sleep to grow properly, so I left her where she was, softly snoring away.

Morrigan glared at me as I walked past her—boy, was I persona non grata around here or what?—and Caoimhe kept her eyes fixed on her lap, ignoring my exit as she recovered from her angry outburst. My dislike of Morrigan wasn't as strong as my disgust for Yum Cimil, but it was close. At least she was openly hostile, letting me know exactly where I stood with her. Yum Cimil never said a goddamned word, which was, somehow, even worse.

I closed the drawing room door, leaving the insistent sound of Freezay's questioning behind me, and took off in search of the kitchen. Zinia hadn't had the patience to wait for me, so I found myself adrift in the semidarkness of the corridor. Luckily the smell of buttery garlic and roasting chicken was enough of a sensory road map to get me where I needed to go. I followed the umami tang of sautéing butter down two long hallways and through a small glass-enclosed atrium until I came to a large rectangular kitchen. Zinia Monroe stood in the middle of a sea of beige tile, a thin human figure pressed up against a Moroccan-tiled island, her hands lost inside a heavy, blue clay bowl full of dough.

"I'm making chicken and dumplings," she said, conscripting me into her culinary world without any further explanation. "Grab that pot holder and take the top off that pot."

I did as she asked, picking up a thick yellow potholder from the tile counter and walking over to the ginormous, 60-inch biscuit-colored Viking Range. Zinia followed behind me, the blue clay bowl in her arms, and while I held the top of the stainless steel stockpot aloft, she began to drop globules of fluffy dough into the boiling liquid.

"It's nice to have your help," she said, her words coming in a staccato burst like gunshot from a semiautomatic, "but I really wanted to get you alone."

I raised an eyebrow, but didn't say anything as she continued to lob dough balls into the slowly thickening liquid.

"I have what you're looking for."

She spoke so nonchalantly it took me a moment to understand what she was actually saying.

"Constance and I were friends . . . It's how she got the job here," Zinia continued, finishing up with the dumplings and gesturing for me to put the top back on the stockpot.

"We had a plan. Then we hit a snafu and now I don't really know what to do."

Zinia set the mixing bowl in the porcelain double sink to soak, then pumped some almond-scented liquid soap into her hands, washing the remains of the dough from her skin.

"Aren't you going to ask me why? What the impetus was for us doing this?" Zinia asked as the hot water sluiced over her hands.

"Okay," I said, not sure what the correct response was in this situation. "Why'd you do it?"

Zinia picked up a dishtowel and dried her hands, turning back around to look at me.

"It's a long story. I'll tell you, if you'd like," she said, putting her hands on her hips and daring me to say no. "Then we can figure out a way to get the book back to you."

"Uhm, it's nice of you to want to give me back the book you stole—" I started to say, but Zinia cut me off.

"Oh, I'm not *giving* it to you," she said matter-of-factly, her eyes magnified by the chunky black frames she wore. "It's a trade."

"A trade?" I asked, beginning to worry where all of this was leading.

She nodded, fixing me with an unreadable stare—one that only made me more nervous about what I was getting myself into.

"I'll return the book to you," she said, "if you return Frank to me."

twenty-one

Frank.

I wondered how one name could bring up such mixed emotions inside me.

When the Devil and my sister had planned their hostile take-over of Purgatory and Death, Inc., they weren't privy to the fact that my old boss, Hyacinth, and her devious Japanese Water God partner, Watatsumi, were parasitizing them. Their intent: to steal Purgatory for themselves—and Frank had been their secret weapon.

Along with Daniel and me, Frank had been one of three possible Death-in-Waitings that could legitimately take control of Death, Inc., and Purgatory if my dad had stepped down from the job or been killed. Unbeknownst to us, Hyacinth and Watatsumi had plucked Frank out of human obscurity and brought him into their fold, keeping his existence a secret. Daniel and I had thought we were the only two possibles competing for the job, so when Frank appeared on the scene, it was a total shock.

While the Devil and my sister did all the heavy lifting, phys-ically hijacking Death, Inc., and doing battle against the com-bined forces of Purgatory and Heaven, Hyacinth and Watatsumi sat biding their time, waiting until just the right moment—

when all the Devil's forces were engaged dealing with my Harvesters and Transporters down in Hell—to break into Purgatory and try to kill me, thus installing Frank as the new President and CEO of Death, Inc., so that through him they could control Death for their own selfish purposes.

Needless to say, we foiled their plans, but I still felt a lot of righteous anger toward the guy (Frank) who'd helped destroy my family and ruin the best and only relationship I'd ever had. Though he wasn't even the worst of the offenders, he'd willingly gone along with the bad guys, using his access to me in order to further their agenda. Oh, he was also the dude who'd finger-banged me in the New York City Subway station—and that one act had ended my relationship with Daniel.

"And why do you want Frank so badly?" I asked Zinia as she stared at me over the tops of her glasses.

The kitchen smelled amazing, the chicken and dumplings simmering over the stove, but it was tainted for me now that Zinia had brought the ghost of Frank into the room.

"You wouldn't understand," she said, dropping her hands to her sides. "I know you think he's a bad boy, but I've known him his whole life. That horrible little man, Watatsumi, and his Valkyrie bitch cohort—may she rot in Purgatory forever—took advantage of him."

I kept my indignation in check, holding on to it to use later as fuel for my righteous anger, but I knew lashing out at her right now would only cut off my nose to spite my face. Besides, there was a little truth to what she was saying about Frank. He *had* been manipulated by Hyacinth and Watatsumi—and even the Devil and my sister—but that didn't excuse his behavior; he'd made his choice and now he was languishing in Purgatorial prison, paying for his participation in the crime. I didn't feel sorry for him, but I understood where Zinia was coming from.

"You give me the book, and in return I get Frank released from Purgatorial prison," I said, repeating the demand just to be sure I had it right.

Zinia nodded, relaxing now she realized I was seriously considering her offer.

"I don't know why that book is so important to you, but

Constance said it was the best bargaining chip we could have," Zinia said, using an index finger to push her glasses farther up the bridge of her nose. "It's why I sold my restaurant and took this job."

Zinia was in over her head. She'd done something she thought was right, but now that there was all this fallout—and death—she wasn't quite sure how to proceed. If Constance hadn't been killed, I'd have been having this conversation with her instead and it would have gone *very* differently. She would've had the upper hand because she knew exactly what the book was for and why I needed it so badly. Zinia was a different kettle of fish entirely. She wanted me to walk her through this, help her to figure out why things had gone so wonky, and in the end, get Frank released and make everything okay again.

"Maybe if you explain to me how this all happened, we can figure out a way to get us both what we want," I said, my gaze flicking around the kitchen, checking to make sure no one was spying on us.

Zinia nodded, happily letting me guide the thrust of the conversation.

"How did Constance know Frank?"

I liked that the kitchen was the warmest place in the house, the gas stove adding a welcome toastiness to the atmosphere, but Zinia was starting to look a bit overheated, the apples of her cheeks an unnatural pink, so I eschewed comfort for fresh air and opened one of the double-hung windows.

"Thank you," she said, pushing a tuft of blond hair out of her face. "I do feel a little peaked."

"So, tell me how Constance knew Frank?" I prodded, curious as to what her story was going to reveal.

She nodded, leaning back against the tiled island.

"I should probably start with me and then move on from there," she began, wiping the sweat from her upper lip. "Most people don't know this, but I had a son. I knew he was *different*, special even, from the very first moment I held him in my arms. And as he grew up, I was proved right."

She paused, frowning.

"Would you like a glass of water? I'm parched."

"Sure," I said, waiting as Zinia got two glasses from one of the oak cabinets and set them down on the island. She retrieved a pitcher of water from the refrigerator and filled the two glasses, each one breaking out in an opaque sweat.

She handed me mine then downed hers, refilling it again immediately.

"I don't know why I'm so thirsty," she said softly, more to herself than to me. "I think it's nerves. Where was I? Oh, yes, my son had an aptitude for magic—not the kind of magic people like you do, but the traditional kind: pulling rabbits out of a hat, sawing beautiful women in half, disappearing from locked boxes. He was an amazing performer, a joy to watch and so gifted."

Zinia paused to down more water, her face still that unnatural shade of pink.

"When my son was nine, I took a position as the personal chef to the world famous aerialist, Alina Petrovosko," she continued. "She was close to retiring, and this was to be her last tour across America. It was a phenomenal experience for Harry— that was my son's name—and he was never happier than that year we spent with Alina. She was lovely, as were the rest of the performers, taking Harry under their wing and encouraging him to work on his act. It was magical."

"What happened to him?" I asked—though I already knew Zinia's story wasn't going to have a happy ending.

"Harry met another boy, the son of a horse trainer, who was a little younger than him and they quickly became inseparable. There were other children traveling with the circus, performers' children, but Harry and his friend, Frank, were too busy with their magic act to notice."

Zinia took another gulp of water, a little of the wetness streaking down her chin.

"A number of the smaller children traveling with us caught chicken pox while we were in Des Moines. Harry had had it the previous summer, so he was one of the few who didn't get sick."

She paused, collecting her thoughts.

"No one knows what happened that night. When he didn't come back to the trailer for dinner, I got worried. I knew I was probably just being overprotective, but he was my only child, so I got security and we searched the encampment. Nothing. He'd disappeared. They found him the next day in one of the big cat cages. A place he knew never to venture by himself—"

"But what about Frank?" I asked, worried she was going to say he was somehow responsible.

Zinia shook her head.

"Sick as a dog with chicken pox. I often wonder had he been with Harry that night if all the horror would've been avoided."

"Did Frank know what your son was up to?"

"He said that Harry wanted to talk to the big cats like he could," Zinia answered. "Of course, I thought it was a joke, that these conversations he was referring to were imaginary . . . It was only later, much later, that I understood what Frank's true nature was. I had no idea he could work magic, not the pretend tricks that Harry did, but the real thing."

"So he was the only link you had to your son," I said and Zinia nodded, her eyes wet.

"We stayed in touch over the years. When he was fourteen, his father died and I offered him a room at my house," she said, "but Frank chose to stay with the circus. He was very dear, calling me every year on Harry's birthday, and I would see him whenever he came through town. He was my second son—one I didn't give birth to, but that I loved as much as if I had."

"And Constance?"

"She was part of the Purgatorial Review Board that oversaw Frank's case," Zinia said. "It's an old story. A lonely young woman meets a man, falls in love with him just as she comes to believe he is wrongly convicted of a crime—"

"He wasn't wrongly convicted," I interjected, but Zinia held up a hand.

"It doesn't matter what you believe. She loved Frank and would've done anything for him. She came up with the plan and found me," Zinia said. "Explained the supernatural world, that it existed and the part that Frank played in it . . . Then she told me what had happened to him. It made so many things clear to me: the conversations he'd claimed to have had with the big cats, for one thing, and a lot of other little pieces of oddness I'd gleaned about him over the years."

"Where is the book, Zinia?" I said. "Someone killed Constance for it and I'm really scared they're going to come look-ing for you next."

"It doesn't matter what happens to me," Zinia said, swal-lowing hard, her eyes red. "You have to promise me that you'll help Frank. I'll do anything you want if you'll just help him."

I didn't know how I was going to do it, but if freeing Frank meant getting the book back, I was sure Jarvis and I could come up with something—a work release program maybe?

"All right," I said, letting out the breath I hadn't even real-ized I'd been holding. "I'll help him."

Zinia grabbed my hands, her papery thin skin hot to the touch.

"Thank you, thank you, thank you," she said, kissing both of my cheeks as a line of salty tears ran down her face. "You have a good heart."

"Not always," I said, but her happiness was infectious and I smiled. "But this time, yes."

"I have to get you the book," she said, remembering she had half of a bargain to fulfill. "It's not here, but I have it, hidden away. Will you meet me by the obelisk in the Assyrian Gardens in ten minutes? It's just past the pool. I'll go straight there."

"Of course," I said, watching as she scurried over to the walk-in freezer on the far side of the room and slid open the door.

Surprised, I watched as she stepped inside it, cold air waft-ing around her.

"Now don't forget! The Assyrian Gardens in ten minutes," she called back to me before sliding the door closed behind her.

She didn't have to say it twice. I wouldn't have missed our assignation for anything in the world.

Intrigued by her odd disappearing act, I counted to ten, then walked over to the freezer and slowly worked the door open, trying to be subtle about my entrance. The cold air hit me like a brick wall, my breath turning to steam as my body tempera-ture dropped five degrees.

"It's freeeezing," I said under my breath, my whole body shivering as I stepped farther into the freezer.

I looked around expecting to find Zinia somewhere inside, but the freezer was empty of life. A few sides of pork hung from the ceiling, but that was the closest approximation to a living creature I could find. The rest of the space was taken up with bags of frozen vegetables and assorted other food items. I searched the inside, looking for another exit, but there was nothing. All three walls were made of smooth, unbroken metal—no hidden doorways anywhere in sight. Frustrated, I left the frozen wasteland and returned to the kitchen.

Where had Zinia gone? I wondered, and then my brain began to hum as a newly born hypothesis began to take shape.

I debated going back to the drawing room to tell Freezay what I'd learned, but the few minutes I'd lost when I'd searched the freezer made it impossible for me to get there, impart the information, and get back to the Assyrian Gardens in time to meet Zinia. I was just going to have to wing it and hope nothing happened to screw up the exchange or else I would have both Jarvis *and* Freezay breathing down my neck.

The kitchen had two entrances: one that led to the interior of the building and one that went outside. I'd taken the former to get to the kitchen, but the latter was going to be the easiest way to get out of the building unnoticed. Before I left, I made an executive decision, turning off the burner beneath the stockpot. I just didn't think leaving food simmering away on a stove with no one watching it was a very a good idea. I knew Zinia was a world-class chef, but she'd been so emotional when she'd left that I didn't think she'd notice if the whole house burned down around her.

I unlocked the oversized door leading to the outside world and pushed it open. The sun was hiding behind a cloud and it was starting to get chilly again, giving me a good indication of how cold it was going to be when the sun finally went down for the night. Unused to the warm California weather, I'd almost forgotten it was autumn and that Halloween was upon us, but the blast of Arctic air was a good reminder.

To my pleasant surprise, I found an empty golf cart sitting just outside the door, the key dangling in the ignition. I looked around, but I saw no one, so I climbed inside. I turned the key, taking the pink rabbit's foot keychain as a sign good luck was in my future, and smiled as the cart roared to life.

Though the weather wasn't what I was used to for this time of year, I could still taste the smoky scent of October in the air as I drove along the pathway that led to the pool. With the wind in my hair, I felt free for the first time in ages and I was hit by the intense urge to chuck all the Death stuff and just find myself a pumpkin patch to go roll around in. There was just something about the autumnal season that made me happy. I could waste away a whole afternoon traipsing through the golden brown of a ripened field, eating a freshly grilled ear of corn as I searched for the perfect jack-o'-lantern-in-waiting. Too bad I wasn't going to get to enjoy Halloween this year. There would be no parties, no trick-or-treaters, no scary movies to get your blood boiling with fear—instead I was going to be helping Edgar Freezay search for a murderer. And as spooky as that sounded, I wasn't really loving the reality-show version of *Clue* I was stuck in, that was for sure.

When I got to the pool, the location of my now-infamous croissant attack, I eased on the brake, hoping the Assyrian Gardens would just present themselves to me. Fat chance of that—wherever I looked, all I saw was Greek and Roman statuary; nothing my eye alighted on was Assyrian.

"Assyrian Gardens anyone?" I said, though I hardly expected a response from the giant Greek statues encircling the circumference of the pool.

It appeared as if I'd taken the cart as far as it could go. The path got smaller when you went past the pool, so abandoning my little battery-powered friend, I got out and followed the curve of the cement pool basin, my sneakers slapping against the concrete edge. Scanning the surrounding area, I was on the lookout for anything that seemed in the least bit Assyrian—and then I saw it, nestled in between the legs of an armless marble Apollo. No, I'm not talking about what you *think* I'm talking about—what I saw through Apollo's legs was the entrance to the Assyrian Gardens.

Cutting through the ring of statues, I followed the path until I'd made my way over to Apollo. Pushing through the foliage that surrounded the statuary, I found myself standing at the top of a short flight of marble stairs. At the bottom was a twisted terra-cotta path that took me right into the heart of the gardens.

Taking the stairs two at a time, I jogged down the path. Demarcating one epoch from the other (Greek from Assyrian, in this case) was a small reflecting pool sitting in the middle of a wide-open space, a primitive-looking obelisk resting on a platform above it. The obelisk showed a frieze of a man sitting astride a horse, his face in profile. It was so unmistakably *not* Greek that I knew immediately I'd found what I was looking for.

"Zinia?" I whispered as I sat down on the edge of the blue slate-tiled reflecting pool.

I got no response, so I tried again, a little louder.

"Zinia?!"

I heard the crunch of shoes on the path and turned around to find Zinia coming toward me, a beatific look on her face. She was carrying a small metal box—and I remembered what Minnie had said about human beings handling the book. Constance had taken precautions, using a lead box to make the book transportable by human hands.

"I have your book!" Zinia called out to me, picking up speed the closer she got. "It's right here in the—"

A shot rang out from somewhere behind me, and instinctively I dropped to the ground—Zinia still too far away for me to help her.

"Get down!" I yelled at her as another shot rang out nearby.

She tried to turn and run back to the main house, but she was frazzled and didn't see the upraised piece of tile in the middle of the path. Tripping over it, she pitched forward and the box flew from her hands.

"Oh, no!" she cried as the box hit the ground, the lid popping open and the book cartwheeling out onto the ground.

It was then, as she crawled along the path, her hand only inches from the exposed book, that I understood what was about to happen next and my mind reeled with horror.

"Don't touch it!" I screamed at Zinia—but she either didn't hear me or didn't trust what I was saying.

Too late . . . her fingers had made contact with the book's cover for the first and only time.

"Oh . . . God," she gurgled, retching the contents of her stomach onto the ground—and then, as I watched with disbelieving eyes, *her entire body spontaneously combusted.*

As soon as the melting began, she let out a horrific wail—like the sound of a thousand kittens mewling as their hearts were ripped out of their bodies. I covered my ears to block out the piteous sound, but that still left my eyes free to bear witness. I stared, unwilling to tear my gaze away, as the skin of her face turned putrid and liquefied off the bone, her poofy blond hair igniting into tongues of orangy-blue flame that turned its tendrils into a sooty, charred black that then disintegrated into ash and blew away on the breeze. Through it all, her eyeballs remained intact, their irises fixed on me, imploring me to do something to help her, but my powers were moot. I could do nothing to save her, nor was I able to put a quick end to her suffering.

Still, I could try and comfort her. Lifting myself off the ground, I crawled to my feet and started to cross the divide that lay between us.

"Get down!" a voice screamed as another shot reverberated through the air, and suddenly I felt the weight of another body slamming into me, wrestling me to the terra-cotta-tiled pathway.

"Get off me!" I yelled as I tried to fight my way free.

"It's me, Cal," Daniel breathed into my ear, his body pressing tightly against mine as he fought to keep me on the ground.

When I realized who it was, I stopped squirming, but my heart continued to beat in frantic bursts.

"We have to help Zinia," I cried.

"I don't think there's anything we can do for her," Daniel started to say.

"I don't care," I said, trying to push him off me so I could go to her on my own.

"Wait, just stop it," Daniel hissed. "I'll go with you."

I relaxed.

"Just do what I tell you," he said and then he motioned for me to follow him as he began to slither across the terra-cotta on his belly.

It only took us a minute to reach Zinia's prone body, but it was already too late. Her suffering was over. The body that had once housed her soul was now a charred mess.

"Oh, God," I said, hot tears flooding my eyes. "She was innocent, Daniel. She was just trying to help someone she loved . . ."

As I began to cry in earnest, Daniel enfolded me in his arms, pulling me tightly to his chest as we lay on the ground.

"It's okay, Cal," he whispered, his lips brushing my cheek. "It's okay now. You're safe with me."

"It's my fault," I said. "I should've protected her."

"It's not your fault," Daniel said, squeezing me tighter. "It's just not."

Suddenly, I felt his whole body tense as he saw something in the foliage behind me.

"What?" I asked.

He shook his head.

"Stay here, I'll be right back."

And then he was off and running, chasing after whatever had sparked his interest. I rested my chin on the ground as I lay there, alone, forcing my lungs to move the air in and out of my chest. I tried not to cry as I fought back the guilt threatening to overwhelm me.

It's okay. You're safe with me.

Daniel's words reverberated in my head as I closed my eyes—the pain and joy inside me so intertwined, they were almost the same feeling.

twenty-two

Daniel had still not returned as the sun began to wane, the afternoon slowly giving way to evening. It was probably for the best since he wouldn't have condoned what I was about to do. I let my hands hover just above Zinia's charred form, then closed my eyes and directed all of my energy into one conscious thought:

Be alive again.

But it was useless—just as I'd known it would be. There was no magic inside me, no ability to use my powers to rip her out of Death.

There's nothing I can do for you, I thought miserably.

Bringing someone back from the dead was never an advisable endeavor. I'd only done it once—and that had been by accident. Jarvis was living proof of what strange things could happen when you wished someone alive again: He'd been a faun before I'd gotten my Death hands all over him, and now, after my meddling, he was stuck in the twentysomething body of a five-boroughs hipster. I couldn't say it wasn't an improvement physically—although I did miss his flashy Tom Selleck mustache—but he was alive and kicking and that was all that counted.

For Zinia, it wasn't even an option.

"Cal?" I looked up to find Daniel standing above me. He was out of breath from running, his hand cradling his left side.

"Don't worry. It's just a stitch," he said when he saw my face, dropping his arm so I could see he was unharmed. "I couldn't catch him, the bastard."

"It was a him?" I asked.

"A very specific him," Daniel said. "He was moving fast, but it was definitely Oggie. I didn't see a gun, though."

"Oggie?" I said, shocked. The Vice-President in Charge of Africa was the last person I would've suspected of attempting to commit murder. "Are you sure?"

"As much as I hate to say it, I'm pretty damn positive," he said, shaking his head. "If he had nothing to do with it, why did he run? It only makes him look guilty."

I sat there on the ground beside Zinia's body, wondering what could make someone do something so horrible. What did Oggie have to gain by killing Coy, Constance, and now Zinia? If he was interested in bringing about the destruction of the human world, well, getting his hands on the book was one way to get the ball rolling, but something felt wrong about that hypothesis. Not that I was the greatest judge of character. I'd been wrong about people before and had paid dearly for my naïveté. This was probably just another episode of *Calliope Reaper-Jones: Pollyanna at Large*—

Shit, the book! I thought.

In the fallout after Zinia's death, I'd totally forgotten about it. I had to find that book before . . . I didn't know before *what*, but I needed to find it.

"Where's the book?" I said, climbing to my feet, tension filling my body. I felt the tendrils of hysteria beginning to grip my heart, but I beat them back into submission. Now was *not* the time to start freaking out.

"Oh, Jesus, the book is what did this to her?" Daniel said, looking down at Zinia's body.

I nodded. Together we searched the area around the body, but to my chagrin, both the metal box and the book it had contained were nowhere to be found.

"It's gone," I murmured as I sat down on the tile, my body starting to tremble from exhaustion and shock. "Someone took it . . ."

"Jesus," Daniel said, sitting down next to me. "What're you going to do?"

"I don't know," I said, leaning forward so I could rest my elbows on my knees, cupping my chin between my hands. "I just don't know. The book's gone and three people are dead. I thought I was getting better at this whole Death thing, but if this is any indication . . ."

Daniel took my hand.

"You're doing a good job—murders notwithstanding—and you shouldn't second-guess yourself."

His words were nice, but they were just words. They didn't make me feel any better.

"Let's go get Freezay," I said, pulling my hand out of Daniel's grasp. "Maybe he can make some sense out of all of this."

freezay had not been a happy camper when we'd found him. The look of pure disappointment on his face when I'd told him what had happened was enough to make me want to go drown myself in the pool. He'd insisted on going to see the body immediately, ignoring my repeated apologies all along the way.

Now, as he knelt down beside what remained of Zinia, it seemed as if his anger had transferred from me to whoever had stolen the book.

"Do you smell that?" Freezay said, crouching down so that his nose was almost touching the pool of vomit Zinia had loosed right before she melted.

Daniel shook his head, but Runt nodded.

"Smells like garlic," she said.

"She was cooking with it, I think," I said, having a hard time dragging my eyes away from the body.

Freezay opened his mouth as if he was going to say something, but then shut it again.

"Freezay?" Daniel asked, but the detective just shook his head.

"All right," Freezay said. "Enough chitchat. Let's go find Oggie and get him to explain his rationale for running away from a crime scene."

"What about Zinia?" I asked, not wanting to leave her body on its own in the middle of the garden. "Maybe we could at least get a sheet to cover her with?"

Dusk was upon us now, the light disappearing faster and faster with each passing second. Pretty soon, we were going to be having this conversation in the dark.

"Here," Daniel said, taking off the light linen jacket he was wearing and draping it across Zinia's torso. "Is that all right?"

I nodded. Pleased that at least one of the corpses was being treated humanely.

"Thank you," I said as we followed Freezay back down the pathway to Casa del Amo.

"Of course," he said, then he reached out and took my hand in his. I squeezed his fingers, letting him know—without uttering a word—how much I'd missed him.

While we were canoodling, Freezay had picked up the pace so that now he and Runt were almost two body lengths ahead of us.

"Anyone had eyes on Jarvis recently?" he called back to us.

"I saw him over by Casa de la Luna earlier," Daniel said.

"What were you doing there?" I asked, my voice low enough that only Daniel heard my question.

"I was looking out for you."

"Oh," I said, very much liking the feel of his fingers laced through mine.

"You have a habit of getting into trouble," Daniel added, his ice blue eyes searching my face as he spoke. "I didn't want anything to happen to you."

Not sure what to say in response, I ducked my head, letting my eyes drift to the ground as I tried to collect my thoughts. I didn't want—no, scratch that—I *couldn't* get my hopes up where Daniel was concerned. If he didn't want to be with me, *really be with me*, then opening myself up to him was a huge mistake. I was going to get my heart trampled on if I mistook him being nice to me as him wanting to be in a relationship again.

Still, I couldn't make myself drop his hand . . . and that meant I was already screwed.

"Runt, can you run ahead and find Jarvis?" Freezay said, interrupting my thoughts. "Tell him to meet us in the drawing room."

"Sure thing," Runt said, taking off down the path, a shadowy blur passing through the twilight.

"Daniel, you and I are going to drop Calliope off at the drawing room and then we're going to find Oggie."

"Why are you dropping me off at the drawing room?" I bristled, not liking any plan that called for me being coddled.

"You can't cause any trouble there," Freezay said brusquely, treating me as if I were a recalcitrant child.

"It's safer there, Cal," Daniel added as we took the long way around the pool, the marble statues looking strangely evil in the gloaming.

"I'm not a child," I said, dropping Daniel's hand and striding ahead of him—and then Freezay—as I let anger fuel my speed. My frustration at being treated like a baby made me oblivious to everything around me, and I slammed right into Oggie without even seeing him, the impact strong enough that it sent us both sprawling.

I fell backward, my head cracking against the edge of a marble pedestal that boasted a statue of the Goddess Athena. My vision tunneled, and for a moment I thought I was going to black out, but then the world slowly shifted back into focus with a startling clarity that made me blink twice. I reached up to make sure I wasn't missing a chunk of my skull, but everything seemed to be exactly where it was supposed to be.

"I'm sorry," I said as I sat up, wincing as I felt the beginnings of a massive headache stirring inside my cranium. "I wasn't looking where I was—"

And that was when I realized who I'd just power-walked myself into. Without saying another word, I threw myself forward, wrapping my arms around his legs so he couldn't escape.

"Let me go!" Oggie cried.

"Not a chance," I said through gritted teeth as he fought to pry me off him.

It only took a second for Daniel and Freezay to catch up to us. They each secured one of Oggie's arms, trying to drag him to his feet, though he continued to flop around like a fish on a line, impeding the process.

"Please, Madame Death, won't you let me explain myself?" Oggie cried, his dark eyes boring into mine. He looked so pathetic hanging there that I started to feel bad about letting Daniel and Freezay manhandle him.

"Go ahead, explain," I said—but I was glad when the guys

didn't release him. I wasn't fully satisfied that he wouldn't run away again given half a chance.

"I didn't kill anyone," he began, his sclera so exposed that his eyes looked ready to pop out of his skull. "I was on my way to meet someone when I heard the shots."

"Who were you meeting?" Freezay asked, shaking Oggie like a rag doll.

"Uriah Drood," he said, letting the name drop like a stone. "I'm sure he's responsible for what happened to the cook."

There was so much finger-pointing going on at the Haunted Hearts Castle, it was beginning to feel like Washington, D.C., had been transplanted to the Central Coast of California.

"Okay, let's go have ourselves a little chat," Freezay said— and bowler hat askew on his towhead, he and Daniel dragged Oggie back to the house.

the drawing room was full of people when we arrived.

Alameda stood by the fireplace, the rigid set of her shoulders clueing me in that something had happened in our absence. Naapi sat across from her on the love seat—a sour look on his face, like he'd just swallowed something exceedingly unpalatable.

Erlik sat in a nearby armchair, glowering over at Yum Cimil and Fabian Lazarev, who stood by the sideboard with an open bottle of bourbon between them as Lazarev made drinks.

"What the . . ." Erlik said as we crossed the threshold, Freezay and Daniel dragging their prisoner behind them—but the large man immediately got up to help Daniel and Freezay settle Oggie into one of the other armchairs.

"Zinia Monroe's been murdered," Freezay intoned, giving everyone in the room the stink eye. "Oggie, here, fled the scene of the crime, so it doesn't look very good for him—"

"No!" Alameda shrieked as she crossed the room and threw herself at Oggie's feet. "He murdered no one!"

"It's all right, my dear," Oggie whispered, stroking Alameda's hair as she wrapped her arms around his waist.

"Stop it!" Naapi cried, pulling himself up off the love seat and crossing the room.

Eyes wild, he grabbed Alameda by the shoulders and ripped her away from Oggie, lifting her bodily in the air by her collar. Oggie didn't take too kindly to Naapi's rude behavior.

"Leave her alone," he said, his voice as calm as a cobra right before it struck.

"She's my consort and you'd best remember it," Naapi spat at him, Alameda wriggling like a cat in his arms.

"I warned you," Oggie said—and then he was on his feet, his fist connecting with the soft tissue under Naapi's chin. The older man wasn't prepared for the attack, immediately releasing his hold on Alameda to clutch at his injured throat. Dazed, he stumbled over to the fireplace and leaned against the mantel for support.

"Don't ever touch me again," Alameda said to Naapi as she scampered back into Oggie's arms.

It was a rough thing to watch play out—an old God losing his woman to a younger, more able-bodied man—but it wasn't really a shocker. Evidently we'd missed the big reveal while we'd been outside with Zinia's body, and I was curious to know how long the affair had been going on and how long it would've continued had Naapi never discovered it.

"Oggie didn't murder anyone," Fabian Lazarev said, turning around so he could glare at me. It was nice to know he'd concretized all his anger and aggression around me.

"Then why did he run away from the crime scene?" Freezay asked.

"He probably assumed you were going to wrongfully accuse him of the crime, so he tried to make himself scarce," Lazarev said, scowling at the detective. "I would've done the same thing. You people are useless. Ineffectual and worthless."

Freezay shook away Lazarev's invective like water off a duck's back.

"Where were the rest of you?" he asked, moving ahead with the investigation.

"Erlik, Naapi, Alameda," Lazarev said, ticking the names off in rapid fire succession. "And myself and Yum Cimil, of course, were in the living room."

"It pains me to say it, but Fabian's right," Erlik said, returning to his spot on the love seat. "We've all been together, thinking there was safety in numbers."

"I have nothing to hide," Oggie said. "I told you exactly why I was there."

"Nothing to hide?" Naapi said as he turned around and pointed at Oggie, his voice scratchy as his whole body shook with rage. "You've just been fucking her behind my back, that's all. But you're right. Nothing to hide there."

"I love him and he loves me," Alameda cried, tearing herself away from Oggie to glare at Naapi.

"Uriah Drood knew about our affair," Oggie said to Freezay—and he had the class to look apologetic about it. "I assumed he was going to try to blackmail me when he asked me to meet him at the Assyrian Obelisk, but he didn't have the chance. When I got there, I heard the shots and fled, fearing for my life."

Well, at least that answers the question as to who Alameda was kissing in the statuary garden last night, I thought as I glanced over at Daniel, knowing that he was thinking the exact same thing.

"Blackmail you?" Naapi laughed. "With what? He came to my room this afternoon and told me everything."

Before Freezay could get into the middle of the *he said–he said* argument, there was a loud crash out in the corridor, followed by frantic barking. Instantly, Freezay and Daniel were moving toward the open door.

"I'm going to beat you silly for this!" I heard Kali yell—and then Horace flew headfirst through the doorway, landing hard, his face two inches from Freezay's feet.

"There's no need for continued violence!" I heard Jarvis say as he and Runt burst in, hot on Kali's heels.

"No need for violence?" she snarled at Jarvis as she grabbed Horace by the chin and lifted him back onto his feet, her eyes never leaving the smaller man's face. "This piece of nonhuman trash is the reason I still smell like skunk stink."

"I understand that," Jarvis said, trying to calm the irate Goddess down. "But hitting him won't make the smell go away."

Kali turned her head, scowling at Jarvis.

"Really, goatboy, that's the best you can do?" She turned to me. "White girl, is that the best he can do? Because what he said just makes me want to hit this guy more."

I walked over to Kali and put a hand on her shoulder.

"Jarvis is right. Let's hear what Horace has to say, and if he can't explain himself about the skunk stink, then you can punch the crap out of him—and guess what? I'll even hold him down for you."

This seemed to appease her and she relaxed her grip, letting Horace go. He backed away from her, his dark eyes amused rather than angry—which made me wonder if we didn't have this whole thing backward. I knew Kali was tough—I'd literally watched her rip people's heads off their necks—but I got the distinct impression Horace had *wanted* Kali to bring him here.

Thankfully, Freezay chose that moment to step in.

He pointed to Oggie and said: "I'm not through with you yet." Then he turned his attention to Horace.

"Skunk spray aside," Freezay said, sitting down on the edge of the love seat. "I have another question I'd like to ask you first."

"You want to ask me why I killed my sister," Horace said softly.

And then he smiled with anticipation, as if he was very much looking forward to what was about to come.

twenty-three

Horace laughed, the sound swelling as it left his belly until it had taken over every molecule of air in the room.

"His sister?" Erlik barked, rising from the love seat. "Who's his sister?"

Lazarev's mouth dropped open and he stared at Horace, understanding dawning on his face.

"Of course," he said, setting his drink down on the sideboard and walking over to Horace. "How could I have not seen it before . . ."

Lazarev trailed off, his voice full of wonderment as he reached out a hand to touch Horace's face.

"I wouldn't be too excited to meet Horace . . . or should I call you Huitzilopochtli?" Freezay asked Horace. "You came to the Death Dinner with every intention of killing Coy, didn't you?"

The gleam of satisfaction in Horace's eye made Lazarev blink in confusion, his excitement dissipating as Freezay's words hit home—and then, without warning, he was on the attack, shoving Horace as hard as he could.

"Why'd you kill her, you bastard!" Lazarev screamed, his hands clawing at Horace's face, trying to rip the other man's eyes out with grasping fingers.

Like he was batting away a fly, Horace reached out and

grabbed Lazarev's bad wrist, twisting it until the Russian screamed. At that point, Daniel and Erlik descended on Lazarev, each grabbing an arm and pulling him away. Lazarev, enraged and in pain, kicked at his captors, alternately screaming obscenities at them and then begging them to let him go so he could kill Horace.

"Please, let me go, let me kill him—"

"Enough!" Freezay yelled, grabbing Lazarev by the collar of his shirt. "Behaving like a lunatic won't bring her back!"

Freezay's words were as about as effective as chipping away at Mount Everest with a ball-peen hammer. Lazarev continued to struggle against his captors, his face mottled with rage.

"Why?" Lazarev spat, the cords of his neck in bas-relief against the smoothness of his throat.

"I didn't kill her," Horace said as he walked over to the fireplace, which was as far away from Lazarev as he could get.

"I don't believe you!" Lazarev shrieked, fighting to break free from Daniel and Erlik so he could attack Horace again.

"Detective," Horace said, appealing to Freezay. "I think you know as well as I do that had I been given the chance, I would've beheaded Coyolxauhqui myself. But alas, someone beat me to it."

Everyone looked at Freezay, waiting for his response.

"Go on," Feezay said, raising an eyebrow.

"Someone has gone to great lengths to make it appear as if these killings were based on Aztec ritual," Horace continued. "Do you really believe I would be so stupid as to implicate myself in such an obvious way?"

"No, I don't, actually," Freezay said. "It would be a real lapse in logic on your part, one I just don't see you making."

"My sister came here to steal the Death book," Horace continued, his gaze lingering on me as he spoke, to the point where I started to feel slightly uncomfortable. "She was under the impression she could use it to call back the spirits of our four hundred dead brothers and sisters, whom I had killed, when, at Coyolxauhqui's behest, they attacked our mother, Coatlicue. They were embarrassed by the circumstances of my inception and Coyolxauhqui incited them to violence. She, alone, escaped the massacre and has been plotting revenge against me ever since."

"The Death book?" Naapi asked, confused. "What's he talking about?"

Jarvis, who was still standing in the doorway, beat me to the punch.

"Someone took the fully annotated copy of *How to Be Death* from Calliope's room last night."

I decided a change in subject was necessary or we were gonna be adding mutiny to the steadily growing list of crimes on this ship.

"You said the murders were *made* to look like Aztec sacrificial killings," I said to Horace. "How can you tell that they're not?"

Horace considered my question for a moment.

"The heart."

"The heart?" I repeated.

Horace indicated that I should join him at the fireplace. I didn't move until I'd gotten the okay from Freezay, who nodded. Apparently he was all for letting Horace have his way.

"It's all right, Calliope," he said. "Horace has no beef with you."

I slowly crossed the room, coming to stand beside the powerful Aztec God, Huitzilopochtli—or Horace, as I'd called him when he was merely the dude who'd served me dinner.

"Look here," he said, picking up the wrought iron fireplace poker and thrusting it into the dying ashes.

At first, I didn't see what he was talking about, but as he sifted through the ashes, I noticed something dark and rubbery stuck inside the grate. I squatted down next to the hearth to get a better look at it.

"What the—" I started to say.

"Lots of fluid in the heart muscle," Horace said, softly, kneeling down beside me. "Makes it hard to burn. Besides, we Aztecs only set fire to the hearts of willing sacrificial victims. It's an honor for them—to have the energy from their souls released back to the sun."

He paused, reaching out and brushing his thumb along my cheek.

"We *eat* the hearts of our enemies, lovely lady."

Needless to say, Horace had made his point.

"I see," I said, unsettled, as I stood up too quickly, all the blood rushing to my head. "Thank you for the explanation."

"Ah, it was my pleasure to serve you," Horace replied, ignoring everyone else in the room as he reached out and took my hand, his lips grazing the swell of my knuckles. Then he whispered: "You might have a look at the freezer. It may prove helpful in finding the real murderer."

He moved to the exit but stopped at the door to give me one more meaningful look. I blushed as his dark, bedroom eyes swept callously over the curves of my body before returning to my face, his cunning gaze making me feel naked and vulnerable—something I didn't think was possible when you were wearing pajamas—and then he was gone, disappearing through the open doorway.

At Freezay's nod, Daniel and Erlik released Lazarev, who instantly shoved them away before striding across the room so he could get in Freezay's face.

"You just let him go?" Fabian Lazarev screamed, cradling his wrist against his chest. *"Are you insane?!"*

Not needing an answer, he took off after the Aztec god.

It was a fruitless endeavor; he was never going to get his hands on Horace, but Lazarev was so full of rage he was incapable of listening to reason. From what I'd just experienced, Horace was a force to be reckoned with—and I had serious doubts that Kali would've been able to capture him if he hadn't wanted all of us to see the burnt heart in the fireplace. Horace intended Freezay to know that someone else was responsible for his sister's murder. I had no doubts he would've slain Coy without hesitation had he been given the chance—it just appeared that he wasn't the kind of man to take credit for a thing he hadn't done himself.

"Now what are you going to do?" Erlik asked, speaking for the room. "You've let a prime suspect go free, which seems rather foolish, if you ask me—"

"There is a method to my madness, sir," Freezay said, interrupting him, a sly look playing across his rakish face. "I promise that all will be revealed in due time."

Erlik opened his mouth to say more, but Freezay cut him off:

"Now, if you'll excuse me. I have a freezer to inspect. Come along, Calliope, Runt."

"Coming," I said as I grabbed Kali's limp hand. I could tell she was peeved at me for letting Freezay release Horace without a fight, but after two tugs on her arm, she finally let me pull her along behind me.

"Damn, white girl," she said. "Don't yank my arm out of its socket."

We stopped in the doorway long enough to see Yum Cimil and Naapi descending on Jarvis and Daniel—and I felt bad leaving my poor Executive Assistant and my ex-boyfriend to deal with all the fallout.

"Let's just sit down and discuss this calmly," I could hear Jarvis saying as we stepped out into the hallway just in time to catch Freezay disappearing down the hallway.

"I know how you got skunked," I said as Kali and I fast-walked toward the kitchen.

Someone, probably Freezay, had been kind enough to hit the lights so that we weren't walking in total darkness, but the iridescent lighting gave the portraits on the walls a pretty eerie vibe.

"Oh, do you now, dipwad?" she said, narrowing her eyes and daring me to answer.

"Yup. You were spying on Horace. You recognized both him and Coy, so you were sneaking all over the Castle trying to see what they were up to."

"You think you're *so* smart, don't you, white girl?" She scowled at me.

"Uh-huh," I said, my voice a stage whisper. "I *do* think I am so smart. So, what did you see?"

"What makes you think I'm gonna tell you anything?"

"Fine," I replied. "Don't tell me. See if I care."

We reached the end of the twisting hallway, the bright lights from the kitchen beckoning us forward, but Kali suddenly grabbed my arm, stopping me in my tracks.

"Wait," she said, adjusting the folds of her sari where it tucked in at her hip—she'd obviously had time to change in between spying sessions, I noticed.

For the first time since the craziness had started, I found myself wondering what Kali had done with my dress. It was an odd thought to have right at that moment, but once it was in my head, I couldn't help but be curious if she'd hung the dress up so it wouldn't get too wrinkled.

"Uhm, you didn't happen to hang my dress up, did you?" I asked, unable to help myself.

Kali gave me a long, incredulous look.

"Think back to the Death Dinner, white girl," she said, deciding to just avoid my question. "You remember when Coy freaked out, yes?"

I nodded.

"She was upset—"

"Yes, she was upset," Kali said, interrupting me. "Because she saw her brother. It was the first time she realized he was here and on to her plan."

"Okay," I said, "but that doesn't tell us who killed her."

Kali pursed her luscious lips together and nodded.

"No, *that* doesn't explain anything," she agreed. "But the fight I saw her having with Fabian Lazarev does."

Now she had me. This was new information.

"C'mon, spill it. The suspense is killing me here."

"Let's go to the kitchen, so I don't have to repeat myself," she said—and I sighed, letting her pull me along in her slipstream.

When we entered the kitchen, we found Freezay and Runt standing by the stockpot. Freezay had the lid off and was sniffing the pot's contents. As we entered, he cocked his head thoughtfully.

"Did you eat any of this?" Freezay asked, Kali's information forgotten as soon as I heard the intensity in his voice.

"No, I only held the lid," I said, my stomach getting all jumpy as I tried to figure out why Freezay was freaking out.

"Thank God," he said, dropping the lid back on the pot so that its clatter echoed around the room.

"Freezay thinks this is what poisoned Zinia," Runt squeaked unhappily.

"Zinia was poisoned?" Kali and I both said at the same time. But then Kali added: "Zinia's dead?"

"She touched the book," I said, trying not to think about Zinia's last few minutes of life . . . and how terribly she'd suffered.

"And Freezay thinks she was poisoned, too," Runt added.

Kali looked bewildered.

"How many people are dead, white girl?" she said, looking at me.

"Three," Freezay called out from where he was rummaging around inside a cabinet. "But it would've been four if Callie had tasted the chicken and dumplings."

He suddenly slammed the cabinet door shut, holding up a small plastic bottle.

"Ah-ha! Here's the culprit."

"What is it?" I asked.

"It's gun bluing," he replied. "Full of selenium dioxide, which, when ingested, proves miraculously fatal."

I didn't think the word "miraculously" was really appropriate, given the situation, but Freezay was oblivious, as usual.

"Well, you should know that Fabian Lazarev and Coy had a huge fight out by the pool last night," Kali said, resting a hand on an outthrust hip and looking pleased with herself. "They were fighting over you and your lover boy, dipwad."

She directed this last sentence at me.

"What are you talking about?" I said.

She leaned back against the counter, arms crossed over her ample chest.

"Lazarev was yelling all over the place about how Coy was cozying up to Daniel more than she was supposed to . . . and by cozying up, I mean doing the nasty and all kinds of bad business."

My gut clenched, the air in the room becoming unbreathable. I must've looked shell-shocked because Runt came over and licked my hand.

"Are you okay, Cal?" she said.

"Oh, I'm . . . that is . . . okay. I mean, we're not . . . uhm, you know . . . oh . . ." I trailed off, my dry mouth no good at forming words.

Kali and Freezay were unconvinced by my show of nonchalance.

"Don't cry, dipwad," Kali said. "It's just a penis."

But it was my penis! I thought miserably.

So, it seemed I had a double standard when it came to the men in my life: I could make a misstep with Frank, but if Daniel had sex with someone other than me, even if we weren't together, it was gonna make me totally freak out.

Damn, I'd really messed my life up. Daniel had been my best friend and my partner . . . and I'd thrown it all away because I was scared of being committed to him. Sure, I could date other men, but no one was ever going to "get me" the way that he did; that kind of relationship was very rare—and then to be sexually compatible at the same time? Well, it was a bloody miracle.

Jeez, just *thinking* the words "sexually compatible" started my brain reeling down the garden path. In my mind's eye, I couldn't help but imagine Daniel thrusting his cock in and out of Coy's tight little body, his face awash in ecstasy as he made her cum in long, drawn-out moans.

Uck! The images were so heinous I wanted to vomit—and they just kept coming, getting naughtier and more intense the harder I tried to shoo them out of my head. I kept freeze-framing on Technicolor pictures of Daniel and Coy locked in athletic poses right out of the Kama Sutra; Coy's breasts jiggling in Daniel's face, their bodies pressed tightly together as they rocked back and forth—

"Grrr!" I snarled, wanting to punch myself in the face so I'd have something else to focus on instead of the imagined slap, slap of flesh pounding away at flesh.

"Cal," Runt said, genuine concern in her voice, "you don't look so hot."

I wanted to cry. I wanted to scream. I wanted to close my eyes and then wake up to discover that someone had taken pity on me and put me out of my misery. For half a second, I was even tempted to down the whole pot of chicken and dumplings, so I wouldn't have those terrible images burning inside me anymore—*because you'd have poison burning inside you instead,* the nasty little voice in the back of my head said—and that's when I *stopped* wanting out of my life and *started* wanting to pummel Daniel silly with my bare fists.

"How could he do this?" I growled. "And with her!? And he lied about it—"

"He didn't outright lie," Freezay interjected. "If it's true, and that's a big if, then it's a lie of omission."

"It's the same damn thing!" I shot back at him, anger cresting over me like a wave. "And I can't believe you're sticking up for him!?"

Freezay held up his hands in submission.

"I'm not sticking up for anyone—"

"Yes, you are," Kali said.

I glared at her.

"And *you*. You're glad about all this," I yelled at her. "You want me to be miserable for the rest of my immortal existence just like you!"

"Callie—" Runt said, but I shot her a "shut it" look and she sat back on her haunches, forlorn.

"God, this sucks so bad," I said under my breath as I fought back the hot tears threatening to spill over onto my cheeks.

"It's not so bad being a miserable mess like me," Kali said softly, and I was so surprised she wasn't screaming at me for my rudeness that I almost forgot to be upset.

"I have a pretty great existence, actually, Callie," she sniffed. "It may not look like much to you, but I have a very fulfilling life."

If Kali had gotten mad at me, calling me every name in the book at the top of her lungs and swearing in Hindi, then maybe I could've held on to my righteous anger—but when she started getting all sniffy and hurt sounding, well, I felt like a total shit heel.

"I'm sorry, Kali, I didn't mean to—" I started to say, but she waved my apology away.

"Your apology is not accepted," she said, swiping at her eyes with the end of her sari.

"C'mon, please don't do this," I tried again, but she was having none of it.

"I'll be in my room enjoying my miserable life if anyone needs me," she said, blatantly ignoring me as she stalked over to the exit. "Happy All Hallows' Eve, everyone but Calliope Reaper-Jones."

There was a blast of cold air as she opened the kitchen door, the autumnal chill of October hitting me full force, and then she was gone, slamming the door with a bone-vibrating *bang*.

"Great," I said, leaning back against the counter. "Well, I really screwed that up, didn't I?"

It was a rhetorical question, but Freezay missed the memo.

"Yeah, you're a terrible friend," he said, then pirouetted on his heel and strode over to the freezer.

"Shall we?"

When neither Runt nor I responded, he turned the handle and opened the freezer anyway.

"Well, I don't know about you, ladies, but I'm curious to see where this thing leads."

Without waiting for an answer, he stepped inside, leaving us alone in the kitchen.

"I'm sorry, Runt," I offered, but she kept her head down and her tail as still as a corpse in a grave. "C'mon, please . . ."

No matter what I said, she still wouldn't look at me—and I thought she was going to give me the cold shoulder like Kali had—but then she raised her head and said:

"Sometimes you're really mean."

Those words broke my heart. Not because they were harsh, but because they were true.

She got up and padded over to the gently humming freezer, her black coat making her seem to disappear in the darkness of the freezer's interior.

"Runt!" I called after her, but she ignored me.

I stood there for a moment, unable to move, and then I followed her inside.

twenty-four

"Wait."

It was a woman's voice, quiet and hesitant. I turned around to find Caoimhe standing in the corridor, her hand clutching at the doorframe. Her dark hair was ruffled, her eyes red-rimmed from crying.

"Is everything okay?" I asked, surprised by how worried I was about a woman I barely knew.

She nodded, her chin quivering as she tried to smile.

"I know you're in the middle of things . . . Edgar, the murders—"

The way she called Freezay "Edgar" made me very curious. It was intimate, spoken as if she knew him well.

"—but after. When everything is settled. There's something I'd like to discuss with you."

She paused, waiting for me to reply.

"Uhm, sure," I said, not really understanding what she wanted of me.

"Good, that's great." She smiled, looking pleased and much less harried than she had two seconds earlier. "Okay, well, that's all I wanted to say. I'll leave you to it then."

She flashed me another brief smile then backed away, hurrying down the hall.

Well, that was bizarre, I thought as I walked back to the

freezer, wondering how much of a head start Freezay and Runt had on me after my talk with Caoimhe.

Apparently, a big one—because when I entered the freezer, the back wall was wide open, revealing a darkened access point into the guts of Casa del Amo.

Freezay and Runt hadn't waited for me, but I noticed Runt's paw prints embedded in a thin layer of frost on the floor near the passage's entrance. Avoiding the hanging sides of meat— the gelatinous half-pig faces, one eye and part of each snout still intact—I kept as close to the boxes of frozen vegetables as I could.

"Guys?" I called out, getting zero response in return.

There were no lights inside the passageway proper, but the fluorescent bulbs in the freezer kind of illuminated its entrance. From what I could see, the passage had been erected out of the same local tuff stone as the rest of the building, so I assumed it had been built into the original architectural plans. Which meant there were a lot of people, including the construction workers who'd built the compound, that knew of its existence— and if the secret compartment in my bathroom at Casa de la Luna was any indication, there were probably more of these secret spaces than just the one I was standing in front of.

"Hello?" I called out again, the thrum of the refrigeration fan sucking up my words.

I stepped into the secret passageway, leaving the smoothness of the freezer floor behind me, the soles of my sneakers squeaking as they tread down a tuff stone stairway leading even deeper into the darkness. It wasn't as cold here as it'd been in the freezer, but it was still chilly enough that I wished I'd brought a sweater to put on over my pajamas. I also wished I wasn't wearing pajamas.

"Runt?" I called as I stepped off the last stair—losing any of the remaining light from the freezer—then using my hands to feel my way in the blackness.

Figuring they were out of hearing range since I still hadn't gotten a response, I soldiered on, trying not to think about what kind of creepy crawly things lived in lightless secret passageways.

"What the hell!" I yelped as I tripped on a groove in the stone floor, my right foot twisting painfully underneath me. I fell forward, throwing my hands out in front of me and willing them to take the brunt of the fall—but I never hit the ground. Two strong arms wrapped around my waist, pulling tight as they lifted me back up.

"Thank you—" I started to say just as the arms tightened around my middle, the pressure on my internal organs increasing tenfold in an instant.

I grunted as my savior/attacker relaxed his grip—he was too strong and bulky to be a woman—so that my whole body slid down the length of his, maneuvering me into a position where he could now easily apply pressure to my chest. Arms trapped at my sides, I frantically kicked my legs, trying to beat my way out of the painful embrace, but my attacker only squeezed harder, compressing my chest like a vise. As I exhaled the last of the air in my lungs, I found I couldn't draw another breath and I started to panic, my useless squirming only making my attacker ratchet up the pressure.

There is something truly terrifying about dying in the dark with nothing to anchor yourself to except fear. The darkness caused my other senses to seem heightened, so that I could actually *hear* the pounding of my heart against my ribs, sluggish at first then picking up speed and energy as it fought to pull the last bit of oxygen from my blood. My toes and fingers started to go numb first, my lungs screaming for the life-giving air it was being denied.

"I want that book," a cold masculine voice whispered in my ear.

I would've told the voice to take a hike, but I was physically speechless from lack of air, so all I could do was kick weakly at his shins.

"Do you understand me?" he said, compressing my rib cage even more tightly.

I nodded my head, weak as a newborn kitten. I understood what he wanted; I just didn't have it to give. Of course, I couldn't tell him that—literally *and* figuratively.

Suddenly, a bone-chilling howl ripped through the air. My attacker tensed, then relaxed his hold on me, and I almost cried because I could breathe again. Inhaling great gulps of fresh air, I relished my ability to expand my lungs past "pancake" position. As much as I wanted to just hang around, drinking in oxygen, I knew this might be my only opportunity for escape, so I took a deep breath and screamed.

Now, I'm not a scream queen, but I have a good set of lungs and I know how to use them. The scream startled my attacker and I used this to my advantage, tilting my head forward then slamming the back of my skull into his vulnerable nose. A gush of hot, viscous liquid poured down my neck and into the back of my pajamas, making me want to gag, but it did the trick. My attacker released me and I fell to the ground, banging my elbow on the floor, but I didn't hesitate long enough to feel the pain. I was instantly rolling onto my stomach, trying to get as far as possible from his reach.

I heard the man scream as something or someone crashed into him—and then Runt was on top of me, licking my face.

"I'm sorry," I gasped, wrapping my arms around her soft neck. "I didn't mean to freak out and be such a bitch."

"It's okay, Cal," Runt said. "But we gotta get out of here and, like, *now*."

I nodded even though I knew she couldn't see me. Gripping the wall, I used it to pull myself to my feet, the sound of scuffling getting closer and closer.

"Get out of here! Now!" Freezay shouted, his words followed by intense grunting and the dull thud of fist connecting with flesh.

"This way, Cal," Runt said. "Grab my collar."

Fumbling in the inky blackness, my fingers grasped at fur until they finally stumbled upon the ridged rhinestones of Runt's collar. I was so thankful that Runt was with me. It was dark, and the lack of oxygen had made me slightly disoriented, so I could never have found my way out on my own.

"Okay, go," I whispered, letting Runt guide me toward the exit.

Behind us, Freezay's muffled efforts to take out the nameless attacker became less pronounced until they were barely whispers in the dark. As much as I was glad he and Runt had come to my rescue, now I was worried he was going to get hurt in my place.

Jeez, would this Halloween never end? I thought miserably.

Moving under cover of darkness, Runt led me through the tunnel until, abruptly, we found ourselves standing in front of the stairway that led to the freezer. My heart leapt and I dropped my hold on Runt's collar in order to grasp the wall so I could keep my balance as we climbed the stairs.

"Thank God," I whispered, never happier to see a kitchen in my entire life . . . but my elation was short-lived: *Someone had shut the freezer door*.

"Crap!" I said, running over to the door and pounding on it with both fists. "Crap, crap, crap!"

Realizing quickly that this full-frontal attack would get me nowhere, I slumped against the door, letting my forehead rest against its cold metal surface.

What the hell were we going to do?

Freezay was probably lying in a pool of his own blood in the middle of the secret passage, a madman might or might not be coming to kill us for a magical book, and Runt and I were trapped in a very chilly walk-in freezer until said madman made his appearance.

Grrr! I thought, wishing, once again, that I wasn't in my pajamas and that I didn't have someone else's blood dribbling down the back of my neck.

I turned around, leaning against the cold metal, then slowly slid down the length of the door until I was on my butt on the floor, pajamas bedamned. I pulled my knees up to my chest, resting my chin between them, exhausted.

"I guess it could be worse," I said, sighing.

Runt came over and licked my hand, then settled down beside me, the warmth from her body a very welcome addition.

"I feel like this whole thing is my fault," I said, reaching out and stroking her neck. "I'm a snafu magnet. Everywhere I go, something seriously bad happens. I can't imagine this was what my dad's life was like. I bet he was amazing at running Death. I bet he never screwed anything up."

"Or maybe it's like that movie, *The Money Pit*," Runt said, interrupting my pity party. "Maybe you're Tom Hanks and you bought the really big fixer-upper house, but maybe your *dad* bought the gigantic Mediterranean mansion fixer-upper and that was even worse."

I loved that a hellhound was comparing my life and career to *The Money Pit*—damn, cable was a beautiful thing.

"So, you're saying my dad could've had it even worse than me?"

Runt nodded.

"Maybe he got stuck in Antarctica . . . while you're just locked in a freezer."

When I didn't respond immediately, Runt added: "Or maybe not."

I shook my head.

"No, you're not wrong. I have no idea what my dad had to deal with, so I should stop being a whiny brat and just chill."

"Like a freezer," Runt said.

"Yeah," I agreed, grinning at the absurdity of our conversation. "Make like a freezer and chill."

"Do you think he's okay?" Runt asked in a tiny voice—but before I could answer that I bloody hoped so, Freezay burst through the entrance, looking a little worse for wear, but alive and kicking.

"He got away," Freezay said, pulling a handkerchief from his back pocket and dabbing at his lip with it.

"I'm sorry I was such a schmucktard," I said, rising to my feet.

Freezay didn't seem bothered by my lapse in maturity.

"Shit happens. But right now, we have to concentrate on getting out of this freezer," he said, side-stepping me so he could try the handle on the door with no luck.

He pulled a paper-thin LED flashlight from of his pocket, squeezing its middle so that it illuminated a (very small) slice of the darkness. Then he motioned for Runt and me to come back with him into the secret passageway.

"All right, back the other way then."

"Where does it lead?" I asked as we followed the guiding beam of the flashlight down the stairway, dog flank bumping into my leg as we walked.

"We don't know. We were almost to the end when we heard scuffling behind us and went back to check on you," Runt said.

We'd only been down in the passageway for a few minutes, but already the oppressive darkness and cloyingly narrow walls made me feel claustrophobic. Added to that was the sense of timelessness I felt as we were shunted deeper underground, the passageway seeming to stretch out endlessly before us in the meager glow of the flashlight. And then, without really being consciously aware of it at first, I began to notice that the tunnel was veering ever so slightly to the left, heading away from Casa del Amo and toward the statuary gardens.

"It stops just down here," Freezay said as we reached the terminus of the passageway: a smooth adobe wall.

"It can't be a dead end," I said, running my hands over the sandy beige surface. "There has to be *something* beyond it— even if it's just a walled-up skeleton."

Freezay shot me a funny look.

"*The Cask of Amontillado*?" he asked.

I shook my head.

"Nope, *The Goonies*."

Grinning, Freezay shone the flashlight around the space, the light creating eerie shadows on the walls, but otherwise it revealed nothing of any consequence—apparently this really was the end of the line. As Freezay worked the flashlight, I ran my hands over the smooth adobe wall, looking for a hidden latch or release mechanism, while Runt sniffed along the crevice in the floor, her tail between her legs.

"I saw Zinia go into the freezer and disappear," I said, kicking the wall with my sneaker-shod foot. "She had to be going somewhere."

Freezay was busy using his fists to knock on the stone walls that butted up against the sides of the adobe wall, listening for the telltale hollowness of a false front.

"I've got it!" Runt cried excitedly, raising her nose from the ground and scampering back the way we'd just come.

Caught off guard by Runt's abrupt departure, Freezay and I chased after her, our pounding footsteps echoing in the darkness, the flashlight beam bouncing crazily along the walls.

"Runt, wait!" I cried, worried whoever had tried to attack me might be lying in wait somewhere in the tunnel, gearing up to finish what he'd started.

"Hurry up!" she called back to us, ignoring the worry in my voice, and we picked up our speed.

When we got to the stairway, she was already sitting there waiting for us, her tail thumping happily against the stone floor.

"What took you guys so long?" she said.

"Ha!" I shot back, leaning forward to catch my breath after the unexpected dog chase.

"What did you find, Runt?" Freezay said, shining the light down on the pup's face.

"I almost missed it," she began. "Zinia's smell is all over the kitchen and on the stairs, but the farther we got down the passageway, the more her scent had faded. At the end, there was no Zinia smell at all."

"Because she never went beyond the stairwell," Freezay said, grinning down at Runt.

"Exactly!" Runt replied.

"Well, where did she go then?" I asked. "I mean she couldn't have gone under the stairs—"

"Yes, she could have," Freezay interrupted me. "If the stairs were actually the real entrance to the secret passage."

"That makes the tunnel we just went down a dummy secret passage," I said, rolling my eyes. "Who *does* that?"

"Someone with something to hide."

Freezay was right—though the idea of a secret passageway being the entrance to another secret passageway may have seemed ridiculous in theory, in reality it was an example of paranoia taken to the utmost extreme.

"So how do we get inside?" I asked as Freezay ran his flashlight beam across the cut stone staircase.

"Easy-peasy—if you just think about how the secret compartment in the bathroom closet worked," Runt said, padding over to the bottom step, which Freezay's flashlight beam was already illuminating. "See how the bottom step is shorter than the others?"

She was right. The last stone step was smaller than its brethren and set into the floor at an odd angle.

"Check this out."

Placing her nose where the two sides of the step met in a sharp-edged right angle, she used brute strength to pivot the step backward, the whole stairwell rotating with it until a flat plane of stone had replaced the stairs.

"Looks like a wheelchair ramp," I said.

"Just wait," Runt said, eager to show us more as she climbed up on the ramp, her nails clicking against the stone as she walked around, sniffing for something.

"Found the trigger!" she called, lifting a paw and setting it down precisely on a small, round depression smack-dab in the middle of the stone plane. There was a click, and then a secret doorway opened up in the stone wall behind Freezay's back, making us both jump in surprise.

"What the—" I said as Freezay stalked past me, flashlight aloft, its LED light illuminating the confines of a tiny hidden room.

The space was only about four feet by six feet—not much bigger than a walk-in closet—but every inch of wall space was covered with the well-ordered spines of a miniature library. Freezay ran the flashlight over the books, stopping occasionally when a title caught his attention.

"*The Vollkommene Geomantia . . . Letters on Demonology and Witchcraft . . . The Malleus Maleficarum . . .*" Freezay read out loud, the low vibrato of his voice eerie in the confines of the odd little room.

"Someone's interested in the dark side of the occult," I said, each title I saw reconfirming my hypothesis. Whoever curated this library had dark tastes, indeed.

"What's that?" Runt said as she jumped down off the stone ramp and trotted past me into the room, coming to a stop in front of something shiny and metallic lying on the floor.

Freezay crouched down beside the pup, lifting the shiny object up into the air by its long golden chain.

"That's the locket we found in the hidden compartment with the book!" I said, taking it from Freezay so I could look inside of it just to be certain. "Yep, same picture and everything."

I started to hand the locket back to him, but he waved me away.

"You hold on to it for now—we need to get back to the other end of that tunnel," he said, and without further explanation, he strode out of the tiny library, taking his flashlight with him so that Runt and I were left in darkness.

"Hurry up!" Freezay yelled, the distance between us increasing until he was only a flickering pinprick of light jogging down the length of the tunnel.

Not wanting to find myself in inky blackness all over again, I felt compelled to run. Runt, who was physically much faster than me, stuck close to my heels. She should've passed my lumbering gait easily, but instead, she was staying nearby, acting as my protector. As the end of the tunnel came into view, there was a blinding flash of light—the kind of flash no flashlight, especially a little LED one, could boast—and I blinked at the sudden brightness.

A moment later we were out of the tunnel—the mysterious adobe wall that had blocked our progression earlier was turned sideways, so we could climb through it.

"Oh my God," I said as I realized where we were.

"It's our room," Runt said, stating the obvious.

We'd climbed through a secret doorway only to find ourselves standing in the space that used to be the fireplace of our bedroom at Casa de la Luna. In front of us, Coy's headless body lay at our feet, a grizzly reminder of why we'd begun this wild-goose chase in the first place.

"Amazing, isn't it?" Freezay said from where he was perched on the end of my bed. "The bodyguard outside has no idea we're even in here."

Without another word, he pulled a long, serrated carving knife from behind his back, its bloody, metallic body glistening in the lamplight.

"Welcome to the last piece of the puzzle," he said.

And then he grinned manically up at us.

twenty-five

"I don't give good head," I said, "if you're thinking of using that thing on either of us."

It took Freezay a moment to understand what I was saying, but when he realized my meaning—and how freaky it looked, him sitting in the middle of a grisly murder scene, holding up the murder weapon—he instantly dropped the knife down onto the bed.

"That's a terrible double entendre," he said, raising an eyebrow in my direction. "I expected something much cleverer from the likes of you."

"It was pretty clever, considering the fact I was worried you were gonna behead me," I replied, eyeing the bloody knife where it lay nestled in the sheets.

"Touché," he said. "And I had no intention of frightening you, ladies. You were just so slow getting down the tunnel. I got tired and had to sit down."

"Where did you find it?" I asked, ignoring the slowpoke comment.

Freezay stood up, leaving the knife on the bed as he joined us, careful to avoid the pool of dried blood on the floor.

"Well, after Runt discovered the hidden room, I had an epiphany," he said, motioning us to move away from the fireplace.

I followed Runt over to the bathroom, both of us crowding inside the doorway.

"It wasn't a blind passage after all, but another trick. I ran back down here and discovered that the mechanism which reveals the hidden library also opens part of this entrance, too," he continued—then he paused unexpectedly and added: "Let's reset the doorway so no one joins us unexpectedly. There are just too many curious people involved in this case."

"How do you do that?" Runt asked.

"Easy," Freezay said. "You see that stand there—"

He pointed to an antique bronze fireplace tool stand sitting slightly askew on the hearth. As we watched, Freezay grasped the top of the stand—tongs, brush, and poker swinging—and pulled it toward the hearth until we heard a soft *click*.

"There we go," Freezay said, the mechanism inside the wall beginning to whirr. To my amazement, the adobe wall swung toward us as the fireplace silently descended back into its spot on top of the hearth, effectively sealing the entrance to the secret passageway.

"That's insane," I said, marveling at the ingenuity of the Castle's architect.

"Insane, yes," Freezay agreed. "Now where was I?"

"You had an epiphany," Runt said.

"Oh, yes! My epiphany," he said, plopping back down on my bed and making the knife bounce. "I ran back here and found the adobe wall askew and your bedroom half-exposed. To my surprise, I discovered *another* hidden compartment built into the brickwork of the fireplace."

The place is littered with the damn things, I thought.

"At that same moment my flashlight decided to stop working, so I stuck my arm and head inside the new compartment, but that only triggered another mechanism and I was lucky enough to get my head and arm out—minus my hat, but plus the knife—before the fireplace finished its ascension into the ceiling."

I felt bad. I hadn't even realized Freezay was missing his trusty bowler hat.

"How did you know that's where the knife would be?" Runt asked, thoroughly engaged by the bizarreness of Freezay's story.

He scratched his head, his eyes shooting back and forth inside their sockets.

"I could lie to you, but what's the point?" Freezay said, running his hands through the shock of blond hair on top of his head so that pieces of dirt and soot littered the floor. "I had a hunch the knife was close, but I had no guarantees it was in that compartment until I stuck my hand inside."

"Why would the murderer just leave it there for anyone to find?" I asked.

"Coy's murderer did not plan to kill her, so there was no premeditation."

"Well, the murderer came in here with the knife, so he had to be planning something—" I said, but Freezay shook his head, picking up the knife and testing its weight.

"Oh, this knife isn't the murder weapon."

He dropped the knife back down on the bed then pointed to the fireplace.

"That poker is."

Runt and I both turned to look at the fireplace at the same time, our eyes locking onto the heavy bronze poker sitting benignly between the tongs and brush. It looked nothing like a murder weapon, but I supposed that was the point.

Freezay stalked over to the fireplace and picked up the poker, holding it out so we could see the flecks of dark brown blood still clinging to its end.

"Resembles rust and blends right in with the aged bronze patina, but I assure you that it's blood."

"Cool!" Runt said, amazed by what Freezay had discovered.

"It was right there in plain sight the whole time," Freezay continued, speaking almost to himself. "I guess I was just really thrown by the head in the bag."

"But that knife is covered in blood," I said, not understanding. "What was it for?"

"The beheading and the removal of the heart were done to throw everyone off the scent. After the murderer hit Coy on the back of the head—an impulse killing probably perpetrated in a fit of rage—he or she ran back to the kitchen to get the knife. They wanted to make it seem as if this were a ritual killing because they knew Horace was here at the Castle and they hoped the evidence would muddy the trail, point us in her brother's direction."

We were missing something—something about the murderer going back to the kitchen didn't sit right—and then it hit me, a series of possibilities exploding in my mind.

"What if Zinia and Constance weren't killed because of the book?" I asked suddenly. "What if they died because they saw something they shouldn't have seen—"

"Like the murderer going back to the kitchen to get the knife!" Runt finished.

"Exactly," I said, pleased with our tag team deductive reasoning.

"You're definitely barking up the right tree," Freezay said, starting to pace. "But why would any murderer in their right mind try to both poison and shoot their victim?"

"To make sure the poison wasn't a dud?" Runt asked, but Freezay shook his head.

"Nope."

When neither of us had another possible answer to Freezay's question, I said: "We give up. Just tell us."

He smiled at me and I knew instantly he wasn't going to give us any more information for free. The jerkoid was going to make us work it out for ourselves.

"We can reasonably assume that Horace wasn't responsible for his sister's death," Freezay went on, approaching the problem from a different angle. "And we can also assume that whoever murdered Coy knew about the secret passageways."

"Someone who worked here?" Runt asked. "Maybe Constance and Coy fought over the book and Constance killed her."

"Another possibility," Freezay agreed. "But that would mean someone else knew about the book—and they killed Constance and Zinia."

"Yeah, there's no way Zinia would kill Constance," I agreed. "They shared a common goal: trying to get Frank out of Purgatory—and if Zinia *had* killed her, then who killed Zinia? The woman didn't poison herself."

Freezay nodded, walking over to the window and drawing back the drape so he could look out into the onyx sky.

"Once again that leaves us with another party—and this

party killed Zinia and probably Constance, too. What else do we know about Constance's death?"

"We know she didn't give Uriah Drood the book," Runt chimed in. "He wasn't lying about that. Otherwise he would have already tried to use it to blackmail you into giving him Naapi's job, Cal."

"Agreed," Freezay said.

"She was never going to give him that book," I said, enjoying the way we were all working together to find the solution. "She'd only told him about her plan, period, because she knew he'd be here for the Death Dinner and he'd have recognized her."

"Well, what I don't understand is why the murderer cut up Constance's body," Runt interjected.

"They were furthering the Aztec ritual killing scenario—" I said then stopped as another possibility occurred to me. "That means whoever killed Coy murdered Constance, too!"

But Freezay wasn't so easily convinced. He pursed his lips together thoughtfully as he considered what I'd said.

"Not necessarily."

"Why not?" I asked, liking the way the plot was thickening around my new theory and not wanting Freezay to tell me I was wrong.

"The hands don't work."

Runt and I looked at each other, not sure what the hell Freezay was talking about.

"The hands?" Runt asked.

"Whoever killed Coy was left-handed," he said. "We noticed that when we turned her over."

I nodded, vaguely remembering Freezay pointing this out when we'd first examined Coy's body.

"But Constance's wounds were different. They weren't made by a serrated knife like the one which beheaded Coy— *and* they were inflicted by someone who was ambidextrous," Freezay said. "The killing cut—the one made to the jugular— was done by someone who was left-handed, while the shallower, nonlethal ones were all done with the right hand."

"Horace is left-handed," I reminded everyone. "Maybe he killed the three of them after all."

Freezay stared at me.

"What?" I asked, feeling like a bug under a microscope as he continued to stare at me.

"Of course! Horace *is* left-handed! You're a genius, Calliope," Freezay said, shaking his head in wonder. "It makes perfect sense."

"What makes perfect sense?" I asked, but Freezay was too wrapped up in his own thoughts to answer me. I looked over at Runt, but the hellhound pup didn't have a clue what Freezay was going on about either.

"Okay," Freezay said, grinning sheepishly at the two of us. "Not my best work by far. I missed a few things here and there, but in the end, the solution to the puzzle becomes clear."

"You know who did it?" Runt asked.

"I know who did it and I know why—and just thank God we'll never have to go to trial because there isn't a shred of evidence that isn't purely circumstantial," Freezay added mysteriously. "Now, we have one hour to put forth our hypothesis and catch a murderer before magic returns to our world and our window closes forever. Are you guys up for a little fun?"

I looked at Runt and knew she was thinking exactly the same thing I was: *Bring it on!*

jarvis glanced worriedly at the clock on the mantel, wringing his hands like a little old lady. I understood his nervousness: It was eleven twenty-one, and we now had less than forty minutes to solve three murders and one count of grand theft larceny before all our suspects magicked themselves out of our jurisdiction and the Death book was lost to me for the next 365 days. Add to that, we were still missing Donald Ali, Horace, and Kali—and I could empathize with Jarvis's paranoia; it was a whole lot of pressure for one ex-faun to bear.

Freezay was a statue, leaning against the mantel, arms crossed over his chest, eyes giving nothing away. He'd personally corralled Erlik, Fabian Lazarev, and Yum Cimil, forcing the three reluctant men into the drawing room, where they were now sitting on the love seat (Lazarev and Yum Cimil) and an armchair (Erlik).

Lazarev still looked shell-shocked, his handsome face drawn and sallow. He kept glaring in my direction with blatant hostility, occasionally transferring the bad vibes over to Daniel, who was standing next to me by the far wall. Yum Cimil was quiet as usual, his elderly countenance and silence lending him an air of annoyed disdain. He definitely wasn't happy about being included in this crazy circus, but Freezay and Jarvis had assured him that he didn't have a choice.

Erlik relaxed in his armchair, his thick legs stretched out in front of him. When he felt my eyes alighting upon him, he yawned, wanting me to know he could care less about the situation or what I thought.

Alameda Jones and Oggie were huddled together on the couch, his arm draped protectively around her shoulder, her head butting up against his chest as he stroked her hair. Her face was streaked with dried tears, her gaze fixed on Naapi, who sat in an armchair by the fireplace, hands in his lap, eyes downcast. I wasn't sure what her intent was, why she was staring so openly at her old lover, but it was unsettling the way her eyes never left his person.

I wasn't the only one aware of Alameda's staring problem; Anjea had noticed it, too. Searching me out, Anjea raised both eyebrows, then looked in the younger woman's direction, her gaze speaking volumes. I nodded and shrugged, feeling strange about having simpatico with the spooky woman from Australia.

Though she'd been MIA ever since dinner, Runt and I had been given the task of finding her and inviting her back to the drawing room with us. To our surprise, we'd discovered her waiting for us out by the pool, her bare legs dangling in the chlorinated water while her owl nestled sleepily against her shoulder.

"Took you long enough," she'd said when we got there. "Been waiting here fifteen minutes."

Fifteen minutes earlier, we'd been with Freezay, making our final plans and divvying up the different guests we were going to have to strong-arm into attending the climax of our investigation. What was so crazy was that the swimming pool was the first spot we'd chosen to look for Anjea—how she could've known our plans literally before we did was eerily disconcerting.

"Sorry," I'd said, not really knowing why I was apologizing.

She'd gotten up and sighed, the owl still nestling in the crook of her neck.

"Death is on the loose and it won't stop with those three," she said, staring directly into my eyes. "I like you, so I tell you as I see it. Best beware and keep your spirit guide close."

As she spoke the words "spirit guide," she looked down at Runt—and I was unexpectedly overcome with the shivers, my body going all cold and achy. My first thought was: *Someone just walked over my grave.* But when I reached down to scratch the sweet spot behind Runt's ears, the shivers disappeared.

"No more words," the older woman had continued, taking my arm, her slender frame light as a bird skeleton as she guided me back to the main house.

We hadn't spoke again, Anjea fending off my conversational advances with a wave of her hand, but when we'd finally arrived in the drawing room, she'd stopped me in my tracks to whisper something into my ear.

"Remember. It's all yours for the taking. Just make sure it's what you really want."

Not waiting for an answer, she'd squeezed my arm, then let me go, striding over to the far corner of the room and sitting down cross-legged on the floor by the sideboard, her back tall as she pressed it against the wall, the owl still sound asleep on her shoulder.

I thought it was fascinating that she and I were the only ones curious enough about Alameda's cuckolded relationship to watch her like a hawk. Everyone else was too busy wondering why Freezay had called him or her here, and if it meant that the murderer was about to be exposed.

Uriah Drood was the first to question Freezay's motives. He'd chosen not to take one of the seats, but to stand by the sideboard only a few feet from where Anjea was sitting. I think he'd picked the spot because it was as far from me as he could possibly get and still be in the same room. He was wary of even looking in my direction, probably worried I'd get trigger-happy with the soda water on the sideboard and douse him with it.

"I hope you've called us all here for good reason," Drood said, resembling a beauty pageant winner the way he was holding his hand on his hip, all his weight resting on his back leg.

Morrigan seconded the query.

"This is ridiculous. You should've had this sorted out hours ago so we could all go home—not that I'm not out of here the moment the clock chimes midnight."

The aggressive redhead stood behind the armchair her girl-friend was sitting in, her fingers tightly gripping the chair back, while Caoimhe leaned forward, just out of her reach. Both women looked pale and worn out and I wondered if they'd been fighting.

Everyone in the room had been beaten down by the events of the past twenty-four hours. If, unlike me, they'd been able to get some sleep, well, it hadn't helped. Only Uriah Drood looked rested, his blubbery body resplendent in a freshly pressed blue and white seersucker suit. I was usually a fan of the summery material, but I was afraid Drood had put me off the fabric in-definitely.

Freezay looked like a wild man, his blond hair sticking up in a coxcomb on top of his head, his green eyes on fire with manic-y exhaustion. He reached up, as if to take a hold of his bowler hat, but when his fingers got to his head, they realized the hat was no longer there and had to settle for running them-selves through his thick blond mop instead.

"I've done a thorough investigation—as thorough as I could manage without magic or the ability to quantify forensic evi-dence in a timely fashion—and I've come to the conclusion that there is a murderer among us—"

"No shit, Sherlock," Erlik said, leaning forward in his chair and resting an elbow on his knee. "Tell us something we don't know."

Freezay paused, and I got the impression he was working very hard to hold his tongue. Finally, his anger under control, he began again.

"Now, as I was saying," he continued, "I think it's best to explore exactly *why* these murders occurred and how they were perpetrated underneath our very noses."

"Go on," Naapi said, looking up for the first time, dark smudges of exhaustion underneath his eyes. "I, for one, would like to understand why all this has happened."

I remembered him asking Jarvis earlier in the night if we

thought his announcement during dinner had caused any of the mayhem. The dark smudges must've been as much from guilt as they were from heartache.

I glanced at Jarvis and he nodded, letting me know he remembered the same exchange.

"Well, it's all very simple," Freezay began. "The book, *How to Be Death: A Fully Annotated Guide*, was returned to Calliope Reaper-Jones yesterday night here at the Haunted Hearts Castle. It had been in Heaven since her father's untimely passing, but with the advent of All Hallows' Eve, the time had come for Death to possess it again."

"It's true," Jarvis said, everyone turning to look at him now. "The book is not just legend. I was a witness to the exchange myself, here in the library more than twenty-four hours ago."

Having said his piece, he closed his mouth and let Freezay continue.

"It was the coveting of this book—this rare and precious piece of Death Arcana—by a number of formidable opponents that lay the groundwork for the commission of these three murders."

"Don't beat around the bush, man," Erlik growled, glowering at Freezay. "Who did it?"

But Freezay wasn't going to be bullied. He was enjoying the spotlight, stretching out the explanation for as long as he could.

"First, you have to understand that the book isn't precisely what it's supposed to be," Freezay said, ignoring Erlik's outburst. "Isn't that right, Daniel?"

All eyes shot over to Daniel, including my own—this was a development I hadn't expected. I had no idea where Freezay was going with this, which meant I had now bought a ticket for the same roller-coaster ride as everyone else.

"That's right," Daniel said, his face serious. "I don't know how you guessed it, Detective, but Heaven and the Board of Death, in tandem with myself, made the decision to replace the original copy of *How to Be Death* with a cleverly forged reproduction after we were informed that an attempt would be made to steal the book during the Death Dinner."

Shock, and then suspicion, filled the room, but before anyone could comment, the door that led to the corridor burst open and Kali and Horace barreled in, a cowering Donald Ali between them.

"Ah," Freezay said, rubbing his palms together excitedly. "So, the guest of honor has finally arrived!"

twenty-six

"It was an accident!" Donald Ali bawled, his nose a bloodied, swollen mess. "A horrible, horrible accident!"

Well, now I know who attacked me in the secret passage, I thought, staring at Donald Ali's miserable face as he sat on the edge of the armchair Kali and Horace had deposited him in, his arms wrapped around himself as he rocked back and forth, misery exuding from every pore.

"Please, you have to believe me," he wailed. "My intentions were never to harm her, but then the book was gone and we argued and I just saw red. The poker was there and I . . . I . . ."

He stopped, unable to go on, his lower lip trembling as he tried to hold back the tears threatening to escape and trickle down his cheeks.

"We found him upstairs in his room," Kali said, addressing Freezay and totally ignoring me. Obviously, she was still pissed at me for being such a bitch. I was going to have to apologize sooner rather than later because I did not want to be on the Hindu Goddess's shit list any longer than necessary.

"He was in possession of this bottle," Horace said, holding up a replica of the gun bluing we'd found in the kitchen that had been used to poison Zinia. "But I was able to wrest it away from him before he swallowed any of its contents."

Freezay plucked the bottle from Horace's hand, nodding his head in thanks.

"And so another piece of the puzzle falls into place," he said, holding the bottle of gun bluing up to Donald Ali's face. "You planned on killing yourself?"

Donald Ali swallowed hard then nodded.

"Without the book," he said sadly, "what was the point?"

"So you admit it was the book you were after," Freezay crowed.

"Of course," Donald Ali replied sadly.

"And is it true, then, to say that Coy had no idea why you actually wanted the book?" Freezay badgered.

Donald Ali took a deep, shaky breath.

"Yes, it's true."

"She thought," Freezay continued, "that you wanted to collect the book, just like you collected so many other rare things. She had no clue how desperate you *really* were. Why you needed to possess it so badly."

Horrified by what he'd done, Donald Ali covered his mouth with his hand and nodded.

"I have Stage Four pancreatic cancer," he whispered. "The book would've saved me."

If Donald Ali expected any empathy from Freezay, he was sadly mistaken.

"When Coy came to you with her plan," Freezay continued, "you realized the book could be your saving grace. Of course, you'd let Coy use it first to exact revenge upon her brother— and then it would come to you and you would use it to make a deal with Death; you would barter the book in exchange for your own immortality."

I scanned the faces of the crowd as they ingested the information, trying to make sense of it all.

"But it wasn't there. Someone had beaten Coy to it," Donald Ali said, his voice cracking. "I didn't believe her. I forced her to take me back to the bedroom even though it was a terrible risk had we been discovered."

"The room was empty when you got there?"

Donald Ali nodded.

"Death and her dog hadn't returned yet—"

"We were walking back with Daniel," I added.

"What happened when you got there?" Freezay asked, waving at me to be silent.

Donald Ali's eyes glazed over, his mind returning to the scene of the crime.

"We got there and the room was unoccupied," he began, his voice soft as a small child's. "Coy had seen God's assistant give you the book while you were in the library. She'd expected you to take it back to your room after the ball and hide it, but no matter where she looked, it wasn't there. I made Coy show me around the room, prove to me that the book wasn't anywhere—I even checked the secret compartment in the bathroom, but it was empty—"

Because Constance had already stolen it, I thought.

"—and then I realized that I didn't believe her. My gut told me that she'd double-crossed me and then I don't really know what happened next, but suddenly the poker was in my hand . . . and then she was lying on the ground in front of me."

"What did you do next?" Freezay asked, encouraging the other man to go on.

"I heard someone at the door, so I dragged Coy's body into the secret passageway behind the fireplace. At first, I didn't know what to do, but then an idea popped into my head. One that would give restitution to Coy for the violence I'd perpetrated against her and, at the same time, save me from discovery . . ."

"You decided to frame Horace for his sister's murder," Freezay finished for him. "That would be Coy's revenge—Horace accused of a sororicide he didn't commit."

"It was brilliant," Donald Ali murmured. "Coy had told me all about seeing her brother at dinner and I knew exactly how best to play the whole thing out."

"You ran back to the kitchen, grabbed a butcher knife, and while Calliope was in the shower, you set your plan into motion," Freezay said.

"I was seen," Donald Ali said softly. "Zinia Monroe was in the kitchen and she saw me take the knife. It was only a matter of time before she put two and two together."

"You poisoned her," I said, a surge of sadness at the futility of Zinia's death. Then, I added: "But why try and shoot her, too?"

Donald Ali frowned.

"Shoot her? Why would I shoot her? I'd already poisoned her. I wouldn't want her to suffer doubly—"

Those words set off something explosive deep inside Fabian Lazarev, and he jumped out of his seat, rage smoldering in his eyes as he attacked the older man.

"You son of a bitch!" Lazarev screamed as he knocked Donald Ali to the ground. "I'll show you suffering!"

He pummeled at the older man's already busted face, fists slamming into bone and cartilage while blood blossomed bright and red beneath his fingers. Grasping the old man by the hair, he yanked his wobbling head up then slammed it down into the floor over and over again.

"Stop it!" Jarvis yelled as he and Daniel attempted to pull Lazarev off Donald Ali.

"Get away!" Lazarev screamed, a hysterical bacchanal refusing to let go even as Jarvis and Daniel grabbed him by the arms, restraining him.

By the time they were finally able to drag Fabian Lazarev away, the other man's face was a pulpy mess, broken dentures protruding from a slackened jaw.

"What the hell is wrong with you?" Freezay shouted at Lazarev as Daniel and Jarvis threw him back down on the love seat.

"He killed Coy!" Lazarev shouted back at him, loosing flecks of bloody saliva from his mouth. "Then he cut off her head and burnt her heart . . . my God . . ."

Lazarev broke down, dropping his face into his palms and sobbing loudly.

"You told them what she was planning, didn't you?" Freezay said softly, placing a hand on the Russian's shoulder. Lazarev shrugged it away, gulping down air as he continued to cry. "I didn't understand why you felt so much guilt until Daniel said someone tipped off the Board . . ."

"I didn't want anything bad to happen to her," Lazarev cried, looking up at Freezay with the pleading eyes of a child. "If she stole the book, it would be the end for her, so I prevented it . . . and then she died anyway . . . and so horribly."

Freezay nodded, letting Lazarev know that he understood.

"You loved her, but you wouldn't be her decoy."

Lazarev took a shuttering breath.

"I refused her, so she manipulated him"—he pointed at Daniel—"to get an invitation to the Death Dinner."

I looked over at Daniel and saw genuine sadness on his face.

"The Board of Death had her under suspicion from the beginning. She's been chasing me for months, trying to work her way in, but nothing ever happened between us. And then I was instructed to invite her," Daniel said, "but that was all. I never touched her. I swear to God."

Lazerev appeared to relax, the notion that Coy might have been true to him throughout the whole sordid affair making him sob even harder.

"You swear it?" he asked, his voice weak with hope.

Daniel nodded.

"I was supposed to keep watch over her, catch her in the act of stealing the book, but I . . ." Daniel paused, looking guilty now. "I failed."

Instead of keeping an eye on Coy when she took off in the middle of the Death Dinner, he'd stayed to look after me. When he should've been following Coy, he was walking Runt and me back to our room. He didn't love Coy after all. He loved *me*.

Kali had been wrong. The argument she'd heard between Lazarev and Coy had been filled with a lover's jealousy—it didn't mean that anything had happened between Coy and Daniel.

I looked over at Daniel, our eyes catching, and it took every ounce of restraint I possessed not to throw my arms around him and kiss him silly. Under no circumstance was now the time for a reunion.

While Freezay and Jarvis attended to the unconscious Donald Ali, Uriah Drood took the floor, lumbering over to the fireplace and claiming Freezay's spot.

"So that's that," he said, running his finger across the mantel. "Donald Ali killed Coy and the others for a useless book. Case closed."

Freezay, who was still crouched by Donald Ali's side, glared up at Drood.

"No, that's not case closed. Not by a long shot."

Leaving Jarvis to tend to the unconscious man, Freezay rose to his feet.

"We know how and why Coy died, but it's only the start of this sordid mess. It's only after her death that the story begins its ingenious twist."

Uriah Drood gawked at Freezay as the detective made his way back over to the fireplace, reclaiming his old spot and sending Drood scurrying back to the sideboard.

"Actually, Mr. Drood," Freezay said, "you played a much bigger role in the events than I'd even realized."

"Me?" Drood said, his eyes wide. "I have no idea what you're talking about."

Freezay turned his attention away from Drood, leaving the larger man to fret over what exactly had been meant by that statement. Then, picking up the thread of the murder plot, Freezay continued the story.

"I have to say it was a very clever plan. So clever it had me stumped until thirty minutes ago when"—he turned to wink at me—"an offhand comment from Calliope elucidated the whole plot."

Like a tennis match in progress, everyone turned their heads to look at me, then back again to Freezay, when he asked:

"How many people in this room are left-handed?"

Freezay narrowed his eyes and repeated the question.

"Who in this room is left-handed?"

Horace was the first to raise his hand, followed by Erlik and Oggie.

"You're left-handed," Caoimhe said—and it was only after her prodding that Morrigan threw in her lot with the other lefties.

"So that means the rest of you are right-handed," Freezay said, pointing out the obvious. "Very interesting."

"What does any of this have to do with anything?" Erlik growled at Freezay. "You have your murderer. Stop wasting our time."

He stood up to go, but Daniel took a step forward, blocking his path.

"No one's going anywhere."

Erlik moved to bypass him, but Daniel grabbed the other man's arm, restraining him so he couldn't go any farther.

"Sit down," Daniel said, his voice even. "Before I make you sit down."

Erlik looked around, hoping to garner some support for his cause, but no one would catch his eye.

"Damn it!" he spat. "You're all cowards."

But he sat back down in his seat, not at all pleased about being stymied from making an early retreat.

"A copycat killer is one who assumes the modus operandi of another murderer. In this case, it was done as a way to conceal the copycat killer's true identity and to place blame squarely on the original murderer."

All eyes were riveted to Freezay. He paused, waiting for a reaction from his audience, but none came. Instead, the quiet in the room deepened and maybe that was reaction enough.

"Once again Horace was the intended victim of this masquerade—but unbeknownst to our killer, he has an alibi for at least one of the murders."

Horace leaned back against the doorway that led out into the hallway, blocking any attempts at flight with his body.

"Kali?" Freezay said, indicating that the Hindu Goddess of Death and Destruction should speak.

Kali struck a pose similar to the one Uriah Drood had attempted earlier, putting his wannabe pageant stance to shame.

"I know Horace by his given name: Huitzilopochtli," she said, moving her hands languidly as she spoke. "Of course, we are not all friends, but most Gods and Goddesses know each other by sight."

"I had no idea who you were," Naapi said to Horace, shaking his head. "Please accept my apologies."

Horace inclined his head.

"No apology is necessary."

Kali glared at the two men, encouraging them to shut up. With her dark hair and flashing eyes, she was not a woman to be trifled with.

"I was talking, but whatever," she said, rolling her eyes. "Anyway, I decided to spy on him, to discover why he was here. I didn't know that the reason was his sister, Coyolxauhqui, who was attending the dinner as Daniel's date."

"I thought you knew all the Gods and Goddesses on sight," Uriah Drood said snarkily.

"She'd had work done." Kali glared at him, the words coming with a defensive edge, and if looks could kill, Uriah Drood would've been a dead man. "Plastic surgery work."

"She'd been hiding from me for a long time," Horace said. "Living amongst the humans for protection."

"We understand," Freezay said to Horace. "Please continue, Kali."

"Like you said, I've had him under observation most of the last twenty-four hours, so there was no way he could've committed the murder of Constance Partridge without my knowledge."

Freezay nodded, and having gotten exactly the information he wanted from Kali, he ended her testimony with a wave.

"So we know that Donald Ali intended to frame Horace by setting the murder scene to resemble an Aztec ritual killing," Freezay continued. "Our copycat attempted to continue the ruse with Constance's murder by slitting her jugular and then, as she bled to death, inflicting a series of shallower cuts to the rest of her body—once again simulating an Aztec ritual killing."

The crowd in the drawing room was silent, but their rapt attention was unwavering. Only Donald Ali (who was unconscious) and Fabian Lazarev (who was still lost in an interior monologue of pain and guilt) were oblivious to the slowly ratcheting tension inside the room.

"Or at least, that's what I thought at first. But I was mistaken—there was no copycat and no intention of making the second murder look like the first. It was only a coincidence that Constance's *torture* killing resembled Donald Ali's handiwork."

Silence. Every breath taken was measured, every heartbeat like the tick of a steadily accelerating metronome.

"Let's look more closely at Constance Partridge's murder," Freezay said, pacing in front of the fireplace, fingers laced behind his back. "Why was she killed?"

"The book," I said.

"Yes, follow the book and you will know the killer," Freezay murmured.

"Follow the book, you say?" Uriah Drood intoned. "Whatever do you mean?"

Freezay stalked over to the large man, intimidating him so badly that he cowered against the edge of the sideboard.

"You've already admitted to me that you engineered the theft of the book—"

"I don't know what you're talking about," Drood said, holding up his hands in acquiescence.

"Liar!" I said, wanting to join in the fight, but Freezay held up his hands for me to stay out.

"Oh, yes, you were instrumental in the death of two women, Constance Partridge and Zinia Monroe," Freezay spat at him, anger lacing his every word. "All so you could get your hands on the *book* and use it to blackmail Calliope into giving you Naapi's job after he steps down."

"So what!" Uriah Drood screamed at him. "I encouraged Constance to steal the damn book! Who cares?"

I wanted to shout at him that *I* cared, but I didn't dare. Freezay was on the warpath and he'd already told me to stay out of it. Runt, who was sitting next to me, whined and I gathered that she felt as frustrated by Drood's behavior as I did.

"You know that she never meant to give you the book, don't you?" Freezay asked, oozing a calmness that was in direct proportion to Drood's hysteria.

"You're crazy," he whimpered. "I had nothing to do with this!"

Freezay reached out and grabbed Drood by the lapels of his jacket, reeling him in like a floundering fish.

"The two of you fought after Coy's body was found, didn't you?" Freezay whispered, his face inches from Drood's. "You argued and she refused to give you the book, so you killed her."

Drood was horrified, his jowls quivering as he shook his head wildly.

"I didn't kill her!" he squealed. "I didn't!"

From the croissant experience, Freezay had learned how well Drood responded to physical intimidation and he used that to his advantage now, agitating the man like a washing machine set on "heavy duty."

"You wanted that book, so you did the only thing you could think to do in the situation. You murdered two helpless women for it—"

"That's not true. *I* didn't kill anyone—"

"Enough!" Oggie said, standing up. "You are hurting the man."

Freezay released Drood, the large man stumbling backward into the sideboard as he turned his attention on Oggie.

"Why do you care what I do to him? Who is he to you?"

Oggie raised his hands.

"You are out of control, Detective," he said. "You have no right to exert physical violence on this man."

Freezay laughed, the sound low and humorless.

"Are you sure there isn't another reason why you wanted me to stop badgering Mr. Drood? One that hits closer to home than just plain old human kindness?" Freezay asked, boring holes into Oggie's face with his eyes, the green irises flashing as they zeroed in for the kill.

"You are mistaken," Oggie said, sitting back down as if that ended the confrontation.

"I don't think so," Freezay replied. "I think you were afraid of what Mr. Drood might say if I pushed him too hard."

Oggie shook his head, amused. Beside him, Alameda Jones was pale, her hand clutching tightly at Oggie's upper arm.

"You speak as though I know of what you're talking, Detective. But I am at a loss. Please explain."

"Yeah, I'd like to know what this is all about, too," Erlik agreed, eyeing Freezay and Oggie both.

"You said that Uriah Drood was blackmailing you about your affair with Alameda. That you were on your way to meet him when the attempted shooting of Zinia Monroe occurred," Freezay said. "But that's not the whole truth."

"That is the *only* truth," Oggie said, unyielding in his resolve.

"You know that the book you have is worthless," Freezay said thoughtfully. "A forgery that can do nothing to grease your way once the Board of Death gets a hold of you."

"We shall see what happens when this night is over," Oggie replied cryptically, eyes narrowed.

"There was another reason that Horace and Kali were so late in getting here. They had another errand to run for me," Freezay said, pirouetting on his heel and turning to Horace.

"The box, please."

twenty-seven

"No!" Alameda screamed as she rose from her place on the couch, her face a twisted mask of fear and rage as she threw herself across the room, slamming into Horace and sending them both sprawling to the ground.

Instantly Freezay and Daniel were in between them, Freezay lifting Alameda off Horace and roughly depositing her into an empty chair. He dropped both hands down onto the chair's arms, squeezing them with his fingers as he used the width of his own body to block her from escaping the seat.

"What do you think you're doing?" he asked, leaning forward so he could really get into her personal space.

"Nothing!" she cried, flinching.

"I don't think that was nothing," Morrigan said as she gazed at Freezay with a newfound respect.

"Shut up!" Alameda yelled, glaring at the other woman.

But the damage had already been done.

"This was all for nothing, Oggie," Freezay said, turning back to look at Alameda's lover, who sat stock-still on the couch, mouth set in a tight line. "The book isn't real."

"Don't listen to him," Alameda called to Oggie as she reached out with a catlike claw and dragged her nails across the side of Freezay's cheek, drawing a ribbon of blood.

Freezay stood up, bringing a hand to his bloodied face, and

Alameda took the opportunity to bolt from the chair. Grabbing a glass bottle from the sideboard—the antique whiskey Donald Ali had opened the night before—she made a run for the window, intending to smash out the glass and escape. But before she could manage to swing her arm, a flash of feathery brown shot through the air. Talons out for blood, Anjea's owl made a beeline for Alameda's head. Screaming as the creature dove into her neck, she raised her hands to her head, trying to extricate herself from the owlet's razor-sharp talons. Panicking, she dropped the bottle and it hit the floor, exploding upon impact, the sound it made like a rifle shot as the bottle splintered into jagged pieces across the floor.

Howling like a banshee, she continued her frantic effort to disengage the owlet from her neck, but as she left the edge of the carpet and hit the slippery tile—the spilled alcohol and glass acting like lubricated marbles—her feet skittered out from under her and her body caromed into the wall, where it bounced once, the velocity of the action reversing her forward trajectory. Arms pinwheeling wildly, she lost her footing and plummeted backward, her head slamming into the tiled floor with a sickening *crack*.

All motion ceased and she lay still, eyes wide open, but staring at nothing as a wash of arterial blood snaked out from underneath the halo of her hair, the gash at her throat turning the whiskey and broken glass scarlety amber. Both Oggie and Naapi ran to her—and there was a moment of uncertainty as they tried to decide who had the most right to be there—but then Alameda took a shuddering breath, her eyes blinking twice in rapid succession, and they both dropped down beside her, each taking a quivering hand.

"*Alameda,*" Naapi whispered, squeezing her hand, but she was gone. The shuddering breath had been her last.

In my brain I heard Freezay say, "*It only takes two minutes to exsanguinate.*"

It had taken even less than that.

it had all started with Uriah Drood. The sniveling worm had been blackmailing Alameda for months, threatening to tell Naapi about her affair with Oggie unless she fed him insider information on Naapi's retirement plans. Of course, after Naapi's announcement at the Death Dinner, the jig was up, and since Alameda now possessed nothing that Drood wanted, he decided it might behoove him to let Naapi know about the affair.

He started dropping hints, whispering tiny bits of information in Naapi's ear, but then Constance had double-crossed him with the book and he'd seen red, his mind settling on how best to get what Constance owed him. He decided he would make Alameda do his dirty work, force *her* to retrieve the book—all in exchange for protecting a secret he had no intention of keeping.

A deal struck, she and Oggie had lured Constance into the library under the guise they could intercede on Frank's behalf with the Board of Death. They'd heard about her effort to free him, thought their input might be helpful—but when they'd asked about the book, she'd gotten cagey and said she didn't have it anymore. That one revelation had sealed her fate: Oggie had pulled out a knife he'd liberated from the kitchen, and while he held her down, Alameda had tortured her, making the shallower, (unintentionally) right-handed wounds. Once she'd revealed the book's whereabouts, Oggie (who was left-handed) had sliced open her jugular, the two of them watching as Constance's lifeblood drained out onto the floor.

Unbeknownst to Alameda, Uriah Drood had already spilled the beans. So while Oggie had followed me to the Assyrian Gardens and lain in wait for Zinia with an antique rifle he'd stolen from the library, Alameda had been confronted about her affair by a devastated Naapi.

It was here, at this point in the plot, that Oggie had had his greatest run of luck. Unbeknownst to him, the rifle he had stolen from the library was filled with blanks, so the shots he fired were literally useless—except they had startled Zinia, causing her to drop the metal box, thus setting the mechanism of her death into motion. As I watched her die, Oggie had stealthily swooped in and stolen the metal box and book, thinking he'd go unnoticed in the ensuing chaos. He never counted on Daniel seeing him as he fled the scene.

It was a small mistake, but it had cost him dearly—and everything after that had been about playing catch-up.

Most of this, Freezay had learned from Oggie while interviewing him in the dining room. He'd filled Runt, Jarvis, and me in on the details later, but he'd thought he could get the most from Oggie by talking to him alone first.

"But why kill them?" Freezay had asked, wanting to know why they'd used deadly force to steal the book.

"The immortality," Oggie said. "With Naapi resigning and rescinding his immortality, she would be mortal again."

"You could've made her your own consort, given her continued immortality through you," Freezay offered, but Oggie had merely shaken his head.

"I already have a wife in Africa who shares my immortality," he said sadly. "This was all I could offer Alameda. A chance to possess a book that might broker her continued existence."

This had seemed to appease Freezay and they'd gone on to other topics, but I'd found myself fascinated by the admission.

For as long as I'd dealt with immortality—my whole life, I guess—it had been the bane of my existence. The attainment of it had caused people I loved to die and it had almost destroyed Death, Inc., from the inside out. And now, once again, it was responsible for the death of three (two of them relatively innocent) people. I understood why mortals wanted to live forever—the loss of self was a daunting thing—but was it worth the sacrifices that people like Alameda had to make in order to possess it?

I just didn't know.

I did find it ironic that Alameda had died on the one day of the year when her immortality was not assured—when soon she would've had a whole lifetime of mortal days to choose from. Maybe, if she'd waited and played her cards right, she could've even met another immortal and begun the cycle all over again. Instead, she'd died on the floor of the Haunted Hearts Castle, a piece of broken glass from an elderly whiskey bottle slicing her carotid artery wide open.

It seemed a fitting death after what she and Oggie had done to Constance—but if I could've rewritten history, I'd have stopped all the death and destruction that happened that night. Even Coy's untimely end seemed like a senseless act. Sure, the Aztec Goddess may have been a bloodthirsty avenger, but her murder, at the hands of a cowardly old man, was just pathetic.

* * *

as i sat in the dining room, the one place in the house untouched by tragedy, contemplating the events of the past twenty-four hours, Freezay came in, looking exhausted.

"They're ready to be taken away as soon as magic returns," Freezay said, putting a hand on my shoulder and giving it a squeeze.

He was referring to Oggie and Donald Ali, the two men who had helped to perpetrate the tragic events of the past twenty-four hours. They weren't the only ones I held responsible, but there was nothing to charge Uriah Drood with since he hadn't physically committed a crime—no, he'd just set two murders into motion with his greed and selfishness.

The fact that he was going to walk free made me ill, but there was nothing I could do about it except keep an eye on him in the future. He was a wily little reptile, but I wouldn't let him get away with anything else if I could help it.

"Hey, you got your hat back," I said, noticing that Freezay was carrying his bowler hat in his hand as he walked around to the other side of the table and took the seat opposite me.

"Anjea's owlet found it," he said happily, tamping it down on top of his head so that it rode low over his blond brows. "I don't know what kind of nonmagic magic the woman possesses, but it transcends the stuff we use."

I didn't think he was wrong on that front. There was something transcendent about Anjea, something unlike anything else I'd experienced in the Supernatural world.

"Anyway," he said, patting the hat. "It's nice to have it back."

"So, the book?" I asked, my curiosity getting the better of me. "How did you know it was a forgery?"

"How did I know it was a forgery?" Freezay repeated, his eyes lively. "Well, I technically *didn't* because technically it's *not* a forgery."

I nearly choked.

"What?!"

Freezay nodded then shrugged helplessly.

"There was no forgery. It was just a little scheme that Jarvis, Daniel, and I cooked up to unsettle our murderers."

I stared at him, at once angry that I wasn't in on the secret and impressed by the ingeniousness of the ploy.

"So the metal box Horace had . . ."

"There was no metal box," Frezay said. "Think back and you'll realize you never saw anything in Horace's hands."

I did exactly what he suggested, surprised by the outcome. He was right. I had never seen Horace with anything in his hands.

"Damn," I said, shaking my head. "There really was no metal box."

"Well, there was a metal box," Freezay said, correcting me. "One with a book and a knife in it—the one used to torture and kill Constance, as a matter of fact—but it was back in Oggie's bedroom, hidden under the mattress. Daniel and Erlik found it a few minutes ago when they were going through Oggie's things."

"So it was only a bluff," I marveled, amazed that Alameda had fallen for it.

"A very powerful bluff," Freezay added. "And now the book is in Jarvis's possession and will be returned to Death, Inc., as soon as it's physically possible. Because it was in no person's hands at the stroke of midnight, it can be returned to you, Death, without a hitch. Amazing how that magic stuff works, huh?"

"Wow," I breathed, unaware that the success of Freezay's investigation had hinged solely upon a complete and utter lie.

Before he could get away, I had something I wanted to discuss with Freezay, but I was uncertain of how to broach the subject. I debated letting it drop, but then I decided just to be plainspoken about it.

"What will you do now?" I asked.

Freezay shrugged, scratching his chin thoughtfully.

"Don't know really. I guess I'll go back to my enforced retirement . . . lots of fishing and eating food that's terrible for me as I enjoy the beauty of the Central Coast."

"You know, you could always come work for me," I blurted out, the idea I'd been mulling around in my head for the past few hours finally injected into reality. "I mean we could use a man like you. It's really just Jarvis, Runt, and my sister, Clio, helping me run the show."

Freezay leaned forward, resting his elbows on the table.

"It's an enticing offer, that's for sure," he said, scooting his chair back so he could stand up. "But one I'd have to think on."

I watched him walk to the doorway, his gait steady and sure. I didn't know what he'd done to get himself kicked out of the Psychical Bureau of Investigations, but frankly, I didn't care. I liked Edgar Freezay exactly as he was . . . and I was gonna find a way to get him on my team whether he liked it or not.

"I'll let you know. And soon," Freezay said, stopping in the doorway for a moment—then he disappeared into the corridor, leaving me alone with my thoughts.

I sat back in my chair, sighing, as I waited for Jarvis and Runt to return. They'd gone to make the arrangements for the four bodies to be wormholed back to Sea Verge, where they would then be cremated and their ashes spread across the Rhode Island Sound.

"Knock, knock."

I looked up to find Daniel standing in the doorway, his lean body looking even more scrumptious than usual.

"Hey," I said, standing up and walking over to him.

"You look tired. Nice PJs, though."

I laughed and then I was in his arms, his lips against mine, our tongues fumbling in the hot wetness of each other's mouths. *God, I'd missed him.*

When we'd had our fill, we broke apart, but kept our hands entwined together, unable to bear even a second of separation.

"I missed you," I said, biting my lip, my throat constricting—and before I even realized it, I was crying.

He reached out, brushing away my tears with his fingers.

"I missed the crud out of you, you idiot," he said, pulling me into his arms and squeezing me tightly against him.

"Really?" I murmured hopefully.

"We shouldn't be apart," he continued, stroking my unruly hair. "I don't care anymore. I just need you in my life. I love you, Cal."

"I love you, too," I whispered.

"Did you really not know it was me?" he asked suddenly.

"Huh?" I said.

"Before the Masquerade Ball, when I helped you up after

you'd fallen. You didn't seem to know it was me, but then I thought maybe you did when you kissed me . . ." He trailed off.

So, Daniel was my mysterious stranger, I thought to myself. *And that meant the lipstick I'd seen on his neck . . . was mine.*

"It was a beautiful mask," I said, not answering his question. He grinned at me, not sure if I was teasing him.

"You're a strange girl, Calliope Reaper-Jones," he whispered as he moved in to kiss me again. But just as our lips met, I heard a *creak* out in the hallway, and we pulled apart to find Caoimhe standing in the doorway, uncertainty rife in her eyes.

"I'm sorry," she said. "I didn't mean to interrupt."

She started to back away, but I broke apart from Daniel and walked over to the doorway, stopping her before she could disappear.

"Wait," I said. Then I glanced at Daniel. "Can I have a couple of minutes?"

He nodded, but I could tell that now that he had me again, he didn't ever want to let me go.

"Why don't I pack and then meet you in your room?" Daniel said, kindly giving me the freedom to do what I needed. "We can catch a wormhole back to Sea Verge together from there."

"That would make me very happy," I said, grinning back at him—and suddenly I didn't want to let him go either.

"I love you," I mouthed to him as he left. He smiled, the sides of his eyes crinkling, and then he was gone, leaving Caoimhe and me to do our business in private.

"I really didn't mean to interrupt," Caoimhe said, looking sheepish.

I didn't want her to feel any worse than she already did.

"It's fine. He was just going anyway."

She seemed to believe me, but she was still nervous as she crossed the threshold and walked toward me.

"You said earlier that there was something you needed to talk to me about?" I asked, getting the ball rolling.

Caoimhe hesitated, licking her lips as she grasped the edge of one of the dining room chairs, holding on to it so tightly her fingers turned white.

"Yes, there is something I need to discuss with you—" She

stopped, raising a trembling hand to her mouth. Whatever she had to say to me was proving very difficult for her to get out.

"Sorry," she said, composing herself. "I told myself I wouldn't get upset and here I am, getting upset."

I wanted to touch her hand, assure her there was nothing she could say that was worth this suffering, but I was afraid to spook her, so I let it ride.

"All right," she began again. "This is a very hard thing for me to say, but I made a mistake a long time ago and I'm hoping that you'll give me the chance to make it up to you. You have to understand my situation, how much I love Morrigan and never wanted to hurt her . . . and your father was so persuasive—"

"Okay, stop," I interrupted, totally confused. "I don't understand. What are you saying?"

She took a deep breath, letting it out slowly.

"Calliope . . . I'm your mother."

The shock was absolute. I couldn't think, I couldn't speak, I couldn't breath . . . all I could do was stare at the woman before me, trying to make sense of the strange sentence she'd just uttered.

"It happened during a Masquerade Ball more than twenty years ago," she said. "I had no idea who the masked man I'd been with was and I didn't care. I wanted a baby so badly I couldn't think straight—and the ball was my only opportunity to make it happen. I knew Morrigan would forgive me once it was all over and I explained my rationale, but I didn't dare tell her beforehand for fear that she'd stop me from doing it."

I started shaking, my whole body vibrating on some unknown frequency.

"When you were conceived, it was the greatest blessing that had ever been bestowed upon me," she continued, starting to cry. "But Morrigan didn't take it as well as I had hoped. How she discovered your father was my partner that night, I'll never know, but she went to him and told him that I was pregnant."

I had to sit down, my legs so weak they could barely hold me. I collapsed into a chair, my throat dry as a bone as I listened to Caoimhe's story.

"Your father wouldn't take no for an answer," she went on. "He and Morrigan persuaded me that giving you to him and his wife would be the best thing for you. You were Death's

Daughter and you would never be safe without his protection. I didn't know what to do . . . so I went to see the great seer, Anjea, telling myself I would do whatever she said was best for you."

"Anjea?" I heard myself saying.

"She took one look at me . . ." Caoimhe laughed—but there was no mirth in it. "She took one look at me and said that one day you would be Death."

Caoimhe stopped again, her eyes wet.

"She said I must protect you at all costs. That you would be the greatest balance the world had ever known."

I started to cry, my heart beating so hard I thought it was going to burst.

"So you just gave me to them?" I almost shouted, anger surging inside me like wildfire.

"I did what I thought was best for you," she cried.

"Why didn't you ever contact me?" I asked, pain snaking through my heart.

"I wanted to, but your mother—the woman who raised you—said no. Once you were theirs, there was nothing I could do."

I suddenly understood so much, why I was so different from my mother and sisters, why I had never really fit into their world. It was like a giant weight had been lifted from my shoulders and I was finally free.

"Please don't hate me," Caoimhe said, her whole body trembling as she stood before me, tears coursing down her face. "Please . . ."

I stood up and ran to her—this alien woman who was my mother—letting her enfold me into her arms. I cried as she held me so tightly I thought I might break, but then she released me and held me back from her chest so she could look into my eyes.

"You are so beautiful," she whispered, kissing both of my cheeks. "And I am so proud of you."

She pulled me back into her arms and we stayed like that, holding on to each other like our lives depended on it (and maybe they did), until Jarvis and Runt came into the dining room, ready to take me home.

epilogue

I stood in my bedroom at the Haunted Hearts Castle, trying to avoid the residual bloodstains left by the night's murderous activities while I packed my bag for the return trip to Sea Verge. Actually, my bag still had Coy's head in it, so this was a loner from Jarvis, but I didn't care. I was just happy to be getting the hell out of California in one piece.

Runt, Jarvis, and Daniel were on their way over, so I was hoping to make quick work of it, but I was finding it hard to concentrate. My brain kept returning to Caoimhe's face, wanting to decipher all the bits of her that were inside me.

Jarvis hadn't been surprised when I'd introduced Caoimhe as my mother. He'd known about my parentage, though not who the woman was, and had been sworn to secrecy on the subject of my birth. At first, I'd been angry with him, but then I'd decided that it wasn't really his place to tell me. In the end, it should've been my father. He should've told me, not left me to spend my life never knowing the truth.

As it was, I was already trying to make up for lost time. I'd made plans with Caoimhe to have lunch the following week—I wanted to get to know the woman who had borne me—and even if it meant I was going to have to spend time with bitchy old Morrigan, too, I knew it was worth it. Caoimhe obviously loved her—and I had no intention of making my mother choose between us. If Morrigan wanted to do that, then it was her business, but I was going to try to make the whole thing as painless for Caoimhe and myself as possible.

There was a knock on my door just as I dropped the last item of clothing into my bag, and I sighed, happy to be packed.

"Come in!" I called, zipping up the bag and setting it on the floor just as I heard the door open behind me.

"I wanted to apologize."

I looked up to find Kali standing in the doorway, looking sheepish.

"Why should you apologize?" I said. "I was the one who was being such a bitch."

She shrugged, leaning against the doorway.

"I should apologize because it made me happy Daniel might be sleeping with Coy and that I got to tell you so."

"Kali, I totally knew that's what you were doing," I said, shrugging. "But it's still no excuse for being mean to you. I was just hurt and I lashed out."

"Well, you were hurt because of me." She sighed. "I couldn't wait to share Daniel's infidelity with you."

"He wasn't my boyfriend, so there was no infidelity," I corrected.

"Yes, theoretically," Kali agreed. "But still, I knew it would hurt you, and I should have been . . . more discreet . . . I suppose."

She was right. She'd hurt me on purpose . . . but, you know what, I'd returned the favor. We were both guilty of hurting the other and the greatest thing we could do now was to forgive each other and move on.

I crossed the divide between us and threw my arms around her.

"Friends, please?"

She nodded.

"All right. Friends again, dipwad."

She kissed me quickly on both cheeks then extricated herself from my embrace.

"I have to go now, white girl," she said. "Horace is taking me to Mexico for the weekend."

"You bitch," I cried, laughing. "You only apologized cause you felt guilty about hooking up with Horace!"

"I'll never tell," she said, and grinning widely, she sashayed right out the door, slamming it shut behind her.

Leave it to Kali to get skunked and meet a man all in the same night, I thought. *Amazing.*

There was another knock, and I raced to get the door, thinking that maybe Kali had forgotten to tell me something about her trip, but when I threw it open, I saw one of the bodyguards—Rat Face—in the doorway, eyes blank, the bloodied point of a sword protruding from his chest.

"I just wanted to make sure you hadn't forgotten about our arrangement," came a cold voice—and then the bodyguard's corpse slid off the sword point to reveal: Marcel, the Ender of Death, standing there, grinning at me.

"You!" I said.

Marcel leveled his sword in my direction. "I hope you will expedite the day and time of our duel so that I do not have to come remind you again."

So the little shit was a sportsman. He wanted to have our duel fair and square; no trickery and no cheating—although he hadn't been above frightening me into getting the ball rolling.

"'Til we meet again," he said, giving me a terse bow. "And I hope that it's soon. So that no more humans have to die."

"Tomorrow," I said, tired of all the bullshit and feeling bad about the dead bodyguard. "We meet tomorrow. I'll have Jarvis send you a location in the morning."

Marcel's eyes flared in surprise.

"Of course," he said, very pleased with the turn of events.

He bowed again, this time with an air of respect he had never shown me before.

"Oh," I called out after him as he sauntered toward the exit. "Don't forget to put on a clean pair of underwear."

He turned around, not sure if he'd heard me correctly.

"Excuse me?"

"Oh, you heard me," I said. "Put on a clean pair of underwear so that you don't embarrass yourself when they undress you at the morgue."

Marcel stared at me, confusion rippling across his face—but when he finally understood what I was driving at, he started to laugh.

"*Enchanté*, Death. *Enchanté*," he murmured.

And then, with a wink, he was gone.

I had one consoling thought as I sat down on the bed, my borrowed bag at my feet, waiting for Jarvis and Runt and Daniel to return and give me hell for what I'd just done: It was nice to know that Marcel enjoyed my peculiar sense of humor—and even nicer still to think that this time . . . *I wasn't joking.*

I still had a lot to learn about how to be Death—and my next lesson would take place sometime, someplace tomorrow. And it wasn't going to involve ball gowns and fancy dinners . . .

From
AMBER BENSON

The Calliope Reaper-Jones Novels

death's daughter

Callie just wanted a normal life, but when her father—
who happens to be Death himself—is kidnapped and
the Devil's protégé embarks on a hostile takeover of the
family business, Death, Inc., Callie returns home to
assume the CEO mantle—only to discover she must
complete three nearly impossible tasks in the realm of
the Afterlife first.

cat's claw

Cerberus, the three-headed dog that guards the gates
of Hell, wants Callie to repay a debt, which means a
trip to Purgatory, Las Vegas, ancient Egypt—and a dis-
count department store. The things a girl has to do when
she's Death's Daughter!

serpent's storm

To protect the Reaper family business, Callie must fight
her sister Thalia, the Devil, and their secret weapon—
someone very close to Callie and very dangerous! This
time, it is *way* personal . . .

penguin.com
deathsdaughter.com
facebook.com/ProjectParanormalBooks